THIS TIME

THIS TIME

MARGARET
JOHNSON-HODGE

SUTTON PLACE PUBLISHERS

Copyright © 2004 by Margaret Johnson-Hodge

SUTTON PLACE PUBLISHERS, INC.
2774 N. Cobb Parkway, Suite 109, PMB 180
Kennesaw, Georgia 30152

ISBN 0-7394-5395-5

Text Design by STUDIO 31

Printed in the United States of America

This book is dedicated to my husband,

Terence Anthony Hodge ...

Amazing Love ...

Chapter One

"Broken heart again. Another lesson learned ..."
The music was too loud, Dajah knew that, but she was in one of her 'got to cleanse myself' moods and Mary J. Blige had both the words and the vocals to do it. "No More Drama," had become the new soundtrack in Dajah Moore's life.

Dajah wanted to say that Rick had done this to her. She wanted to point a finger at Gina, Rick's ex-girlfriend, and Kanisha, Rick and Gina's daughter. But the truth was, Dajah had done this to herself. She had decided to get with a man who had a child with someone else. Dajah was the one who had given up her heart and soul to make it work, creating nothing but heartache for herself and a second chance between Rick and Gina.

Rick, Gina and Kanisha now had the victory and Dajah had been left all alone by the roadside even though, with words at least, Rick had picked her.

"I chose you," Rick had uttered that December morning. But his words had come a little too late. Too many days had passed while Dajah waited for Rick to make up his mind. Within that void, Dajah had returned to her center. She'd returned to who she'd been before Rick happened.

The Dajah before Rick had never done 'share.' The Dajah before Rick had never considered getting with a man who had a child with someone else. Yet somehow, Rick had managed to change all her parameters. He wiped away all of her set boundaries and in a heartbeat, Dajah had found herself not only involved with Rick, but in love.

Together they had managed their way through the baby mamma dramas that Gina had forced upon them. Together they had navigated a life where Rick's daughter Kanisha became their center. For a little while, it seemed to be working. But then Gina had changed, going from a loud, uncouth, uncaring young mother to a woman who understood that the only way forward was to grow up.

Gina's growth, maturity and new-found goals had been the start of it, changing how Rick saw her, changing how Rick saw Dajah. And though, in the end, he still desired a life with Dajah, Rick's daughter came first and Dajah couldn't be second.

Stop thinking about him. But it was all Dajah could do. In the three weeks that had passed since she walked away. In those three weeks since she had uttered into the phone that cold almost Christmas morning *"But I don't chose you,"* and felt her own heart break over her decision, Rick was all she could think about.

Mary J. was gearing up, the power of her voice, "Go 'head. Go 'head," was diesel driven. Mary urged, forcing the ugly conflicts from her soul. Dajah sang along, wanting them gone too.

She stood in the middle of her living room, head back, arms out, mouth opened. Face pinched, body racked in ethereal pain, Dajah sang along. Hungry for the deliverance, desperate for reprieve, she bellowed, *"I need a peace of mind, peace of mind ... "* as Mary wailed it.

Caught up, her feet left the floor, making her bounce and buck. Caught up, she didn't hear the ringing phone. Caught up, she wasn't aware of the commotion she was making over the heads of Mr. and Mrs. Merriweather, owners of the two-family house Dajah lived in.

Dajah was in the midst of revival and nothing could take her from it because the Spirit had her. The Spirit of Redemption. The Spirit of Salvation. The Spirit of 'everything's gonna be alright.' She couldn't stop.

Dajah couldn't finish one second before Mary J. Blige did. She could not close her mouth, cease the motion of her feet. She could not stop waving her arms, the jerking of her neck. She was a hostage and only the end of the song could set her free.

As the soft drifts of the soap opera theme song faded, she came back to herself. That's when she heard knocks on her door. Panting and out of breath, she opened it, knowing who would be there and why. The music had been too loud, her stomps too hard for it not to be her landlord.

"We heard all this stomping Dajah," Mr. Merriweather began.

Dajah tried to smile, but that took more energy than she had. "I was just doing some exercise. I guess I got carried away."

The older couple stared beyond her into the apartment, noses aloft for whiffs of marijuana, eyes keen for signs of destruction.

Mrs. Merriweather scrutinized her. "And the music was loud. We rang you and everything."

Dajah nodded, caught. "Sorry. It's my favorite song. I must have turned it up too high."

"You're a good tenant Dajah. All the years you've been here, we never had any trouble with you. But blasting your music and stomping over our heads isn't acceptable. You understand?"

"Yes, I understand and it won't happen again."

But that's all Dajah wanted — one more round with Mary. Mary and the music. Mary and the Spirit. Mary and the Holy Ghost fire save-me-Lord-Jesus music. Because for those few minutes, she felt born again. For those few minutes she had the hope.

For those few minutes Dajah had the peace Mary J. Blige had sung about. And that's all Dajah really wanted. She wanted some peace.

If she had known what would become of her life two hours after her soul revival, Dajah would have played the song a second time, possibly a third. If she had known what she'd be facing before the night ended, she would have shored up more reserve while she still had the chance.

But she hadn't and three simple words turned Dajah Moore's world upside down.

Three simple words snatched the rug from under her feet and sent her tumbling. Three simple words — *think about it*, slipped her back into a time and place she swore she wouldn't travel anymore. The deliverer of that detonation: Rick Trimmons.

Dajah had walked away from Rick, the drama and the madness. She had said 'no more' to Rick's baby's momma Gina and all that mess that situation entailed. That almost Christmas morning in 2002, Dajah had spoke words that broke her own heart but she had survived it. At least she thought she had.

She never suspected later on that evening that Rick would pull up to her place in the black SUV and ring her bell. Dajah never considered that she would answer the ring and open the door to him. She didn't count on just the sight of him jump-starting her heart.

But it did.

Her doorbell had rung. She had gone downstairs to answer it.

Without checking, she opened the door and saw him there. Dajah blinked in surprise. "Rick?"

"Hey."

She blinked again, the sight of him, a shock to her senses. Her defenses failed her. Her resolve vanished. Her face crumbled and Rick, sensing her sapping strength, reached out and took her into his arms.

The feel of his hands sliding about her waist, the touch of his fingers dancing on her spine, turned every bone in her to Jell-O. She leaned into him, her face burrowing in the soft weave of his North Pole down. Nose deep against it, she became lost in the best of times, the worst far, far away.

It felt good. Delicious. Real. Rick holding her like that made all the sorrow, the loneliness and the deep sense of betrayal less valid. It made the horrors fade in the distance, infusing her with good times.

There at her front door, light spilling behind her, the dark night before her, Dajah surrendered. She surrendered because after three weeks of not having it, she needed Rick's embrace.

It seemed a lifetime before she pulled away, gathering pieces of herself lost in his arrival. Eons zipped by as she righted herself, tried to still her heart, her mind full of too many thoughts.

Her head moved side to side. Her forehead furrowed as she forced words from her mouth. "This isn't right. You're not supposed to be here."

That there were tears in her eyes surprised neither of them. Something deep and real had been cleaved when she left him. In this moment, a healing was taking place. But the tears in her eyes served a purpose. It reaffirmed what Rick felt and thought. No, they weren't finished.

A lump formed in his throat. Rick swallowed, gazing at her. "I made a lot of mistakes Dajah. I know that now. And I know I'm not supposed to be here. I know you said we were over, but I couldn't stay away. I couldn't. Y'know?"

Yes, she did. It was in the very air she breathed. It swirled up around her like a tornado on the horizon. Despite the oncoming danger, she couldn't turn away. Her body grew tense, bracing for the impact.

"I was so wrong about everything," Rick went on to say. "I

should have never put Kanisha before my own happiness. I should have never made you second. I know what's important now and what's important is you. I came to ask for a second chance."

What had been forgotten came back at the mention of Kanisha, Rick's five-year-old daughter. Suddenly the hard cold truth of what life had been like with Rick was front and center — none of it pretty.

Sorrow spun into anger. Relief churned into disbelief. "Another chance to do what?"

"Make it work right between us."

Dajah's head began shaking again, but it was with a different conviction than before. Conflict and confusion disappeared. "It's too late for any of that."

"Will you think about it at least? Just think about it. You don't have to tell me now. Take some time, as much as you need. But at least think about it."

Dajah stood in her doorway, the chilled January night rushing past her, mocking the warmth of her sweat pants and the cotton top she had on. She hugged her chest, ran fingers along her exposed forearm, looked beyond Rick, seeking answers.

She settled her gaze and fixed her eyes on the man who had disturbed so much in her life. She took in the one who had made her break so many rules, she'd stop counting.

She wasn't supposed to be here in this place. She wasn't supposed to be entertaining any new possibilities with Rick. Although she had walked away brokenhearted, she had walked away. Her life was never supposed to involve him ever again.

"Please?" Rick asked again, his voice more plea then question and Dajah found herself back in the struggle. "Will you at least think about it?"

In the weeks since she said goodbye, Dajah had struggled to combat her loneliness. She'd struggled to live her life in truth. She'd struggled to hold onto optimism that somewhere out there, the next man was waiting for her even as memories of Rick haunted her every minute of the day.

Dajah had struggled with accepting that she still loved and missed him. She'd struggled past all the times she wanted him still. She'd struggled not to call and struggled with the notion that leaving him was best. But this moment was the hardest struggle of them all.

Because I still love him.

There it was, her bottom line. There it was, her ultimate truth. She had promised herself no more lies. No more half-truths. She had promised herself last New Year's that, from that point on she would be honest about everything. And the truth was, her love for him had not decreased one iota. The truth was, she had to look into his eyes, those eyes, and admit it.

She knew all that she would see when she did. Dajah knew all that she would feel. The love between them had been real though crippled. *Real and still there*, something whispered. *Still there and right in front of you. All you have to do to see it is look.*

She did and the impact was as powerful as she imagined.

She found herself drowning in the big, wide, dark-brown pools of his eyes. Drowning in those little boy wonders, so deep and endless, they looked back lit. *Allen Iverson* eyes, came an after thought.

"What about Gina?" she found herself asking.

"What about her?"

"You were getting closer to her when we broke up."

"Was. Not anymore. That's finished."

"Finished?"

"Done," he affirmed.

"Why?"

"Why what?"

"Why are you so sure this time?"

He took her hand, raised it to his lips. Kissed the back of it. "Because you're the only one I love."

Dajah snatched her hand as if burned. Rubbed it, erasing the feel of his lips against her skin. She didn't want any mementos after she closed the door to him. She didn't need any part of him to linger.

Fixing him squarely with her eyes, something hard glowed in their depths. "I'll think about it," she said quickly, stepping back and closing her front door. With trembling fingers, she locked it, leaned against the wood, her heart thrumming in her chest.

He had messed up. He missed her. Things had changed and he wanted a second chance. The question was — did she?

Chapter Two

The walls of the kitchen in the third floor apartment glistened with wet paint. The air held the smell of paint fumes.

"It's not too bright?"

Gina stood in Tarika's tiny kitchen, taking in the burnt orange walls. It was a bit too busy for her eyes, but sometimes the last thing a friend wants to hear is the truth. "Nah, girl. It looks just like the magazine."

Gina Alexander had learned a few things in the last year. She had learned that nothing about life could be taken for granted, certainly not her friendship with Tarika. She had nearly lost a life-long buddy and now that she had gotten her back, she was doing everything to keep her.

"Okay, we have to let this dry and then rag roll the glaze."

"I'm going to have to leave soon."

"Already?"

"I been here four hours," Gina offered.

"Yeah that's true." But Tarika wasn't able to hide her disappointment. She had hoped that they could do her kitchen like the people on TV did — in one weekend. But neither she nor Gina had ever really painted before and it took a while to get a rhythm going.

There were a lot of firsts for both women. At twenty-three, they had finally grasped the concept of doing for yourself. And being about something was the only way to go. Up until a few months ago, their days had been spent smoking marijuana and slugging down forties.

But mostly what Tarika recalled were the days when Gina was just a nasty bitter bitch who was always unhappy and cursed like a sailor. While they both had come far, Gina had come the farthest.

"We can start again next Friday night," Gina decided. "We should be finished by Saturday. Then we can make us a nice dinner and really celebrate."

Tarika smiled. "Sounds good." She took the paintbrush from Gina and dumped it into the old porcelain sink. Putting the lid back on the paint can, Tarika picked up the glossy page ripped from a decorating magazine. She compared the kitchen in the picture to the one she was standing in. Sighed. "I would love to have one of them aluminum refrigerators."

"You will," Gina offered. "You work hard. Just save up your money, right?"

Tarika looked at her friend. Warmed. "Right."

The cab came to a gentle stop. Gina paid the driver and got out. She looked up at the house and it seemed to be looking at her. She hated the dark-brown wood shingles.

In the daytime they looked delicately carved and the color of cocoa. At night they become black and had a fish scale look — like the Adam's Family house — Gina thought with a shiver.

If the outside of the house felt murky, the inside felt just as gloomy. Gina found herself envying Tarika's tiny little third floor apartment. At least it was full of light.

When a stupid choice had landed Gina in jail and she lost custody of Kanisha and the second floor apartment in Rick's house, she needed a place to stay. Jefferson, her mother's friend and surrogate father had offered her his home.

With no other place to turn, initially it had felt like a godsend. Now it felt like a mausoleum. Heavy drapes on the windows. Large, oversized antique furniture filled the house. The place was just too dreary for her taste.

When Gina had suggested to Jefferson that he get new furniture and change up the drapes, he looked hurt. "My wife picked this out," he told her in a soft voice. But she's been dead three years, Gina wanted to say but didn't.

She never brought it up again. Tried to ignore the shadows and gloom she felt inside the walls. But every time she stepped through the front door, she felt like she was entering a tomb. A tomb of doom was how she came to see it lately, something she had confessed to Mrs. Jones, her court-appointed counselor.

When Gina had gotten in trouble with the law, the Courts had appointed Gina a counselor. The idea was to offer Gina intervention, giving her someone she could talk to when the stresses of life became too much.

Since that time Gina had sat in Mrs. Jones' office more times than she could count. On one of those visits she had talked about how depressing Jefferson's house was.

"Be grateful you have some place to live," Mrs. Jones told her. "Not many men would take in a child, especially a grown child that's not even theirs."

It amazed Gina that though Jefferson wasn't her daddy, he acted like he was. For years Jefferson had insisted to Doreen Alexander, Gina's mother, that Gina was his child and for just as many years, Gina's mother had insisted that Jefferson wasn't.

Even when the truth came out in all its ugly stinging wonder, Jefferson had still claimed Gina as his own.

Back when Gina's mother was young, she entertained a lot of men and Jefferson had been just one of many. While Doreen never took much precaution with birth control with most of the men she saw, relying on them to do the right thing, she always insisted Jefferson used something because he had been a married man.

When Gina's mother turned up pregnant, she didn't know who the father was, but she knew for certain it wasn't Jefferson. But there was no convincing Jefferson of that. He proclaimed Gina his in the womb and went on to proclaim her out. Though he went home to his wife every night, initially his free time had been spent being a daddy to Gina.

Having Jefferson around so much cramped Gina's mother's style and by the time Gina was five, Doreen ran Jefferson away for good. Even though he was gone, he never forgot Gina or Doreen. Decades later, when his wife passed away, he came to look them both up.

Initially Gina hadn't remembered Jefferson. She hadn't remembered the old man who made her her favorite breakfast and took her places. But when he told her he was her father and Gina's mother told how he wasn't, the memories came flooding back to her.

It was easy to slip back into the roll he had carved into her life long ago. She didn't call him daddy, but she felt it every time the word 'Jefferson' left her mouth.

Gina let herself in and closed the door behind her. "Jefferson?" she called out.

"I'm in the kitchen."

She moved through the dim house and found him sitting at the table, the little black and white TV playing, a plate of food before him. "You hungry? I made dinner."

"What you make?"

"Meatloaf. Mashed potatoes. Green beans." Her favorites.

"Yeah, I'll take a plate." Gina took off her coat, hung her pocketbook on the chair. Sat. Jefferson got up and began fixing her plate, humming a little melody as he went along.

Rick knew things.

He knew that dropping by Dajah's house that night and talking about the changes in his life would not be enough for her. He knew that after giving her half truths about himself and his heart when they were together, Dajah needed to see something that said he was on the up and up this time.

A big sore point had been the second floor apartment of his house. No doubt getting the house with the idea that Gina would be able to live upstairs, over his head and not meddle in his love life had been a breaking point.

Even after Gina had blown the apartment by getting in trouble, Rick had left the apartment empty. Though Dajah tried to get it rented to anybody who would take it, Rick never really tried. Dajah never came out and said he was holding onto that apartment in hopes that Gina could return, but both Dajah and Rick knew it. Unfortunately, the knowledge had come to Rick a little too late.

That's why Monday was an important day for him.

Monday would become proof positive that he had changed. It would be proof that he understood where he had gone wrong with Dajah and was willing to fix it. He was going to show the second floor apartment to a fellow corrections officer from his job.

If everything worked out, by the following weekend, the place would be rented.

The idea of getting a two-family house had seemed like a good idea at the time. It would have allowed Rick to always see his daughter and give Gina the space she needed to live her own life, something she had always done even when she shared his two-bed-room apartment.

On paper the idea was ludicrous, but in his head it was doable. Rick began working as much overtime as Department of Corrections allowed and began stockpiling money for a down payment. When he met Dajah, he found a new urgency to execute his plan and made it happen.

Everyone knew it wouldn't work except Rick.

Gina invaded on Rick's privacy every chance she got. She used Kanisha to do some invasion as well. It became too much for Dajah and she walked away from Rick. When Gina was arrested for child abandonment and Kanisha was placed into the foster care system, Dajah's heart softened. She gave Rick another chance.

With her arrest, Gina couldn't be around Kanisha, which meant she could no longer stay in the upstairs apartment. Dajah saw it as an end to the Gina drama. But it turned out to be a new beginning.

A beginning that never got past "Go," as far as Rick was concerned. For a hot minute around Christmastime, getting back with Gina had crossed his mind. But the dust had settled and Rick's vision was clear.

Gina had been his past. Rick wanted Dajah to be his future.

Renting out the upstairs apartment would be the first step.

"This is nice Bro," Wilcox, a C.O. from Rick's job was saying as he looked around the second floor apartment. "This is real nice."

Rick nodded. "The person who used to live here before kept it pretty clean." Which was the truth. Gina had loved the apartment and treated it like a treasure.

Wilcox walked through the dining room into the kitchen. "How do you feel about noise over your head? 'Cause you know I got two little ones."

"How old?"

"Six and three."

Kanisha would have some playmates. Rick might even have a babysitter. "I don't think that'll be a problem."

Wilcox went to the main bedroom. Looked out the window. Liked the view. "It looks good, but my wife wants to take a look before I sign. I'll bring her by tomorrow."

"Sounds good," Rick said, shaking his hand.

Second chances came in all sorts of measures. Gina Alexander had had more than a few in her lifetime.

But the biggest one she'd ever received was when she had gotten a job at the central library on Merrick Boulevard in Jamaica, New York. At twenty-three, it had been her first place of employment and though the work was menial and the pay was low, for the first time in her life, Gina had some purpose in her life. She embraced it.

Like all the other Friday afternoons before, Gina was tired from her long workweek. But there was a pep in her step as she exited the glass doors, spotting Rick's SUV parked up the street. Besides getting the chance to spend some time with Kanisha, for the next two mornings Gina wouldn't have to get up at the break of dawn.

Easing into the passenger seat, she turned and smiled at her daughter. "Hi baby."

"Hi mommy."

She glanced at Rick. "Hey."

He didn't return the glance. Simply muttered "Hey," and pulled away from the curb.

There hadn't been much between them since the end of last year. Rick had become standoffish as of late. But Gina ignored it as best as she could, concentrating on her daughter, like now as she shifted in her seat. "How was your week? You had a good week in school?" she asked.

"Uh huh."

Gina dug in her purse for her cell phone. "What you want from the Chinese restaurant?"

"Chicken *wangs* and fries."

"Rick you want something?" He shook his head no, eyes never leaving the road. Gina punched buttons on her cell. "Yeah. I want to place an order for pick up. Give me an order of wings, fried well. Don't want them bleeding near the bone, with French fries. Then I want some beef lo mein with broccoli and garlic sauce. Give me a Coke and a Sprite too. How much? Okay."

Gina pitched her phone back into her bag. Studied Rick's profile. "You busy Sunday?"

"I don't know. Why?"

"I got these tickets for the Ice Capades from my job. Free. Out at Nassau Coliseum. Figured we could take Kanisha."

In truth Rick wasn't busy, but he wasn't up to taking in the Ice Capades. "I don't think I can make it."

Gina blinked. "Oh. Well maybe Jefferson can take us."

Rick remained mute.

Gina changed subjects. "I'm going to the Chinese restaurant up on Farmers. You know, the one I always go to?"

"Yeah, I know."

She studied Rick's profile for another second or two, then cast her gaze out of the car window.

Mother and daughter sat at the kitchen table eating their take-out. With concentration Kanisha worked the end of the chicken wing bone, gnawing into it, in search of the marrow.

Gina took the bone out of her hand. "Don't eat that Kanisha. It'll cut up your stomach."

"But I like that part."

"Don't matter. You not suppose to eat bone." She pitched it onto her plate.

"I'm getting new friends Mommy."

"New friends? Who?"

"Two little girls. They moving upstairs this weekend. I ain't met them yet, but they'll be there when I get home on Sunday."

"Upstairs? Where we used to live upstairs?"

Kanisha nodded her head emphatically. "That's what daddy told me."

"When did he tell you this?"

"Before."

Gina stared at her child, her brow furrowed. Kanisha stared down at her plate until she heard her mother sigh. Only then did she pick up her next chicken wing and take a quick bite, her mouth chewing quickly as if it were her last one, hoping whatever it was that was bugging her momma wouldn't last.

* * *

Twenty minutes later Gina was on the phone with Rick. "You

couldn't even tell me?" There was hurt in her voice with brushes of tears.

"I was going to," Rick defended.

"When?"

"Look Gina. You know I can't carry that house by myself. You know I was going to rent it out sooner or later."

"I ain't saying you weren't, but you could have told me."

"Why? What difference would it make?"

"You know I loved that place."

That he did. But things were different now. He had a point to make and renting the apartment was the first step. "Yeah, but you blew it, so don't be trying to put that on me."

Silence. Rick could hearing her breathing and thinking, but little else.

"I got to go," he decided. "I'll see you on Sunday." Rick disconnected. Gina hung up too then made another phone call.

"Stop crying," Tarika was saying a few minutes later. "Ain't nothing to be crying over."

"But he knew I wanted that place."

"You even tell him that?"

No Gina hadn't. She had insinuated and hinted, but had never come out and said it. She didn't think Rick would let her move back. She told Tarika so.

"Why else you think it stayed empty so long? He was probably waiting for you to ask and when you didn't, he just went ahead and rented it."

"But why didn't he tell me he was gonna do that? He ain't even mention it. Kanisha did."

"Maybe because he thought it didn't matter to you one way or the other."

"That shit was mine and he just like gave it away."

"It was yours but it's not anymore. You just got to deal with it."

But there were other parts of Gina's sadness, other parts that she was too scared to speak out loud. Like how Rick was drifting further and further away. That not even Kanisha seemed to keep him tethered.

"It ain't right Tarika. That just wasn't right."

"Well why don't you call him back and ask him can you have the place?"

"He gonna tell me no."

Tarika couldn't even argue the point. Didn't try. "I'm sorry girl."

But the words didn't have any impact.

It was always hard on Gina when Rick came to pick up Kanisha on Sundays, but this Sunday felt harder.

Gina was beyond pretense that it didn't matter. Beyond pretense that it didn't hurt. She opened the door to him red eyed. But if Rick noticed, he didn't say anything about. Just asked if Kanisha was ready.

"Yeah, she ready, but I want to talk to you."

"About what?"

"You could have told me Rick. Given me a chance to rent it."

"And how were you going to pay the rent?"

"Don't even go there. You know Jefferson would have helped."

"And what would've happened if he stopped paying? I can't be carrying you like that no more."

"I ain't asked you to carry me. I could have figured something out." Tears sprang from her eyes. She wiped them. "You know how hard I'm trying. You know how much I changed. I loved that apartment. I couldn't ask to have it back."

"Oh, so I was supposed to offer it to you?"

In her eyes laid the answer, supported by those moments they had shared since Christmas. They had slept together three times since then. Three attempts to give their crumbled past a new birth. But they never quite succeeded and there had been no fourth.

Since then Rick's eyes seemed to ignore her more than they acknowledged. Still Gina held onto the notion, the idea that Rick knew how much she loved that apartment. Even though she wanted it, he would have to do the asking.

"I'm sorry Gina, but they're already moved in."

Her face turned ugly. "You ain't sorry Rick. You ain't sorry 'bout nothing. So don't stand there and tell me you are." She headed for the stairs. "Kanisha! Kanisha! Your daddy here."

* * *

Gina sat on her bed, one leg dangling off the edge. She was trying to get her emotions in check. Trying not to throw away months of good over a half a day of bad. She wanted to run out into the streets and cop.

She wanted to smoke a few joints, down a forty. She wanted to inebriate herself away from the pain. But to do that meant turning her back on all she had accomplished.

She hadn't indulged in months. Gina hadn't self-medicated in a while. But there was no doubt she wanted to. No doubt she felt she needed to.

There was no doubt that the world she had wrangled her soul to create was changing and not for the good. No doubt that the world she had once seen as hopeful was starting to dim.

Chapter Three

*T*hink about it. It was the new singsong playing in Dajah's head. Think about it, all she had been doing since the night Rick rang her bell. Think about it — a tight box she couldn't get out of.

The pros and cons of it all raced through her like her car raced down the Southern State Parkway. Another workday begun, her head was in thick debate as she headed to her office at General Management in Seaford, Long Island.

She hadn't mentioned it to anyone. Dajah was afraid that just talking about it would reveal the huge doubt that she now harbored. Before Rick showed up, it had been so small and tiny she barely noticed it. Before Rick, she could swat it away with a flick of her emotional hand.

Now there was no swatting. Now it stole her thoughts and kept them hostage. Now it made every waking second of her life a huge debate of will I or won't I. Should I or shouldn't I? Could I?

Could I was the hardest, the trickiest, the sneakiest, the most deadliest because there was no doubt she could. No doubt she could just click her heels and make the previous failed attempt vanish. There was no doubt that she could pick up the phone anytime and say, "Okay, we can try again," and before twenty-four hours had passed, Rick would be right by her side — *without the Gina dramas.*

That was all she wanted just over a month ago. All she needed, she was certain. She needed Gina out of their hair, gone from their life. Rick was claiming that's just what he had done. He'd made the bad part go away.

But would Gina really stay gone?

Dajah exited at the Seaford exit and made a right. Heading down Old Country Road, she moved through a couple of traffic lights and made a left. Driving slow, she found a parking space and cut her engine. Buttoning up her coat, she slipped on her gloves and her hat for the short, stingingly cold walk across the asphalt to the building of glass and steel.

Like every workday morning, she spied Mr. Elias, the old, past-retired black man who worked as the janitor of the building. "Good morning, Miss Moore," he offered as she headed toward the elevator.

"Good morning Mr. Elias. How are you?"

"Just fine."

The elevator door slid open. "Well have a good day," Dajah said, stepping inside.

"I'm sure gonna try, Miss Moore."

Their conversations never changed. The same words, in the same tone had been shared five mornings a week for the past eight years. Like coffee and a bagel, it had become a part of Dajah's routine.

Much hadn't changed since she started working as an accountant, except maybe her cubicle. It used to overflow with plants and cacti but was now empty of the simplest of flora. The four walls that greeted her as she entered were the same as when they had gone up.

She hadn't consciously killed off her spider plants, cacti and Wandering Jew. There had been no real malice as things withered and died. She simply forgot to water them. And then when she did, she gave them too much, resulting in root rot.

When her little fuscia and orange head cacti got soft near the bottom, unable to support the weight of its top. When they leaned, then keeled over, she didn't replace them. She simply threw them away.

When her ever-expanding Wandering Jew began yellowing in places, Dajah didn't bother to remove the dead leaves. When all the green was gone and the plant became a tangle of cocoa brown, again she didn't replace it. She just tossed the whole thing into the garbage.

Plants used to be her life.

Not too long ago they surrounded her at work and at home. But when her four-foot ficus tree had died, something left her and her love of plants disappeared. *Wrong. When Rick turned your world upside down, your plants became unimportant.*

She pretended not to notice their absence, but she did every time she came to work and every time she walked through her front door. This was what being with Rick meant. Losing important things in your life, like your dignity.

Dajah had had tons of it before she became involved with Rick. Barrels full. No man had ever walked over her, because she wouldn't allow it. No man had ever mistreated her, because she would not tolerate it.

The slightest suggestion of any mistreatment and Dajah would get in the wind. But not with Rick. Nope. No sir. *You hung in there and hung in there and even when you were holding on by your finger nails, you were still holding on.*

Dajah turned away from the thought. Besides, it was a new day now. What was past was past. A new venture was before her. She just had to decide if that's what she really wanted.

If someone had said that they would give her a million dollars to describe the color of a winter's night sky, Dajah would be out of a cool mil. She could never describe it. She never could pinpoint the exact color it was.

Dajah had tried for as long as she could remember. She had tried to put a color to the shades of deep luminescent blue that filled a New York skyline on a clear winter's night.

She tried to pinpoint what made it so special to her, what its ambience was. She couldn't. All she knew was in the winter time, on her drive home from work, she'd look up and see the incredible dark blue with flecks of white stars and something in her would go soft.

Now as she drove home, her eyes flickered back and forth from the sky to the road, the sky more important.

Jennifer Carpenter who had lived on Dajah's block when Dajah was a child used to called Dajah a sky freak. "You're a sky freak," Jennifer would bellow, those many years ago, when day would move to dusk and Dajah would stop whatever she was doing to gaze up.

Dajah hadn't been fazed by the name calling back then and she wasn't fazed by the memory now because Jennifer Carpenter had it right. Dajah was a sky freak.

Skies. She loved them. Sunsets — her favorite. So much so, if it was setting and she could see it, she'd stop whatever she was doing to watch it. In the warmer months, going to Jones Beach was her mainstay.

Wintertime had caught her out there too after her breakup with Rick.

Dajah glanced at the road and then looked back up at the sky. She thought about Jennifer Carpenter, sunsets and Jones Beach. Realized a trip was overdue.

With no checks expected and the end of the month approaching fast, Dajah knew there was nothing in her mailbox she would be really interested in. Just bills and junk mail. She opened the black lid and reached inside. Getting a good hold, she pulled the mail out.

She peeked inside to make sure nothing was stuck and saw a large legal-size envelope jammed around the sides. Curious, she worked it loose and checked for a return address. There was none.

She could tell by the denseness that there were quite a few pages. Dajah opened it on the way upstairs.

It took her a while to understand what she was reading, a while to connect the names and address on the page to what it all meant. It was a copy of a lease, signed and dated a few days ago for a three-bedroom apartment in Jamaica.

No, she didn't know the tenants Wilcox and Eva Stevens, but she knew the landlord. Rick had done what she thought he never would — rented out the second floor. But more importantly, he had made sure that she knew.

Dajah had kept quiet about the latest Rick matter, but this newest action sent her to the phone. She made a call to her best friend Frieda.

"A lease?" Frieda was saying a few minutes later.

"Yes. A lease. *The* lease. He rented out the second floor."

"And he sent you a copy."

"Yeah."

"Because?"

Dajah didn't want to say it. She wanted to discuss everything but the 'why.' Too late, she realized that she would have to tell it all. Talk about Rick coming to see her and asking for a second chance. Dajah would have to talk about how she didn't tell him to take a hike, but she'd think about it. She took the Fifth. "I don't know."

"There has to be some reason."

"Who knows. But he shouldn't have sent it. This is personal legal business. I shouldn't be having this."

"So what are you going to do about it?"

"Nothing."

"So what are you going to do with it?"

"Throw it away. I should have never gotten it in the first place."

"But you haven't talked to him since last year, right?"

"Well, no."

"No?"

"No."

"When?" Frieda wanted to know.

"When what?"

"When did you talk to him?"

Dajah swallowed. "Last week."

"Last week and you didn't tell me?"

No, Dajah hadn't. It was a can of worms she wanted to get settled within herself before she went ahead and shared it with the world. "I didn't want to say anything."

"Why not?"

"It's supposed to be over."

"Well, I think the fact you kept it a secret says it's not. So what did he say?" Dajah sighed. Broke it down to her friend. "Sounds like he's serious. I mean, he did rent out that apartment."

"Yeah, but that doesn't mean I'm going back."

"I don't see why not."

Dajah couldn't believe her ears. "Wait. Hold up. What do you mean you don't see why not? You know what it was like, Frieda. You know how jacked up that situation was."

"Key word — was. Was isn't is and, based on what I'm hearing, it's different now." Silence came from the other end. Frieda knew how cautious her friend could be, but she also knew that her friend really loved Rick. Despite the mask Dajah wore for the world, Frieda knew Dajah missed him. "Look, all I know is you went through a lot to be with him, but if the man is making changes in his life to make it work between you two, I say give him another shot."

"But that's the thing Frieda, how could I even begin to believe him? I mean he lied to me before."

"No, he lied to himself."

"Same difference."

"Fine. Think that way. But let me just say this. Love, real love is getting rarer and rarer these days. I say if it's there for you, take it."

But the words were easier to hear than to accept.

Since childhood they had been friends and since childhood, Rick had come to rely on the wisdom of his best buddy, Nelson. So it wasn't surprising to find Rick sitting in Nelson's basement apartment nursing a beer.

Dajah would have gotten the lease by now. She would have gotten the proof that he meant business. But he hadn't heard from her and couldn't bring himself to call. So he'd headed over Nelson's house to spill his heart.

"You tried. It didn't work. You have to let it go," Nelson's advice.

"How? She's all I want!"

"Yeah but you have to respect her choice."

"You want to know the funny thing?"

"What's that?"

"For a hot minute, when Dajah left me, I thought that maybe me and Gina could work things out."

"Gina?"

"Yeah. I mean she's changed Nelson. She's changed a whole lot. She doesn't get high anymore. She takes real good care of Kanisha now. Has a job and everything. For a hot minute, around Christmas time, I was thinking, yeah, we can do this."

"Because you were rebounding, bro, that's all. Dajah left you, Gina was there. Christmas. Nothing more, nothing less." Nelson gave him a stealth look. "Besides, the fact that you finally rented the apartment says a lot."

"Exactly. But Dajah's not seeing it."

"And you can't make her."

Rick looked sorrowfully at his friend. "I blew it, didn't I?"

"You did what you thought was right and you can't fault yourself that ... but you do have to accept the fact it may be over."

"She did say she would think about it."

"Yeah, but she might come back with a no. Regardless, you need to get on with your life. You've been living for other people for a while. It's time you do *you*."

* * *

Without a doubt Mike Rusk was a rookie. He had stink hours, worked the roughest cell block at Rikers and inmates tried to mess with him all the time. He hadn't learned the fine art of exerting authority without losing his cool and often left the prison frustrated.

But for all Mike Rusk lacked as a newly hired corrections officer, he was barely twenty-two and rumored to be a DJ. This was the reason Rick approached him as his shift ended and Mike's was starting.

They had only seen each other in passing. Had exchanged just a handful of words in the few months Mike had been there. Still Rick felt comfortable in approaching him about the best clubs Queens had to offer.

Taking Nelson's advice, Rick wanted to get into the swing of things.

"Depends on what you into," Mike had told him. "You into chicken heads, then you definitely want to check out The X-Spot. You want straight up hip hop, then you need to go to C.I. on Merrick. If Reggae's your thing, shoot over to Soca on the Ave. The mature crowd goes to After Seven."

"Mature?" Rick asked.

Mike chuckled. "Yeah, you know, that 'over thirty' crowd."

"Where's it at?"

"On Linden."

"I hear you DJ."

"I do my thing when my schedule allows."

"So where do you spin?"

"I be up at a joint on Sutphin sometimes, but this weekend, I'm going to be right here."

"And After Seven, it's tight?"

"Tight as it's going to get for Queens for someone like you."

"Someone like me?" Rick wanted to know.

"No offense, but a cat your age don't want to be up at a club with cats my age. It ain't a pretty sight."

Mike knew of what he spoke. Having been in a lot of clubs, too often he'd seen some old dude past thirty, dressed wrong, talking wrong, trying to get with somebody that was only a few years older than what would qualify as a baby sister.

The eighteen-nineteen-and twenty-year olds didn't want anything from men like Rick but the cash in their pocket. Unless Rick was looking to get shook down, he needed to stay away.

Until then Rick didn't take offense to certain segments of their conversation, but Mike's words raised the hairs on the back of his neck.

"My age?" Rick asked nonplussed.

"Yeah, yours. A cat like you roll up in there and you gonna be taken for everything you got and don't."

Rick took in the reed-thin young man in the fresh-from-the-factory uniform. His lip curled. "A cat like me." It wasn't a question but Mike nodded his head like it was. He wasn't taking back a thing.

Rick loosened up. Smiled even. He was past thirty but he wasn't dead. What did he care what this knucklehead thought? "Thanks bro." Rick headed towards the second of five locked exit gates as he made his way away from the prison block.

But the more he walked, the more the conversation came back to haunt him. Just yesterday he had been as young as Mike. In a blink of an eye, he had grown older. Between those two spans he saw how poorly chosen dreams had eaten up his life.

Rick knew he had to stop that.

The next day at work, Dajah stood at the massive shredder, feeding it a document she never should have gotten. There were a bunch of "never-should-haves" as far as Rick was concerned and this was just one more.

As the fast spinning steel blades cut into the lease agreement, Dajah found herself back to that moment in her life where an absolute no had become a maybe. She saw herself that night as Rick must have seen her — scantily dressed and scared to the teeth because instead of taking her car to Manhattan, she had decided to take the subway; a subway that had gone out of service two stops before hers.

It had been that mishap that had made her walk up the subway exit to David's place.

David. More failure in her life.

Two years ago, David, had been her boyfriend, perfect in every way. Too perfect. There had been no dramas. No highs, no lows. Just smooth sailing. What woman didn't want that? *Me*, Dajah almost said out loud. *I didn't want it. It bored me. Good old stable fun-loving honorable David got old.*

Dajah had ended things with David, but the two remained friends.

A year after her decision, she still hadn't found anyone close to be being what she wanted. So that night the train went out of service, she had headed towards David to see if the fire could be relit. But she had been too late.

David had just met someone new and he had been on his way to meet that new somebody. Rejected, Dajah had headed off to the diner up the street. Rick had wandered in there too. The rest was history, hers and Rick's, as disappointing as it was.

The trip down memory lane struck a cord inside of Dajah. Leaving David had been a big mistake. Had she made the same with Rick?

Think about it.

She had no other choice now.

Chapter Four

Dancing.

Dajah knew exactly the last time she had — New Year's Eve at Frieda's boyfriend Barry's house. It was almost February. It had been a minute too long. Besides, she was feeling stagnant. Movement, motion, working up a sweat would do her good.

She called Frieda, asking if she and her boyfriend Barry were up to some clubbing that weekend. In truth Frieda could have taken it or left it, but a good friend was a good friend. Frieda told her sure.

The minute Dajah got off the phone, she was in her bathroom mirror, checking out her eyebrows — they needed waxing, and her braids — they were a week short of being redone. If she could get an appointment for early Saturday morning, she could be out of the shop by mid-afternoon. She made a mental note to call her braider.

Friday night caught Dajah standing in her bathroom, the sink littered with real and fake hair. She had been taking out braids since she got in from work. Four hours later, she was still at it.

Of course she'd taken some breaks in between, eating some dinner, just plain sitting down on the edge of the toilet seat. But for the most part, she had been in the bathroom, taking out too many micro-braids.

It was always a little startling to see just how jacked up her hair looked when she took the braids out. Her hair stood out from her head like porcupine quills intertwined with greasy white lint. Flakes of dead skin covered her from forehead to chest and as always, her arms felt like they were going to fall off.

What price beauty?

Past midnight, Dajah found herself with just three more to do. She hurried up and got the braids loose, reached over and turned on the shower. When the water got hot, she stepped in, head going under the fast spray, making her sigh.

It felt good. Real good. Damn good. She could have stayed that way forever, head hanging under the spray, but there was hair to be washed, detangled, dried and greased. It was already close to one in the morning.

Shampoo in hand, her fingers were working more magic when she thought she heard a noise. No, not a noise, a specific noise. Her doorbell.

Head full of shampoo, eyes closed against the sting, Dajah reached blindly for a towel and found one. Turning off the water and stepping on the bathmat, she grabbed her robe and hurried out the bathroom, her eyes finding the clock. Twelve forty-five, just as she thought.

Twelve forty-five was the witching hour.

Twelve forty-five was the time Rick used to ring her doorbell after he finished his shift at Rikers Island. A corrections officer, he had worked the four p.m. to midnight shift. Forty-five minutes after his shifted ended, he would be at Dajah's door.

Like now? she wondered as she opened her upstairs apartment door and made her way down. She was halfway there before she remembered she hadn't made a decision yet and to see him now, drippy-wet and butt-naked under her robe, was a bad idea.

She headed back up the stairs and slowly went to the window. Gently, she eased back a blind and looked out into the night street. Nothing but parked cars, none of them the black Navigator he drove.

She was about to turn away when something caught her eyes, taillights glowing feral in the dark. By the time her brain registered the information, the vehicle was turning the corner, but she was certain she'd seen it — the black SUV.

The Italians had done it with pizzerias and bakeries. The Jews had done it with delis and diamond shops. The Asian population had done it with fruit stands and nail salons. The East Indians, with gas stations and fast food chains.

Immigrants coming to this country had found a void in the service industry and filled it, making their way through the American Dream. It was now the women of Africa's turn, hair braiding stores popping up like street vendors on nearly every corner.

Dajah entered the shop, every braider's chair filled, with half a dozen more clients waiting. Like so many others, she wore a hat to cover her wild spiky hair. Catching Abena's eye, she waved and took a seat on the hard folding chair. Picking up a magazine, she flipped through its tattered pages.

Outside, the world was going by with the quick pace of a sunny but cold Saturday morning. Sunshine was all any shopper needed and Jamaica Avenue was filled with people willing to spend their hard-earned cash on good sales — perceived or actual.

Dajah alternated between the magazine and the world outside. She was just about to flip the page when she saw something that stopped her heart — Rick and Gina — together. Together and talking. Together and not looking unhappy at all.

"Dajah, Dajah, come. Come."

It took her a hot second to realize Abena was calling her to the workstation; another hot second to disconnect from her thoughts. Taking one last look out the window, Rick and Gina disappearing from sight, she made her way to the chair, wishing for X-ray vision.

"You think she gonna like them?"

"What's not to like? They're Baby Phat, right?"

"Yeah, they are."

"And that's what she likes, right? Baby Phat?"

Gina nodded her head, sensing an argument and not wanting one. The last time she and Rick had gone shopping together, had gone anywhere together, had been last Christmas. Being out in the daylight with him felt good.

"Yeah, she'll like them." They bypassed McDonald's, Gina cramming her neck to look inside.

"Tarika still works there?" Rick asked.

"Yeah, she still hanging in there. She got a promotion and everything."

"Umm."

"I know you want to get back home and stuff, but could we go down to Margharita's? I'm dying for a slice of pizza."

It was early and Rick had more than enough time to take the long block down, but he found himself sighing and glancing at his watch anyway.

"We don't have to stand there and eat. I can eat it on the way back to the car. Just that I've been feinding for some for awhile."

Rick thought about the stop he had to make to Hack's, the men's clothing store he favored and how crowded the barber on Guy R. Brewer was going to be later. He wanted to get his SUV detailed too. But even with all that to do, he couldn't make time an issue. Could not use it to tell her no.

"I got to run to Hacks anyway, so while I'm heading over there, you can run to Margharita's, get your slice and we can meet back up on one-sixty-four."

Gina could but it wasn't about the pizza. It was about sharing a meal with Rick. She shook her head. "Nah, never mind."

He looked at her cautiously. "I thought you were fiending for a pizza."

"Nah, I'm cool."

That night Dajah stepped into the dance club, Frieda and her boyfriend Barry by her side. She was determined to get her party on. She was going to let it all go, including any chance with Rick. She had seen the truth this morning and truth was all her life would ever be about again. Gina wasn't gone at all.

Dajah wore her suede buckskin skirt with the tassels at the hemline and a black knit midriff that showed her belly button. Rounding out her outfit was her suede buck high-heeled boots. She was ready for some serious dancing.

She had barely entered the club when the music claimed her. Her head started moving, her fingers started snapping and she walked along, shaking to the beat. Someone tapped her shoulder. Asked her for a dance. She told Frieda and Barry she would catch them later. Went to the dance floor.

Dajah was out there for five records before she gave into the sweat on her face, the fast beats of her heart. She thanked her dance partner and went to find Barry and Frieda. Taking a seat, she flagged a barmaid. Ordered a drink.

"God that felt good."

"I bet it did," Frieda told her.

Another man approached the table. He extended his hand to Dajah but she declined. Winded, she just wanted to sit a few records out. Chill.

Two more men came by before her drink arrived. To each of

them she politely said no. Frieda leaned over. Sniffed at her neck. "What do you have on? You're just pulling them in."

Dajah laughed. It felt good to be noticed. "Maybe it's because for the first time in a while I'm free. No lies, no drama. No trifling men." The last part empowered her. The last part, a new pact she'd made with her soul.

Barry reached into his pocket and pulled out his sunglasses. "You're glowing so bright you blinding me."

Dajah laughed again. "Don't hate."

"Oh, I'm not hating."

She flipped her hand. "Forget you." She was turning away from Barry when another hand appeared. 'No thank you,' was already on her tongue when she looked up.

"One dance, that's all I'm asking for."

Dajah blinked. She looked at Frieda quickly. Looked back up at Rick. "No."

"One dance Dajah? Just one?"

"Which part of 'no' don't you understand," she said hotly.

Barry stood up, extended his hand. "Hey Rick."

Rick leaned over and hugged him. "Hey Barry. Good to see you." His eyes found Frieda's, unsure of her reaction, relieved to see a smile on her face. "Hey Frieda."

"Hey Rick."

Rick looked at Dajah, but her eyes were elsewhere. He looked at the empty seat. "This taken?"

"Yes." Dajah insisted.

He didn't sit down. "Well, it was good seeing you all."

"Same here," Frieda and Barry said quickly.

Rick took one look at Dajah, then slowly headed off. Reality had taken hold and now he knew. Dajah had made her decision and it wasn't the one he hoped for. Her reaction confirmed it. Obviously she just hadn't gotten around to telling him yet.

Frieda looked peeved. "Damn that was cold."

Dajah's eyes flashed back at her. "Was it?"

"Yeah, Dajah it was. All the man did was ask you to the dance floor."

"It's a whole lot more than that Frieda."

"Yeah? What is it then?"

Dajah shook her head, refusing to speak it. There was no way in the world she was going to admit to her friend that once again, she'd been had.

Her drink arrived. She picked it up and took a long sip, feeling Rick's eyes on her. Despite herself, she began looking back.

Was she looking for him or just looking? Rick wasn't sure as he stood behind a row of bodies three deep at the edge of the dance floor. The way her head was moving around, the way she seemed to be studying faces, it looked as if she were looking for him. A good sign?

Rick couldn't trust his instincts.

"Must be interesting."

Rick looked over, saw a pretty woman standing next to him with eyes like sunshine and lips like two slicks of caramel. "Excuse me?"

She smiled, showing a gap between her teeth. "I said, must be interesting."

"What?"

She cocked her head. "Whatever you were thinking about."

He couldn't help but smile. "I guess you can say that."

A hand extended his way. "I'm Faith."

He extended his own. "Rick."

She took a deep breath as if it took all her effort to speak her next words. "So Rick, did you come to think or did you come to dance?"

"I came to dance."

She took his hand. The contact warm against his palm. "Well, come on, let's go."

A while since he had shaken a leg, Rick found himself winded after three records. He begged off the dance floor.

"Let me buy you a drink," Faith offered.

He took in the sunshine eyes, the creamy lips. Nodded. "Sure."

They made it to the bar but there were no seats. They stood off to the side nursing their drinks, making small talk. "Never seen you here before," Faith confessed.

"I guess because it's been a while."

"How come?" Rick looked away. "Oh, is it a secret?" She smiled. "I like secrets."

"Do you?"

"Yeah."

"Why's that?'

"Because it keeps everybody guessing what the real deal is, that's why."

"Really?"

"Absolutely."

"So what's your secret?"

She shook her head, eyes never leaving his. "Can't tell."

"Why's that?"

"Some things you just need to keep to yourself."

Mysterious. Rick didn't know why he liked that, but he did. He relaxed a bit. "So what's so bad about your secrets?"

"Now didn't I just tell you I'm not telling?" Her eyes glittered, witchy and beckoning. Rick felt his dick get hard. Her hand brushed over it. The surprise touch, electrifying.

She saw his eyes widen. Cocked her head again. "You want to go somewhere?"

"Do you?" his voice thick.

"I wouldn't be asking if I didn't." She looked off. Looked back at him. "You know where the Capri is?"

He did. It was a little motel on Sunrise Highway. "Yeah."

"Let's go."

Faith looked sumptuous in her clothes. Out of them she looked even better.

Rick laid on the Queen-size bed, boxers on and nothing else, staring at her.

"You like?" she asked.

Yes, he did. Rick had only slept with three women in his whole life and seeing Faith stand there, naked, curvy, luscious and brown made all of them long-ago memories.

She moved to the bed, eased him back. Straddling him, her thighs cupped his hips. She began moving her pelvis like a belly dancer, wave after wave of shiny black hair, dewy fuscia lower lips in his line of vision.

He reached for her but she shifted away from his grasp. Carefully she got to her feet and stood, a tower of womanhood over him. Rick sat up, nose-dived between her thighs, rubbed his face against the thick, damp bush.

Wet, drippy wet, the inside of thighs glistened in the soft light. He slipped a finger into her, wishing it could be his tongue. He worked it in and slowly, each withdrawal making a sucking sound.

Rick went on that way until her eyes pinched for a final time and her legs started to tremble. Reaching over, he got a condom.

"You don't need that," she insisted.

"Yes, I do." It was a fire dousing moment, a streak of bright light in the smoky dimness of lust, but Rick was too far to turn back, too deep into it to stop. Underwear off, condom on, he eased her back against the bed and slipped into her hot wetness. Rode away his demons in the magic of her thighs.

Barry held her coat and Dajah slipped into it. "Ready," she announced as the three friends headed out into the night. Her shoulder was anticipating contact, her ears, buzzing for the calling of her name. Her arm tingled for a surprised grasp; her hand, the same sequence.

But as Dajah, Frieda and Barry walked up the block to Barry's car, as their footfalls took them further and further away from the club, the sensation faded as a new one emerged.

Dajah silently chided herself for even thinking it. Her face drew tight, angry at herself for even considering it. It was just her ego, she knew this. Just her ego wanting Rick to appear from nowhere begging for another chance, a chance she would not give.

Payback was a hard thing to resist and though she had gotten some, Dajah wouldn't have minded a little more. She would have loved to have Rick begging one more time.

Chapter Five

The morning sun was bright and harsh, though most of it was hidden by the thick drapes when Rick opened his eyes the next morning. Even in the gloom he could see the hunched over body going through his wallet. Saw a bankcard being lifted from its slot.

"Hey. What you doing?"

She turned, his card in her hand, mouth opened, caught.

"You ripping me off, is that what you're doing?" Rick asked, getting out of bed, making his way towards her.

"I was just going to run out and get us some breakfast," Faith answered, still pretty in the soft gloom.

"Without asking me?" Rick snatched his card from one of her hands, took his wallet from the other. He watched her as he back-tracked toward the bed lamp and clicked it on then went about the business of making sure nothing else was missing.

"You a cop?" she asked, his off-duty revolver suddenly in her hand. She was pointing the barrel his way and he hoped she hadn't removed the safety.

"Put that down." He didn't say it as a command, more as an afterthought, hoping the nonchalant tone would disarm whatever thoughts she was thinking. But seeing her standing there butt naked, with his gun between both her hands, that strange glittery look in her eyes, he realized two things immediately.

One, he didn't know her from Adam and two, she was a bit crazy.

"What if I don't want to?" Faith asked with a smile. "What if I said I want to blow you to fucking smithereens." She turned the barrel towards herself. "This thing got a silencer?" She waved the gun between herself and him. "Hey, I could do us both. You feel like living anymore Rick? I sure as hell don't. Maybe I'll just shoot myself."

Basic training had taught him how to disarm someone. And

though it had been a while since he had had that training, Rick knew he had to try.

"Why you want to shoot yourself? You got everything going for you."

"Everything?" She chuckled. It was a weird demented sound. "Everything. Yeah, you right about that. I got every damn thing. Good, bad, and more bad." She waved the gun to and fro. "Want to know what I got? Want me to tell you what I really got? Maybe after I tell you, you'll want me to shoot you too."

A chill moved down his spine. New fear replaced the old one. Rick wanted to run to the bathroom, turn on the hot water, open that pack of hard itchy soap and wash until he was raw.

"You forget too easy Rick," Faith went on to say, the gun comfortable, too comfortable in her hand. "Remember when I told you about secrets?"

Rick swallowed, sweat gathering on his face. He understood how he got in the situation but he didn't understand why. All he had been trying to do was live a little. "Put down the gun," he offered, mouth dry.

Her face pinched. "Put it down? Why should I? See, you should have taken the hint, but no, you had to be a greedy boy. And now that greed's going to cost you."

"Wait," was all he got out of his mouth before she pulled the trigger. The click made his eyes close and stunted his heartbeat, but nothing else.

Eyes shut, heart momentarily stopped, when it started it again, the recaptured beat stung his chest. Rick's mouth opened, laboring for breath. Then his eyes opened and when they did, he took in Faith, standing there, the beautiful brown skin beauty with the barrel of the gun aimed at his head.

"I never took off the safety." She pitched the gun on the bed. Went around the room snatching up her clothes. Slipping her dress over her head, she left the room barefoot, panties, bras and shoes in her hand.

Most of the time Dajah didn't dream and when she did, it was the un-intrusive kind. She had learned long ago not to research Freud when they didn't make sense. She had learned that dreaming of your high school was as common as dreaming about the house you grew up in.

Dajah had learned to forget them the moment she awakened. She had never searched for signs or clues in the mind journeys that came with sleep, but this dream had been different. A bit too real.

She had been in the upstairs apartment of Rick's house, boxes everywhere, her name written in magic marker on all of them. There were so many boxes that she couldn't see anything else. They crowded around her like a skyscraper city, floor to ceiling, making everything shadowy.

Someone was calling her from downstairs, the voice urgent and insistent. She knew she had to get to it but she couldn't find the door. Like a mouse in a maze, she moved through the narrow isle of cardboard towers, feeling more lost with each step she took.

And then they began to quake, the paper box city began vibrating as if an earthquake was occurring. She looked up and saw a box falling towards her and she covered her head. One second before it reached her, she woke up.

Dajah awoke with her heart beating too fast in her chest. Fear was choking her, so much so, she started coughing and more than a few seconds passed before she could stop. Swinging her legs out of the bed, she sat on the edge.

She sat trying to still her heart, corral her thoughts, squash her fears, the image of her inside the apartment crammed with boxes as fresh and real as the mattress beneath her.

A bird was tapping on the window.

Rick wished it would stop because it was disturbing his sleep and all he wanted was to sleep. He didn't want to be awake and thinking. He didn't want to be awake and revisiting. He wanted sleep to take away consciousness, but the woodpecker's rap was becoming insistent.

It's glass stupid. Can't peck glass. Rick strained to hold onto his slumber.

"Wreak. Wreak."

Did woodpeckers talk? Not only was the dumb-ass bird tapping on the wrong thing, it was trying to say something.

"Wreak."

The bird was confused and its confusion was interfering with his zzz's. Rick opened his eyes, threw back the covers and went to his bedroom window. Raising the blind, the dull gray afternoon light hurt his eyes and made him squint. But it was the sight of his father's face peering up at him that made him jump.

"You didn't answer the phone. We were worried," his mother began the moment he opened the front door. They were looking at him curious. Three pairs of eyes sizing him up with trepidation.

"Sorry," he muttered, rubbing his face. "I didn't hear it ring."

"You sick, daddy?"

Rick looked at his daughter wedged between his mother and father. Felt new fears dance along his spine. He tried to smile, but the effort failed him. "No, just a little tired."

His father came through the door, Kanisha second, his mother bringing up the rear. "Too much fun last night?" Mr. Trimmons wanted to know. But it was obvious from his expression that he didn't think that was the real cause.

"Yeah, too much."

"We were waiting for you to come pick up Kanisha and when you didn't, we called. It started snowing, so we decided to bring her by ourselves."

"Snowing?"

"For the last two hours."

It was then that he noticed the melting flakes on his daughter's knit hat, the ones clinging and blending with the gray of his father's head, and on his mother's silk scarf.

"Can we make a snowman daddy? Can we?" Kanisha wanted to know and the last thing Rick wanted to do.

He wanted to get back into bed and pull the covers over his head. He didn't want to think about what had happened to him this morning, how he almost lost his life to a woman who looked good but was crazy. And worse.

It was the 'worse' part that had him in its clutches. *Remember what I told you about secrets ... after I tell, you'll want me to shoot you too.* He had been careful. He had been safe, *except for my finger. My finger all up in her ...*

He had scrubbed his hands until they were raw. Had scrubbed his body with as much gusto. When he came home he took another shower just for good measure, dousing himself head to toe with antibacterial soap.

But antibacterial soap didn't kill everything.

"Can we daddy?"

Up until last night, he had only slept with three women. Did that justify a death sentence? Three women, becoming four, did that mean he deserved what had happened to him, what could happen to him?

Up until last night, he had always done the right things. Rick had never done a one-night stand. Had never tested those waters. But he did last night. Was it a crime? Hadn't Nelson told him to start living his life. Wasn't that why he had gone to the club in the first place, to start some living?

"Daddy?" Kanisha was talking, but Rick wasn't hearing her. He was too deep in his thoughts.

Faith had looked okay. No, she looked better than okay. How could he have resisted that? How could he have resisted a woman who was offering up some pleasure without all the formality and rigmarole that normally went with bedding someone new?

How could he have ignored the way she touched him last night at the club around all those people or how she poonany-danced over him?

"She talking to you Rick. Kanisha's talking to you." He snapped out of it. Caught his father's worried eyes. "Your daughter's asking about building a snowman. I promised her you would when she got home."

Rick looked at his mother, back to his father and then at his daughter. Wanted to cry. Didn't. He cast off his gloom. Forced a smile. "Sure we can. Let me get some clothes on. You go get your boots."

Rick knew from yesterday that Kanisha's boots were too small but the discomfort had been okay because it meant playing in the snow. Going off to school was a different ball game and as he struggled to get them over his daughter's shoes, she winced and moaned.

With force and might he attempted to get them on, already tired even though it was just a little before seven in the morning.

Yesterday, as was required by law, he had shoveled the sidewalk in front of his house and had cleared the path to the door as well as the steps. This morning when he awoke, it had been as if he hadn't touched it and Rick had to shovel again.

Everything in him ached because of it and he was in no mood for the prisoners of Rikers Island. He wanted to call in sick and tried to, but his supervisor told him that outside of a death, he had to report to work.

"They too small daddy," Kanisha said as Rick struggled to get the second boot on.

"I know they are baby, but you have to wear them today."

"But they hurt."

"You only have to wear them to school. Then you can take them off, okay?" He got the second boot on and felt Kanisha's agony as she stood and walked a few paces, her gait awkward. "I'll buy you some more later."

But later was too far away to be considered. Kanisha looked down at her hurting feet and looked back at her father. She saw the pain in his eyes, her five-year old wisdom telling her it didn't have anything to do with her too small boots.

By the weekend, the side streets, sidewalks and main streets had been cleared of snow. Along busy avenues, piles of it sat icy and gray and storeowners spent their day spreading salt over slick patches.

By the weekend, the beauty of the late January storm could be appreciated without the hassle of maneuvering in it and Dajah took advantage of the opportunity. She headed to Jones Beach where a different world greeted her.

Drifts of white were everywhere. Patches of untouched snow sat as perfect as when it first fell. Footprints, dozens of them spotted the board walk in orbs of brown. The seashore held small glaciers, curved from water meeting snow. The sun dazzled off of the whiteness, making sparkling confetti in all colors of the rainbow.

Dajah stood at the boardwalk, absorbed, in tune. A few brave souls passed by her, but in that moment she felt one with the world.

"Makes you wish you were a kid again."

Dajah looked up. Smiled uncertain. She didn't hear the tall black guy approach, but he was now standing three feet away. "Do I know you?"

"No. But I figured there had to be some connection between us. I mean how many people come to the boardwalk in the heart of winter with snow no less?"

Dajah looked closer, trying to determine if the man before her was a friend or a foe. His eyes held bemusement and it unnerved her bit. She found herself looking around.

His hands went up, big ones covered in dark suede gloves. "I'm harmless," he offered with a smile. "I'm just out here walking my dog. I'll go if you want me to."

She didn't notice his canine, but there at his feet sat a beautiful animal. Its red coat glowing in the lowered sun. She looked back at him. Older then she was, but not unkind on the eyes.

And he did have it right. Nobody else she knew or had ever known came to the beach in the wintertime. She looked away, converting a smile. "No. I believe you."

He extended his hand. "I'm Jeff? And you are?"

Despite herself, she smiled, blushed even. She realized he was coming on to her, that his approach, the whole bit, was a come-on. It felt good to get a hit after not getting one in a while. The other night with Rick didn't count.

"Dajah."

He nodded as if she had confirmed some assumption. "Yeah, you look like a Dajah."

"Really?"

"Really."

"Now just what does a Dajah look like?"

"You." He smiled. Showed his teeth. Not pearly, but at least they were straight. He reached down, patted his canine. "And this is Kelly."

With it's red coat and long body, there was no doubt the dog was an Irish Setter. A pretty one. She told him so.

"Yeah, she's something special."

"A girl?"

"What other kind of dog is there?"

She laughed again, tickled. Looked back up at Jeff, eased. "Well, a male dog for starters."

"Yeah, if you're female."

She blinked. Held up her hand. "Hold up. Are you calling me the "b" word?"

"You mean beautiful, sure, I'm calling you that."

Her cheeks rose a third time. She shook her head. "Do you always make yourself so comfortable with folks you don't know?"

He extended his hand again. "Hi, I'm Jeff."

"No, I'm not shaking your hand anymore and yes, I know who you are. You're Jeff."

"And you're Mya."

Her eyebrow raised. "Who?"

"Mya, I mean Dajah." But suddenly he wasn't so confident. He looked off, taking the joy of the moment with him.

Dajah looked away too.

Jeff's glove hand came down on top of the canine's head, his voice breaking the stillness. "You ready girl?" The dog stretched its neck in reply. Jeff found Dajah's eyes, smiled, but there was a touch of sadness in them. "It was nice meeting you."

"Nice meeting you too."

Soon man and dog were trotting up the snow covered board-walk. Dajah found herself watching until they were just specks on her horizon, part of her wondering if they were coming back.

There was a warmth inside of her now, the kind she hadn't felt in a while. Real comfort. Real ease. Not music inspired, not meditation inspired. Nothing forced, just natural, like breathing. For those few seconds with Jeff, things inside of her had reassembled, became whole again.

Because he's a nice guy. Easy and assured. Drama-less, I bet.

She found herself looking back in the direction he had gone. Wondered about him, wondered a lot about him. But mostly Dajah pondered if they would ever get the chance to meet up again.

Other things compounded as she nestled in her thoughts. Things like the empty spaces of her life and what she could do about them. A thought came to her and stayed. On this journey back to her center, she knew just where she would start.

When her four-foot high ficus tree had died last year, because she had been paying too much attention to Rick, Dajah let it go. Sort of.

She convinced herself that it was just a plant and in the scheme of things, Rick and Kanisha were more important and if her ficus, affectionately called "Baby" died, it was no biggie.

But the truth of the matter was every time Dajah stepped into her apartment after its demise, every time she glanced by the double windows and saw the spot her ficus tree used to occupy, she was filled with guilt.

Dajah had not replaced "Baby" because for the longest time, she felt she wasn't worthy of another tree. It was the same reason she had not replaced the plants in her office. She had mishandled her responsibilities and felt bad about it.

Dajah loved greenery. So much so, "Greenhouse" was the moniker she used on internet chat sites. But Rick and his mess had changed that innate part of her and she had given up on green thumbing.

Until now.

Now, it was all she wanted. Now she wanted to fill her spaces with life-growing things. The urge was so deep she went straight to Valley Stream when she left the beach and headed to Home Depot. It was time to start putting back the pieces of her life.

Moving through the automatic doors of the huge orange and white warehouse, Dajah stopped to ask where the plants were. She moved through the store until she reached her destination. There before her were dozen of ficus trees awaiting her selection.

One called her name. Whispered: *Dajah*. She went up to it. Joy, rushing her. Four feet tall, three feet wide, her heart went out to the ficus before she got close enough to touch. Flagging down an orange-vested salesperson, Dajah bought the tree and paid the extra sixty dollars to have it delivered the next day.

She deserved some joy in her life again. Dajah was finally about getting it.

Chapter Six

The bag of marijuana shifted as Gina searched for a clean bra. For over a week it had been tucked into her underwear drawer. That and the rolling paper. She had gone so far as to cop but she hadn't smoked it yet. Every day she wanted to.

Gina had worked hard for this new place in her life. She had worked hard to do the right things. Her counselor, Mrs. Jones, had told her that there would be good times and bad times and no matter what, she had to cling to the good.

But the good was fading.

There had been layoffs at the library. It seemed like every week somebody was getting their walking papers. Every time Gina went to work she never knew if she was going to be next or not. It made her whole day tense.

She had tried to talk to Rick about it. Gina tried to share her concerns, her worries, her fears with Rick, but emotionally and mentally, he was in some other place. And with the hours her friend, Tarika was working, catching up with her was difficult.

There was a knock on her door.

"Yeah?"

"I just wanted to make sure you was up."

"I'm up," she shouted, wishing Jefferson wasn't home. The idea of a nice thick spliff made her mouth water. She couldn't do it now, but maybe later. Later, when Jefferson wasn't around. Later, when the big old house held just her in it. Right now she had to get ready for work.

Kanisha knew something was going on with her daddy. She just wished she knew what it was.

It was a different Rick that picked up Kanisha from after-school care, a different Rick who was irritable and no fun at all. Kanisha was used to anger from her mother but never from her daddy.

Now as she sat at the kitchen table, cutting out pictures from magazines, she felt his presence like one of those summer storms that turned the sky black. It hadn't struck yet, but she knew it was coming.

She needed help cutting out the picture of the dog, but her mouth wouldn't work. The safety scissors weren't very sharp and she had a lot more to cut out. She had to cut out an egg, some food and something that started with "G." She was working on her alphabet book and she just wanted to get it done. If she finished, she could go upstairs and play with her new friends.

"What you doing Kanisha?"

"These scissors don't work."

"What do you mean they don't work? They were working a minute ago?"

"They not cutting daddy."

"Or maybe you aren't trying."

Her head dipped. She fought back tears. Kanisha tried to make her eyeballs take them back in, but a tear slipped down her cheek.

"What you crying for?" Kanisha wouldn't answer. Couldn't. Her father had that tone in his voice that scared her. "I asked you a question? Answer me."

She couldn't even pick up her head to look at him. Just stared at the table, tears wetting the rough ecru construction paper beneath her.

He grabbed her arm, hard enough to get her attention. It was the feel of Rick's big hand around the tiny arm that cut into his anger. It was the feel of Rick's thumb closing over his fingers, the tiny bit of flesh between, that made him pause.

He let his daughter's arm go, his heart beating too fast. Gingerly he laid a hand on her shoulder. Felt her stiffen. Rick drew back. Got up from the table. He went into the kitchen, resting his hands against the counter. Hung his head.

Rick was there for a while.

"Something wrong with daddy," Kanisha was telling her mother days later as they stood at the door watching Rick's Navigator leave the curb.

But Kanisha wasn't telling Gina nothing Gina didn't already know. He had said few words to Kanisha before he left. Rick had barely kissed her forehead. There had been no hugging, no talk of missing her for the two days she would be with Gina. None of that.

"He been mad and mean all week," Kanisha went on to say. "What's the matter with him?"

Gina didn't have a clue. But misery had a fondness for company. Her life wasn't that great, why should Rick's be?

"Huh Mommy, you know?"

"Do I live with him? What you asking me for?"

It had been a while since she had heard that tone in her mother's voice. A while since she'd felt the simmering rage. Kanisha looked at her mother and grew quiet. Without words, she followed her mother upstairs to her room, not even asking if Granddaddy Jefferson was home.

Rick drove, feeling like a dead man. He drove, his mind in a thousand directions, barely paying attention to the stop signs and traffic lights. Four days since he had taken the AIDS test, he still had three more to go.

He didn't think he could last that long.

He had been taking the test twice a year for the last few years, but this time was different. This time he had come close, too close, to a person possibly infected. Possible? She so much as said she was.

His world had unraveled. In a blink of an eye, he had found himself in a chaos of which he couldn't escape. He wanted relief from the pressure point inside his head. He wanted ease from the cauldron of fear that had taken up inside of him.

He wanted Monday to be here so he could find out if he had AIDS or not. Rick wanted to beat himself senseless over his stupidity. His whole life, in that moment, felt like one long road of ignorance.

He should have never gotten together with Gina. He should have never had had a kid with her. He should have never put his daughter before his happiness. He should have never let Dajah go.

He should have never gone to the motel with that woman. He should have never let his lust get in the way of sensibility.

A car horn sounded. Rick looked up and saw a car heading his way. He had drifted into the opposite flow of traffic. Turning the steering wheel hard to the right, more car horns erupting around him.

Pulling over, he put his truck in park. Hung his head. Tried to gather his thoughts.

He never saw the unmarked car pull up behind him. Never saw the two plainclothes officers approach, hands on their guns. All Rick knew was the silence was interrupted by raps on his window.

Looking up, he saw a badge pressed to the glass.

Rick sat in the back of the unmarked car, the sounds of life muted. He felt the eyes of people walking by, feeling as guilty as they perceived him to be.

At least they hadn't cuffed him.

Rick knew police procedure. Knew that the officers hadn't followed it. They were supposed to have asked for his license and registration first, instead of hauling him out of the car like that. But he also knew his shiny less then two-year-old Navigator, the blackness of his face and the erratic way he had been driving made them forgo procedure.

He knew that too many black men had been gunned down for less offenses too.

He had been forced to the back of his truck, pressed against it and his legs were kicked apart.

The officer had been in the middle of patting him down when his off duty revolver was discovered strapped to his ankle. Before Rick could explain, he was face down on the ground with a knee in his back.

He tried to talk with his cheek pressed into the asphalt, but his words came out mumbled and the officer was shouting for him shut up. All Rick was trying to tell them that he was a C.O., a corrections officer and was licensed to carry, but when the service-issued revolver was pressed to his skull, he hushed.

He was forced to stay that way, on the ground, knee in his back, gun to his head until his wallet was found. Inside was his badge and without apology, they had hoisted him to his feet.

Still, they had taken his gun, his wallet and his keys and he was ordered into the back of the unmarked police car. They had to make sure his info checked out. His license and plates were being run and though he knew they would find nothing, it was bad that he had been stopped.

Now as he sat in the back seat, the radio squawking loudly, he studied the back of the two patrolmen's heads, experiencing, for the second time in his life, what it felt like to be on the wrong side of the law.

For the nine years he had worked as a corrections officer at Rikers, Rick had felt little pity for the prisoners there. But in that moment, he was right there with them.

"Ten-Four," the officer said into the walkie-talkie. Turning to his partner, the officer nodded and the partner got out of the squad car.

Going around to the passenger door, the cop opened it and handed Rick his wallet. "You're free to go."

But the moment demanded more. The moment demanding a heartfelt apology and Rick's mouth was opening before he could think. "That's it. That's all you got to say?"

"I said you're free to go."

"Where's the goddamn sorry?"

The officer stared at him and Rick stared back. They were both officers of the law, both supposed to be on the right side of things, but the color of Rick's skin and the color of the officers was the valley between them.

Rick scooted out the back and snatched his wallet, his keys, his gun. He stared at the officers badge number and committed it to memory. Looking at the officer a long time, Rick headed back to his vehicle.

The Cambria Heights neighborhood of low houses, trimmed hedges and quiet streets seemed all the quieter as Rick stood at the side door of the ranch, waiting for Nelson to answer. He knew Nelson was home because his car was in the driveway. What he didn't know was why Nelson was taking so long to answer the door.

"I'm coming," Rick heard as he laid on the bell. The door opened halfway, Nelson appearing, sweaty and out of breath. "Hey Chief. Wasn't expecting you."

"Can I come in?'

Nelson glanced down the basement steps. Glanced back at his friend. "Bad time man."

"Company?"

"Yeah."

"Sheena?"

"Yeah." Nelson looked at him closely. "You okay?"

"If you call being roughed up by five-O and possibly contracting AIDS okay, then yeah, I'm straight."

Nelson sighed. Nodded. "Wait here." Disappeared down the basement stairs.

There was no real dislike between them and they had always been civil to each other, but there was no missing the eye-cutting Sheena passed on to Rick as she hugged Nelson goodbye and hand-waved towards Rick before heading up the basement steps.

"Sorry man," Rick said, the two men settling on the couch.

"No thing." But both men knew it was. "So, what's going on?"

Rick had come to Nelson many times in the past. He had poured his heart out, asked for advice and drop more than a bucketload of Gina drama on him. But not even that extensive history made the telling of Faith any easier. "It felt good," he ended up saying. "Not just good. But right. The way she just came up to me . . . going to the hotel. I felt like that was the way it was supposed to be."

"Fantasy yeah. Real life?" Nelson shook his head.

"I know that now."

"Should have known that then. You got to learn to read people better. No matter how fine a sister is, no woman in her right mind is going to do that — tip off to Motel 6 with you five minutes after you met. And if she wants to, then you definitely need to leave that alone."

"I was trying to live my life, like you said I should do."

"Live your life yeah. Be stupid about it . . . " Nelson didn't finish. Changed his words. "Look, I know you been feeling all cooped up lately. I know you were just trying to get back into the swing of things. You made a mistake, but don't beat yourself up over it. And besides, you were covered right? Bottom line is this. You were just trying to do something good for yourself."

"Was I? Was I really?" Rick shook his head, confusion thick. "It's like I don't even know me anymore Nel. And that's some scary shit." Scary, a word Rick had never used before. "There's so much going on inside of me now, so much."

Nelson nodded. Allowed Rick to speak.

"I look at my life and see all the messes. I thought I was cleaning it up, but it's like I missed the most important thing."

"Dajah."

Rick looked at his friend, eyes wild, greedy in the affirmation. "Yeah. How did I lose that?"

"How, why, when. It doesn't matter 'cause she's gone. And I think, no, I *know* this whole thing is about her being gone."

"I saw her."

"Saw who?"

"Dajah. That night at the club. I didn't even know she was going to be there, but she was and I couldn't stop myself from going over to her table. Even after she basically told me to go away, I was still standing there. That ain't me Nelson."

"She tell you what she decided?"

Rick shook his head in disgust. "No, she didn't come out and tell me to have a nice life, but from how she was acting at the club and considering it's been over a week, I can see the sign post."

"Okay, so she gone and now you have to accept that. The sooner you say it's over, the clearer your head's going to get. Till then?" Nelson shrugged.

Hardball. Nelson knew his friend needed it even if his friend wasn't trying to hear it. Nelson switched subjects. "Now what about the police thing. What are you going to do about it?"

"Nothing."

"So you just gonna let it slide?'

There inside of his friend's eyes Rick saw a different fire, deep, bottomless. Rick knew the source. Knew it went beyond what happened to him. As a young black man behind the wheel of a BMW, Nelson had been the victim of 'driving while black' too many times to count.

"The shit happens ... I know. Been on the other side myself." Rick didn't wear the NYPD uniform, but he felt a part of the league. Pressing charges would say differently. Pressing charges would take away the sense of security.

"That doesn't make it right."

"I said I wasn't going to do anything."

"You sure?"

"I'm sure."

There was no missing the disappointment on Nelson's face.

The mist shot out of the nozzle, fell softly to the gather of green leaves below, coating them in a gray fuzz. Moving around the tree, Dajah aimed the spray bottle and pulled the trigger again. "Feels good right?"

That she was talking to her plant wasn't anything new. Over the last few weeks, she found herself talking to her ficus like it was a good friend.

"I'm so happy you're here, yes I am. And you're just growing and sprouting." She bent down, touched a new shoot. "See there? You like being with Dajah, don't ya? Yeah, you like being here. Well, I like being here with you too."

Better, that's what was going on inside of her these days. Dajah was feeling better about life and things. She felt clearer, focused, on point. *Even with no one in my life, my life is still pretty good.*

She thought about the boardwalk, about the man named Jeff. She relived the moment and wondered what went wrong. *He got my name wrong and everything changed, but up till then ...*

Up till then, it was the most stimulating moment she had shared with a guy in a long time. Up till then, she could have stayed out there till midnight just talking. He was confident, funny and smart, all the traits she liked.

"Cut it Dajah, stop thinking about some man you don't even know," she found herself saying out loud. But it wouldn't be first time she'd done that and she had no doubt it wouldn't be the last.

Chapter Seven

Gina sat on the bathroom toilet, lid down and window open. Even though the cold air was making her shiver, there was no denying the mellowness the moment was giving her.

She sucked on the spliff as if her life depended on it. Eased back against the cool porcelain of the toilet tank. Jefferson had gone off to Atlantic City last night and Kanisha was asleep. She finally had her peace.

It was her third spliff for the week. By all accounts, she was keeping it under control. Times used to be when she'd have three, four a day. Three in just five days was a sure sign of control.

Her whole life was work and having Kanisha on the weekends, nothing more, nothing less. Having some weed every now and then wasn't hurting nobody. If anything, it helped.

"Momma. I'm hungry."

Gina cracked one eye open but couldn't get the other to work. Sleep was calling her and hard. She closed her eye.

"Momma. I'm hungry."

"Go ask Jefferson to get you something to eat."

"He ain't here."

Gina remembered. He had gone to Atlantic City with her mother. Wasn't due back until later in the day. Still, the bed felt warm and she was drowsy. She wasn't up to moving just yet. "Go see if there's cereal."

"I checked. There is none."

"I'll get you something in a little while," Gina offered, burrowing under the covers, falling back fast asleep.

At five and a half, Kanisha had the dos and don'ts down to a science. She wasn't supposed to touch the stove. She wasn't supposed to turn on the gas or even use the microwave. But hunger was

an insistent thing. At Kanisha's age, it didn't know how to go away.
It just kept knocking inside her stomach.

Though her mother said she would fix her something 'in a
minute,' a bunch of them had passed already and her mother was
still fast asleep in bed.

That was the reason Kanisha was downstairs in the kitchen,
looking into the refrigerator for something to eat. There was half a
pack of bacon, and a carton of eggs. There was a jar of Welch's
grape jelly on the door and a whole loaf of bread.

Kanisha stood staring into the refrigerator trying to figure out
how she could eat without touching the stove. Without turning on
the gas. Without using the microwave.

All of it was 'hot.' 'Hot' cooked stuff. She needed to find
another 'hot.' Closing the refrigerator, she looked around. There
was the faint hiss of steam coming from the cast iron radiator. That
was a 'hot' and she wouldn't be turning nothing on to use it.

Going back to the refrigerator, she took out the bacon. Opening the pack, she took two slices of raw pork and laid them on the
curve of the radiator. She jumped back, expected hot grease to pop.
But the meat didn't even sizzle.

It just laid there, the white and pink strip unchanging.

She had seen bacon being made before and knew she would
have to "turn" it. Getting a fork, she pierced one strip and flipped
it. Standing back, she waited for the smoke to erupt. For the sizzle
to come. But the only thing that came was the faint smell of raw
meat.

Maybe the 'hot' of the radiator wasn't the same 'hot' of a stove.
Maybe that's why the meat just laid there, getting a bit translucent
at the tips. Maybe she would have better luck with an egg.

Kanisha went to the refrigerator and got an egg. Cracking it
against the edge of the radiator, she poured the contents over the
two-inch wide bar. It slipped down the side and onto the floor.

A mess. She had made a mess. She always got into trouble for
making messes.

Kanisha grabbed the roll of paper towel, pulled off six sheets
and dropped down. Inching her way closely to the bottom of the
radiator, she looked beneath it. It was dark down there. Dusty too.
The heat was really hot and she knew if she tried to get to the egg
she would burn herself.

Kanisha got up from the floor, threw the unused paper towels into the garbage and concentrated on her bacon that didn't look so pink and white anymore, but more brownish. She thought about toast and got two slices of bread. Folding them over the curve of the radio cores, she pressed them until heat reached her fingers. Then she 'turned' the bacon again, mouth watering in anticipation.

Hunger alleviated the warning signals that the mouth and tongue sent out. Hunger made the matter of getting substance into the stomach more important that the safety of the substance. This was the reason Kanisha was able to chew the rubbery half cooked bacon, munch on the dusty, dirt-smeared warm bread.

This was the reason she ate without hesitation or question, downing it with a glass of orange juice. A minute after she had finished her meal, her stomach began to hurt. A minute after she had consumed her breakfast, she had to throw up.

She didn't make it to the bathroom. Only got as far as the living room when the contents of her stomach let loose, sending a projection of half cooked meat and dirty warm bread smeared with too much jelly across the Persian runner.

Kanisha clutched her stomach, fell to her knees, mouth open, throat straining. Helpless she remained on the floor, vomit coming out of her with force, the muscles in her whole upper body, piano-wire taut.

"Kanisha?"

She wanted to look up, but she couldn't. Vomiting had her in its grip. But even in the midst of her upchucking, relief was moving through her. Grandpa Jefferson was home. He would make her better. He would take care of her. Clean up all the messes she had made before her Momma woke up.

Jefferson never yelled. Never.

If something made him mad, he got sad, but never angry. So it was hard for Kanisha to hear all that he was saying to Gina as Kanisha laid in Jefferson's bed, a wet, runny bowel movement and some ginger ale making her tummy feel more settled.

Even though Kanisha couldn't hear what Jefferson was saying, it must not have been nice because her mother was yelling and cursing. Screaming about she was a good mother and Kanisha should-n't have done what she'd done, which confused her.

She knew she had made two messes, but she hadn't turned on the stove or the microwave. She just tried to get something to eat.

"I'm tired of this shit. God damned tired!" Gina bellowed. *Tired of this shit* was a pre-curser for change. *Tired of this shit* always signaled a not-so-good situation getting worse. It had been a while since Kanisha had heard her mother say it, but the meaning was always the same.

While it wasn't rare for Jefferson to drop Kanisha back home, it was rare that Jefferson came inside, sat down on the couch and had a talk with Rick. But that was exactly what Jefferson did.

He drove Kanisha home. Rang the doorbell and waited for Rick to answer. He greeted Rick warmly, asked if he could come in. That he needed to talk to Rick about something. "It's important," Jefferson said softly.

It was obvious from Rick's expression that he didn't want to hear anything Jefferson had to say, but he let the old man in any-way. He told Kanisha to go to her room and she went, but she kept her ear glued to the door.

"Gina's heading for trouble again," was how Jefferson began.

"That's on Gina."

"No, it's on you too."

"What Gina does and doesn't do don't have nothing to do with me Jefferson."

"Well now, that's where you're wrong. What Gina do and don't do has everything to do with you because it has everything to do with Kanisha."

"Something happen?"

Jefferson sighed. Nodded. "She been messing with that pot again. And today when I got in, Kanisha was sick all over the living room because the child was hungry and cooked bacon and toast on the radiator."

"What?"

"You heard me. Her momma in the bed, dead to the world and Kanisha downstairs trying to cook pork on the radiator."

"She okay?"

"Yeah. She threw up. Had a bowel movement. I gave her ginger ale but you need to be watching her stool to make sure she ain't get no worms."

"So what's Gina saying about all this?"

"What she always say, it ain't her fault. Kanisha should have waited till she got up. But a hungry child is a hungry child and Gina should have gotten up like she was supposed to." Jefferson looked off. "You know I love that girl like she my own. And I took her in 'cause I know she got some good in her. But as of late it's like the good is being wiped away. And as much as I love her, I can't be having no nonsense up in my house."

"What do you want me to do?"

"Talk to her. She'll listen to you."

"And if she don't?"

"You got to at least try. If not for her, for your child." Jefferson stood up. "I'll let my own self out."

Tarika had given her the key in case of an emergency. "In case something happen to me," she had told Gina. Gina had never used it before but she couldn't stay in Jefferson's house another minute.

She knew Tarika was at work and so she let herself in. Walking up the three flights of steps, she unlocked the door at the top and stepped inside. Soft light greeted her as it spilled in from the kitchen window. Thick white candles, their wicks burnt at the tips, left behind the faint smell of Vanilla.

Gina headed towards the bedroom, the queen-size bed with the damask comforter, her destination. Stripping down to her underwear, Gina slid into the cool comfort and closed her eyes. She didn't toss, she didn't turn, she just gave into the weariness that claimed her. When she woke up, it was past six in the evening.

The ten hours Tarika put in behind the counter at McDonald's was exhausting, but coming home to her own place made the taxing times worthwhile.

The neighborhood she lived in wasn't the best. Even the house her third-floor apartment was in wasn't too kind on the eyes, but there was no doubt that heaven, her haven, lay behind the door and Tarika was looking forward to relaxing after her long shift.

Her apartment was by no means large. Typical of an attic space, her bedroom, kitchen and living room railroaded from the front of the house to the back. But she had made it into her refuge with paint, muslin, dried bamboo, stalks, shoots and vases half the height she was.

She had invested in copper pots, tasteful but cheap reprints and throw pillows. She burned scented candles, read decorating magazines and played music that she liked to sing along to.

She kept bottles of chilled inexpensive wines that were sweet to her tongue and easy down the throat. She had reinvented herself.

Gone were the days where life had no meaning and her days were getting high and not much else. Gone were the days where she lived in her Uncle's dark, dank basement because she had no place else to go and having a job was as faraway from her life as China.

Tarika was about something these days and had put her money where her mouth was. She worked hard to carve the life she lived and was rewarded every time she stepped through her own front door.

But she nearly went into shock when she came in and found a sink full of dirty dishes, crumbs on her kitchen table and the scent of marijuana in the air.

Gina coming out of her bedroom, eyes red and higher than two kites completed the shocking picture. "Hey girl." So overwhelming was the scenario that for a minute Tarika couldn't get her mouth to work. "Waz 'zup?" Gina asked with a syrupy grin.

"What you doing?"

But Tarika knew what Gina was doing, the joint in her hand sending up curls of gray smoke, said it all.

"What you mean what I'm doing? I was waiting for you."

"You smoking, up in my house?"

"Shit nigga, it ain't like we ain't toked before."

"Put that out."

Gina reeled back. "What?"

"You heard me. Put that shit out — now."

"Alright ... damn." Gina moved to the sink, pitched it into a bowl of water. Looked at her friend. "What you looking at me like that for?"

There were dozens of reasons but Tarika couldn't find the exact one. "How long you been here?"

Gina scratched at her head as if digging up thoughts. "Wha? Since this afternoon?"

Tarika looked around her, the air fouled, her kitchen, a mess. "And you couldn't clean up after yourself."

"I was going to do it."

"When? This place was clean when I left. Look at it."

"I said I was going to clean it."

"Clean it when Gina?..smoking in my house. Dirtying up my place. I don't want to come home to this."

"Damn girl, what you getting' all upset for. I said I'd clean it."

"That ain't the point."

"I thought you'd be happy to see me."

Tarika stared at her. "Why you even high? You don't do that no more?"

"I ain't high."

"The hell you aren't."

"I ain't high."

Tarika stared at her. Gina stared back. A war of wits. A war of wills. "What happened?" Gina looked away. "What happened Gina?"

"Ain't nothing happened."

Tarika took a step towards her, then another, each approach slicing off a bit of resolve. Each approach causing the expression on Gina's face to change. Tarika stopped a few feet away. "Tell me," she said softly.

Gina looked at her, arms folded, mouth set. Tarika touched her shoulder. "Tell me." Gina didn't answer, just sort of leaned in. Tarika took her in her arms. Held her, Gina's tears dripping along her shoulder.

She blubbered like a baby.

Gina lay against Tarika, her words incoherent. Tarika strained to understand. But the only part she got was, "I'm trying. I'm mutherfucking trying."

Tarika eased her back. "Stop crying."

Gina sniffled. Sniffled again. Brought the back of her hand across one eye, then the other. "The shit ain't right Tarika. I ain't tell her to do that."

"I know."

"And Jefferson, Jefferson ... " the rest was lost to a voice with no power.

"Breathe."

Gina did. Then again and again. "I ain't tell her to try and cook no damn bacon on no radiator."

"I know."

"I told her to wait. Ain't my fault if she couldn't wait."

"She was cooking bacon on the radiator?"

"Yeah. I was going to get up and make her something, but she wouldn't wait."

"She okay?"

The truth of the matter was Gina didn't know. After her argument with Jefferson, she had left the house. "I guess so."

"You don't know?" Gina looked away. Tarika sighed. Pointed to her living room. "Let's go in there." Allies again, they sat close to one another. "You can't be letting stuff like this happen Gina. Kanisha was taken away from you once. You want that again?"

"No."

"And smoking. When did you start that?"

"Just started."

"You got to stop."

"I need something, Tarika. I need something to make life feel good. I ain't got no man, no life. Nothing but work. You ain't never around. What am I supposed to do?"

"Be responsible Gina. That's what you supposed to do."

"I'm trying," she implored.

"Well you got to try harder. You want to go back to how and what you was, huh? I know I don't. And smoking ain't about nothing ... how we used to be, about nothing. We're something, somebody now. We don't want to lose that."

"You something maybe but I sure as hell don't feel like it."

"Life ain't hard, just different. And no matter what you say, it's a thousand times better than before."

"For you, yeah. You got your own place. You got a real life Tarika. What I got?"

"You got me," Tarika said softly. "You got me. You got Kanisha. Jefferson. We all love you. We all care about you."

But it wasn't enough. Deep inside, Gina needed more.

While Tarika let Gina stay at her place for one night, the next day she made her go home. "All your life you've been running away from stuff. It's time for you to face it. You have to go and face Jefferson. Face what you did."

It wasn't what Gina wanted to hear, but Tarika was firm in her decision and so Gina went home that Sunday. She went home uncertain of what she would say to Jefferson. She went home uncertain of what Jefferson would say back.

But he had no words for her, not real ones. He simply said that he was disappointed. That she had to do better and he would appreciate it if she didn't smoke that stuff in his house.

He didn't wait for her to speak. Didn't wait for her to express herself, tell her side of things. He didn't wait to hear the apology she had worked on during the cab ride home. Jefferson simply turned and went to his room. Gently closed the door.

The Monday Rick had waited for finally arrived. Like much else in his life, circumstances had brought him here. Circumstances had put him before his HMO doctor. Neither man cared for the other. Rick felt his doctor was distracted and overworked and his doctor saw Rick as just another patient to get through.

But as the single word left his doctor's mouth, "Negative," Rick could have gotten up and hugged him. "But please be advised that a negative result now doesn't mean a negative later. You should continue to take your test twice a year as always." The doctor opened a drawer. Took out some pamphlets. "Here are some brochures I would like to give you."

But Rick didn't want them. "No, I'm cool Doc."

"You called some weeks ago saying you were involved in some risky behavior. Perhaps you should take these with you."

Rick stood up. "I made a mistake. That's not going to happen again."

The doctor wasn't going to argue. "As you wish." He put them back into his drawer.

When Gina had left for work Monday morning, Jefferson didn't say anything to her. He hadn't come by to knock, saying, "Are you up?" He hadn't wished her a good day at work or anything. His silence hurt her.

When she came in Monday afternoon, for the first time ever, Jefferson wasn't there to greet her and there was no dinner on the stove. He didn't even leave a note.

He'd be back later Gina decided as she made her way up to her room. She'd just wished he'd hurry up and get home. Suddenly it felt empty without him.

The doorbell rang.

Gina wasn't expecting anyone and hoped it was Jefferson. That maybe he forgot his key. But it wasn't Jefferson. It was Rick.

"Can I come in?"

"I don't care." And she didn't. The gap between herself and Rick had grown wide. Where once she'd felt that there might be a second chance, Rick was doing everything to say there wasn't.

She didn't know why he was there but gave herself the chance to find out as they went into the living room. Took seats.

"Jefferson came and saw me," Rick began.

"I didn't tell her to do it."

"I'm not saying you did, but she ate raw bacon because you were too tired to get up."

"I made a mistake."

"But it was a dangerous one Gina. You are already on probation. If Kanisha had gotten sick, what do you think would have happened to you?"

"It's not like I did it on purpose Rick. Damn ... "

"I thought you had given up the curse words."

"Damn ain't no curse. It's in the Bible."

"Yeah, it is ... " He looked her over carefully. "What's going on Gina? You were doing so well. Now I hear you smoking weed again, cursing, being slack with Kanisha."

What was going on? A whole lot of stuff, but Rick really didn't care, so she didn't feel the need to share any of it. "Nothing's going on."

"It must be something."

"I said nothing, alright."

"No, it's not alright."

Her eyes blazed at him. "Why? You don't care."

But he was supposed to. She was the mother of his child. He used to love her. But sitting next to her now, she could have been a third cousin, a neighbor down the street. Sitting next to Gina, he felt far removed. Rick looked away.

"Can't even look at me, can you? I ain't nothing to you, am I?"

Rick searched his brain for the right words. He tried to find sympathy, kindness. Something that made her words untrue. Couldn't.

Her voiced snapped at him. "Anything else you got to say?"

No, nothing else. Rick was finished. He was so finished with Gina, so removed, so unconnected to the woman next to him — the mother of his child that he just wanted to get out the front door.

But this went further than Gina. Like Jefferson said, what she did affected them all. How she acted, didn't. The rights, the wrongs, a part of his pie too. He should be in her corner if only for his child.

He made his hand go to her shoulder. Forced himself to massage the flesh there. "You'll be okay Gina." Her head leaned against it, short curled hair tickled his skin. Heat rose from her. Drifted his way. Loneliness tap-danced on his spine. Connected with other parts of him.

Rick did not stop Gina as she took his hand. Did not stop her when she put it on one of her breasts. Rick did not take his hand back as she moved it slowly. Nor did he halt the hand that reached for his zipper. Delved itself deep inside.

In Gina's bedroom, Rick was in Gina.

She felt tighter than he could ever remember. Even through the condom he could feel her slippery heat. The way she rolled her hips, clung to him, moaned hard and long against his ear, spoke volumes about her need.

His eyes were closed so he could not see her desperation, her need to get there, he himself caught up in the same rapture, but there was no emotion. It was pure sensation, pure lust. Not a drop of deep feeling was with him.

"You love me Rick?"

The question landed on him like ice water. He grew soft but Gina didn't stop her motion. Did not allow her own question, his inability to answer, the lost erection, to halt her.

She thrashed and moved, desperate, alone. Rick, so out of the mix, nearly slipped out of her but her hand latched onto his buttocks like a vise.

Sadness rushed him. A hollowness filled his gut, Gina was beneath him but she was all by herself. It seemed a lifetime before her orgasm arrived, but in truth, it was less than a minute, her contractions forcing his soft penis from her, he rolling, moving to the corner by the wall.

Rick was embarrassed. Unsettled in the worse way, her question *'you love me?'* not lost, not gone, but still there above him as Gina struggled to catch her breath.

He wanted to get up, but didn't know how. Sorrow pressed him down. This was the real farewell, the final goodbye. Rick knew he had to tell Gina before he left.

"We're over Gina."

"I know that."

"It's different for us now."

"I said I know it. Damn. I don't need no fucking lectures, alright?"

"I wasn't trying to lecture you Gina. I just wanted to make sure you understand."

She sucked her teeth. "I ain't stupid Rick. We was over before we got started. So save your words, hear? Just get your shit and go."

The door to his prison laid wide open. Rick wanted to dash. But he took his time as he got off the bed. Forced himself to slowly slip on his jeans. Headed to the bathroom. Ridding himself of the condom, he wrapped it tightly in toilet paper and pitched it in the garbage can. When he got back to the room, Gina was crying.

In the light from the street lamp, she looked vulnerable and lost. In the soft nearly obscured light of the street lamp outside the window, she looked as young as the day he met her.

There were a few things Rick could not handle. Tears of a woman was one of them. Despite everything that said 'go,' he went to her. Dropped down before her. Took her hands from her face. Asked her not to cry.

"It ain't right Rick. This shit's not right. I'm trying. I'm trying so mutherfucking hard and you acting like it ain't worth nothing." She looked at him, her eyes, wet and dismal. "How come it ain't enough? How come I'm not enough? I've changed and she gone. How come you don't want me?"

The truth was it wasn't about Gina or Dajah. It was about him. After thirty-two years of living for others, he was about to live for himself.

"It has nothing to do with you."

"Don't tell me that shit."

"What we had and what we got are two different things now."

"How come I don't get a second chance?"

Her memory had failed her. Over the years Rick had given her that and more. Over the years, Rick had doled out second chances like the sun rose and set. There was no more in him to give.

"It's just not like that for me any more." He stood up. "I'm sorry." Taking up his shirt, and his jacket, Rick left.

Chapter Eight

The commercials were everywhere. The more Dajah tried to flip channels to escape them, snatches of violins, silhouettes of elegantly dressed couples, the more she ran smack dab into them. *Give her something she will never forget ... show her how much you love her. This year give her something that she will remember always ...*

It was enough to make Dajah want to puke.

February 14th had become a big commodity and it was milked for everything it was worth. Whether you were in love or wanted to be, there was no denying the impact of those diamonds and flowers ads.

If you were in love, it made you glad. If you were out of love, it made you sad or mad. Either way it affected you. Either way it made you respond, feel something. Most of the time it made you want.

Dajah had seen the candy box displays pop up in her local supermarket and silk roses springing from the counters of news-stands. She had come across more red-tie Teddy Bears than she wanted to ever see and whole sections of card racks were filled with red and white.

She wasn't in love, wasn't even close to getting it and she didn't want to think about it. But it was all television and radio seem to know and so she was inundated from all points.

She changed the station to the Discovery Channel. Watched as ocean creatures of the deep floated through murky water. Down in the darkness of the ocean there was no February 14th. She envied that.

Rick did not believe in signs.

He had never looked to occurrences in the outer world to give him insight to his inner. But as he drove home, fiddling for some music on the radio, he hit upon the record "Free Man" and found himself singing along.

"I'm a free man," he insisted to his windshield. "I'ma free man, talking 'bout it."

It was an old record. He had barely been six when it had made its debut back in the seventies. But hearing it now, he was feeling it like he had been too young to feel it back then.

For the first time in his life Rick felt unchained, unbound, soaring like an eagle. For the first time in his nearly thirty-two years of living, possibility for anything and everything coursed through him.

"Don't hang up."

The insistence in his voice caught Dajah by surprise. The power behind it halted her. Despite herself, she wanted to know. "Tell me why I shouldn't."

"Because I understand. I get it. I know what you need from me and I'm finally in a position to give it to you."

"Position." It wasn't a question.

"Yeah."

"And what position is that?"

"A free man. Totally, one hundred percent free."

"I'm happy you realized that. Really I am. But you took me through some changes. I'm not trying to go back there."

Less than two weeks to Valentine's Day and bent on truth, Dajah didn't want to be alone, but the bigger truth was she didn't want to be with Rick either. There was something better out there for her and if she was lucky, she would get it, or it would find her. Either way, Rick was out of her picture forever.

"You still telling lies and I don't have any use for them or you," she went on to say.

"Lies? What lies?"

"What lies? How about Gina being gone from your life, but that Saturday when we were both at the club, I saw the both of you walking down the Avenue."

"The Avenue?" he was confused.

"Yeah, you know, Jamaica Avenue. I saw you and I couldn't believe you lied to me again."

"I didn't lie. I'm not with Gina anymore."

"So what were you doing with her then?"

Tossed for a loop, Rick didn't know. Couldn't remember. "I don't know."

"Yeah, I bet. I'm hanging up."

"No ... wait ... just wait ... give me a minute."

"To think up some more half-truths?"

"No. I'm trying to remember."

"Good-bye Rick." She was pulling the receiver from her ear when she heard his voice come through the receiver, loud and panicked.

"We went to buy Kanisha some clothes."

"Some clothes." It wasn't a question.

"Yeah. She's sprouting like a weed and me and Gina ... "

"You and Gina ... my point exactly. There isn't supposed to be anymore you and Gina."

"What you want me to do? She's Kanisha's mother?"

"Exactly Rick. Exactly. Gina will never be out of your life for just that reason and I don't have to put up with none of that mess anymore. I'm hanging up. Don't call me anymore." Dajah did just that. Sat back against her sofa and folded her arms. Not mad, not hurt, not upset.

Just relieved.

There was no mystery about how she'd come to be where she was. There was no mystery but there was anxiety and hope. Hope, if it was the right kind, could empower. Hope, if it had a real foundation beneath it, could elevate, make everything seem better. Clear out the haze and let a new future be gleaned.

Dajah had the hope. It was deep inside her now and she cradled it secretly as she walked the boardwalk of Jones Beach, the day not as cold as before; the snow mostly gone. Clumps nestled around light poles and midsized lumps dotting the sand, but most of the area was clear.

It took some calculation to get the arrival time right. She couldn't come too early or too late. Doing the math, she had arrived at the boardwalk with the sun just fifteen minutes from setting.

There were a few things she didn't know and she tried not to let the unknown invade her too much. Besides, even with her cautiousness, she knew nothing beat a failure but a try.

Dajah strolled the boardwalk and came to rest in her favorite spot — right by the steps that led down to the sand.

She looked out into the ocean, happy to see more winter flockers moving around. Kids raced skateboards along the weathered wood and couples strolled, close and tight. She forced herself not to look around, but to study the crashing waves, the sun slinking deep and brilliant in the sky.

She didn't check her watch, but she could sense the minutes moving by at a snail's pace. The cold began finding the warm parts of her and she knew that she couldn't hang around too much longer.

Doubt slipped in. Her chiding mind stroked its presence.

Did you really think he would be out here? Did you really think that you could make a chance meeting happen again?

The truth was Dajah did. The truth was that something about him said he would be here today, he and his dog and he would see her and remember those few seconds they had shared and perhaps share a few more.

But now as the sun moved into the void of heaven and earth and darkness began to press up around her, she knew that she didn't have that kind of power. *Go home.* She didn't want to. She didn't want to leave, another week of nothing before her.

Go on home fool. That stung and it got her feet moving. Yes, she was being foolish, something she wasn't supposed to be anymore, *remember? Remember you promised yourself you wouldn't be stupid about anything ever again?*

Dajah moved down the boardwalk, the parking lot her destination. The cold seemed deeper, and her trip felt like a waste of time. She tried to find some optimism for the lonely Saturday night ahead. But all she saw was going home, getting into her pajamas and watching TV.

Maybe get on the net. Visit some sites. Check my e-mail. Dismal.

Something caught her ear. Something dragging along the boardwalk at a fast past. Something metallic. Dajah turned her head, peered into the gloom. Saw a dog in motion heading her way. Stopped and waited for its approach.

Jeff watched his dog sprint. He hoped that the person frozen in the distance wasn't afraid of dogs. He had had too many bad experiences, like the one out at Far Rockaway Beach. That's why he preferred Jones.

He didn't expect too many people out on the boardwalk because it was nearly dark. He didn't expect Kelly to slip loose either. He had planned on setting her free once they reached the sand, but Kelly had other plans.

Jeff meant to get out to the beach earlier in the day, but he had gotten in so late that morning, he had slept past noon. There had been errands he had to run and by the time he and Kelly headed out, it was later then he liked. But he had no choice. A setter had to run free.

"Kelly!" he called, but the dog paid him no mind. Chain dragging, four paws flying, Kelly continued her race. "Kelly! Stop!" It was a useless word because the only word his dog knew was 'sit.' Telling his dog to 'stop' was like saying 'purple.' It held no meaning.

Breaking out into a sprint and avoiding the bits of ice patches along the boardwalk, Jeff took off after his pure breed, knowing his dog would get to the person before he did.

Dajah saw the dog leap. Knew where the paws were going and braced herself. The impact almost knocked her over, but she laughed away the near mishap. "Kelly," she exclaimed, scratching the red head through her gloved fingers, moving her face from the reaching tongue that wanted to lick.

"Hey, how you doing girl?" she asked, soul lifted.

"Sit Kelly! Sit!"

Dajah looked up. Saw Jeff running her way. Cupped her hand and shouted "She's not bothering me."

She noticed things in his approach. Dajah noticed how long his legs looked beneath the cut of his short down jacket. She noticed how big his Timberland boots were and they were made of a dark leather. But mostly what she noticed was how there was no recognition in his face that was pinched in annoyance.

He came up and grabbed Kelly's collar. Kelly's tail wasn't sure if it wanted to wag or be still. Big, wet brown eyes looked up at its master and back at Dajah. A doggie whine followed.

"I'm sorry," Jeff muttered, winded.

"For what?" Dajah said with a smile. "She remembered me. I'm flattered."

"Remembered you?"

"Yeah, I met you guys a few weeks ago. Right over there." Dajah pointed in the direction of her favorite spot. Jeff studied her. It unnerved her that he hadn't remembered what she had considered a great exchange. "You came up to me and said something about it makes you wish you were a kid again."

Memory leaped him. "Oh, yeah, right. Dajah."

She nodded, relieved a bit. "Yeah, Dajah. And you're Jeff and that's Kelly."

He smiled. "The mind goes first."

"Or something."

He looked about him. "You're out here by your lonesome?"

"Yeah, why?"

"It's nearly dark. Not many people around."

"I came to watch —"

"The sun set, right." He nodded. "Yeah, I remember now." He considered her, eyes fully into hers. "So how was it?"

In truth Dajah couldn't remember. In truth, she hadn't paid it much mind. She had been too busy waiting for him to show up. "It was ..."

"Umm. I was planning to get out a little earlier, but you know what they say about plans."

"Yeah, I do."

He looked around him. "I almost didn't come, we left so late. But Kelly, well, she has to get her run on, being a setter and all. Apartment life isn't really for a dog like her. She's not the type that likes to be cooped up."

"I bet."

"Well, I better get down to the beach."

"The beach?"

His smile came again. "Yeah. I set her loose on the beach. Let her run, chase seagulls for a few minutes. It gets all that energy out of her."

Dajah gazed towards the ocean, the sand a band of darkness. "It's pitch black. How can you see?"

Jeff shrugged. "Not as dark as you think." His eyes slipped towards hers. "Come join us. You'll see."

"Down there?"

"Yeah, down there."

Suddenly she wasn't so sure. In truth she had been with him for less then a minute and didn't know him from Adam.

He saw the hesitancy in her eyes. Sweetened his pot. "I tell you what. You join me and Kelly for a few and then I'll take you to this place that serves the best hot chocolate in the world."

"In the world," she stated, nonplussed.

Three fingers of his right hand went to his forehead. "Boy Scout Honor."

"A Boy Scout. It figures," the idea to her liking.

Dark, cold, but exhilarating.

There on the wide strip of wind-blown beach, Dajah raced, the crash of the waves a soothing symphony.

She had no intention of joining the game of Frisbee. She had no intention of tossing it to Kelly and having Kelly return it full of dog slobber. She couldn't even see where the Frisbee went off to it was so dark, but Kelly had no problem finding it.

Soon Jeff was rushing her for the hard plastic disk; an impromptu game of duck and maneuver springing up between them. He had started out just grabbing her arm, but soon he was putting her into arm locks. The sensation, not bad at all.

The night was pitch-black. The tall lights along the boardwalk providing the only illumination by the time they headed back to the parking lot. Blood pumping, sweater gathering, euphoric and near spent, she leaned against the hood of her car, catching her long awaited breath. "That was some workout."

"Yeah, it gets the blood pumping."

"So, okay. Where's this place with the greatest hot chocolate in the world?"

"Up on Sunrise."

"Sunrise runs forever, can I get an address or even a town."

"It's simple. When you come off the Causeway, take the Southern State to the Valley Stream exit. Come off and hang a right, take that down about four exits, make a left."

"Wait, that's too much to remember."

"You have your cell with you?"

"Yeah."

"Be back." He headed to his car, opened the door and reached in. A few seconds later he was coming back with a piece of paper, his cell number on it. "Here. My cell number. If you get lost, call me."

Dajah took the number. Looked at him. "This hot chocolate better be the bomb," words that held no merit. Hot chocolate was the last thing on her mind.

Tires crunched over gravel. Headlights swept the clipped hedges at the parking lot's edge, disturbing their shadows. A car door opened, another and then both were closing, the sound ricocheting through the night.

Dajah's hands slipped easily into the pockets of her sheepskin coat. She waited for Jeff to reach her. Kelly yelped from behind the rolled up car window. A cold night, she hoped the dog would be okay.

Jeff came up to her side. "Ready?"

"Sure." She felt something more to his question than just entering the eatery. Felt a new doorway was opening. Liked the sensation.

Going up the marble steps, Jeff held the door open for her and the warmth and the smell of the diner engulfed her. A young woman with big hair dyed a light-consuming shade of black grabbed up two menus and headed their way. "Smoking or non-smoking?"

"Non," they said together. Laughter followed their synchronization.

"You don't smoke?"

Dajah frowned her face. Shook her head. "Who does?"

Jeff liked that answer.

Sitting in the vinyl booth of the warmly lit diner, Dajah discovered things she hadn't fully seen during their brief times at the beach. Under the glow of overhead fixtures, Broadway bulbs and recessed lighting, she saw Jeff completely.

The eyes were soft and brown, his face, long and hairless. The hair on his head was closed shaved and his ears pixied at the ends.

"Stop staring," he said with a smile.

"I wasn't staring."

"Sure you were."

"Okay, I was. It's the first time I'm getting a real good look."

"I hope you like what you see."

Dajah smirked. "Maybe."

"I'm starved. What about you?"

"My stomach is over here growling."

He waved towards the menu. "Feel free to order whatever you want."

"You sure? Cause I could probably eat the whole kitchen right about now."

"Knock yourself out."

Dajah opened the menu, knowing what she wanted before she even looked. "Cheeseburger platter, with melted cheddar and bacon," she declared.

Jeff put down his menu. Gave her a quizzical look. "I was going to get the same thing."

"I guess I'm psychic."

"I guess you are." Jeff summoned the waitress, gave the orders. Looked at Dajah. "Twenty-eight?"

She blinked. "Excuse me?'

"Your age. How old are you? Twenty-seven, twenty-eight?"

"Thirty-two this year." He nodded to himself. "And you? What, thirty-five?"

Jeff laughed. "I wish."

Dajah frowned. "Thirty-six?" Jeff hiked his thumb up a few times. "Thirty-seven?" His thumb continued to punch the air. "Thirty-eight?" She was still wrong. "Thirty-*nine?*"

"Bingo."

She leaned back against the red vinyl booth. "No, you can't be."

"Oh, but I am. At least come November I will be. For the moment, I'm still thirty-eight."

"You don't look that old."

"Thanks."

Her head shook. "No seriously. I thought you were about thirty-five."

He shifted onto a hip, "I can show you my drivers license," reached for his wallet. She stopped him.

"No, I don't need to see it." Still she found it hard to believe she was attracted to a man so close to forty. Like other rules, dating someone too much older wasn't what she did.

"You want to leave now?" he asked, a knowing smile on his face.

"No, it's not that."

"Then what is it?"

Dajah tried to pinpoint the what. Found it. Another rule she was about to break. "It's just me and my silly notions."

"Which are?"

She leaned forward. Hands out. Palms up. "I have these rules, about dating."

One brow raised. "Dating?"

Oops. She'd put the cart before the horse. Too late to take it back. Dajah went with it. "Yes, dating. And there's these rules."

Jeff gave her a smile that was mostly disbelief. "We're dating?"

"Well, no, not dating dating, but I mean, hey, we're here together and you're paying for my meal."

"I am?"

She stared at him, caught off guard. Flustered. "You said."

"Hot chocolate."

Hands that had been still against the table, took flight. "No, you just told me not a minute ago ... "

He reached over, grabbed her wrist, settled their movement. "I was just playing with you Dajah."

She took her hands away. "Yeah, well I didn't like the joke." Nor did she like how he had gotten her twisted up, or his reaction to her using the word 'dating.' He asked her to the diner and was paying for a meal — that was a date as far as she was concerned.

She told him so. "First time, last time, this is a date Jeff. You invited me to eat with you and you're footing the bill."

"That I am."

"So don't be trying to act like it's not."

His brow went up. Fire. He liked fire. Spicy women always intrigued him. "You don't bite your tongue do you?"

"Not anymore."

"I like that."

But suddenly Dajah wasn't sure if she did, or if she still liked him. She looked out the window, trying to settle the disturbance inside of her.

"Hey."

She heard him but pretended that she didn't, even though the way he said that one word came as soft and as gentle as a lover's touch. Even though he said it as if they had been together forever and they'd just had another spat and he knew he was dead wrong and was ready to make amends.

"Dajah."

She continued to stare out towards the glass, the nighttime pressing her reflection back at her, the hurt that dripped in her eyes. She didn't know him from Adam and already he had the ability to stir things up inside her, sending her stomach and her heart churning and not in a good way.

"I didn't mean any harm."

But so many other people in her life hadn't meant any harm and had hurt her anyway. She didn't want that anymore. She fixed her eyes on him, the fire inside of them, roaring. "You didn't mean any harm, but you 'harmed' me anyway. I just got away from a toxic person. I'm not looking to invite any more in."

The hurt in her voice surprised him. It was Jeff's turn to be caught off guard. "Inviting any more in? It's just a meal?"

She checked herself.

He was absolutely right. It was just a meal. She didn't know his last name, where he lived or anything. And yeah, they had spent some fun time on the beach in the pitch dark and yeah, she had his cell number on that piece of paper she tucked into her purse, but that was it.

Lighten up. She did. Shook her head. "I'm sorry," she managed after a while. "You're right. It's just a meal."

He changed the subject. "Let's talk about something else."

"Like?"

"Well, what do you do?"

She was happy to see that he had moved beyond her outburst. Wanted to know more about her. Gladly she obliged. "I'm an accountant."

"Head?"

"No, assistant. I work for this firm out in Seaford."

"You like it?"

"I love it. I've always had a thing for math." She risked a look his way. "What about you?"

"Architect."

"Really?"

Jeff chuckled. "How come everybody seems so surprised when I tell them that? Like I'm not smart enough to remember equations and draw lines on paper?"

"Because you don't meet one everyday."

"True."

"... One cheeseburger, cheddar, bacon. Medium rare."

They both looked up. Jeff indicated the space before him. "That's mine."

"Be careful the platters hot." The smell of grilled vegetables, seared meat and hot fries filled the air as the platter was lowered.

"And this must be yours," the waitress said to Dajah.

"Yep," her answer as she reached for the salt.

Twelve minutes later, the meal was a memory. Jeff sat sipping his Seven Up, Dajah, a Coke.

"That was good."

"Yeah, it was."

Jeff glanced at his watch. Dajah did the same. Not late, it was just a little before six.

"Thanks for the meal," she told him.

"My pleasure ... I mean that."

"Mine too."

"Dajah what?"

She was glad he finally asked. "Moore. And you?"

"Gingham. Jeffrey Gingham."

She smiled. "Sounds important."

"Oh, I am."

She laughed, head shaking, liking the moment. "You are too much, you know that."

"That's what they say."

Dajah looked down at her plate, wanting much in the next second and refusing to suggest any of it. "Well, I guess it's time to go."

"Yeah, Kelly's been in the cold car for a while. I better get her home."

Jeff flagged the waitress. Handed over his credit card. Standing, he took Dajah's jacket off the hook. Held it while she slipped into it.

"A gentleman," she murmured.

"Is there any other way to be?"

They stood outside in the parking lot, shivering, hesitant to part.

"Same time, same channel?" he asked, small talk over.

"What, you mean the beach and dinner?'

He shrugged. "Something like that. It was nice having someone to keep me company. Not many people can get with the beach in winter."

"Sure."

"Next Saturday then, around five-thirty?"

"Okay." But it seemed a lifetime away.

"Great. I'll see you then."

Jeff turned to walk away. Dajah called out to him. "Wait."

He turned, expectant. "Yeah."

"Don't you want my number, I mean in case something comes up?"

"You have mine, right?"

"Your cell, yeah."

"Well give me a call if you can't make it."

Dajah didn't like that scenario, but it was a bit of information she decided to keep to herself. "Okay. Good night."

She got into her car and turned on the engine. Made sure she was the first one out of the parking lot. She went through a green light and got stopped at the next red. Looking back into her rear view mirror, she hoped for a sight of Jeff's car, but it was nowhere to be seen.

Chapter Nine

Monday morning, the drive to work was different. Monday morning, Dajah had come off what she considered a great weekend and with another promising one ahead of her, the commute seemed to take no time at all.

She was almost there. Almost back to the Dajah she had been before Rick.

With her cautious cloak back on, she refused to put all her eggs in one basket. She wasn't pinning a ton of hope that the business between herself and Jeff, whatever it was, was gold at the end of her long awaited rainbow.

But what Dajah did allow herself to feel good about was their impromptu meal. She allowed herself to feel good about their night romp on the beach, the invite to do it again. That much she allowed.

She didn't tell Frieda. Didn't mention it at all when she called Sunday night, wanting to know how her weekend went. She had put the horse before the cart too many times already and she saw no sense in doing it again. Whatever became of her and Jeff would become of them.

Dajah the cautious was back in action and it felt good to have her there.

By Wednesday, the need to call Jeff just to confirm they were still on was an itch she was dying to scratch. By Wednesday, the need to just call to hear his voice, get a good laugh, was strong. But Dajah had been at the deep end before and she managed not to take the leap. Hard as it was, she continued to resist.

Rick had steered her off of her course, but she had managed to get back on and she was determined to stay there. It was no easy feat, not by any means, especially since she felt good when she was with Jeff. She liked him and his style.

After Rick, Jeff seemed to be just what the doctor ordered. Despite all that, despite the promise of what could be, Dajah was going to do it the way she used to do things — slowly without rush.

She had showed too many cards that night at the diner. She was going to make certain it would be the last time Jeff ever peeped them again.

It wasn't the expression on the woman's face, or the man's, that caught Jeff's attention. It was the diamond and the intensity of the violins that did. He didn't even realize he was staring at the TV until Kelly came up to him, leash in her mouth, snout nudging his hand.

He refocused.

It was nothing but pure hype anyway. The boys of Madison Avenue had mastered the insinuations of love well, but that was all it was, insinuation. He had bought Mya such a diamond. Did it give them that happily ever after that just rolled across his TV screen? Nope.

He wondered, as he had done at least once a week for the last four years if Mya had found the happiness she hadn't been able to accept from him. Jeff wondered, as he did too often to count, if Mya's life was okay.

He wondered if she was still married. If she had any children. If the man he had seen by her side at the outside wedding at a local park, been able to succeed where he didn't. Jeff could not stop the bitterness his questions brought.

The last time he had seen her, she had tried to explain it to him, speaking a whole lot of yang-yang about letting go, and moving on; mumbo-jumbo about 'what was' couldn't be 'what is'. It had been like standing next to Gandhi and didn't help his broken heart one bit.

Even then. Even knowing she had changed, knowing that her feelings for him had changed, he had still wanted her. But she was in a different place that didn't include him.

Since that time, he had danced around real relationships, giving just enough to keep a woman interested but never enough to make it deep. Like a blind man, he had moved forward by senses instead of clear sight, something that didn't bother him until now.

At thirty-five, Jeff had felt he had the rest of his life. But now that thirty-eight was soon turning to thirty-nine, he felt more than half of his life was over.

Pushing away those thoughts, he leashed up Kelly and the two of them headed out of the apartment building. The cold dark night swallowed them as they headed for the nearby park. He thought about Saturday and the woman called Dajah.

Cute. Young. Spicy. Reminded him a bit of Mya. *Stop lying to yourself. She reminds you a lot about Mya. Even her name had you trippin'.* But lying to himself was no longer an issue. There were so many he told himself in the last few years, he'd stop counting.

It happened four years ago, but it still felt like yesterday or at least last week.

He had loved Mya like he had loved no other, so much so, he asked her to marry him. She said yes and wedding plans were being made, then she did something that made their happily-ever-after go away forever — she slept with another man, *and told me about it.*

That had been the knife stabber. That had been the thing that cut his heart to bits. It was bad enough she cheated on him with a wedding date set, but the fact she came out and told him was devastating. *Because she didn't want you and the only way to make you go away was to do what she did.*

Jeff got that part. Had gotten that part soon after her confession. What took him a hot minute to understand was what she'd done had nothing to do with him, but everything about who she was at the time. She didn't feel she had any self worth, so there was no way on God's green she could accept that he thought she did.

He forced himself to get over her. He thought he was succeeding, or at least convinced himself he was. So much so, that when she tried to come back, he sent her packing. But he never got over her. Never stopped thinking about her. He stopped a lot of other things in his life though.

He tugged on Kelly's leash. "Come on girl, let's go on home."

A few minutes later, Jeff was letting himself in his apartment, Kelly dashing off for the water bowl. The phone was ringing as he let himself in and in no real rush to answer, he took his time getting it.

He checked the caller ID and saw the number on the display. Tonight, he just wanted quiet, so he didn't return the call.

Calling to Kelly, he took loose her leash and hung it in the closet. For the first time in a while, he felt a pull, the type that had been missing too long.

Dropping down to his hands and knees, Jeff reached into the closet and began pulling out shoeboxes. The bottoms of suits, jackets and coats bounced against his head making the search uncomfortable, but he didn't stop until he found what he was looking for.

Soon the long, wide cedar trunk was before him. Just touching it made him pause. Just placing his hands on it made him sweat. It had been years. Four in fact. Nearly fifteen hundred days since his true passion had been given free reign.

Weeks, months and years had come and gone since he felt the need to commit his visions to paper, but here he was, down on all fours, inside the deep, dark closet, wanting to do just that.

He grabbed the box, pulled it out. The unstained cedar was dark in spots with age, but the latch was still coppery bright. Inside was so much. Inside, a lifetime of private drawings few had glimpsed.

Jeff reached for the latch, lifted it up. He dug his nails under the slight give and opened it. Dozens of tubes of acrylic paint, lead pencils, round canisters of all sizes holding his old artwork greeted him. But it was the thick pile of sketches he was most interested in.

Somewhere in the gather was a portrait he had not looked at in awhile. Somewhere in the gathering, old hurt remained. He was ready to look at it. Confront it. Jeff was ready to look into the face that had turned his world upside.

He needed to baptize himself in the memories of her good, bad or indifferent. Jeff needed to recall that day she had sat in his living room, bashful, near shy, as he committed her image to paper. He needed to revisit what it had felt like as he recreated her, pencil stroke by pencil stroke. He had evaded the moment for way too long.

But he couldn't.

Instead he found himself taking up the sketchpad that was so old the edges were ecru and crumbly; ruffled through the box until he found a chocolate brown pencil.

And there on the floor, he leaned back against the wall, put the pad against his bent legs and sketched a new portrait, his pencil not stopping until it was complete.

Clock watching.

Dajah had done it a few times in her life, but not often enough to count and the phenomena felt foreign to her. Foreign and scary. Foreign and exciting.

She had plans to sleep in late Saturday, get up around noon, do some housecleaning, shower and dress then head for the beach about five-thirty that afternoon. What ended up happening was she had tossed and turned all night, woke up before the sun did and laid in bed until she couldn't stand it anymore.

She got up, brushed her teeth and threw on some sweat clothes. Got on her living room floor and did some stretches. She did some sit-ups, some leg lifts and all the other exercises she had learned over the years that didn't require too much noise over her landlord's head.

Then she hopped in the shower and made some coffee, sipping it as the sun rose.

She stood at her bedroom window, leaned against the jam, the painted wood cool against her shoulder, watching the sky change from the pretty dark blue to streaks of pale pink.

Dajah was grateful that the sun was rising, that it wasn't snowing or cloudy and the day was presenting itself perfectly for her afternoon with Jeff. But mostly she was grateful that those too long, dragging-its-butt seven days were over.

She was extremely thankful that her weekend, her Saturday would involve more then hanging out with Frieda, doing housework and having television to keep her company. Dajah was thrilled with the idea she had another date.

Pulling away from the window, she took her empty cup to the kitchen. Looked at the clock, her watch begun.

Light diffused the branches of the tall pines of Jones Beach, sending shafts of orange goldenness in strips of white across the front of her car. Turning off her engine, Dajah recognized the creamy Lexus. Smiled.

She had gotten to the beach early. So had Jeff.

Though the car was empty of both man and dog, she knew that beyond the spread of tall trees, beyond the boardwalk, they awaited her. She also knew that the fact that she hadn't called him once the whole week added a certain anticipation to her arrival. In truth, Jeff didn't know if she was coming or not.

But that notion was cancelled a few minutes later as she joined them on the sand, Kelly spotting her first, Jeff second. It became a thought with no merit when Jeff reached into his jacket pocket and pulled out a small paper tube, saying simply, "For you."

The fact that he had something for her, whatever that something was, said he knew she would be there, or, at least, had no reason to believe she wouldn't come.

She took it. Twice as wide as a cigar holder, and as long as a twelve-inch ruler, curiosity had her. "What is it?"

"Open it and find out."

She looked at him, the smile on his face wavering. Dajah looked back at the tube and took off one glove. With her nail, she eased the plastic covering off and looked inside. Frowned. "I don't see anything."

"Oh it's in there. Look again."

She did and noticed paper tightly wound against the edges. Using a finger, she snaked it out, the paper curled into her hand. Suspicion had her fully. "What is it?'

"Just open it." There was an eagerness to him that infected her. Hoisting the tube up under one arm, Dajah slowly unrolled the paper, not believing the face she saw looking back at her. Her mouth, opened.

He placed a glove finger to it. "No, don't say anything. Don't say you like it, don't. Just take it okay? Something from me to you."

She couldn't honor his request. She had to ask the one question that demanded an answer. "You drew this?"

"Yeah, I did."

"When?"

His head shook, eyes closing for a second, shutting off her probing, her deep need to know. "No more questions."

"I just want to know."

"I drew it. Does it matter when?"

Yes it did. She tried to figure it out. After a few seconds, a time frame came to her. It had to be between last Saturday and this. Somewhere in that time frame he had sat down and drawn her from memory.

Dajah looked back at the sketch. It was beautiful, *too beautiful to be of me*. But obviously Jeff didn't think so.

She rolled it back up, slipped it into the canister and opened the flap on her pocketbook. But even as she stuck the edge between the wallet and her cell, she knew that bag wasn't wide enough to hold it.

"I'll hold it." Jeff took it from her hand and slipped it into his jacket pocket. Snatched up the Frisbee and called out to his dog with a whistle. Getting Kelly's attention, he pitched the hard bright orange disc into the air.

"Tell me something?"

They were back at the diner, hot chocolate before them, cheeseburger platters being prepared in the restaurant kitchen.

Jeff looked up from his mug, saw her expression, eyes shiny, curious and delving. "Something like what?"

"Stuff," Dajah answered, her eyes dancing from his. "About you."

"Like?"

"Well, where do you live for starters?"

Her question surprised him. He was certain he had revealed that much about himself. But the way she was waiting for his answer, for his 'something', he realized he hadn't. He smiled, embarrassed. "Jamaica."

Her brows went up. "Really?"

"Yeah. Apartment complex on Merrick, near Baisley."

Dajah knew where that was. She passed it often. It was a few miles north of Rick, a few miles east of her own place. "I'm in Cambria Heights," she offered.

It was his turn to probe. "Where?"

"Two Hundred and Twenty-seventh Street."

"I know where that's at. How long have you been there?"

"What, eight years now? And you?"

"About twelve."

Twelve years. Since she'd been a freshmen in college. She moved on with her excavating. "What else. Tell me something else."

He understood where she was going and why. There was still mystery between them. Dajah was out to fill in some blanks. He sipped his hot chocolate, looked off to gather loose notions about himself. "I was born and raised in Jamaica. I went to John Bowne High School and graduated from Baruch."

"John Adams and Stonybrook."

One of his eyebrows raised. "SUNY, huh?"

"Yes, SUNY. There's nothing wrong with SUNY."

"CUNY is better," Jeff insisted with a smile. But they both knew in the scheme of things, in how colleges were really ranked, the State Universities of New York were considered better than the City Universities of New York.

Her eyes danced, her tone insistent. "Don't hate."

"Oh, I'm not hating."

"Yeah you are," she pulled back some, delivered a smile. "But I ain't mad atcha."

His eyes did a slow sweep of her face. "I'm not mad atcha either."

She looked away, a blush coloring her butternut-brown cheeks. Motion pulled her attention.

"Cheeseburger medium-rare?"

Dajah looked up, saw the waitress, the same one from last week. "His," she found herself saying.

"And you must be the well?"

Dajah nodded, leaned back allowing the hot plate to find its home. She looked down at it, risked a look at Jeff, but he was busy getting the ketchup, his attention fully on the platter before him.

Moves.

Dajah was waiting for Jeff make them — or, at least, make one. She was waiting for him to ask for her home number, an exact address where she lived. She was waiting for him to mention next Saturday and another beach date. She was waiting for him to extend their time together beyond the meal that had come to an end.

But he seemed to be in a hurry. Halfway through his meal, he began checking his watch. She had barely gotten her last bit of French fries in her mouth before he was asking her if she was ready. Her answer — *yeah* — had barely finished before he was flagging the waitress.

He was in a rush no doubt, as he stood up, got her coat and waited for her to stand up too. He looked at his watch two more times before they left the diner, a third as they stood by her car giving up the formal goodbye.

"I had fun," she offered, her words so standard, they felt stale before they left her lips.

"Yeah me too," but his eyes weren't on hers, they were beyond them, his sights on something else, somewhere else.

"So we're going to do this again? Next weekend maybe?" The chilled night seemed chillier as she waited for her answer. Her question, the one he himself had asked just last weekend, seemed to catch him off-guard.

"Next weekend?"

"Yeah." Dajah was smiling, but there was no joy in her at all. There was panic and un-easiness and all those funky feelings she hated when uncertainty was looming, but not a single drop of delight.

"Er, I'll have to see."

See what? she wanted to ask but didn't. She nodded, swallowed, kept her smile fixed. "You'll call me, or something?"

Jeff nodded absently. "Yeah. I have to go." He turned away from her, her voice calling her back.

"But you don't even have my number." It pinched her to say those words. Pinched her that he didn't even know that. It pinched that even though he was less then three feet from her, emotionally and mentally he was already gone.

He turned, jerky, his feet with one set of orders — move, his mind, with another — wait. He found her eyes, saw her confusion, dabs of hurt and released his breath, a plumb of white racing from his nose.

He took two steps, closing the space between them. Knew some of what she was feeling as she studied the ground. "You still have my cell number?"

"Yeah."

"Leave your number on it."

Writing it down would be easier. Writing it down would make it more personal. Dajah found her ground, stayed there. "No, take it now." She dug into her pocket book, found an old supermarket receipt and her pen.

She leaned over her car and wrote her name and number. Turned and gave it to him. Her eyes brushed his, full of a fire she didn't want to possess. "Call me," her last words as she turned. Unlocked her car door. Got in.

The red lights seemed endless.

The more Jeff tried to beat them, the faster they seemed to come.

He glanced at his dash, muttered under his breath. Sighed and looked at Kelly. "There's no way I'm going to make it."

On paper, it sounded reasonable. On paper, it worked itself out. But the reality was, he had spent too much time on the beach with Dajah and now his whole schedule was off. It was quarter after six and he had to get home, get showered and get dressed.

He was supposed to be picking up Lisa in twenty minutes, the Broadway show *Aida,* their final destination.

With a curtain call of eight p.m., there was city traffic to get through and parking to be found. It hadn't been his idea to take in the show, but he had told Lisa yes, he would go. She had made a point of telling him the tickets cost her a pretty penny and if he even thought he couldn't make it, he needed to tell her before she made plans.

Jeff had swore up and down that he would and could, but as the red digits of his dashboard clock moved to six-twenty-three, he knew he just made himself a liar.

It was rare that he got caught up on his timing, because timing was everything. He basically had a smooth ride in these last years. He had never been caught up. Always stayed on his schedule, but Dajah had tripped him up.

Big time.

It would be another twenty minutes before he got home, and another half hour before he could head out again. He would need fifteen minutes to pick up Lisa and fifty minutes to make his way into the city.

By the time they parked and made their way to the theater, it would be, at the earliest, going on nine o clock. The show would be halfway over and there was no sense in that. Picking up his cell phone, he dialed Lisa, bracing himself against her barrage.

She cursed him out for exactly forty-seven seconds, then hung up the phone, the whole experience less painful then he imagined in the aftermath.

It took Jeff a minute to realize why. A couple of seconds to understand what was going on inside of him — relief. A great big chunk of relief. A smile broke out on his face. Ease found him.

He looked at the scrap of paper sitting in the cup holder and smiled some more. Felt something in his pocket and realized he still had the drawing. At the next red light, he turned on his overhead light, picked up the paper and punched numbers into his cell.

She wasn't home yet, that much he knew, but she would be soon enough.

Dajah drove in a fog, a cold, dense, bone-numbing fog.

How could something so good turn so bad on a dime? How did Jeff just turn on and off his connections with her so easily? She got an answer and didn't like it.

She got an answer and didn't want to believe it. *Because I'm not that important to him, that's why. I'm just some crazy-ass fool who is willing to hang out on the beach with him in the wintertime for the price of a cheeseburger platter.*

Nine dollars and forty-seven cents — her new worth. Not even an even ten spot. She didn't know when she became so cheap, only that she had. Without notice, without scrutiny, she had allowed herself, her time, her presence, her energy, to be bought cheap.

Well, he did draw you that picture. But she didn't even have that. It was probably still in his pocket.

A laugh left her, but it was choked in pain. There wasn't anything funny about it. *And you're carrying on as if there was something real about it. Carrying on as if you were his bomb-diggity when all you really are is a body to keep him company.*

She was supposed to be beyond all that mess. She was supposed to have reclaimed the Dajah she used to be, but in a blink of an eye she saw she hadn't changed anything. She had only gotten worse.

One time, shame on them; two times, shame on her. Dajah knew that there would be no third, not as long as she lived and breathed. This evening was the last time for her and Mr. Jeff. The absolute last.

Her answering machine was blinking when she got in. In no mood to talk to anybody about anything, she ignored it while she shook sand out of her boots and from the inside of her pants.

Standing in her tub, she felt down right stupid. Beach in the wintertime. *Girl, you done lost your mind.* It wouldn't have been so bad if she had gone to do her thing — watch the sunset. No, she had gone to do *his* thing — keep his old ass company.

She didn't even like men too much older then her. Dajah had set a cutoff in that regard. If a man was more then three years older, she couldn't hang with him. But once again she had set aside her personal goals and for what?

Two damn cheeseburger platters?

Because that's all she really got when you look at it. Two damn cheap-ass meals. Anything else she had perceived wasn't the actuality, like, a *nice guy I could get to know better. A nice man with no issues, who was funny and smart and not bad on the eye.*

She thought that's what she'd gotten, but as she stepped out of her tub, sand granules littering the bottom, she was seeing the real deal. Didn't like it.

She stopped in front of her bathroom mirror. Looked at her face. Tried to see where the word stupid was stamped. She couldn't see it, but she could feel the letters burning, as if the branding iron had just left her skin.

It has to be somewhere, why else would I let myself be played like that? Maybe only men could see it. Maybe she needed male eyes, or male genes to make it out. Whatever the reason, it was a part of her.

Dajah needed to find a way to remove it.

Seven thirty-six.

Jeff looked at the clock and looked at the phone. Maybe she didn't get home yet? Maybe she made a stop somewhere? *No, maybe the way you were trying to make your great escape pissed her off.*

He didn't want to remember how she looked, the vibes he felt from her when they parted, but the fact that she didn't return his call made it front and center. *What did you expect? You expected her to be glad about being dumped like that? You expect her to okay with how you switched gears like that? That's not how she rolls and you know that.*

No, she wasn't the run of the mill. Dajah wasn't like the other women he saw. She was feisty and bold. She didn't take no nonsense or B.S.

That's what he liked about her. A like that was growing stronger as the seconds ticked by and he found himself on phone watch. When was the last time? Jeff couldn't remember.

He turned on the television. Tried to keep his eyes glued to the screen. By seven-fifty nine, he couldn't take the wait any longer. Going through his wallet, he found the slip of paper with her number on it.

Taking a deep breath, he started dialing again.

The tea was hot, sweet and splashed with fresh lemon, just the way Dajah liked it. The movie on Lifetime was emotional and heart tugging, just the way she liked it. Even though Dajah knew how it would end, she still enjoyed watching it unfold.

It wasn't the greatest way to spend a Saturday night, but it calmed her.

Watching the story of a woman left for dead by a man and exacting revenge was just what the doctored ordered. For that hour and a half, Dajah's problems would seem tiny compared to the character on the screen. *At least nobody tried to poison me.*

Not literally anyway.

Her phone rang.

She looked over at the display and saw "caller unknown." Probably a telemarketer. She ignored it. Heard her own voice say she wasn't home and to leave a message. Distantly heard the beep and then the voice.

Jeff's voice.

She spilled her tea sitting up. Dajah was on the edge of her sofa in no time, contemplating picking up before he finished. At the last second she decided not to.

"It's eight o'clock and I was wondering what you were up to? I know this nice Jazz club in Brooklyn — good music, good food. I was calling to see if you were interested in going, but it doesn't look like you're home. Maybe some other time."

He hung up.

A Jazz club in Brooklyn. A real date. The chance to get dressed up and go out. A Jazz club. She'd never been. Didn't even like Jazz but the going out part had her.

She went to her phone, played the other message. The one that had been waiting for her when she got home. Jeff, asking what she was doing later. Jeff, calling her twice. Jeff, Mr. Flip-flopper, who just a half an hour ago, Dajah swore would never see her again.

She erased both messages. Settled back against her couch and fixed her eye on the TV, the images holding no importance to her. None at all.

Chapter Ten

Jeff was getting a Big Mac when he really wanted a New York Strip steak.

He knew it before he set out the following Sunday, stopping at the ATM before he got to his final destination. He had to make things right between himself and Lisa. Money always talked. It would cost one hundred and fifty dollars — reimbursement for theatre tickets never used, plus another thirty-five if they decided to take in a movie.

Depending on Lisa's mood, he might not have to do the movies, but she always made him come out of his pocket when he made her mad.

The whole routine was old hat, a road so familiar, a trip so well traveled, they could travel it backwards and in their sleep. The whole issue of pissing her off and making up with her was routine now. He was used to it and nowhere, in the true sense, did it even matter.

Lisa was like an old pair of bedroom slippers, ready for the garbage heap, but still comfortable to schlep around in. It was familiarity and assured comfort that kept him tethered to her. Real love never popped up in his equation.

He knew it and he hoped she knew it too, though it was hard at times to tell. They had been seeing each other for four years, she learning his rules of dating quickly. She understood his concept of 'I'll see you when I see you' and only really balked when he broke a date. Like last night.

Still, as Jeff parked his car and headed up her walkway, the sensation of reaching for seconds plagued him. Dajah hadn't returned a single phone call he'd made. She was whom he wanted to be with. Lisa was whom he got, her face appearing behind the glass pane, annoyed.

"Sorry about last night," he began, waiting for the storm door to be unlocked. Three seconds later it was swinging open. Jeff accepted his Big Mac — Lisa, while visions of sinking his teeth into the New York Strip — Dajah, drifted through his head. Accepted it as he drew an unyielding Lisa close to him, his mind everywhere but with her.

Dajah could tell it now because she had the victory. She could get on the phone and have a gabfest with Frieda, because the revenge was finally hers.

"... Twice," she was saying, excited and annoyed in the same breath. "He didn't call and ask me out once, but twice. I wasn't going anywhere with him."

A good friend, a long-time friend, Frieda was hearing something different in Dajah's voice. Still, she played her part. "Well, good for you."

"Damn right good for me. I swear Frieda, these fools had me standing in my bathroom mirror looking for the word stupid stamped on my forehead. How could they feel they can mess with me like that?"

"Because men are who they are."

"Well, they better ask somebody," Dajah said animatedly.

"So, he's an architect?" Frieda wanted confirming, which surprised Dajah none. Frieda was hung up on white-collar titles. When she'd first heard Rick had been a corrections officer, she had a small fit.

"Yeah, that's what he says."

"Well, he did draw that picture of you."

A picture she had forgotten to take with her. Dajah had an answer for that too. "He probably does it for all the women he's trying to play."

"You really think he was playing you?"

"What else can I believe? One minute he's all in my Kool-Aid and the next ... "

"I guess you're right."

"I know I'm right." But her friend's responses and the questions were sprinkling Dajah with a little doubt. "I know he was just playing me Frieda."

"Yeah, probably."

"Don't matter. He won't get the chance again."

Frieda didn't really believe that. She didn't think Dajah believed it either.

As far as Gina was concerned, the silence had gone on too long. Too many days had passed since Jefferson had said two real words to her.

Every day when she came in from work, she'd hope things would be different. Every day as she turned her key and stepped into the gloomy house, she prayed he'd have a change of heart.

But Jefferson was still on his streak as she let herself in that Monday evening. There was the smell of dinner coming in from the kitchen and Gina had followed the scent. Spied Jefferson at the table, finishing up his meal.

"Hey," she'd offered, getting no response. "I said hello Jefferson." But there was no reply. Storming out of the kitchen, Gina went upstairs, ditched her coat, her bag and her shoes. Tromping down the stairs, she bypassed the living room and entered the kitchen, her voice full of fire.

"I ain't air." The words cut through the kitchen like steel, sharp and glittery. It was aimed at the back of Jefferson's head. "I said I messed up and that I was sorry. How long you gonna ignore me?"

Jefferson turned slowly around in the chair, a mug of tea not too far from his lips. "You say you sorry, but are you sorry enough not to let it happen again?" It was the most words he had said to her in days and despite the condemnation, Gina was happy to hear he was speaking. "'Cause that's all I really want to know. Will you let it happen again?" He was looking at her, not too kindly, but not so disappointed either. The displeasure Gina had seen for days, gone.

"I love Kanisha. I ain't trying to hurt her. It was an accident. And I'm sorry." Gina didn't mean to cry, but standing there, with Jefferson's eyes on her, made her weepy. She wanted him to get up and hug her, tell her everything was okay. She needed to know that he still believed in her if nobody else seemed to. But her answer wasn't the right one and so Jefferson looked away.

"I ain't invisible. I got feelings. I matter." But she might as well have been talking to the refrigerator, the old vinyl floor, because the only person who seemed to be listening was herself.

* * *

Kanisha sat at the little table, oversized Lego's before her, the square she'd made not as interesting as when she had begun to construct it. Her teacher's assistant, Ms. Wample, was across the room, her head in a magazine, but Kanisha could sense the words she was reading wasn't holding much interest for her either.

Kanisha was still trying to master the concept of time, but she knew her father was late because the short black line on the clock was between the six and the seven and the long black line was almost to the twelve.

She had never been at the after school center when the short black line was past the six. She had never had to sit in the classroom, all her other classmates gone and Ms. Wample reading a magazine in the corner.

She felt Ms. Wample's stare more so than saw it. The five other times she had looked up to meet it, she had seen such disappointing annoyance in the teacher assistant's face that Kanisha immediately felt guilty about something. She just wasn't sure what.

Change in her young life wasn't new. Since she could remember, stuff was always getting changed. But this was a new kind, a different kind. Normally it was her mother who brought the changes. Now it was her father.

He was different. There, but somehow not there. Like his body had lost the insides of him. Kanisha did not know the meaning of the word distracted, but she felt it every time she was in Rick's presence.

Mrs. Jamison, the center director, popped her head in. " I just got off the phone with him. He'll be here soon." She turned her attention towards Kanisha. "Get your things on Kanisha. Your daddy's on his way."

Like the stares, Kanisha felt the relief inside of Ms. Wample more so than she saw it. Up until then, she had liked Ms. Wample. Up until then, Ms. Wample always seemed to have an extra smile just for her. But today, this afternoon, as the short black line and the long black line went places Kanisha had never seen them go before inside of her classroom, the extra smile was missing. As Kanisha went to her cubby and retrieved her coat, she hoped it would be back tomorrow.

"I don't know where the time went," Rick was saying eleven minutes later, Kanisha secure in the back of the Navigator, he behind the wheel. "I made a stop, lost track of time," he added, uncomfortable in his own skin.

The P-Spot on Queens Boulevard had never seen him until today. The idea of going, to get a lap dance, had never crossed his mind until today. Somehow Rick found himself in a booth in the back, a strange woman shaking her ass in his face, his wallet a hundred dollars lighter.

He found himself with hands itching to touch the firm round hips and a hard-on that threatened to break through the material of his slacks, when he remembered that he was supposed to be somewhere else. That he was supposed to pick up Kanisha.

The traffic on Queens Boulevard had been a horrendous nightmare and the flow along the Van Wyck seemed nonexistent.

Rick had nearly been to the day care center when his cell phone shrilled. He knew before he picked it up that it was the director calling, asking him where he was. He also knew that the delay was costing him a dollar a minute. By the time he got there, he owed them seventy dollars.

Mrs. Jamison, the dread-headed, thirty-something director had always looked at him glowingly. Privately and publicly, she had applauded Rick's determination to be a good responsible dad.

But this breach had her looking at him in a whole new way and it wasn't good.

Rick stared out into space, trying to gather thoughts that were too illusive to grasp. Behind him hot dogs boiled in slick orange water and from the oven came the smell of grease and potatoes. A simple meal of hot dogs and fries, there wasn't a drop of real nutrition in it.

Slack was fast becoming his middle name. He was half-assing left and right. And going to that strip club?

He got the potholder, opened the oven and took out the fries. He put hot dog buns on plates, loaded them with hot wieners. He scooped fries on the side and grabbed the bottle of ketchup. Taking the plate with him, he called out to Kanisha to come and eat.

The next morning as Gina got ready to leave for work, she bumped into Jefferson in the hallway. She didn't say anything and neither did he, but for a split second, she saw a splash of regret in his eyes.

It gave her hope that they were moving beyond her indiscretion and gave Gina some comfort during her workday. Eager to get home after her workday ended, she boarded the bus wanting nothing more than to get home.

The house normally had a few lights burning when she got in, but not a single one could be seen as she came through the gate. Walking up the steps, she used her key, pushing back the door to stilled darkness.

She didn't even smell dinner cooking, just the scent of dust and radiator heat.

She had seen Jefferson's car in the drive, so he should have been home. But the silent, dark house felt empty.

She ran her hand along the wall, flipping on the foyer light and made her way into the living room. She clicked on table lamps and headed to the kitchen. Flipped on the overhead.

Gina looked around at the cleaned kitchen, not even a glass in the sparkling sink. She was hungry and wasn't up to cooking. She searched the refrigerator for something to eat. Finding nothing, she was in need of something quick. She decided to run out to the Chinese restaurant.

She thought about Jefferson. Wondered if he had eaten. He wasn't talking to her but she would at least ask if he wanted anything from Haung Wah's.

Gina made her way up the stairs, certain Jefferson was napping when she heard no sounds from behind his bedroom door. She raised her hand, knocked. Called out "Jefferson," and waited for a response.

Hearing none, she knocked again, called his name and again received no answer. "Jefferson? You in there?" She tried the knob. It gave easily. "Jefferson," she called again, moving the door back slow. A bad smell hit her nose. Gina's eyes scanned the bed. Saw it empty.

She looked around the dark room trying to make out shapes. Saw a strange lump on the floor, the rest of it hidden behind the bed. Even as her mind told her what it was, Gina refused to believe it.

Even as it insisted: *What you think that smell is?* She refused to conceive it. Instead she turned and ran down the hall. When she got to the steps, she ran down them too. She stopped long enough to unlock the front door and swing it back wide.

She didn't stop to close it. Didn't stop to lock it. She just kept on running even as her chest began to burn and tears blurred her vision.

Gina ran, barely pausing at traffic lights, moving through the Hollis, Queens' neighborhood deftly. She didn't stop until she reached her mother's house, ringing the doorbell like the house was on fire. When her mother answered, Gina collapsed into a heap at the door.

Doreen Alexander was known for a few things, but compassion wasn't one of them. She had never been loving, had never been gentle, but the sight of her only child in a heap on her front step, wailing and moaning, changed that for her.

In a heartbeat, Doreen Alexander was down on the step too, taking Gina into her arms, asking her what happened, asking her what's wrong, wiping tears, the snot that bubbled from Gina's nose.

"You got to talk to me Gina. Tell me what happened." But Gina couldn't talk "You got to tell me Gina. Tell me what happened," her mother insisted, pulling her back, searching her face.

Gina blinked, tried to find her breath, her voice. It took a couple of tries before she could. "He dead Momma," as far as she got before sorrow locked up her throat.

"Who dead?" but in that moment Doreen Alexander knew.

"Jefferson," Gina said with a shutter.

Doreen released Gina. Her arms landed dully by her side. Doreen's body went numb and she stared out in space. Her mouth opened a bit. Her head shook slowly. "Dead? Jefferson can't be dead?"

But he was and it took the women a little while to get grounded, snap out of their shock. Doreen came around first, rising from the stoop. "Come on," she said but Gina didn't budge. "Come on now. Get up. We got stuff to do."

Running her hands over her face, Gina got up.

The block was filled with the oily swirly lights of four patrol cars and an ambulance, cutting into the evening darkness. Outside of the house, neighbors had gathered in overcoats and bathrobes, peering into the door, open wide, revealing just the stairway.

Doreen and Gina pushed their way through the crowd. A patrolman stopped them. "Are you a relative?"

Both women nodded their head. "We the ones that called," Doreen said quickly, wanting nothing more to get up those stairs before they brought Jefferson out.

"Brother?"

"He's my daddy," Gina said quickly.

The officer looked her over. His brows raised. "Your sisters are already inside."

Which confused Gina for a minute. She had no sisters.

It came to her half a second later, that the officer was referring to Jefferson's real daughters. Daughters who never really liked her. Daughters who had always looked at her sideways. Real flesh and blood daughters who never really understood Jefferson's attachment to Gina and no doubt grumbled about her between themselves, *because Jefferson wouldn't allow no disrespect when he was around.*

But Jefferson was gone.

The thought made Gina's chest hurt. Made tears fill her eyes. "I got to get in there," she said, pushing past the officer and running up the stairs.

Her bedroom door, which she was certain had been closed, was now open. Inside two officers were going through her dresser drawers. She had a nickel bag of weed in it. She backed away from the room.

"That's her," came a voice from up the hall.

"Gina Alexander?" A plain clothes detective asked as he approached. Instinct made her back up. She bumped into the wall. "Are you Gina Alexander?"

"Yeah, that's her," one of Jefferson's daughter's said.

Gina hadn't seen her when she came up, but she saw her now, the face, a wide bowl of chocolate-pudding fury. She scowled at Gina with rage, her big body ready to spring. She was old enough to be Gina's mother, but Gina knew, in that moment the woman didn't care.

In that moment, the idea of a forty-something year old woman beating down a twenty-three year old made no dif.

"Gina Alexander, I need to speak with you," the detective said again, his steps cautious, his hand on the handle of his gun.

Gina got her feet moving. In a second she was flying down the stairs. But another officer grabbed her before she could make it outside. Grabbed her and turned her, both wrists in his hand, her whole body pressed against the wall. "Now just calm down young lady. Just calm down."

"What you doing? What you doing to my child?" Gina's mother insisted.

The upstairs detective came running down, stepping in to help keep Gina against the wall. "We just want to talk to her, Ma'am, that's all." He directed his voice to Gina. "Now we need you to calm down, okay. If you don't, we will cuff you and book you. Do you understand?"

Gina nodded, relaxed. Allowed herself to be turned around slowly. The detective indicated the living room. "Let's go in there." Taking a seat on the edge of the chair, he was direct. "Why did you run?"

Gina's lips grew tight.

"Answer the officer," Doreen Alexander insisted. But Gina seemed willing to do anything but.

"Now we can do this the easy way, or the hard, so I'm going to ask you again. Why did you run?"

Gina's lip trembled. "'Cause I was scared."

"Scared of?"

Doreen jumped back in. "That was her daddy. Him dying like that was shocking." Until that moment, Doreen had denied the feasibility of Jefferson ever really being a father to Gina. But here she was, rising her to daughter's defense. Gina looked at her mother, but Doreen Alexander simply looked away.

"According to the two women upstairs, Jefferson wasn't any real relation to you, is that true?"

Gina's eyes snapped to the officers, hurt and defensive. "Yes, he was. He was my daddy."

"Not according to the deceased daughters. In fact the daughters are saying you took advantage of their father's kindness. That you served time and use drugs, is that true?"

"Tell the truth Gina," her mother warned.

"I didn't serve no real time. I'm on probation and yeah, I smoked some tree."

"They also suggested we needed to interrogate you. They seem to think you were somehow responsible for the decease's death. That you knew he had a lot of money in the house and you did something to him so you can get your hands on it."

"I ain't did nothing to Jefferson. I loved him."

"Well, according to his children..."

"I'm his too. He loved me just as much." Tears came again. "I ain't did nothing to Jefferson. I'd never hurt him."

"For your sake, I hope not." The detective eased back. "We have to wait for the M.E. It might take a while. In the meantime we would appreciate it if you wait here with us till he arrives."

"The M.E.? That can take hours?" Doreen Alexander warned.

"You're absolutely right, but right now, Miss?"

"Alexander."

"Right now Miss Alexander, we have a dead man upstairs and his daughters are saying she did it. Until we get some idea about how he died, no one can go anywhere."

Gina's eyes dusted the ceiling. "Can I go to my room?" She wasn't feeling well and her head hurt like crazy. Besides that, she wanted to hide the marijuana if they hadn't found it already.

"That's a potential crime scene, you need to wait down here."

"Well can I at least go look at him? I didn't get a chance to look at him good."

"Sorry, but as I said, it's a potential crime scene up there."

"But they up there. Why can't I go up?"

"That was their father."

A second plainclothesman came down, whispered something into the other policemen's ear. The policeman looked at Gina, looked at Doreen. Got up. Was gone for a while.

Past midnight, the house took on a surreal feel. Sitting in the kitchen, an open container of takeout before her, Gina was overcome with a bunch of emotions. She had listened to the sound of footsteps over her head. Heard people in her bedroom, drawers opening and closing, furniture being moved.

It took her a while to realize that they hadn't found her stash. If they had, they would have arrested her by now for possession.

What had her now was how anybody could even think she would do something to Jefferson. That she would kill him over some money.

What money?

Jefferson had always given her a few dollars when she needed it but he wasn't rich. Gina knew he got a pension and Social Security, but she didn't know a thing about 'his money.'

"Eat something Gina," her mother insisted. "You got to keep up your strength."

"I can't eat." She got up from the table. The uniform officer put his hand on his gun. "Just going to get some juice, damn." She went to the refrigerator, taking out the ice tea.

She was drinking it before she realized who had made it. Jefferson had. That added to her sadness. Tears came with a new intensity as she poured the rest of the contents down the sink.

A wail came from behind her. She turned to see her mother's mouth opened in a big wide 'O', her eyes pinched. Doreen had been holding off on her sorrow and holding on to maintain her composure, but there in the silence of Jefferson's kitchen, her grief set itself free.

Gina dropped the glass. It shattered against the porcelain sink. The cop jumped at the sound. Gina rushed to her mother and held her, deep and close, in a way she never had before.

Where did the night go?

Gina wasn't sure, only that sleeping upright on the sofa wasn't as harsh as the morning sun that came through the window when her mother woke her.

"He here," Doreen said in an anxious soft reverence. Gina squinted, rubbed at her eyes. Looked around. Remembered. Let tears leak from her eyes. "He just went up."

"Who?"

"The M.E."

The words shook the last bit of sleep from Gina. She had to go to the bathroom. Told the officer. He nodded and followed. Kept the bathroom door ajar with his foot as Gina used the toilet.

She wanted to take a shower. Wanted to look into her room, but that wasn't allowed. They had taken skin samples from her hands and from beneath her fingernails. They had questioned her a dozen times, asking over and over what she'd done and didn't do when she got in from work.

Gina had talked about being hungry, wanting to let Jefferson know that she was going to the Chinese restaurant and the smell that hit her when she opened his bedroom door.

She told it more times than she wanted to remember — the running, the fleeing straight to her mother's. That her mother had phoned the police.

She talked about the relationship, or at least what she knew, between her mother and Jefferson and how he wasn't her blood father, but he always wanted to be. Gina shared how his real children never liked her and how he had taken her in when she had no place to go.

But none of it seemed substantial or important now. The M.E. was, at that very moment, checking Jefferson over to make sure she hadn't killed him. Checking his cold, dead, defecated body to ensure that Gina hadn't poisoned him, or stabbed him or shot him in some indiscriminate place.

Gina came out of the bathroom, looked down the hall towards Jefferson room, glanced at her own, a new realization striking. No matter what the outcome, no matter what the M.E. found, Jefferson, her protector, her would-be father, was gone.

The footsteps coming down the stairs were heavy and quick. Three sets in all, they didn't pause, didn't come into the living room, but continued outside. Soon after, additional footfalls were heard.

"Miss Alexander?" Both women said yes. "Preliminary findings suggest that Mr. Carter died of natural causes. He was a diabetic and had hypertension. The M.E. could find no signs of foul play, so we are letting you go."

Gina's face pinched. "Go? Go where?" This was where she lived. And while she didn't have any plans on staying too much longer with Jefferson gone, she wasn't ready to evacuate it right now, this second. "I live here."

"Yes, his daughters said as much. But they asked me to inform you that they want you to vacate the premises. They asked me to tell you that it's their wish that you pack up your things today."

"Where am I supposed to go?"

"That, I can't tell you."

Doreen Alexander spoke up, a fire in her voice. "She ain't got to leave today this minute. She done lived here more than thirty days, so she got tenant rights. They can't make her leave now."

"That's true. But if you want my advice Ms. Alexander, I would suggest you try and find some other place to stay. Neither of them were happy about you being here and technically this is their father's house, which means it will become theirs shortly. No, they can't make you leave right this minute, but they can make your staying here hard."

"She got a right to be here," Doreen insisted.

"I've informed you of their wishes and you know the law. The rest is up to you."

But there were more pressing needs inside of Gina. "Can we go see him now?"

The officer nodded, the two women made their way up the stairs.

Chapter Eleven

Rick stood in his kitchen, washing up the few dinner dishes. He was glad that he was almost through. He had helped Kanisha with her homework, fed her a decent meal, got her into the tub and finally into bed.

He had a headache the size of Montana and all he really wanted was to go lie down. As soon as he finished washing up the dishes, he planned to do just that. The headaches had gotten frequent of late and he had taken some aspirin a few minutes ago.

He was waiting for the medicine to kick in, but instead of relief, he felt his stomach getting queasy. Ignoring it, he moved around the kitchen, wiping countertops as his head throbbed with every beat of his heart.

Everything was wrong in his life, from the choices he made to how he was living them. Thinking about it made his head hurt all the more.

In the last few weeks his life paralleled a hip hop video, complete with hoochies, ho's and strippers. *Let's not forget the crazy-ass woman who dropped her drawers and put a gun — your gun — to her head or that police beat-down you nearly got.* The only thing missing was throwing back bottles of *Cristal* and flashing the *bling-bling.*

Rick found himself marooned, not knowing who he was, where he was going or how he was going to get there. He winced against the head pain and swallowed back nausea. Laid the dish rag across the sink. Stomach lurching, throat constricting, he knew he was going to throw up.

Running to the bathroom, he barely got the toilet seat up before vomit poured from his mouth. Far away, he heard the phone ringing, but caught in the middle of upchucking, he was in no position to answer.

* * *

Doreen Alexander stared at the receiver for a second then hung up.

She wished for the hundredth time that Jefferson was still alive. Doreen wished he hadn't died and was still just a few miles away. Jefferson could help Gina. He would know what to do. He would get her off the couch. Get her eyes to focus.

Doreen didn't have a clue.

She had tried anger. She had tried harsh words. She had tried holding her, but none of it worked. Gina was still shell shocked. Still sitting on the couch staring at nothing. She had been there like that since they returned home.

She had been fine until they returned to Jefferson's house the next day so Gina could get a change of clothes. Fine until they discovered Jefferson's daughters had changed the locks and had Gina's possessions in plastic bags dumped on the dead lawn.

When Gina rang the doorbell, they didn't even open the door, just hollered through the wood that she didn't have no business there and she needed to get gone. When Doreen had asked about funeral arrangements, she was told it was none of her damn business and she needed to get gone too.

When Doreen insisted that Gina had tenant's rights, she was told Gina had jack. When Doreen threatened to call the police, she was told to, "go right ahead, we ain't scared of them or you."

It was at that point that Gina grabbed up her plastic bags, her mother picking up what Gina couldn't carry. Coming back to Doreen's house, Gina had dumped the bags in her old bedroom and taken refuge on the couch. That had been four hours ago. Gina had moved only to go to the bathroom.

Doreen looked at the clock and picked up the phone one more time. It rang unanswered. This time she left a message.

Rick was rinsing out his mouth when the phone began ringing a second time. He spat into the sink, splashed his face with warm water and dried it with a towel. Whoever it was, he wasn't up to talking.

His stomach was quiet but his head was still raging. The only thing he was up to was lying down.

* * *

Rick was sleep, or at least in the semblance of it when the phone jarred him awake. It had taken a while just to get to the REM stage and the last thing he wanted was to leave it. He looked at the clock, saw the hour — a little after midnight. He reached over. Picked up. "Yeah."

"Rick, it's me."

Sleep left him. "Miss Alexander," he said, sitting up.

"Been calling you all night."

"Sorry."

"Listen. Jefferson dead."

Rick blinked. "Excuse me?"

"Jefferson. He dead and Gina over here, like a zombie on my couch. She been here, just sitting, barely blinking, for hours."

"Jefferson's dead?"

"Ain't that what I said? Gina ain't taking it well. Them damn kids of Jefferson done thrown her out and everything. And she's taking it bad and I can't do nothing for her. I need you to come and try to talk to her or something."

Or something. Rick was terribly sorry that Jefferson was dead. He liked Jefferson. Knew he had been a good person. That he had a faith in Gina that nobody else possessed, but Rick's life with Gina was supposed to be over. If it didn't involved Kanisha directly, he wasn't supposed to have any parts in Gina's life.

"Rick? Did you hear me? I need you to come over here."

"Now?"

"What the hell you think. Girl been sitting on the couch for hours, only moving to use the bathroom and I can't do nothing and Jefferson dead ... " Tears. They came through the wire quick and sharp.

"What am I supposed to do with Kanisha? If you say Gina's like you say she is, Kanisha don't need to see that."

"Take her to your momma's or somewhere, but I need you over here now Rick. Right now."

Rick fell back against the bed, not muffling his sigh. "I'm on my way."

He didn't take Kanisha to his mother's. He took her upstairs to his tenant's. He wasn't sure just how long he'd be gone, but he promised to be back before daybreak. With clothes hastily tossed onto his back, Rick headed towards Gina's mother's house, an unwilling rescuer to Gina's latest predicament.

The lights were burning. Even an outside fixture that Rick had never seen clicked on was shining. From the street, the house looked like a party was going inside.

Rick headed up the walkway, then the stoop. He was about to ring the bell when the door opened, a worried, nearly petrified Doreen Alexander opening the door. "She still on the couch."

Rick entered the house, ill memories of previous brief visits accosting him. He tried to prepare himself for Gina. Tried to think of what he could do and say that her own mother seemed incapable of. Came up empty. He wished Jefferson were still alive.

Gina didn't look up when he entered. She didn't acknowledge him when he called out to her. She just sat there looking out straight. If he didn't know better, he would have sworn she had taken a hit too many of *Wet*, the reincarnation of an old drug with a new twist that included marijuana, PCP and embalming fluid.

Too much *Wet* made people freeze like that. 'Stuck' was the slang name for the condition. In recent months he had seen more than one prisoner 'Stuck.' A trip to the infirmary cured it.

He knew Gina used to smoke and Jefferson said she had gone back to the nasty habit. What Rick didn't know was if she had moved onto the marijuana/PCP/embalming concoction. He hoped not.

He went to her. Sat next to her. There was still no response. "She been doing anything?" he asked Gina's mother.

"Nothing but sitting there."

"No I mean, drugs. Smoking anything?"

"I been with her since yesterday. She ain't smoked nothing round me. And if she tried to sneak it, I'd smell it. No, that ain't no drugs. That's grief." With that, Miss Alexander brought her hands to her face and left the room.

Rick leaned into her face. "Gina. Hey. Gina." He snapped his fingers in front of her face. She blinked, but that was all. He tapped her shoulder. "Gina." Shook it a little. Still no response. Rick looked around him, unsure what to do next.

Worse case he would call 911, say he had a catatonic. Worse

case, he would call 911 and the let the hospitals deal with her. *But if she's been smoking ...* her probation would be rescinded and back to jail she would go.

He dropped down in front of her. Took her shoulders into his hands. Shook her. "Gina. Gina." Rick shook her some more, her head too rag-doll loose to his liking. He went on shaking her, raising his voice "Gina!" until he was bellowing.

His spit landed on her eye. She blinked quickly, seemingly trying to focus. "You see me Gina?" Rick asked quick, anxious. "You see me? Come on now. Look at me. Look at me!" She blinked a few more times before her eyes closed, as if for good.

A tear slipped past the fold, then another. Her throat bobbed and a soft mewl left her. Instinct made him reach forward. Instinct made him draw her near. Jefferson's words, *"What Gina do and don't do has everything to do with you because it has everything to do with Kanisha,"* shifted his heart. Jefferson's words, opening what had been closed.

He made sure Gina was in the third bedroom before he went upstairs to get Kanisha. Past one in the morning, he was tired and already knew that tomorrow, he would call in. His excuse, "my father-in-law died," adequate.

Jefferson wasn't Gina's real father and Rick had never been legally married to Gina, but life had taught him that real-life situations bit you in the butt no matter what the law had to say about it.

Kanisha had been asleep and so Rick carried her downstairs and tucked her in. He was about to turn in himself when Gina appeared at his bedroom doorway. "I'm scared Rick. Can I sleep with you?"

His immediate reaction was no. His immediate reaction was too much would happen if she did. His immediate reaction was that in her state, she would want what he promised he'd never give again.

"Can I?"

Even in the gloom he could see the wetness on her face. She just lost her daddy, or the only one she'd ever known. Rick nodded, took the third pillow off his side of the bed and placed it on the other.

Gina got in and scooted next to him, her breast and belly to his back, her arms clinging to him tight. It felt wrong. So wrong he could not relax. Get comfortable. Shifting away from her, he eased her in the other direction and spooned against her.

Rick ignored the penis that swelled at the contact of the warm flesh. He made sure his hands stayed on her belly and far from her breast. He laid there with halted breath, hoping Gina wouldn't start moving against him. Hoped she would keep her own hands to herself.

Five minutes later when her snores came, he knew he was safe.

The next morning, Rick eased his arm from beneath Gina, pins and needles in his fingers. He had slept the whole night with Gina laying on it. It hadn't been comfortable but when he tried to ease it from beneath her, she had instantly awakened, taking his arm and putting it back.

Uncertain of this new day, Rick went to check on Kanisha who was fast asleep and then went to use the bathroom. He made a mental note to call her school and his and Gina's job. None of them would be any of those places today.

He was coming from the bathroom when he saw Gina. She stood in his doorway, worse for the wear. Eyes puffy, hair astray, she looked tossed about.

"Hi," she said

"Hi," he offered back

"You getting ready for work?"

"I wasn't going to go in today."

"Oh."

"Yeah, I figured, I'd, you know."

"I ain't in on the arrangements or nothing. They wouldn't tell me when or where."

"Who?"

"Jefferson's daughters," her face crumbled. "Told me it wasn't none of my business and I wasn't wanted there."

"Of course it's your business."

"They don't think so. They think I'm nothing to him. But I was a lot," she seemed to be convincing herself more so than him. "He loved me. Just like them. I was his daughter too."

"You still are Gina."

"How can I be when I don't know when he's gonna be buried or where? How can I say goodbye if I don't know where he's at?"

Rick thought about it. He could pull some strings, get the information from the officers that had arrived on the scene. "Don't worry. We'll find out."

"Them heifers ain't gonna tell us."

"They don't have to."

Four hours later, Rick had the information. Wallington's Funeral Home on Sutphin Boulevard had the body. But it wouldn't be for long. They were shipping Jefferson south to North Carolina.

"When he leaving?"

"He's scheduled on Delta first thing tomorrow. Today they'll do the embalming to get him ready."

"So I can't see him."

"I know this C.O. who got a cousin who I think works there. Maybe I can get in contact with him. Maybe you can go by and see him."

Gina's eyes grew wide, plaintive. "You'll come with me right? Come with me so I can say goodbye. I don't want to go by myself."

Rick's idea of fun wasn't death, or anything to do with it. He had seen enough of it in prison. Every so often someone would hang themselves or got shanked and he would have to go and retrieve the body. Death wasn't pretty. He told Gina so.

"He's going to look gray. He's not going to look how he'll end up in the casket."

"I don't care about that Rick. I just got to say goodbye."

"I'll see what I can do."

How do you explain death to a five year old? How do you tell them that someone close to them, someone they loved, someone they saw often was no longer around?

You tell them they were up in heaven and let them spend minutes of the time staring at the sky trying to find them. You prepare yourself for their frustration when they can't.

Rick was trying to do that but he was tired of Kanisha's outbursts and her tears. He called his mother to see if Kanisha could come over for a little while, "to give me and Gina some breathing room."

Rick's mother wasn't thrilled at all that Gina was even there with her son. Rick's mother had never cared for the loud, brash, street, way too young Gina and that opinion wasn't changing any time soon. But Loretta Trimmons bit her tongue, said okay.

So on the way to Wallington's Kanisha was dropped off at Rick's mothers, armed with a few toys and a Happy Meal. Then they headed to the funeral home in silence.

They entered the double glass doors, asked for Chuck and a few minutes later, they were being led down into the basement. Gratefully, all the doors were closed, no unwanted glimpses of the dead in various stages of final preparations.

Most of the doors said "Authorized Personnel Only" and one said "Showroom". There was no telltale odor in the air and the walls, painted a pastel yellow, invited the warmth of the overhead lights and the table lamps about the room.

But beyond the plaster and sheetrock, a chilly somberness hung in the air. Beyond the walls of soft yellow, the dead waited.

Gina and Rick were told to wait and soon a body bag was being rolled out to them. Huge, parts of the bag spilled over the side of the gurney.

Chuck offered warnings. "He hasn't been embalmed yet. He's been kept cold, but not embalmed, so you might get an odor."

But Gina didn't care about that. What she was concerned about was how that huge lump in the oversized black bag amounted to Jefferson. She was trying to equate it with the voice that asked five mornings out of a week, "You up yet?"

She was trying to equate the lumpy black Hefty bag with the man who took her in when no one else would. Who insisted that he was her real daddy when he wasn't. Who gave her money when she had none. Cooked her food, cleaned her room and just cared about her when she'd felt nobody else in the world ever would.

"Can I see him now?"

"Sure." Chuck eased the huge zipper back sixteen inches. Stopped. Shifted the gather of thick plastic. There he was, Jefferson looking as he often looked when he took a nap.

Rested.

Not gray. Not smelly. Not dead. But in the middle of a good sleep.

Gina moved in closer, Rick by her side. "I'm sorry Jefferson," Gina's first words. "I'm sorry you went away mad at me. I'm sorry I messed up. I'm so sorry." Tears choked her. She lifted a hand to touch his face but Chuck stopped her. Shook his head no.

Gina nodded. Moved fingers to her mouth. Kissed them. Blew it towards the gurney. "I love you Jefferson. Even when I was mad I still loved you. You know that, right? You know that, don't you?"

Chuck stepped in. "I have to take him back now."

Rick took Gina gently at the shoulder, turned her about face. Chuck stood sentry, making sure they were half way up the stairs before he zipped the back bag up. Wheeled the gurney away.

When they got back to Rick's, Doreen Alexander was waiting in her car for them. She got out when they pulled up, moving fast and brisk their way. "Where y'all been? I've been calling all day."

Rick and Gina exchanged looks, a silent agreement passing between them. "We took Kanisha to my mother's. Stayed a while," Rick offered. To tell Doreen that Gina went to say goodbye to Jefferson without her knowledge would cause a huge argument. It was best if she didn't know.

"Them women came to the house first thing this morning." Doreen fixed her eye on her Gina. "They keep on talking about the money. They keep saying that you took it."

"I don't know about no damn money," Gina defended.

"That's what I told them, but they insisting Jefferson had a big fat bankroll up in the house and they can't find it. That you must of taken it."

"I ain't take shit."

Rick stepped in. "Calm down Gina."

"No. God damn it. No. I'm tired of this shit. Jefferson dead and I can't even go to his funeral and all them stink-fat-black-ass bitches can talk about is some money? Their father, my daddy, dead and all they can think about is some fucking money?"

"That's enough Gina."

"No, it ain't enough. I'm tired of them and their mutha fucking bullshit."

Rick took her by the shoulder. "Come on. Let's go in the house."

The three of them went.

Inside Doreen told them more news. "They saying if you give it back, they'll fly you and me down for the funeral. Tell us where Jefferson gonna be buried."

"I ain't got no money, Momma. I swear to God I don't."

"He ain't never said nothing to you about any cash?"

"No."

"Oh."

The way Doreen said 'oh' made Gina take notice. "You know about some money?"

Doreen shrugged. "Ain't a million dollars, but yeah. I know of it. That weekend Jefferson went to Atlantic City. He brought home about a hundred thousand. He was supposed to put it in some kind of a fund. As far as I know he did, but them heifers saying he didn't. Said he told them he was going to do it first thing next week."

Gina's mouth hung open. "So there was money in the house."

"Was. He ain't tell me where he put it. And he made me promise not to tell you."

"I wish the fuck he would have 'cause I would have told him to deposit the shit. Now they thinking I'm a damn thief." She fixed miserable eyes on her mother. "I ain't never stole from Jefferson. Never."

"I know."

Rick got into the foray. "Anybody else knew about it?"

"Well if his daughters knew, I'm sure his grandkids knew and all them had keys," Doreen offered.

"And I bet you, I fucking bet you, that's who got the money. Them damn grandkids 'cause I seen them and they ain't for shit. They done probably spent it all up by now."

"You probably right."

"Next time they come around, you tell them to check their own funky kids."

"I did and they swore up and down that their children wouldn't do no mess like that."

"Oh, but I would right? Fuck. Them."

"Alright Gina, that's enough." Rick said sharply, having heard enough.

"I'm sorry Rick, but how they gonna blame me?"

"They shouldn't, but you don't want to pick up the bad habits you dropped because of them."

"Rick's right Gina. You can't be letting people mess you up now. You doing too good to be turned around."

Gina looked at her mother. Compliments from her were rare. Doreen looked away. Stood. "Well, I guess I'll be going. If I hear anything else, I'll call you. They don't know where you are and I ain't telling."

Chapter Twelve

In many ways, Jeff's life was a series of fence-straddling and with music, there wasn't much difference. He listened to Hot 97 as much as he listened to KISS-FM. He liked to hear the latest music as well as taking trips back in time with the Golden Oldies.

Still the song that came from his car radio as he made his way to the cleaners caught him by surprise. An old tune from the sixties: Martha Reeves and the Vandella's "No Where To Run" had him doing more than bopping his head and singing off key. It had him thinking.

"Got nowhere to run to bab-bee, got no where to hide."

It was his newest theme song.

Perhaps it had been his tune for a while, but up until recently, he never claimed it. Jeff never saw his social life as a series of ducking and weaving. He never considered the fact that he refused to see just one woman at one time as anything more then how it was for him.

Dajah had changed that.

Dajah had changed much. She had him doing things and feeling things he hadn't done or felt since Mya. She had him reexamining his life in ways he never wanted to before. She had him wanting somebody, really wanting somebody.

Whether it was just the thrill of the hunt or the joy of the pursuit, Jeff didn't know and wouldn't know until that time came. But what he did know in the weeks since he had seen her, talked to her, been in her presence, she was all he could think about.

With Valentine's Day fast approaching, his phone had been ringing like dating central, the various women in his life vying for the perfect spot — the evening of the Fourteenth.

2003 was a special year with regards to the Day of Love. It fell on a Friday. It would be seven more years before that happened and the different women took alternate dates when he balked, saying he wasn't sure what his plans were. They asked for the evening of the Thirteenth, the afternoon of the Fifteenth. All day on the Sixteenth.

The women in his life knew that pinning him down wasn't a good thing, so they offered up alternatives, each wanting to spend some quality time with him around Valentine's Day, if not on it.

It was sad really, how desperate they could get. But that desperation was the very same thing that allowed him to see them as he wished and not at all if he didn't. Jeff understood their eagerness to set a date. They would need it as proof to their friends that they were important to him and if they couldn't snag the actual day, they could always wave the before or after days as affirmation that they really mattered to him.

They did, in a way. All four of them. Lisa, Jill, Syretta and Joy all mattered. Each had something the other didn't. But none of them had the real stuff that made his heart sing. None of them had real backbone. Not even Lisa, who he had been seeing the longest.

Occasionally they would whimper or shout, occasionally they would insist they couldn't go on sharing, but none of them had walked. None. Because even when they did get up the nerve, within a month or less, they'd be calling him up asking: "What's up?" as if they had never stepped.

Jeff had remained guilt-free in his roulette dating because he had never tried to tell those women he loved them. He had never tried to press upon them that they made his world spin. When he was with them, he was fully with them and when he wasn't, he wasn't.

For the last few years, Valentine's Day was just too much hype and not enough substance. But now that was changing. Now he didn't want to toss the purpose of the day away. This year he wanted something substantial.

Dajah came in from work, tired, cold and hungry. Winter seemed to just be getting started even though it was more then halfway over. That's how it was in New York. Just when you thought you couldn't take another bone chilling day, Mother Nature came along and showed you just how wrong you were.

Yes, there were nice things about the season, like when snow was falling at night and you looked out your window and saw everything covered in white, the world outside muffled, everything sparkling like diamonds. And the winter skies ... with smog cut back to a minimum, the beauty of an early evening could be both seen and appreciated.

There was something downright delicious about coming in from the cold, the smell of heat drifting up your nose, the warmth rushing your face likes small kisses. But while you were out in it, battling the low temps, there wasn't much niceness to it at all.

All of those things were the least of her problems. The inconvenience of winter didn't matter. The upcoming Friday had her front and center, something she was reminded of every time she went to a supermarket or turned on the TV.

The whole world was gearing up for Valentine's Day and the preparations were in her face everywhere she looked.

Last year she had David to share a meal with. She had even shared his bed, though nothing happened. And as mocking as that evening was — her sitting up with a man she tossed away — at least she had not been alone.

Unlike this year.

This year she would be resigned to stay home on that Friday night and be okay with it. This year she would have to say *"Nothing"* when her co-workers asked what she had planned for the evening.

This year, there was still no Prince Charming in her life to buy her roses or wine and dine her. Give her that card that *says it all*. This year, Dajah would be all by her lonesome, which, when you got right down to it, was her choice, but that didn't make it feel any better.

Hurrying up the stairs to her place, she put her key in the lock, the darkness complete, except for the little red flashing button on her phone; the little red flashing button that said someone had called and left a message.

Moving through the shadows, she hit play. Heard. "Valentines Day? Are you busy?"

"Go for it."

It was exactly what she expected Frieda to say, so there was no surprise there. What was surprising was how she had had the very same thought.

"If the man wants to spend some time and money on you on Valentine's Day no less, I say why not?" — which had been Dajah's second thought.

"Because I'm suppose to be finished with him?," her voice more laughter than question.

"Well be finished with him after Valentine's Day. It'll sure beat being alone." Which was the ultimate truth. "Go out with him and if you still not feeling him, then you don't have to see him anymore after that," Frieda's advice.

"Kind of sounds like I'm using him."

"How? He asked you, remember? Obviously it's what he wants."

"True."

"So hang up with me and call him."

Dajah sighed. "I don't know Free."

Frieda laughed. "Stop lying. You knew before you called me. You just needed me to tell you yes, so I'm saying it — yes, go for it."

Dajah went.

He answered on the second ring, an anxiousness coming through the wire as he muttered the word, "Hello?"

"Jeff?"

"Dajah?"

"Yep, the one and only."

"You got my message."

She laughed. "Which one?"

"Ouch."

"Yeah, ouch," she declared. "How you gonna act like I'm not there one minute and the next, you calling to get together?"

She was calling him on it. He didn't mind at all. "Busted."

"Dag on right you're busted. I heard those two pitiful messages and I wasn't even going to waste my time calling you back."

"But you did."

"Only because you owe me, so I figured why not Valentine's Day."

It was his turn to laugh. "Oh, I owe you?"

"Yeah, you owe me. So where we going?"

"Where would you like to go?" She didn't know. Told him so. "Well, there's that Jazz club I mentioned before."

"Yeah, I'm listening."

"They have a nice little combo, the food's great and we would-n't have to trek to the city."

"They have dancing?"

"No, it's a jazz club."

"Oh."

"Don't worry. You're going to love it."

"How do you know?"

"Trust me."

He hadn't earned that yet. She pressed on. "So, what time should I be ready?"

"Two Hundred and Twenty-seventh Street, right?"

"Yeah, off of Franny Lew."

"You're about eight, nine, minutes from me. If I swing around and pick you up around eight, we can be there by eight-thirtyish, nine."

"And make sure you bring my picture."

"Picture?"

"Yeah, the one you did of me."

Jeff looked across the room. Saw it on his drafting table. The beauty of it making it hard to part with. "I don't know what I did with it."

"What do you mean, you don't know? How can you not know?"

"I'll just have to do another one." His phone beeped.

"Yeah, I guess you will."

"Are you always so demanding?"

She laughed. "Is that a problem?"

"No, not at all."

"Good."

"So you really weren't going to call me?"

"Nope."

"Not ever again?" His phone beeped again.

"Is that your phone?"

"Yeah." He glanced at the display screen. "Just my boy. He can call back."

"Your boy, huh?"

"Yeah."

"What's his name?"

"Who?"

"Your boy. The one whose call you're ignoring?"

"Casey."

The phone beeped again. "Must be important. He's calling back."

"Nah, it's never important. I can holla at him later."

A second beep. "No, holla at him now. I can't stand the interruption."

"You sure?"

"Yeah, I'm sure."

"So you'll call me back?"

"Nah, you call me back when you get finished with Casey."

"You'll be home?"

Dajah laughed. It felt good to be riding high in the saddle again. "Where else am I'm going to be on a cold night like tonight?"

"Okay. Talk to you in a few."

"Okay." Dajah hung up the phone, shook her head, her smile wide enough to hurt her cheeks.

A few miles away, Jeff looked at his display, saw the number that really wasn't Casey's and headed to the kitchen to fix some dinner. The phone rang four more times before he could even sit down and eat.

He didn't bother about picking up.

Ding! Dong!

Jeff heard the bell, knew who it was and debated on whether or not he would answer it. He did a heart and soul check, deciding if he wanted to be bothered or not and decided last minute it might be better this way.

With Valentine's Day just a few days away, it would be better to give Lisa a little something now so she won't be mad when she didn't get anything later. He pressed his intercom, asked who, like he didn't have a clue and buzzed her up.

She arrived at his apartment door a minute later, winded and hot under the collar, asking him why he didn't answer her call. Jeff didn't say much, just sat down to finish his meal as she rattled on about how unfair it was.

Seven minutes later as he finished up his dinner, Lisa was sitting there watching him eat, her anger all gone.

When Jeff got up to take his empty plate to the kitchen, she was on him like white on rice. Half an hour later, he and Kelly were walking her to her car, promising to call her later, a time span they both knew had no real merit.

Before the night was through, Jeff made four other phone calls, three getting the bad news that his Valentine's Day was booked, the fourth making plans in her head on what she would wear.

Chapter Thirteen

Gina, in the middle of her bereavement days from work, ignored the movements of Kanisha and Rick readying themselves for another day of school and work. She was looking forward to them being gone. She needed some serious thinking time anyway.

While Rick had given her the use of his third bedroom, he had told her straight out that she would have to find a permanent place of her own. Gina wasn't surprised when Rick told her she had to leave, but she was a little hurt.

While he hadn't professed a change of heart, in the last few days she had seen a return of his kindness.

He knew the situation she was in. Knew that she could not go live with her mother, that there were few real options she had. She thought to ask Tarika if she could stay with her a while but sensed that Tarika wouldn't let that become permanent.

Her job at the library only brought in about twelve hundred dollars a month and she would need at least half of that just to get a room somewhere. Unless she found another job, she would not be able to live on her own.

The problem was Gina wasn't trained for much. She didn't even have a high school diploma and outside of the library job, she had never worked a day in her life. The job market wasn't pretty at all and layoffs were abundant.

Gina needed a plan. Needed to prioritize things, get her head in order. She had mourned but now it was time to get busy. Her main support was gone and nobody was going to help her. Gina had to help herself.

She decided to put in an application at the Magic Johnson Theatre. She could work there part-time after her regular job and not have to travel too far.

Taking the bus up to the Avenue, Gina ignored the street vendors selling ten-dollar bouquets of roses out of used chitterling buckets as she walked down the street. She ignored the huge over-stuffed teddy bears propped up on milk crates and roses made of milk chocolate.

When she got to the theater, she was told she had to come back on Saturday. "Manager's off today," she was told, which depressed her even more.

On her way back to her bus, she looked away from the crowd of people in the card store, the folks that gathered around the dingy white buckets of bouquets. This day meant nothing to her because she didn't mean much to anybody else.

It was just another Friday as far as she was concerned, a point well-taken later that evening as she sat around the dinner table with Rick and Kanisha.

In no shape, form, or fashion was it a lavish dinner but it was a hearty one. The takeout from the Rib Shack on Linden Boulevard consisted of a slab of ribs, potato salad, cornbread and collard greens.

"Can I have another?" Kanisha said, a gnawed, nearly-to-the-marrow spare rib bone in her hand.

Rick held up the box. "Sure. Help yourself."

Wiping his hands of sauce, he went and turned on the television. Rick took a seat and sipped his soda. On the coffee table there was a crudely cut out heart made of red construction paper, the only indicator what the day was.

"Know what I just thinking about?" Gina asked, breaking the silence.

"What?" Rick asked absently.

"That big ol', I mean big ol' box of chocolate you gave me one year, remember? It looked bigger than me and it must have been like a hundred pieces of candies inside."

Rick did remember, but the memory brought no joy.

"You remember, right?"

He nodded. Muttered, "Yeah."

"And that bracelet you brought me too. Lost it like a year later."

That bracelet Gina was referring to had been a tennis bracelet and it cost Rick a pretty penny. It had been the last time he bought her any jewelry. *Did she ever take care of anything you gave her?*

Rick got up from the table. "Tired. I'm going to bed. You'll do the kitchen?"

Gina looked at him three seconds before she answered. "Yeah."

Rick headed to the bedroom. Closed the door. He wasn't really tired but he couldn't be around Gina another minute. It wasn't anything she was doing, just simply all the things she didn't do, should have done over the years that was piling up in his mind.

He needed to put some distance between them.

Rick got into bed and turned off the lights. Staring up at the ceiling, his past was bitter, his present, unhappy and his future, unknown.

The pullover, or what Dajah could see of it, was a nice shade of brown, not too dark, not too tan. It complimented the hue of Jeff's complexion, emphasizing his clean shave. He didn't sport hair anywhere on his face.

She liked that.

She also liked how his smile was easy, how his cologne drifted in the air as she opened the door to him. Dajah didn't have to touch the black of his leather to know that it was buttery soft. Knew he had a sense for what women did and didn't like as he handed her a bouquet of tulips.

"For me?"

"Yeah, roses are so overrated."

"Better put this in water, come on up."

Jeff followed behind her, the sway of her hips, well in his reach.

Her apartment of soft yellow walls, bamboo wicker accents and the huge tree, spoke to a deeper part of him. It was a refreshing break from most of the other women's apartment he had seen, which had been full of blacks, grays and sharp angles.

He moved to the tree. Touched a leaf. "A real tree."

Dajah smiled. Nodded. "Most definitely. I could never have a fake one up in my place."

"Nice," he murmured.

"Let me put these in some water, grab my coat and then I'll be ready."

Jeff took in the abstract art on her walls. Recalled his own self-drawn originals. He thought about the one he had done just recently, considered how she re-stirred passion in him.

"This is really a nice touch," he heard her say from the kitchen, cabinet doors opening and closing. Water running.

"I figured you'd like them."

"You figured right."

Reaching in his pocket, he took out the tube, inside the sketch he had done of her. He had it ready when she returned.

"My picture," Dajah offered, delighted.

"Yeah."

She took it and smiled, affirmed. Placing it on her coffee table, Dajah planned on getting it framed.

The mimosa was a pretty shade of orange and delightful on the tongue. Dajah had had the champagne and orange juice drink before, but this particular one tasted better than she ever remembered.

"Must be the champagne," she shouted across the din of the live jazz band.

"What?"

"I said it must be the champagne," she shouted again. "It's the best I've had."

"Yeah, their drinks are pretty good."

They were in the Fort Green section of Brooklyn at a jazz club which tonight, violated occupancy laws by having more then the maximum seventy people in its place. Small, intimate, warm with a good vibe, Dajah had never been big on jazz, but the three-piece ensemble was giving her eargasms.

"How did you find this place," she shouted again.

Jeff cupped his hand to his ear, the horn solo reaching its crescendo.

"I said-,"

Again his hand was cupped to his ear, as he mouthed the words, "I can't hear you."

Dajah got up, taking her chair with her and put it next to him. She reached for her drink and put that before her too. Moving the whole of her body against him, her mouth stopped an inch from his ear. "I said how did you find this place?"

"I like jazz," Jeff's answer.

She nodded, pulled back some but not enough to break contact.

Jeff's arms found the back of her chair. His fingers landed on her shoulder. They stayed that way, close and connected, until the set ended.

Jeff was taking the long way home.

Instead of getting on the Brooklyn Queens Expressway, or driving down to the Belt Parkway, Jeff maneuvered his car down Atlantic Avenue. Three lane roads gave way to two as the subway rose up out of the ground, dividing north and sound bound traffic.

They passed by auto shops, three story walkups and upholstery stores. The vehicle glided them past project housing, West Indian restaurants and Boys and Girls High that held Afrocentric festivals in the summertime.

Four in the morning had settled the world into a late night/early morning demur of delivery trucks, gypsy cabs and a handful of passenger cars. A few people were out walking alone or in groups and young men hung around twenty-four-hours stores, but most of the world had gone away.

"Had a good time?" he wanted to know.

"Had a great time. I've never done a jazz club."

"Never?"

"Nope. Dance clubs yeah, but just sitting back, listening to some jazz?" Her head shook lazily against the headrest. There was a gentle, sexy weariness to her. She looked a yawn away from sleep.

"I see I have a lot to show you."

"Uh hum," she murmured, eyes closed.

Jeff wondered if she was sleeping. Studied her as he waited out a red light.

"I'm not sleep," she offered, though her eyes didn't open.

"Oh."

She shifted in his direction as much as the seat belt allowed. "Just resting my eyes."

"So if I hear you start snoring ..."

Her eyes flew open. "I don't snore." But in truth she really didn't know. No one had ever said so. Her eyes closed again. To say that she was comfortable with him, enjoyed him, liked him, was an understatement.

He was smart, good looking, intelligent and fun. He was witty, offered a whole new world for her, things she had never considered, like taking in a jazz club.

Dajah found herself appreciating everything about him, from how he dressed to how he talked. She found she liked having chairs pulled out for her, doors opened for each entry and, exit. She liked how good being close to him felt, without worry that he would misinterpret the action.

He had showed up on time, wasn't married and didn't have any kids. He dug the beach as much as she did and wasn't pressuring her about anything.

"What are you thinking on so hard?"

Her eyes opened. "You."

"And?"

"I'm liking what I see," she said genuinely.

"Ditto," he answered back.

One minute they were taking the scenic route down Atlantic Avenue and the next they were parked in front of her place.

In the half shadows that fell from the street lamp, Dajah's lips danced in a strip of light. "It was wonderful."

"I'm glad you enjoyed it. Happy Valentine's Day, " Jeff looked off. Looked back at her. "And I'm not coming in."

"Oh? Who said I was asking you to?"

He smiled, lips firm over the white of his teeth. "It's not that I don't want to, but I'm not going to rush you."

"That's cool." But even as she said it, she didn't mean it.

Dajah wanted to be rushed. She wanted the magic of this night to continue into late afternoon. She wanted Jeff in her bed, in her arms, between her thighs. She wanted to be putzing around the kitchen later on in the day cooking them something to eat.

And later still, she wanted a long, slow goodbye that curled her toes as they shared a hot, syrupy kiss at her front door. Still the time wasn't now. Dajah undid her seat belt.

Jeff touched her cheek. Closed his eyes as his mouth met hers. No tongue, no moisture, just lips against lips. A gentle pressure, soon he was pulling away. "Good night."

Dajah smiled. Held his gaze. "Good night." Got out the car and gave a wave. She did not look back at him as she unlocked the front door. Did not look back as she stepped inside then closed it. Dajah didn't look out of the peephole as she secured the locks. Just made her way upstairs, eager.

What are you feeling? How are you feeling?

Jeff was feeling the way he always felt after a good first date — elated, a little turned on, highlights of the evening moving through his mind, being compared, matched up against his first date with Mya.

They too had gone to a club, ate good food, chilled with good music. On his first date with Mya, they had debated about the merits of Al Jarreau's face maneuvers when he sung versus those of Rachelle Ferrell.

Did Dajah even know who Rachelle Ferrell was? Did she know the difference between fusion and contemporary or just how deep Miles Davis really was? Would she want to know or even care?

I never done a jazz club ... almost thirty-two and she never had? A woman as smart and on the ball as she seemed never sitting down to good music? So what else hadn't she done? What else didn't she know? Was he supposed to become this great teacher of the world and she an eager pupil?

For the first time all evening Jeff felt disappointment. For the first time since he had picked Dajah up, he felt a little disillusioned. For the first time, the age thing snagged on his soul.

But a deeper part of him wormed through. The deeper part that called a spade a spade and didn't allow B.S. *You searching for reasons why it won't work 'cause you too afraid to see if it will.*

Everybody's not Mya. Everybody's not going to take your heart and put it in a meat grinder. That girl is digging you and you trying to set it up so she won't. She gave you such a good time, you didn't even try to sleep with her. When's the last time you did that?

Sleeping with women on the first date was a given. There was something wrong if he didn't. But he had opened his mouth and said no, he wasn't coming in. He had opened his mouth and declared he wasn't going to pressure her.

And she's stirred things up in you. Things you pushed away for years. She has you sketching again. She has you being a gentleman again. And don't try and tell me you didn't feel like Big Willy when she confessed it was the first time she had gone to a jazz club. Don't even try.

Jeff reached for his cell phone. Hit a few buttons. Listened to it ring three times before the receiver was picked up.

"Hello?"

"You sleep?" he asked.

"No, just washing my face."

"I had a great time too ... I wasn't sure if I told you that or not."

"No, you didn't."

"Well, I just wanted to let you know."

Silence, each of them holding on, waiting. Each of them listening and hoping. Each of them wanting.

Jeff spoke. "You're a good thing for me Dajah. And I know moments might come where I might act like I don't know that, but I wanted to let you know."

"You're a good thing too."

He smiled. "So what are we two good things supposed to do next?"

"Dinner." She decided.

"Dinner?"

"Yeah?"

"When?"

"Tomorrow. My place."

He would have to cancel some plans, but he didn't care. "You're going to cook?"

"No, we're going to cook, together."

"Who says I can cook?"

"Can you boil water?"

"Last time I checked."

"Then you can cook."

"What time?"

"Five-ish."

"That's a long ways from now."

Dajah smiled. "Not that long."

"How about breakfast?"

"Breakfast? That's like in four hours."

"I could make a U-turn."

"Yeah, you could."

"But I won't if you don't want me to."

She wanted him to. But she wouldn't allow it. "Let's just stick with dinner."

"Dinner it is."

Saturday found Gina back at the Magic Johnson Movie Theater. The manager was there and she was able to fill out an application. Within the huge movie complex, she was certain there were more than enough jobs, whether it was taking tickets or sweeping up spilled popcorn.

In the 'position desired' box, she wrote "whatever is available." She couldn't be picky. The movie theater was only one of a handful of business that would allow her to work an extra twenty hours in the evening.

She could leave the library at five and work in the movie theatre from maybe five-thirty to nine-thirty. She'd be dragging by the time her work day was over, but she had to start somewhere.

She took her time filling in the application, determined to be careful and neat. The manager looked at it for all of thirty seconds then told her he would be in touch. Heading back up Jamaica Avenue, Gina made a stop at Tarika's job. She wanted to share her news.

"Go somewhere," Tarika said agitated, pushing Antonio away. For the last few weeks since he had started on her shift, he was always in her face.

He wasn't even kitchen staff, he was maintenance, but he always found some reason to be in the galley, whispering things in Tarika's ears while she put lettuce on Big Macs. All up on her while she moved batches of frozen fries near the fryer.

Her co-worker, Stef, said Antonio liked her and Tarika was thinking the same thing, but she didn't have time for him or his nonsense. She had no use for a man still acting like a little boy.

"You liked the candy?" Antonio asked eager.

In truth she did, even though she had acted annoyed when he had given it to her earlier that day. She had taken it and tossed it into her locker without so much as a thank you, but had gone back on her break to look it over.

A twelve-inch box shaped like a heart, she knew he had gotten it half-price. The day after Valentine's Day, everything was half price. Still it was the only thing she had gotten.

"Did you?" he went on to ask.

"Not really," Tarika answered.

"Oh, but you took it right?" He studied her, his smile crooked. "That's okay though. I know you frontin'. You gonna go home later, get on the phone with your girl and talk about how sweet I am, I know you are."

"I'm not even gonna be talking about you."

"Yeah, you are." He looked Tarika up and down from head to toe, as if the oversized Tennis-style shirt and the polyester pants she had on was a halter top and a G-string. "Damn girl," he muttered, licking his lips L.L. Cool J- style.

Despite herself, Tarika blushed but she turned her head so he wouldn't see it.

Tarika saw Gina before Gina saw her. She didn't know Gina was going to drop by, but she was glad to see her. There was still a touch of sadness to her friend's face and Tarika knew it would be a while leaving her.

As far as Tarika was concerned, Gina had just lost her father. Tarika knew what that felt like. She had 'lost' her father too, except he was still alive. She hadn't seen him in years.

Tarika left the fryer and moved towards the counter. "Hey girl."

"Hey." Gina looked around her. "You got a minute?"

Tarika nodded, tapped her manager, held up three fingers and then slipped under the counter. They took a booth. "What's up?"

"I put in an ap."

"An ap where?"

"At the Em Jay's — Magic Johnson's Theatre."

"Ain't you still at the library?"

"Yeah. But they don't pay me enough and I need another gig so I can get a place of my own."

"Oh." Tarika sensed that Rick wasn't going to let Gina stay with him long and she couldn't see Gina's mother taking her in either. That left her.

"I ain't welcomed at Rick's and you know I'm not trying to live with my momma."

"So when you have to leave?"

"Well he told me he'd give me a few weeks, but I could tell he want me gone sooner than that. And I was thinking," Gina said carefully, "that even if I get the second job at the theatre, it's gonna take longer than that to get paid. And I might need some place temporary."

Tarika tried to keep her face neutral. "I don't know Gina. I mean my place ain't no bigger than a minute. There's not a whole lot of room up there." Gina had stayed there for less than a day and had the place looking a wreck.

Tarika had worked so hard to get it. So hard to make it nice. She couldn't have her refuge messed up like that.

"It wouldn't be for long, Tarika. I mean, I figure, if I work two weeks at the theatre right? I'd get my first paycheck and then I can move."

Math was never one of Gina's strongest points, but it was Tarika's and she didn't know what numbers Gina was using, but even with the nicest of landlords, nobody was going to let you move in with a measly two hundred and fifty bucks, about all Gina would be bringing home if she worked part time at the theatre for two weeks.

Tarika lowered her head, her voice, keeping her eyes fixed on Gina. "Two weeks would only give you a deuce and a quarter. You'd need at least a G." The knowledge stunned Gina. She blinked. "Not to mention getting your utilities turned on. Everybody's gonna want a deposit, Con Ed, the phone company, everybody and that's what, another couple of hundred?"

Gina's face changed. Tears were on their way. Right there in McDonald's in front of everyone, she was about to cry.

"Look, you got your library job right? So, just start saving now. Figure you'll need about twelve hundred, right? And you bring home, what, at least a grand a month, right? So okay. You start now and by the time you get your first paycheck from EmJays's, you should be set right?"

Gina looked at her, eyes damp. "You think so?"

"I know so. I did, right?" But the truth was, it had taken Tarika four months of determination and hard sacrificing. She wasn't certain Gina had the same drive.

Quick break over, Tarika stood. "I got to get back behind the counter."

"Go on. I'll check you later."

She wasn't back at the fryer a minute when Antonio was appearing at her side.

"See, I told you."

Tarika turned up her nose. "Told me what?"

"That you'd be bragging to your girl first chance you get."

"Negro, please."

"Yeah baby, that's right beg me."

Tarika looked at him, unable to keep her smile straight. "You'sa fool, you know that."

He leaned in close, his mouth to her ear. The warm breath against her, titillating. "Be anything you want me to be."

Tarika tried to take the smile off her face on the bus ride home, but the box of chocolate wouldn't let her. The teasing Antonio gave her, the way his breath had felt against her ear, wouldn't let her either.

She shook her head, lips tight over a smile.

He wasn't even cute. Wasn't very tall and didn't seem to have much of a body either. A scrawny little runt with a peanut head and a thousand bumps beneath the skin on his forehead, that's what he looked like. And he was goofy to boot.

He was so not her style. So not her type. Not like Sha-Keem, tight and muscular like a bulldog. Sha-Keem, with eyes just like the rapper Nelly, kind of gritty, kind of slitty, but with a touch of softness when he didn't think anyone was looking.

Antonio was so not like Sha-Keem, who would sex her until she thought she was dying and going to heaven and then would go on and sex her some more.

Even though he had broken up with her a while back, not once did she stop thinking about him. Sha-Keem had told her to her face that she deserved better and he wasn't the one. In the months since, he hadn't shared two words with her. But not once had she come home, wishing Sha-Keem was there to meet her, or at least, was on his way.

She imagined him with a good honest job, sporting khakis and clean, white work shirts. Tarika imagined them together, building a life, Cosby-style, but without the kids. But a third-ranking drug dealer couldn't reach 'Huxtable' heights, especially if they felt there was nothing more or better out there for them except slinging drugs.

Thinking about Sha-Keem, the life they had had together, the victories (when he got out of jail) and the losses (she had miscarried with his child), made her think of all the between times. Those moments when it was just him and her down in her Uncle's dark, dank, smelly basement that she used to call home. It made her think about how it felt to snuggle up close to him.

Thinking about the good times with Sha-Keem made Tarika think about how there had been no one since. She looked down at the box of chocolate and pulled off the cellophane. Opening it, she saw everything was covered in the same shade of chocolate.

Won't know what's in 'em if you don't take a bite. Tarika picked one at random, bit into it, a sweet, caramel center surprising her tongue.

Chapter Fourteen

The dinner Dajah had prepared had been consumed, the lights were now low, candles burned, music played and the wine was perfect. But it was the wonder of Jeff's kisses that had her head spinning.

"Look at me."

He was asking her to pull down the stars and the moon. Asking her to turn water into wine. He was asking Dajah to do something impossible to do.

There was too much greatness about him. Too much greatness in him and Dajah found herself tossed up and turned about. Her emotions were like water drops on a hot frying pan, jumping and boiling all over the place.

She was in no position to look at him. No position to fix her eyes dead center his, not with her heart beating too fast in her chest, her body, moist, damp, pulsating. He would vaporize her with one look. She kept her eyes averted.

"Come on. Look at me."

She shook her head no, the comfort of her couch, the comfort of Jeff, the wonder of the evening, a great undoing for her.

He lifted her head. Placed his in direct line with hers. Her eyes became Mexican jumping beans, moving and hopping all over the place. Dajah broke away, stood up from the couch. Adjusted the fit of her peasant blouse, turned slightly to ease one breast back into the cup of her bra.

She did not tamper with unzipped jeans, the panties wedged to one side. But she ran her fingers through her braids, head shaking. "Too fast."

The make-out session they had just embarked on on her couch made her feel like it was 1987 and she was back in her bedroom with Herc, her first real boyfriend and her parents were gone. What she'd just done with Jeff had her feeling the same way she felt when she'd been 16 and a ways from going all the way.

Jeff, there on her couch like that, transformed her back to teenhood where eager hands and hot little bodies wanted to solve some of the mystery of sex, but not all of it. Hands — his, hers — everywhere.

"Too fast to look at me?" Jeff asked.

It sounded stupid even to her own ears. She was going on thirty-two and way past grown. She did want Jeff badly. But she was trying to hold on to what he had said just the night before, about not rushing. To look at him, squarely in his eyes, in this moment would make saying 'not now' impossible.

"I'll be back." She went to her bathroom and closed the door. Holding onto her sink, Dajah leaned in. Studied her face. Her lips were swollen. The iris of her eyes, tiny pinpoints. Her neck was flushed red.

She was so ready for sex that just adjusting her underwear, rezipping her pants gave her a rush, a troubling thing. *You can't do this now.* But beyond that door sat the man who was saying she could.

Dajah felt caught between a rock and a hard place. Wanted a third option. She was trying to figure one out when there was a knock on the bathroom door and then the door eased open.

Before her heart could take the next beat, Jeff was behind her. His body pressed to her spine, his arms wrapped around her waist. The sides of his hands nestled up under the weight of her breasts.

There in the bathroom mirror she did what she couldn't do seconds before. She looked at him, the impact as dazzling as she feared. She felt the beat of his too-fast heart, his heat, his desire. Forced words out of her mouth. "Okay, I looked."

She tried to pull away, succeeded in only being turned, leaned against the bathroom sink. "Too soon, Jeff," she managed, wiggling from him. Stepping away, stopping at the doorway, her resolve a little firmer. "Way too soon."

She left the bathroom. He followed, the both of them stopping like adversaries in a final war when they reached her living room.

Dajah found courage. Voiced her heart. "You think I don't want to? You think I haven't since last night? But I don't want to risk what's going on between us now. I don't want to mess anything up by getting close too soon. You said you wouldn't rush me, so don't okay?"

He nodded. "Okay."

"You mean that?"

"I mean it."

"No hard feelings?"

Jeff smiled a bit, "Just one." Shook his head, laughed. "Just joking, but yeah, I mean it." He looked at his watch.

Was he ready to leave? Her heart sunk. Lifted when he asked about television.

"I want to catch the scores."

She reached over and tossed him the remote. Went over to the stereo and turned off the music. Dajah turned on lights, blew out the candles. Snuggled against him, content as ESPN rolled across the screen.

The number of women mad at Jeff rose to three by the time Sunday afternoon arrived. He ended up canceling dates just to spend time with Dajah. There had been no Saturday afternoon movie with Joy, no Saturday night dinner with Jill. By the time Sunday rolled around, he knew there would be no dinner at Syreeta's place either.

New territory he was stepping into, Jeff was going with his flow. He wasn't sure how it would all turn out in the end, what it meant or anything. All he knew was that he liked being with Dajah and she liked being with him. For the moment, it was more than enough.

So Sunday, around noon, Jeff found himself on the phone, sending apologies to Syreeta. "I can't make dinner," he told her.

"You can't?" She always seemed surprised when he had to break a date. Not angry, not hurt, just surprised.

"Yeah, something came up but maybe we can get together next weekend."

"Sure." Out of all the women, Syreeta offered the least resistance. Out of all the women, Syreeta never pushed.

"I'm sorry about this," and in some ways Jeff was. He was sorry that she took so little and gave so much. He was sorry that such a nice woman as herself got caught up in a nowhere relationship. But mostly he was sorry that even though she knew all of that, she didn't try change it.

"I understand."

After the phone call, Jeff got dressed and headed out to Jones Beach with Kelly. The day was cloudy and gazing towards the ocean, there was no clear line between heaven and earth, but to Jeff, his horizon was shining brightly.

Dajah was coming over later. It was his turn to play host. He couldn't think of anything he wanted more.

Baby steps. Remember them?

Dajah was trying, but stretched out on Jeff's couch, fresh strawberries being dipped in melted chocolate and eased into her mouth, made it difficult.

How she ended up there, shoes off, stocking feet pushed up under the weight of his thigh, her head against the arm of the sofa, eyes closing as she took sweet bite after sweet bite, didn't matter. Only that he was seducing her, carefully, slowly, one chocolate-dipped strawberry at a time.

This was how it was supposed to be. This was how she was supposed to be treated in the warm comfort of his place on a lazy winter afternoon as the wind howled outside, making being inside all the better.

Dajah was supposed to be here like this, a third date and just kissing between them. No sex, not yet, but every meeting stirring up anticipation.

"More?"

Her belly was full. She told him no.

"You sure?"

"I'm sure."

He picked up the wine. Poured some into the glass and handed it to her. Dajah leaned up a bit, took a sip, eyes closing. "Mmmm. This is good."

Jeff sliced some cheese and laid it on a cracker. An indoor picnic for a bad weather day was what he called it. Dajah loved the fact that he could even think that way.

The CD stopped. Jeff got up and put in another. Soon a sexy sax filled the air.

"Who's that?"

Jeff lifted the CD cover. "Kim Waters."

"Nice."

"Yeah." A thought popped into his mind. Stayed. "He's going to be here in the city. Want to go?" In truth he had promised to take someone else, but plans were being changed by the minute. What was one more?

Her eyes lit up. "I'd love to."

Hours later after Jeff walked Dajah to her car, kissed her good-night and promised to call, he came back inside and went to his phone. Reconnecting it, he checked his messages.

He had six.

Chapter Fifteen

The following Monday when Gina got in from work, both Rick and Kanisha were already home. Rick was in his room, behind closed doors and Kanisha was sitting at the dining room table, schoolwork before her.

"Where's your daddy?" Gina asked.

"In his room."

Gina took off her coat, hung it in the closet. There was no smell of anything cooked coming from the kitchen. "He make dinner?"

"Uh unh. You help me with my homework?"

"You haven't done it yet?"

"Uh unh. I asked Daddy and he say to wait till you got home."

Gina looked in the kitchen, not a pot of nothing in it. She looked back at her daughter. Her blood boiled. "How long you've been sitting there?" Kanisha shrugged. She didn't know. "He give you a snack or anything?"

"Uh unh."

Gina looked down the hall at the closed door. Looked back at the kitchen, then fixed her eyes on her daughter. "So you ain't ate nothing since you got home?"

"Two cookies, but they was stale."

Gina hooked her bag on the chair. "You want a peanut butter and jelly?"

"Ain't no bread."

With a suck of her teeth, a twist of her head, Gina headed for Rick's bedroom. She gave it three raps before she opened it. A lump under the covers was what she found. "Rick. Rick!" She moved closer to the bed. "Rick!" She shook him hard. He came to wild, arms swinging.

"What? What?"

"What? I'll tell you 'what?' Your child been home almost an hour and you ain't even seen to it that she had a decent snack and since when she got to wait for me to come home to get help with her homework."

He eyed her with insolence. "You here now." Turning his back to her, Rick put his head back on the pillows. "You do it."

"What the fuck you mean I'm here. Yeah, I'm here, but whether I am or not got jack to do with taking care of Kanisha. She up there starving and you in here sleeping like it's all right."

He turned, sat up in the bed. "I had a headache, Gina. Okay?"

"Oh, so Kanisha suppose to starve 'cause you got a headache?"

"Look Gina. I just needed to lay down for a bit. What's the big deal?"

"The big deal is you starting to act real shitty about being a father, that's what the big deal. Like Kanisha ain't nothing special, that's the big deal."

"That's crazy."

"Is it? I seen it. Seen it with my own eyes. Bit by bit you just letting Kanisha go."

"What are you talking about?"

"I'm talking about you and how you've changed. Even Kanisha noticed it. Said you act like you ain't even here half the time. I ain't never known you not to give that girl a snack when she gets in from school, not to do her homework with her. I don't know what's up with you, but you better get your priorities straight. That little girl is your child. Your daughter. Yours. We ain't got no bread and there's nothing for dinner, so you best get your black ass out that bed and handle your biz-ness."

With that Gina left the room.

Another takeout meal before them, Rick eyed Gina none too kindly from across the kitchen table. "How soon can you find yourself some place to live?"

"Momma moving?" Kanisha asked

"Because me and you here together isn't working out."

"Is she daddy?"

Gina glared at Rick, or the man that used to be Rick. She no longer knew him. No longer understood him. No longer liked him. "Kanisha talking to you."

"Yeah, and I'm talking to you."

"Huh Daddy? Is she?"

"Answer her," Gina insisted, not liking Rick's expression, the sullied mood.

Rick dragged his eyes to his child. "Yeah, she moving."

"Can I go with her?"

The question surprised him, but it didn't stun him. Rick didn't expect it, but realized he didn't mind the possibility. He looked at Gina. "She want to come live with you."

"You want to leave daddy?" Gina asked Kanisha.

The furious way in which Kanisha nodded left no doubt. But more importantly, the way Rick had answered Kanisha's request put the cards on the table.

"You finished eating?" Gina asked her daughter, forcing a calm she wasn't feeling.

Kanisha looked down at her plate. Back at her mother. "Uh huh."

"Then go scrape your plate and get ready for bed."

Kanisha went.

Gina waited until Kanisha's bedroom door closed before she spoke. "You want her to come with me, don't you?"

"Obviously she'd be happier with you than me."

"Listen to you talk. Can you even freaking hear yourself? What is up with you?"

"Nothing ... I'm just tired."

"Tired? Of what? Raising your daughter. Your Kanisha? Since when, because the Rick I knew went through hell and high water to keep her."

"Key word: *knew*." Rick looked down. Sighed. Looked at Gina. "My heads fucked, okay. For a lot of reason, no reasons at all, it's just fucked. And I can't deal with nothing now. Kanisha want to live with you, I can't handle her now, let her."

"And where am I supposed to go?"

"Get your own place."

"With what money?"

"I'll give you the money."

"What about the courts?"

"What about them?"

"I ain't got custody, you do."

"We go back and petition them for joint."

"Won't that take a while?"

Rick's face twisted up. "I don't know?"

"Suppose it does? I mean, it might take months."

"And?"

"You don't want me here that long."

"Well, Kanisha can move in with you anyway."

Gina looked at him hard. She looked at Rick in a way she had never looked at him before. "What's going on?"

"I don't know Gina. I honestly don't know."

"Maybe you need to talk to somebody."

He shook his head against that suggestion.

"You miss her that much?" she found herself saying.

Truth rolled from his tongue like water. "Yeah Gina, I do."

"She know?" He nodded. "But she ain't coming back, is she?"

"No, she's not."

Gina was silent for a minute. "You can't stop living because somebody don't want you. You can't lay down and die because you can't have who you want. If they gone, they gone."

Rick sniffled, blinked a few times. Searched for a silver lining. Couldn't find one. Moved on. "I'll find out about the petition this week. In the meantime, you start looking for a place to stay."

"Is that legal, me taking Kanisha before they give me custody?"

"You have visitation rights, right? Anybody find out, we'll just say that I needed a break and so Kanisha was staying with you for a while."

If Gina had any doubts before, she had none now. Rick the honest, Rick the law abider, Rick the truth teller, was becoming everything but.

For Gina, Tuesday felt no different then Thursday; her workdays now came and went without real notice. Little in her life seemed special. She resigned herself to that fact as she unloaded books off the cart.

"Gina?"

She looked surprised to see her mother standing there. Doreen Alexander had never come to her job. It must have been serious. There had been too much in Gina's life already. She wasn't up to any more.

"Momma? What you doing here?"

"I need to talk to you."

Gina looked around, abandoned the shelf of books she had been working with and slipped from behind the counter.

"This came in the mail."

Gina looked at the envelope, saw her mother's name on it and that it was from HSBC. She knew that HSBC was a bank. She had seen a couple of their branches around. They used to be called Marine Midland.

"It's got your name on it." Doreen looked around again. Nodded toward an empty table. "Let's go sit."

Mother and daughter made their way, sliding out chairs, sitting across from each other. "Open it."

Gina slipped her hand inside, pulled out a letter. Read it silently to herself, though her lips moved. Her brow furrowed, relaxed as surprise took her. "This real?"

Doreen nodded, sighed a little. "Yeah, but they mention a passbook. You ever see a passbook?"

"What's a passbook?"

Doreen wondered what kind of world had her child grown up in that at going on twenty-four, she didn't know what a passbook was. "A bank book."

"Oh."

"You never seen one when you was at Jefferson's, have you?"

"Nah. I ain't seen no bank book. Even if I did, I wasn't paying no attention. That was Jefferson's business."

"Then it must be in the house. You still got a key?"

"Yeah, but it don't work. They changed the locks."

"Maybe they didn't change all of them."

"We can't go up in there, Momma."

"Why not? They ain't served you no papers right? And legally you were there for more than 30 days. You got a right to go back there."

"Supposen somebody there?"

"Even more reason to let you in. You kept any old mail, anything with Jefferson's address on it addressed to you?"

Gina thought about it. "Probation stuff."

"Where's it at?"

"I don't know."

"You think you left it in the house?" Gina shrugged. "Well, that don't matter none. You got tenant rights. Till they take you to court, you got a right to be there."

Gina looked at her mother, looked back down at the letter, the one that said there was a mutual fund in her name for eighty-nine thousand dollars, courtesy of Jefferson. She couldn't help but wonder that if he had left her that much, how much he'd left his real children.

The music was loud. Too loud.

Rap music rumbled past closed windows and secured doors, a sign that somebody was inside of Jefferson's house.

Gina looked at her mother and her mother returned her look with indignation. Gina began laying on the doorbell. It took a few minutes before the door opened.

The smell of marijuana rushed past them. The red-eyed young woman who answered looked at both of them with a near blank expression. She was one of Jefferson's granddaughters but Gina couldn't remember which one. "You come for the rest of your stuff?"

The rest? Gina didn't know she had anything left. "Yeah," she said quickly.

"Wait here."

The door closed in her face. It was only seconds but it felt like minutes before the door opened up again. A box, big enough to hold six bottles of wine was presented to her. The label said "Cordon Bleu."

Gina took it, laid it down. Remembered something. "And I got boxes in the basement too."

The young woman looked at her, looked back over her shoulder. Stepped back and let her in, Doreen behind her.

The music was ear-splitting. Around what used to be Jefferson's living room half a dozen people were strewn. Some on the couch, others in the chairs. Some sat on the floor, the smell of marijuana, heavy.

Gina and her mother moved past them, headed to the basement without words. Once they were downstairs, Doreen Alexander let go of her thoughts. "Jefferson's probably rolling over in his grave. Them nasty-ass, good-for-nothing heifers in his house like this."

But Gina wasn't listening. She was looking for boxes, those few household items she had brought with her when she got out of jail. Not much, but at least she was in the house. She would think of a reason to go back upstairs to her room, but for now she was searching out her boxes. She was relieved when she found them.

She took one, her mother the other, both women heading back up the stairs. Stepping into the living room, Gina searched for the one who opened the door. Both of Jefferson's granddaughters looked so much alike, it was hard telling them apart.

Both were on the petite side, wore microbraids and were the color of double-dipped chocolate. Neither of them seemed to have had a happy moment in their lives and they wore their misery like it was a badge of honor.

Gina couldn't remember their names because she really never wanted to know them that well. So she looked around, squinting in the gloom, the music hurting her ears, her lungs assaulted with smoke.

"You need something?" asked a voice from behind her.

Gina turned, looked into the face of the granddaughter that opened the door. "Yeah. I think I left something upstairs."

"Ain't nothing up there. All your shit's gone. That my room now."

"Yeah, but I'm sure some of my CDs fell behind the dresser."

The woman looked at her, looked at someone across the room. A hand came up, "Let her look."

"Alright, but don't be touching my shit, hear?"

Gina nodded and made her way, her mother behind her. Doreen headed toward what used to be Jefferson's bedroom, Gina on to what used to be hers.

She barely recognized it.

Clothes strewn everywhere, three ashtrays overflowed, the smell of indulgence of too much of everything clung to the walls. Gina wanted to cry. Didn't. Going to the dresser, she dropped down to all fours.

Looking underneath, she did see some of her CDs that had indeed fallen to the floor. She also saw a manila enveloped taped to the bottom. She peeled it off the wood and tested the contents with her fingers. Even before she opened it, she knew one of the items. But it was the other thing she'd found that almost let loose her tears.

Gina and her mother came back down the stairs, Gina waving the four found CDs in her hands. "I got them."

The granddaughter came up to her, hands out. "Let me see. I gotta make sure they not mine."

Even as the woman snatched them, Gina had already decided she would not put up a fight. If the chick wanted the CDs, she could have them. The other item, the envelope tucked and folded into her jacket pocket was worth more than any CDs.

"They had the funeral?" Doreen found herself asking.

"Yeah, last week."

"Was it nice?"

The woman stopped her label checking, casting Doreen Alexander with a caustic eye. "What you mean, was it nice? How a fucking funeral ever going to be nice?"

Gina forced her arms, her tongue to be still.

The woman handed Gina back one CD. "This here one is yours, these other three mine."

Gina didn't bat an eye. Just said okay. Gathering up one box, her mother the other, they turned and left.

At nine o'clock on the dot, the doors to the HSBC were unlocked.

At nine o' two, Gina and her mother entered. Documents were presented. Information was cross-referenced and the money market account was divided between a new money market and savings account.

Doreen Alexander kept quiet throughout the entire process. For the first time in her life, Doreen Alexander got to see up close and personal the deficiencies in her daughter's life. There was no time to learn like the present, so she didn't interfere.

She didn't suggest anything. Made no comment or gave advice about what Gina should do with the money. Gina had to learn to handle her business.

Still, it gave Doreen ease of mind when the bank officer suggested Gina take the one account and make it two, allowing part of her money to continue to grow while having the other part accessible to her.

Doreen and Gina were riding down Parsons Boulevard heading

back to Rick's place when Gina broke the silence. "He was a good man, wasn't he?"

"Yeah, Jefferson was a very good man."

"You miss him?" Her mother said nothing, but Gina could hear her swallow a lump in her throat. "I miss him. Miss him bad." Gina hung her head. Cried a little. Her mother let her be.

They were nearly to their destination when Gina asked her mother to drop her off on Guy R. Brewer. "I need to find a place to stay. There's a real estate office over there."

"You need to find a place to stay where?" Gina shrugged. She wasn't sure. "Well, first thing you need to decide is where you want to live. You want to be near transportation. You don't want to be somewhere where you have to take a bunch of buses to get around."

Gina hadn't thought about that. Just finding a place for her and Kanisha had been her only concern. There was school to think about. Kanisha was in the middle of a school year. Gina couldn't just take Kanisha out now, which meant it had to be somewhere close. "Damn."

"What?" Doreen asked.

Gina was about to tell her but remembered that what she and Rick were going to do had to be hush-hush. "Nothing."

"You want me to come with you?"

Gina looked at her, smiled. "No Momma, I got this one." Got out of the car.

A wiser, more mature person would have thought about buying their own home with the nice sum left by Jefferson. But Gina's world didn't extend that far, so the idea never came to her. Others things didn't enter her equation either, things like figuring out what she could and couldn't afford.

It wasn't until Gina was sitting inside the real estate office, her application filled out, did she 'do the math.' It wasn't until the realtor, an older black man with light-brown colored skin and swirls of brown around the eyes, reminding her of a cinnamon bun, asked her how much she could afford did Gina even realize that she needed to figure it out.

She asked for a calculator. Entering the number 40,000.00, she picked the number 800 to divide it by. Gina came up with 50. She then went on and divided 50 by 12 and got 0.24, which confused her. Puzzlement danced on her face.

"Anything wrong?"

Gina looked up at the cinnamon bun face. Faltered.

He reached for the calculator. "What are you trying to calculate?"

"Well. I got like forty G's, right? And I'm trying to figure how long I can pay my rent if I'm paying about eight hundred a month."

The man worked his fingers over the calculator. "Four years and some change." He didn't look up.

"That's it?"

"I'm afraid so." He picked up her application. "You are working right?"

"Yeah."

"You will have the job for a while?"

"Yeah."

He flipped the application. The brief scanning he had done suddenly demanded a closer look. "You left this part blank."

Gina knew which part. The part about ever being convicted of a crime. "Yeah, I know."

"Have you?"

Suddenly the cinnamon bun face wasn't looking so sweet. Gina snatched her application and stood. "I changed my mind."

When Gina got home, there was an envelope for her from the Magic Johnson Theatre. They appreciated her submitting an application but they would not be able to hire her at this time.

It didn't matter now. In fact, she was relieved. She never liked the idea of working two jobs and thanks to Jefferson, she wouldn't have to.

She waited until Rick came in with Kanisha and she had spent a few minutes asking Kanisha about her day before she told Rick about the money.

"You rich, Momma?"

"Not rich, rich, but yeah, I got some cash."

That seemed to please Kanisha. "Can we go to Toys R Us?"

"It's not that kind of rich, Kanisha. Besides," her eyes found Rick's, "we gonna use this money to get our own place."

"That's a good thing," Rick said.

Gina wasn't expecting Rick to throw himself at her feet and beg her to stay, but she didn't expect the agreeableness in his eyes either. She was hoping for some conflict in his expression. There wasn't any.

Telling Kanisha to go to her room and close the door, Gina fixed her eyes on Rick. "I'm gonna need your help."

"Help how?"

"Getting the apartment. I can't get a lease because I got a record. You gonna have to get it."

"My name on the lease." It wasn't a question and it wasn't what Rick wanted either. The last thing he needed was a screwed-up credit report and that's all he saw happening. He didn't see Gina keeping up with her rent payments. He saw her being late with the gas and light bill. Fiscal responsibility had never been her thing and Rick had little faith she had any now.

"It's the only way, Rick, if you want me gone."

He felt it then. They both did, the final link severed, the broken past fully snapped in two. Whatever had kept them bonded, whatever had made their struggles worthwhile, was gone.

In that moment they were simply two people standing in the same place, but headed in different directions. In that moment, who they were to each other mattered little. Not even the child they had born could keep them linked.

"It's nice."

But it wasn't, not in the sense of layout or natural light. It wasn't like Tarika's place where you felt a definitive peace even if you weren't looking for it the moment you stepped through the door.

The second floor apartment of the house on One-Hundred Sixty-seventh Street was empty and bare, but both Gina and Tarika knew the moment the furnishings were brought in, it would feel tight and claustrophobic.

They knew the living room would welcome a couch but begrudgingly admit a chair, the TV and its stand. Gina's queen-sized bed would make navigating the front bedroom difficult and though the coat of paint was fresh, it couldn't hide the cracked walls or the chipped wood around the doorframes.

Gina and Tarika knew that the juvenile bedroom set that complimented Kanisha's bedroom at Rick's place would never fit the one she would soon have here. They both knew the apartment would never be cozy.

In no sense did it match Gina's dream, in no way did it make her feel welcome. But it was what she could afford even with the money from Jefferson, and like Rick and Tarika both told her, it was a start.

The din of Riker's Island was loud and intrusive. Around Rick, hundreds of prisoners engaged in their life of lockup. Inmates outtalked each other, engaged in verbal disagreements and used the only real freedom they had — their voices.

Rick didn't want to call his lawyer from the jailhouse. But by the time he got home from work, Jacob Maitlin was out of the office and Rick needed to get the joint custody papers filed.

Rick had used Maitlin when he was facing jail time over Gina's lies and though it had cost him a pretty penny, Jacob Maitlin, as he had proclaimed, was the best. He had connections inside the court system that ran deep and he would be able to speed the joint custody petition along quickly.

That's what Rick wanted — he wanted quick. He wanted Gina to do what he had been doing for too long by himself, take responsibility for raising their child.

"Jacob?" he yelled into the plastic receiver. "It's Rick. Rick Trimmons ... yes, I know it's noisy. I'm on the job. But listen, I need your services again ... "

The court petition, set in motion, would take some time before it became final, but as far as Rick and Gina were concerned, joint custody of Kanisha was a done deal.

With Gina and Kanisha gone, it took a few days for Rick to get used to no one being there when he got in from work. With nobody living there but him, it took a few days for him to find things to do as the late afternoon shifted into the evening.

He watched sports on TV and ate a lot of takeout. He turned on the light in Kanisha's bedroom and left the door open. He called Nelson and talked until he ran out of things to talk about. The knowledge that he was all alone crept up on him. When it did, it was painful

He forced his soul into a new role. It led to long thoughts about his life, where he was going and where he had come from. It nudged his heart about how much he missed Dajah, all that he'd blown.

But like dropping out of college and not getting his degree, it became one of those things he regretted but was forced to accept. Dajah had made it plain enough. She wasn't coming back.

Rick knew the statistics, knew that logistically there should be at least ten women out there who would be happy to hook up with him but he wasn't ready for another relationship. That much he knew.

Chapter Sixteen

Though the eatery did massive business, employee turnover was just as considerable. For most, working behind the counter at McDonald's was just a steppingstone to somewhere else. No one really came with lifelong plans to stay and so it wasn't unusual to see new hires every other week.

In the seven months that Tarika had worked there, quite a few people had quit and quickly been replaced. But the latest hire caught her attention like no one had in a long time. The latest hire had her sneaking peeks and buzzing with anticipation.

Six feet tall, the color of cinnamon, there was a confidence to the guy being led around the galley by Byron, her manager. One look at him and you knew McDonald's was just a pit stop. One look at him and you knew he had a real future and was working double time on it.

Tarika turned away, went back to shaking up the large wire basket, hot grease and French fries spitting up before her. She heard Marisa's soft laughter, a heavy accented "Nice to meet you," and knew that she was next to be introduced.

Her heart jumped a little and she shook the basket again, eyed the timer to see how much longer the French fries had to cook.

"And this is Tarika," she heard to the side of her.

She turned, automatically wiping grease from her hands against her polyester slacks. Extending it, Tarika offered, "Hi," her smile bright, her eye contact brief.

"This is Justin, our new part-timer. He's a college student at York."

College student. He looked like the type. Tarika's eyes scanned his one more time, her lips battling to hide her teeth. Before the moment could fully register, Byron was taking Justin to the front counter.

The timer on the fryer beeped and she banged the basket a final time, lifting it and dumping the hot fries into the metal holder. Shaking salt over them, she scooped up a medium and a large order.

In five more minutes, she would be off work. In six, she would be meeting Antonio. In fifteen minutes they would be standing at the ticket window at the Magic Johnson Movie Theater, off to see "Blame It On Eva." Tarika liked L.L. Cool J. They came from the same neighborhood.

She also liked the idea of having a date. It had been way too long since her last one.

Antonio was taking her to the movies. He would pay her way in and get her snacks. He would sit next to her in the darkness of the theatre, maybe kiss her, hold her close.

Antonio had broken down her defenses even though Tarika tried real hard to ignore them. He wasn't as 'cut' and solid as she liked, but there was something in his eyes when he looked at her that made her feel special. Something that made her heart beat a little faster, that made her remember those times with Sha-Keem.

It would be nice to have somebody, even if it was just to take in a movie, chill at her place; last thoughts as she abandoned the fryer and clocked out.

"So, you dug it?" Antonio was asking her hours later, the Nacho's with extra cheese, Coke and Gummy Bears, a faraway memory in her grumbling belly.

Tarika did. She liked the movie very much. What she didn't like was how she had paid for the both of them. She didn't like how Antonio 'must of forgotten' his money as they had stood at the ticket window.

"So, we gonna shoot over to your place?"

It was part of the date, wasn't it? The unwritten law that said that's how things went? Spent a few hours out of doors and a few more in?

"Are we?"

But Tarika wasn't feeling that or him. Doing anything with Antonio was now firmly out of the picture. "No, we ain't going to my place."

She broke away from his arm. "Check you tomorrow." Her feet picked up speed as she made her way down Jamaica Avenue, his shouts of, "Hold up," ignored.

* * *

Company was so far and few in between that when the doorbell rang, for a minute Gina didn't know what the sound was. It was Tarika. Gina opened the door, let her in. "Hey girl."

"Hey." Tarika barely looked at Gina as she passed by. Just made her way up the stairs like she lived there.

"What's going on?"

"I got played."

"Played?"

"Yeah. That damn Antonio."

"Antonio who?"

Tarika realized she hadn't even mentioned Antonio to her best friend. *With good reason,* she realized. *Nigga wasn't shit.* "This cat on my job."

"The counter guy?"

Tarika chuckled, sucked her teeth. "No. This cat still cleaning toilets ... I can't believe I actually thought something could happen."

"What happened?"

Tarika spilled her beans starting with Antonio's flirting and ending with him 'forgetting his money.' "Then he had the nerve to ask about coming to my place." She was angry but that wouldn't last. Sadness was just a few heartbeats away.

"He ain't nothing Tarika. Forget him."

Tarika wanted to. She wanted to forget the whole thing, but come morning, no doubt he'd be back in her face grinning and talking smack and every time he did, it would be a painful reminder of how she tried to make something out of nothing and got less than nothing in return.

It was just the way it went sometimes.

The next day, her fear was realized as Antonio moved up on her. "You ain't talking to me?"

Tarika glanced over at Antonio. Rolled her eyes. "I said 'hi.'"

"You mad at me or something?"

"Nope."

"So why you ain't looked at me longer than two seconds."

Tarika shrugged.

"You pissed about the movie thing?"

She cut her eyes at him. Went back to placing hash browns into the basket.

"I thought we had a good time."

She lowered the basket into the grease, stepping back to avoid the pops and sizzles.

"... Tony, get back to work."

Antonio turned, eyed Byron the manager who was stuffing Egg McMuffins into the bag. "An-TONE-nio. My name's Antonio, not Tony."

"Well, Mr. An-TONE-nio, can you get back to work? Tables need to be bussed and the bathrooms checked." Antonio gave his manager a hard look. Walked away.

Byron looked at Tarika. She held the look briefly then looked away, understanding everything Byron could have said, but didn't.

No Antonio wasn't the 'one', but she knew who she wanted the 'one' to be. Justin, 'College' as she called him in her head, would be her choice. Cute, smart and real proper talking, he mostly kept to himself. Beyond 'hi' and 'bye,' there wasn't much conversation between them. Even if there were, Tarika wouldn't know what to say.

She had never really talked to a guy like him. What would he want with her anyway? She had the booty but not the beauty. And she had never gotten past tenth grade. She had nothing to offer him.

She looked up on the monitor, saw orders for three supers, two mediums and a small. Got back to work. She sensed College moving by her more so than she saw him; his cologne, a dead giveaway.

Everyone else showed up funky, uniforms reeking of old grease and cooked meat. But not College. He never smelled that way. He always smelled fresh and clean. Just like that Outkast song. Tarika wondered if he liked OutKast.

She wondered what was on his CD player. What his favorite color was? But mostly what she wondered as he caught her staring, if he had any idea how she felt?

Two and a half weeks?

Had it really been seventeen days, five dates, eleven phone calls and not a drop of sheet action? Even as Jeff asked himself the questions, he knew the answer — yes, it had been.

Almost there a few times, he had not quite crossed the finish line, Dajah always managing to pull back, pull away, get up, put some piece of her clothing back on. Dajah always managing to stop in the middle of their heat, offering 'not yet,' a 'not yet' that surprisingly, he didn't mind hearing.

It wasn't about sex anyway when it came to her.

It was about other things, like intelligent conversations and serious debates. It was about her ability not to go with his flow, but to stand firmly inside her own. It was about her having a real backbone and not being afraid to flaunt that fact.

Like now as they sat in her living room watching sports, she hating the Los Angeles Lakers with as much passion as she loved the Philadelphia 76ers.

"Two years ago they tortured my boy Iv," she confessed, "and I never forgave them for that. They need some of their own medicine. This season they got it."

"Your boy Iv?"

"Yes. Iv as in Iverson."

"Don't tell me. Its his eyes right?"

"Oh my God yes."

"And his basketball skills don't matter."

"Of course they do," she stated. "But he also has heart. When the Lakers were giving him a pounding back in 'O one, and he was getting beat up, he never quit. That takes heart."

"Heart."

"Yeah."

"But all ball players have that."

"Not all of them. I mean they should but I've only seen a few who really do."

"Such as?"

"Jordan for one. I know this was his last season, but where do you think the game of basketball would be without him? That's something people forget. He reinvented the game."

"And nobody else helped."

"Nope. Just Mike."

"Well what about the new kids on the block. Folks like McGrady?"

Dajah turned up her nose. "T-Mack got skills and so does Kobe for that matter, but none of them are Mike. Never will be."

Jeff shook his head. "So you're saying Michael Jordan is it?"

"Yeah. Mike is and will always be the Man."

He laughed. "If you believe that, then you don't know."

"Don't know what?"

"About ball."

"Yes I do. In fact, I can tell you who isn't going to get a four-peat this year."

"Okay Mrs. NBA, tell me who isn't going home with the 2003 ring."

"The Lakers," Dajah said, affirmed.

"You're mad, aren't you?"

"No, I just know of what I speak."

"Then how can you even say the Lakers aren't going to take it?"

"Because this season's been hard on them and you saw what Yao did to Shaq that first game. The Lakers are getting weak."

"You must have missed the one last month. Yao got like four points the whole game. Shaq got thirty-nine *and* won."

"That's only because Yao ran out of steam."

"Out of steam, got taken. Same dif. Nobody can take on Shaq."

"Don't tell me you like Shaq."

"Love him."

Dajah's face screwed up. "Oh yeah, that's right, a Lakers fan."

"Any other type to be?"

"Well, your Lakers' in trouble," Dajah said pointing to the television.

"It's just the first quarter. They got plenty of time."

Dajah flipped her hand. "Whatever." Picked up her juice. Took a sip, charged.

When the game was over and Jeff's Lakers lost, Dajah was double-charged. She jumped, hooping and hollering around her living room. "What I tell you?" she asked, that fire dancing in her eyes. She leaned forward, put her hand to her ear. "What? You say something?" Jeff just smiled at her. "I thought not."

The late hour caught up with her. It was going on eleven. She yawned, apologetic. "I'm beat." His cue.

He stood. "Yeah, the hour is late." But even as he said that, he knew he would be making a stop before he got home. Jeff knew that Syreeta came to expect the late night visits, a pattern he began a week after he started seeing Dajah.

Being with Dajah wasn't about sex, but that didn't mean he

didn't want it after he left her. He always did and chose the path of least resistance — Syreeta.

Dajah moved into his space, into his arms, accepted the lips, the tongue, that made soft music inside her soul. Pulled back when the heat between them reached fever pitch. "So, we're on for Jones this weekend?" she wanted to know.

Her baby steps were back. She was taking things slow, her own little calendar in her head. Three weeks — twenty-one days would come and go before she gave up that part of herself. Last count, they still had four days to go.

"I have to check the weather. They're talking about an ice storm."

She laughed, snuggled up to him close. "If there is, then we'll just have to stay in."

And there it was, the signal that Jeff had been waiting for. He kissed her lips lightly. "I'll give you a call tomorrow."

"Yeah, you do that."

Rick turned off the television and got into bed. He wasn't tired, he wasn't exhausted. He wasn't anything. He wasn't bored, he wasn't lonely. He just felt as if he had stopped existing, for life certainly had stopped for him. Not a drop of anticipation did he have about anything.

He was the walking dead these days.

He worked, he came home. He ate and went to bed. He woke up in the morning and went to work. No more, no less.

He hadn't even spent time with Kanisha last weekend because he just hadn't been with it. Like a hermit, Rick had spent the whole weekend inside, watching TV and pigging out. He had become a recluse from the world. He found it was a safe place to be and initially he didn't mind.

But he was starting to mind now, the full matter of his situation was starting to nibble at him. He was thirty-two, but he might as well have been seventy for all he did with his life.

He gazed around the darkened bedroom, heard the squeak of springs over his head. Gazing up, Rick tried to remember what that felt like, what it felt like to make love to someone you loved and loved you back.

Images of him and Dajah filled his head, sweet, wonderful,

kind, loving, giving, understanding, Dajah. He saw them eating out, staying in, going places, doing things. Rick conjured up the memory of the love fire that danced in her eyes when she looked at him then forced himself to remember how, too many times, he had seen just as much hurt.

He thought about how she had stayed by his side through thick and thin, even when there was no reason to remain at all. It had been love, real love, that made it possible. Love, deep and as real as the mattress beneath him, supporting him, nurturing, holding him up.

And I blew it.

He had never known a woman like her and had no confidence that he would ever meet someone like her again. If he had only known … but he hadn't known, didn't have a clue.

He wondered where she was, what she was doing and whom she was doing it with. *Not me,* came the thought, sour and bitter. *Never with me again.*

His phone rang and hope leaped into his soul. Racing to sit up, he took the receiver, put it to his ear. "Hello?"

"Trimmons?"

"Yeah."

"Clayton. You interested in doing a double tomorrow?"

Overtime. Once upon a time his whole life had been about it. About making some money and keeping some money, his eyes on it like his eyes should have been on Dajah.

"You interested?"

Rick didn't see why not, he had nothing else to do.

When Gina opened her eyes that Friday morning, the only thing different was that she had grown a year older. It was her birthday and she was now twenty-four. For the first time since she'd met Rick, there would be no Hallmark card sitting on the dresser for her or gift boxes wrapped in pretty paper.

Kanisha would not be coming into her room to sing an exuberant happy birthday song. In all likelihood, Kanisha wouldn't even know what the day was.

Rick had made all that happen. He wasn't around anymore. But his absence had some merits.

In losing a relationship through death, Gina found one in life.

She rediscovered her daughter and her daughter began to discover her. Gina and Kanisha spent their time together in a way they never had before.

They played board games, watched TV together. Talked about their day. Bonded.

But even with their new-found closeness, Gina was certain Kanisha didn't know what the day was. Gina hadn't mentioned it and Kanisha hadn't been around Rick in weeks. Tonight that was going to change. Tonight Gina was going out and Kanisha was going to be with her daddy whether she liked it or not.

Kanisha didn't.

With Gina fully in her life, Kanisha neither missed her father nor asked about him. Gina knew it was a stage; that the time would come when Kanisha would want him around. This evening would be the start.

She was going to a dance club with Tarika to celebrate and Rick was babysitting. Neither Rick nor Kanisha seemed pleased with the idea, but Gina didn't care. Father and daughter had been apart too long already. It was time to get those bridges mended.

"You're going to give me a hug?"

Kanisha looked up at her father, shrugged and went to him. She put her arms around his waist. Squeezed once and stepped away. Rick reached for her backpack. But she took it back. "I got it."

They headed out of the after-school center, made their way to his SUV. Kanisha got into the back and Rick reached for her seat belt. "I can do it," she insisted. Rick let her be. Got into the driver's seat.

"So, what will it be? McDonald's for dinner?"

Kanisha shrugged.

"Don't tell me you're going to turn down your favorite meal?" She shrugged again, eyes everywhere but on him. "You mad at me?"

That got her attention. Her eyes latched onto his, sizzling. "No, you mad at me."

"I'm not mad at you, Kanisha."

"Yeah, you are."

"Why do you say that?"

"'Cause you don't care about me."

"Of course I care about you."

"No you don't."

"Since when did I stop caring?"

"Before. Before I went to live with Momma. You stopped doing stuff with me and everything."

"I was going through some things Kanisha. It wasn't that I didn't care. I was just ... " He could see his words weren't fazing her. Rick got out and got into the back seat. He reached for her, but she resisted. He let her be.

"Who's my number one?"

She shrugged again, little arms folded tight, lips pinched.

"What do you mean you don't know? Who's always had my heart?"

She shrugged a second time, eyes blinking.

"You don't know? No? Well I guess I'm gonna have to tell it. Maybe I'll get one of those big-old billboards and put a sign up there that says, 'Hey everybody. Kanisha Adera Alexander is my number one.' Think I should do that?"

"Ummh."

"What?" he put his hand to his ear. Leaned in towards her mouth "I'm sorry, I can't hear you." Her head shook no. She wasn't going to answer. "I don't understand head shake." He tickled her side. She squirmed. "Ticklish?" He tickled her other side. Kanisha moved about but her lips were firmly clenched.

He tickled her chin when she was certain he was going for her side. He tickled her side when she was certain he was going for her chin. Soon Kanisha was giggling all over the place.

"See, I told you you were ticklish." He stared at her until he caught her eye. "I love you Kanisha. More than ever." His throat filled. He swallowed. "I hurt you Kanisha and I'm really sorry that I did. Really sorry."

She reached for him. Rick welcomed her embrace.

Chapter Seventeen

The Rubba Dub was bumping.

Though mainly a Reggae club, the clientele was a mix of various nationalities, all below the age of thirty and the music was a nice blend of dance styles. Neither Gina nor Tarika had ever been there, but Tarika suggested it was time to try something new.

"It's crowded up in here," Gina shouted into Tarika's ear.

"Sure is," she said, scanning the crowd.

No more than a wish, no more solid than a hope, Tarika was looking for Justin. A lot of people from York hung out there and he seemed like the type to get out every once in a while. Maybe this night he decided to get his groove on. Maybe this night he would get to see Tarika in a way that working the fryer at McDonald's didn't allow.

"Which way?"

Tarika pointed towards the back. "Let's go to the bar."

Tarika had on new clothes and her shoes were straight out of the box. She had put on beige lipstick, lined them in brown pencil and applied enough lip gloss to fry chicken. Her earrings were gigantic hoops and she sported a cap.

Gina had gone the denim route, with hip huggers, a thick rawhide belt, boots and a peasant blouse that rose three inches above her navel.

There was no doubt that their outfits were working because they were asked to the dance floor a dozen times before they reached their destination.

"What you drinking?"

It had been a hot minute since Gina had had a real drink. She searched her mind for something different. Looking over, she saw someone sipping something blue. "What's that?"

Tarika shrugged. She tapped the woman on the shoulder. "Excuse me, what's that you're drinking?"

"A Hpnotiq."

"A what?"

The lady moved her drink from her mouth, leaned over and shouted. "A Hpnotiq. Taste a bit like a blue Alize."

"Thanks." Tarika turned, translated it in Gina's ear.

"Sounds good. I'll take one of those."

Tarika flagged the waiter. "Let me get two Hpnotiqs." Turned back around and scanned the crowd.

It was all the way live.

Hundreds of bodies gyrated to Sean Paul's "Gimme the Light," some even lying on the floor. A booty and pelvis show, neither of the women could wait to get out there.

The drinks came. Tarika paid and handed one to Gina. "Happy Birthday girl," she shouted. Raising their glasses they clicked and took a long sip. Before the glasses were halfway empty, the two of them were on the dance floor.

After dancing nonstop for six records, Tarika and Gina left the dance floor and headed to the ladies room. Huge and long, most of the stalls were occupied. They stood before the mirror, touching up their make-up, rearranging the lay of their hair.

"You having fun?" Tarika wanted to know.

"Sure am." Gina stood back. Checked herself in the mirror. Caught sight of Tarika. Smiled. "Thank you, girl."

"Ain't no thing Gina. What else we supposed to be doing on your birthday?"

Gina leaned against the wall of the club, her nose turned up like she smelled something bad. "What?"

"Me say whatta fine woman like you du up in dis 'ere place?"

Gina looked at the man with the wild dreads and the piercing black eyes. Shook her head. "I can't hear you?"

"Me say whatta fine woman like you du up in dis place?"

She pulled back, face still pinched. "What am I doing here?" He nodded. "Celebrating," she shouted back.

It was his turn to go deaf. "Wha?"

She leaned in closer, shouted, sweet essence oil drifting from his dreads. "Cela-bray-ting."

"Ya? What ya celabrating?"

"My birthday." He said something else to her, but between his accent and the music, Gina couldn't understand.

He took her arm. "Come."

Gina understood that action if she couldn't quite hear the word. She pulled her arm back. "I ain't going nowhere with you."

He smiled, revealing perfectly white teeth. "I'm not going to hurt you, just want to buy you a drink." Perfect Queens, New York, English. No accent, no choppy words.

She gazed at him. "You was playing me?"

He smiled again. Looked down. Looked up. Extended his hand. "Hi. I'm Collin."

It took her a minute to take his hand. "Gina."

They sat in the outer bar where the music wasn't so invasive and a normal conversation could be held. Before her was a pretty drink layered in orange, green and yellow. The taste was multi-layered as well. First there was the sensation of slurping a slushy on a hot summers day. Next came a sweetness that reminded her of candy, and finally a tartness reminiscent of lemonade without enough sugar.

Gina looked towards the dance floor. Felt his stare. Wondered how she was going to get away. He wasn't her type. On the dance floor he was fine. In idle conversation, he was okay. But now she was sitting across from him, she wanted to take shears to his various sized, not very neat dreads.

It was obvious he was a real Rasta, or on his way to being one. True Rasta's didn't get their dreads professionally twisted. They just let them grow however they wanted and there was no doubt that the sixteen-inch gather on his head had come the natural way.

"You don't like my hair."

"Excuse me?"

He smiled that smile again. "I said, you don't like my hair, *right?*"

No she didn't. She also didn't like how his accent switched back and forth. But she was loving the drink. "It's a little funky."

His lips turned down a bit. "You prefer the fake look then."

"Not fake. Just done."

"They're going anyway."

That got her attention. "Going where?"

He raised his hand, made scissors out of his fingers. "Snip, snip."

"For real?"

"Yeah. It's time. Had them for a while, but people react funny to them. They can't seem to find the real Collin behind them."

Gina looked at him. Imagined him a close clean haircut. "Yeah? So who is the real Collin then?"

"I'm surprised you're asking."

"You brought it up."

He leaned back into his chair, one long lean leg stretched out. "Let's see. The real Collin. He works in a warehouse in lower Manhattan loading furniture onto trucks all day. The real Collin? He's a guy who came to the club all the way from the Bronx because he heard it was so hot. He came all the way from the Bronx to hear some good music and spotted this woman on the dance floor. He liked how this woman looked so much, he waited until she finished dancing, disappeared and came back to ask her to the dance floor.

He scooted up in the chair. Leaned in close. "Collin, who came all the way from the Bronx who came to the club in Queens because he heard the music was hot and spotted a woman on the dance floor who he liked so much that he waited out his time has discovered that after talking with this woman, he likes her even more, so much so, he bought her his favorite drink that he doesn't share with most people."

Despite herself, Gina smiled. Despite everything she felt was wrong with him, something about him intrigued her.

"Yeah?"

"Yeah." He leaned back again. "Okay, I've told you about Collin beneath the dreads, how about telling me about Gina, the woman behind the pretty lips and sexy eyes."

Taking another sip of her drink, Gina obliged.

Tarika was walking around the club looking for Gina when up ahead she saw College, a Heineken in one hand, the other in his pocket, talking with a group of guys. She debated with herself to walk by, say hi, or just go back the way she'd come. Something about him scared her and excited her.

Intimidation.

Tarika had no doubt that given the chance, she could love him into the next lifetime. She had no doubt that given the chance, she would give her heart and soul and anything else she had to make him happy.

She knew she would do cartwheels and somersaults to keep him. She would be willing to give away large chunks of herself. Big chunks, dangerous chunks, boulder size pieces until there was nothing left to her.

But he seemed to be the type of man worthy of it. The type who would return the favor and together they could be just one big bowl of a whole lot of giving.

She was more than a fry cook at McDonald's. More than a menial wage high school dropout whose former lover had been a drug dealer. She was more than a woman who as a child had been bounced from relative to relative because her mother didn't want her.

She wasn't certain where that 'more' was, only that she possessed it. Would College be able to see that? Would he be willing to try to? Or would she just be the ghetto girl flipping burgers to him?

Tarika looked at him. Got scared and walked back in the direction she came from. She circled the edge of the dance floor and came up on the other side of the club. Slipping past the crush of bodies she moved to the outer bar and spotted Gina sitting at a table with some dread headed man and stopped in her tracks.

Head back, gums showing, Gina was laughing out loud. The man was holding her hand, merriment dancing on both their faces. There was no way Tarika could interrupt that moment. No way could Tarika intrude on her friend's joy like that.

She turned to go back into the dance area when she felt a hand on her shoulder.

She turned, her heart jarring. She blinked, tried to get her mouth moving. It opened, but no sound came out. She closed it.

"Hi."

"Hey."

"Funny running into you here."

"I'm celebrating a friend's birthday," she said quickly.

"Oh." He took a step back.

"Yeah. She's around here somewhere."

"Oh?"

"Yeah."

Jay Z's "Excuse Me Miss" bumped through the room. "You want to dance?"

"Love to."

It was taking Kanisha twenty minutes to read a ten-page book. A children's book, Rick knew the story backwards and in his sleep, but he struggled to listen, to stay awake. He had worked overtime this week and he was feeling it.

A little past eleven at night, he was tired, his eyes were hurting and all he wanted to do was close them.

"The ... li ... li ... tle. The little red he ... he ... hen ran ... up ... up the ...," she twisted the book Rick's way. "What's that word daddy?"

Rick blinked, focused on where the little brown finger was pointing. "Road."

"Ro, ro, road ve ... ve ... very slow."

Rick shifted on the bed. Got comfortable. "I'm just going to close my eyes so I can see the pictures in my head while you read, okay?"

"Okay."

In three minutes he was fast asleep. A minute later he was snoring but Kanisha kept on reading until she got to "The End."

The two men stood on the sidewalk, a warm front bringing in a thin veil of mist making the late night/early morning look smoky. They had sized each other up at first meet and knew immediately that they would never be buddies. It was the women in front of them that allowed their close proximity possible at all.

One stood close to Gina. The other put some distance between himself and Tarika. Tarika looked up the street, searching out headlights in the mist. She wasn't sure of much in this moment except her feet were tired and she wanted to go home.

She wasn't sure if College wanted anything more than the few hours of dancing they had had, or if the next time they met up at work, he would have more than a 'hello' to give. What she did know was he seemed uncomfortable standing there with her, even though he had promised to wait until her cab arrived.

Gina's giggle drew her attention. Collin was whispering something into Gina's ear. Tarika envied the ease between them. She wished she and College had the same.

Justin shuffled his feet along the wet sidewalk, hands thrust into the pockets of his leather. He too gazed up the street, a bit tired from dancing. His body was buzzing with the need for sleep.

He had had a good time with Tarika, but he didn't know if he wanted to pursue it. She seemed street wise and her friend was definitely ghetto. From the way Tarika talked she had never mastered good English and she seemed a little rough around the edges.

She was cool to hang with and he did enjoy the time they had spent in the club. But beyond that, Justin wasn't sure. She was the type of girl his father would frown upon.

Justin Edison, Sr., had hopes and dreams for his son and had let his expectations be known. At an early age, he had drilled time and time again the road he expected his son Justin to travel. Justin's mother was more understanding. She felt Justin should find his own way, but her husband ruled the roost.

A ghetto girl wasn't supposed to be a part of Justin's journey, still there were things about her he liked.

Sweet: there was an underlining innocence to her that appealed to him. Most of the girls he'd met had little interest in what he had to say. But Tarika did. Justin had gone on and on about himself and she had sat quiet and attentive, drinking in his every word. But could he bring her home to his father?

Now as Justin stood on the sidewalk outside the club, he thought about his car parked two blocks away. A '94 Corolla, it was a hoopty for sure, but he had worked a whole summer to buy it and despite the ripped upholstery and the dents, it was reliable.

He debated with himself to offer them a ride, but decided against it. With going to school full-time and working part-time, Justin wasn't looking to complicate his life and though he liked Tarika, their worlds seemed too far apart.

"You don't have to wait," Tarika said, sensing his need to leave. "Gina's here. So's her friend. We'll be okay."

"You sure?" Justin asked, relieved.

Tarika forced a smile. "Yeah. See you at work."

College hesitated for a moment, moved his body a bit as if he wasn't certain if he wanted to go or stay. His eyes brushed hers, then he was saying goodnight. Heading up the street, he vanished in the mist.

"You crazy."

Tarika looked in Gina's direction, eyes wide, heart racing. "I'm not crazy," she insisted, defensiveness finding her.

"Not you, Tarika. Talking about this fool." She pointed to Collin. Collin, whose smile was so wide, with teeth so white, for a moment Tarika wondered if they were real. Collin, who was so close to Gina and looked so pleased to be there, it was as if they had been together a lifetime.

"He left?" Collin asked, his smile less bright, something else dancing in his eye.

"Yeah."

"Then he the real crazy one."

Tarika wanted to agree, but the weight in her heart would not let her.

The cab cost Tarika more than she wanted to spend, but she was just glad to get home. Past five in the morning, she knew the breakfast she had planned to make for Gina would become lunch.

Gina stood in front of Tarika's dresser, studying herself in the mirror. "I don't know about him."

"About who?"

"Collin."

"What you mean?"

"I mean he was cool and all 'cept for them nappy-ass dreads in his hair. But I think he was doing a lot of frontin'."

Tarika unzipped her skirt. "What you mean frontin'?"

"You know how a cat will be all in your face like you the best thing since white bread? Cats like that always hiding something. Acting like you all they want when they got something else going somewhere else."

"You think?"

"I know."

"But you had a nice time, right?"

"It was a'right."

Glancing over her shoulder, she quickly studied the back of her. "Now who's 'frontin'?"

Gina laughed. Slipped her blouse off. "Yeah, you right. I did have a nice time." She turned and faced Tarika. "What about you?" Tarika shrugged. "You digging him?" Tarika shrugged again. "I ain't judging you. I'm just asking a question."

"Yeah, I am."

"Why?"

"'Cause he's so smart."

"Hell, you smart."

"But he ain't like everybody else."

"Why?"

Tarika shrugged again. "Because he gonna be something someday."

"You something now."

"I don't mean like that."

"What? Because he talk proper? Just because he talk good don't mean he's better ... you got to stop selling yourself short, Tarika. You are as important as everybody else, I don't care how they act. Don't let that nobody run over you, hear?"

"It ain't even that kind of party, Gina."

Gina fixed her eyes on her friend. "Make sure its not."

Despite her weariness, Tarika couldn't fall asleep.

She wasn't used to sharing her bed. Gina snored liked a rhino and the night would not let her go.

When College had asked her to dance, she had assumed he'd dance with her a few records and then go off and find new partners. When Kelly Rowland's, "Dilemma" came on, she was afraid to look into his eyes. When Nelly came in with his rap, she snuck a look. College had been looking back.

When "Dilemma" faded into D'Angelo's, "How Does It Feel?" and she went to walk away because slow dancing was intimate — the song itself as intimate as a song could go, things they hadn't shared, hadn't had the chance to try out, became real as College reached for her hand and gently pulled her back to him.

Tarika found herself pressed against him, pensive about how hard she pushed against his body, determined not to get lost in his embrace, the music. But closing her eyes became easy. Leaning her head against his chest just as simple, things he didn't seem to mind as his grip on her tightened and her mind took flight.

She was seeing D'Angelo in all his stripped wonder, abs and muscles that she never knew a man could possess, twitching and shifting as he sang, pursed his lips, looked down to whatever was going on beyond the camera.

It was easy, so easy, to imagine what the video did not show. Easy to feel every twitch, slight buck that D'Angelo made. It became mixed up, tossed together, the vision of D'Angelo and his bare chest singing, moments with Sha-Keem, the feel of College pressing her close. It became mixed up and soon she was clinging to College, unafraid to let him know with her body what she wanted from his soul.

Then that song faded and he was easing from her, asking her if she wanted something to drink. They left the dance floor and went to the bar. Found seats, sipped, Tarika's eyes falling on his lips as he talked and talked and talked.

But afterward, when it was time to go. Afterwards when they had left the smoky magic of the club and were out on the sidewalk to wait for her cab, the connection she'd felt was gone.

All she wanted was to have it back.

This was why sleep would not come despite the lateness of the hour, the weariness of her. This was why she tossed and turned, looking for comfort, for ease, unable to find it for a long time.

Chapter Eighteen

Saturday found Rick wanting things. Mostly he wanted to be easy like Sunday morning. He wanted to get over his hump.

He knew he was on his way there because he actually enjoyed spending time with Kanisha and she seemed to enjoy spending time with him. But that moment was short lived.

Kanisha got up early, washed her face and brushed her teeth. She put her clothes on, made breakfast and kept her attention between the cartoons on the television screen and the front door.

The wall that had come down between them reappeared. Rick knew why. The life he and Gina had led was filled with uncertainty. Life had shown Kanisha that nothing lasted forever, not even the fun she had last night with Rick.

Sure her daddy was fun last night but that didn't mean he was going to be fun this morning. So Kanisha emotionally tucked herself away from any possibility of disappointment, setting her sights on her new sure thing — her momma.

When Gina had come to pick her up, Gina seemed to be beaming. Rick asked her about it and she confessed to him that she'd met a guy at the club. "He awright," she offered, but Rick sensed he was much more then 'awright.' The fact that Gina was even mentioning him said a lot.

Everyone was moving ahead with their lives except him.

Plopping himself down in front of the television, he flipped channels until a commercial caught his eyes — a man with a "six-pack" bench pressing. Rick had seen the commercial before, but this time it really caught his attention as the image of a woman with superb gluts filled the screen.

Glutes. Glutemaximus, that muscle beneath the skin of the derriere. Rick used to have them. He used to be 'stacked in the back.' In high school, he took weight training his entire four years.

High school. Nearly fifteen years ago?

The past always had a way of holding him down. Being by himself gave him some thinking time and in the process, he realized he put himself in situations that would guarantee some type of drama.

As he sat there watching the commercial, why he did that to himself came. By always having external congestion around him, he didn't have to deal with the internal. He didn't have to deal with what was really going on inside of him.

But the dramas were gone now. He was living without them and it was a strange and difficult terrain.

Fancy black letters filled the screen — *Bally's*. "Get fit for spring," a voiceover on the television was saying. A number flashed across the screen.

Get fit. Get in shape. Get it together.

Rick made a mental reminder to do just that.

When Dajah awoke Saturday morning, the sun was out and the sky clear. The possible ice storm hadn't materialized and for that she was glad.

A full day, she was meeting Frieda early for some shopping and Jeff later at his place for their weekly trip to Jones Beach to let Kelly romp.

It was feeling good to her, the whole business between herself and Jeff. Taking Kelly out — more icing on the cake. Dajah liked how Jeff was allowing them to get to know each other before they took the next step.

She liked how attentive he was and had yet to disappoint her. There were a few times when she called and he didn't answer, but she never pressed him about it and he always called her back.

Just good for me, she was thinking, as she pulled up to Frieda's apartment. Later in the day, long after the afternoon had said hello to evening, Dajah knew she was going to find out just how good the goodness got.

The two women walked along Jamaica Avenue, the Old Navy store, their destination. They maneuvered around the thick Saturday traffic, hundreds of shoppers entering and leaving stores.

"So, it's going good?" Frieda asked.

Dajah's face broke out into a smile. "Better then good. Three weeks today and we still haven't done it."

"Either the man has the patience of Job or Jesus done come back."

"Stop it," Dajah insisted, showing teeth and gums.

"He's on the up and up, right?"

"Yeah. He said he wasn't going to rush me."

"I think it's time I meet this Jeff."

Funny. Dajah was having the same thought.

Jones Beach behind them, the sunset, glorious and gone, Jeff, Dajah and Kelly piled into Jeff's car and headed back to his place.

Dajah felt like a blindfolded hostage as Jeff opened his apartment door, Kelly scooting past both of them, off to the kitchen, the sounds of lapping reaching them before the door was closed.

She had been here before, of course. Had reclined on the sofa, been fed chocolate-dipped strawberries. But the next step was about to begin.

They both knew it.

"You want something?" Jeff asked, taking off his jacket. Dajah told him no. "I'm going to make myself a sandwich."

Cabinet doors opened and closed. Silverware jangled as he went about making himself a turkey and Swiss on white. Jeff piled on what looked like a pound of meat onto the mayonnaise-smeared bread.

"You think you got enough turkey on there?"

Jeff looked at the sandwich, at Dajah. "Yeah, why?"

She moved into the kitchen, pointed to the half completed sandwich. "That wouldn't even fit in my mouth."

"Not finished yet." Jeff added four slices of Swiss cheese, another dollop of mayonnaise and sliced tomatoes.

"You are not serious."

"Yeah, I am."

"Can you even hold it in your hand?" The sandwich looked five inches thick.

"I do it all the time."

"Go like this," she imitated, her hands holding an invisible sandwich. He did. She measured the thickness of the sandwich and the space within his hands. Found there was room to spare. "I guess you can."

"Well, you're measuring the right place."

Her brow went up. "Excuse me?"

"It's not the feet, it's the hands."

"What's the hands?" but she knew.

"Are you spending the night?" he asked, out of the clear blue sky, taking a bite from his sandwich. It had been the unspoken word between them, but Jeff wanted to make sure.

She was planning to, of course, at least get some bedtime, if not the whole night. It was her turn to get things clear. "Am I?"

"I would like you to."

She shrugged, body tingling. "Then I guess I am."

Good and deep, that's how Jeff felt inside of her. Even with the condom on, she felt all of him as she clung to him, holding him hostage with her legs.

Dajah moaned, moved, made music and motion. She felt him contract once, twice, three times and knew his end was near. She stilled him with her hand. Whispered, "Don't move." He breathed heavily against her, parts of him spasming. "Relax," she offered. "Just relax."

It took him a moment to stop his trembles, heed her advice. They were still, bodies on fire; speaking a special language. Intensity built. Fire within fire formed. A rapidness came into them, the sweet release on its way.

Jeff wanted to move. He wanted to glide. Every nerve ending begged for redemption, but Dajah's hand, firmly on his buttock insisted that he didn't. A gasp escaped her, her orgasm starting, taking him along for the ride. Jeff shut his eyes, his whole body trembled and strained as he came in the midst of her climax.

He fell on her, crushing her chest, halting her breath for a few seconds. Then Jeff was rolling off, the two of them longing for a cool breeze.

Morning took her by surprise.

Different bedroom, different bed. Different morning sun making different patterns against the ceiling, but mostly it was the face lying next to her, eyes closed, lips slightly parted. The face, unsheltered, unprotected. Open, honest and aged.

She had always seen Jeff clean shaven, but this first morning with him, Dajah could see the bristle of a five o'clock shadow, how some of it was gray. Not a lot, but enough to say he was no longer young.

Dajah didn't want to be caught staring. She closed her eyes. But they opened again. She studied the bits of white in the slight bead. There was a fuzzy shadow lining his cheek, his chin, the hollow beneath his bottom lip.

"Stop staring."

That he wasn't asleep, had been playing possum as she had her un-thwarted look made her feel guilty. But she managed a come-back through a smile she wasn't feeling. "I wasn't staring. Just scoping."

His eyes opened. The few hours of sleep they had had, showed like brown gossamer in the corner of his tired eyes. "Scoping?"

Dajah shifted, turning until her back was to him. She nestled against his chest, not wanting to see the tiny white new growth. Not wanting to dismantle the wonderfulness she'd felt with him. "Checking you out, yeah."

"And?" His question came against her head, his breath warm through the mass of braids.

"And, nothing."

"Nothing." It wasn't a question.

"Nope, not a thing."

"Not even how tired I look with so little sleep?" Thick into her lie, she shook her head no, concentrated on how warm his skin felt against hers. "Or the fact that I need a shave."

It was an opening he was giving her. Dajah decided to step into it. "Well, yeah, the shave thing."

"And I guess the gray surprised you."

"A little bit."

"Surprised me too the first time I noticed it. Now?" he shrugged against her. "It happens to the best of us I'm sure."

"What?"

"Going gray. One morning you're all black and then the next, you notice a tiny little strand of gray. First instinct is to pluck it. A few weeks later its back and has invited some friends. After a while there's so many, you can't pluck. So you do other things."

"Like be clean shaven."

"Yeah. But I'd rather have gray on my face than those other places."

"Like your head?"

"Yeah, that too."

Dajah nestled closer to him, his sleepy giant stirring against her back. "Where else?"

"Take a guess."

She did. Laughed. "Are you serious?"

"Serious enough. I never really thought about it, going gray down there, y'know? Then I saw it for myself. And I was like 'wow,' I guess all hair goes gray."

"So you're gray down there too?"

"Not a lot, but yeah, at least quarter of a dozen."

Quarter of a dozen. Three. Not really enough to count. "That's not too bad."

"Hungry?" he asked.

"No, just a little tired."

"We did get to bed late last night."

"We sure did."

He eased away from her, glanced at the radio alarm clock. "A little after eight."

"That's all?"

"Yeah."

"Too early to get up."

"I agree."

"Be back." Jeff got out of bed, and headed for his bathroom. He was in there a good while before he returned. He kissed her lips gently. "That's the other thing about getting older."

"What?" she asked.

"Morning breath."

"I didn't notice."

He smiled at her. "One day you will."

Tarika was certain she had dreamed the whole thing. She was certain that that night at the reggae club where she and College had danced fast and slow, shared drinks, had been a figment of her mind.

She had not been expecting great things when they met up at work a day later, but she didn't expect the way he barely looked at her when he had come on his shift; how he seemed to look more at the poster of Ronald McDonald than her when he'd said hello.

Tarika made herself cool with it even though it felt like a five-hundred-pound weight was nestled on her shoulder the whole shift. She made herself okay with it every time they passed each other or shared the same space.

By day three, she couldn't pretend that it was okay. By day three, she just wanted to pin him in the corner and make him tell her why he was acting like they had never partied together. By day three, everything inside of her was turmoil and jumbled up. It had to be released.

When he took his fifteen-minute break, she took hers too, entering the break room carefully, trying not to let the hostility she felt rise up.

It was obvious he had planned to do some studying by the little workbook in his hand, but whatever class he was trying to cram for would have to wait.

"You want to act like nothing happened the other night, that's fine. But if that's what you plan, then you need to come out and say it."

"Nothing happened the other night," he insisted, his eyes never leaving the pages of his book.

"Oh, so we didn't dance. You didn't buy me a drink. I didn't listen to you talk for hours about yourself?"

He took a breath, released it. "Since when did a few hours together at a club mean something?"

"Since when you can't even look me in my face?" He looked up at her, daringly so. Put his eyes back to his book. "You know I used to think you was something special. But standing here having you ignore me, tells me you ain't no better than nobody else."

"I never said I was."

"You're absolutely right." She turned and left the break room but she could not leave behind the envy she felt at his ability to thoroughly disconnect.

Tarika had seen much growing up. One of the most pertinent things she'd seen was a man's ability to emotionally detach at a drop of the hat. She had seen her mother's boyfriends do it, had witnessed guys do it to her friends and had been victim of the same too many times to count.

The men who did it the most successfully always had a hard edge to them. An, "I-don't-give-a-shit-'bout-nothing" attitude. College was different, or at least she thought he was. The fact that he was in his third year of higher education at least suggested a better understanding and reasoning.

Fifteen years of education should have made right and wrong simple. Being all hugged up with her on the dance floor and then sharing his life with her wasn't something you did with someone you didn't want to know the next day.

But that's exactly what College was doing and it made her feel cheap. Tarika hadn't slept with him or anything, but the sensation was the same. He had her feeling like a one-night stand.

"What you doing with that nigga?"

Tarika didn't see Antonio standing there until she closed the door. He scared her. "Damn," she muttered, her hand to her heart.

"What you doing with him?"

"What you mean what I'm doing with him?"

"You dropped me for that?"

Tarika blinked. "Excuse you?"

"I said — ,"

"I heard what you said Antonio and I don't know what you been smoking but it's really none of your business what *I* do."

"He ain't right for you, Tarika."

"Oh, like you are?" She pushed past him. "Nee-grow, get out of my face."

Tarika called Gina on her break. "Forget him," Gina told her. "If he can't see the jewel you are, you need to drop his ass like a bad habit."

College had dropped himself, so that wasn't the problem. The problem was Tarika found it hard to accept. She had never been delusional. She had never seen silver linings where there was none. But she had never met a guy like College

"It don't make sense to get all twisted in some cat that ain't studying you. Am I right? Take Collin. He talking all this smack about what we gonna do. You think I'm paying it any real mind? He got to show me, because talk is real cheap."

"Yeah? What he saying?"

"He gonna take me to Jamaica. He wanna take me and Kanisha to the circus. Mess like that."

"It doesn't sound like mess, Gina. Sounds nice."

"Yeah? You taking me to Jamaica? Show me some tickets. You taking me and Kanisha to the circus? Take us. I ain't believing nothing till I see something."

But even inside of Gina's tirade, Tarika could hear she liked the possibilities. "So when is he going to do all this?"

"Exactly. When?" Gina sucked her teeth. "Got to be about more than talk before I start investing myself."

"So you dig him?"

"He a'right. He supposed to be coming over this weekend."

"Y'all going to hang out?"

"That's what he say. But like I said, I'll believe it when I see it."

Chapter Nineteen

Rick wasn't certain of what he expected the first day he stepped into the fitness center in Long Island City. He did know that he didn't look fit. The love handles that had started to bloom at his waist surprised him when he took time to look at himself naked in his bedroom mirror.

He knew his stomach had gone soft, his arms a bit flabby. Rick knew he was technically out of shape, but was determined to get it all together again. He appreciated that nobody seemed to notice him; that no one gawked or stared.

The people there were about getting their own selves right. By the time he was introduced to his trainer and started working on his fitness, he was relaxed. That had been three sessions ago.

Now as he laid against the black vinyl, covered in sweat, the muscles in his arms trembling as if palsied. Rick gritted his teeth and pushed the one-hundred and twenty-five pound bar up, struggling just as much to lower it to his chest without letting it crush him.

"Good," his personal trainer said.

It might have looked good, but it felt like hell. There would be no second attempt. Rick muttered "take it" and felt a huge wave of relief as the bar was lifted from his hands.

"How are you feeling?"

Rick closed his eyes, exhaled. "Like crap."

His trainer hit him on the shoulder. "Okay, catch your breath and then we'll move on to the treadmill," which Rick hated the most.

When Rick had joined the gym, it had been with the idea he would come in and workout on his own schedule. But they had been running a special and he was able to get a personal trainer for two weeks free of charge.

His name was Dirk. He was tall and built, with dirty blond hair and brown eyes. After he had put Rick through his first series, Rick began to think of him as "Dick." As the sessions went on he gathered a bunch of names in his head: Dick Head. Dick Face. Little Dick. No Dick MF.

Rick never said it out loud. At the end of the first day, Rick swore that he would not go another session with him. But on the second day when he tried his own workout, his body felt like it was missing out on something. Rick ended up seeking Dirk out.

They were now well into the second week and though Rick didn't like Dirk a bit more, his body loved him, even as it struggled through the workouts.

"Twenty minutes okay?" Dirk asked as he set the incline and speed on the treadmill.

"Sure."

"I'll be back."

Rick began to run. "I'll be here."

Three minutes later his surroundings faded away. Three minutes later it was just him and the motion of his body. Three minutes later, Rick felt at one with himself. Liked it.

Rick finished up the last of his Linguini and clam sauce and signaled the waiter. A great afternoon had become a great evening.

After his workout, he had gone into the sauna. After the sauna, he had taken a massage. The hands of the masseuse felt so good on his overworked muscles, he swore it was better than sex.

Leaving the gym, he headed to his favorite Italian restaurant in Astoria, unabashed and unconcerned about dining alone. He was given a booth which gave him privacy and comfort, and feasted.

Meal over, he felt full, complete and relaxed as he left a nice tip and headed for his SUV. Windows down and music pumping, Rick headed home. He was learning to live alone and liking it.

Dajah came in from work, tossed her bag, kicked off her shoes and checked her machine. No message. Sometimes there were some waiting, sometimes not. But it was all good, as far as she was concerned.

She'd been seeing Jeff regularly and things between them were going nicely. He did back off a bit from their marathon dating, but at least one day out of the weekend, they spent together. Sometimes they caught up with each other midweek.

She liked him a lot, but the "L" was still some time away. That suited her, it was the way she preferred it. She was taking baby steps, just like she used to do it, and the whole matter of Rick and his mess was beginning to feel more and more like some long-ago dream.

"Hi, Baby Two," she murmured, going over to her ficus. "How was your day?" she asked, caressing some leaves. She dropped down and tested the soil, mashing dirt between her fingers. A little dry — she headed to the kitchen and filled an empty jug with water.

Coming back into the living room, she bent down, pouring the contents into the dirt. Next she got her spritzer and gave the leaves a good spray. She turned on the radio, went and changed her clothes, then headed back into the kitchen, dinner in her head.

She cooked up a burger, laid the top with cheese, shook some greens from the bagged salad and ate. When dinner was over, she washed up her dishes, sat down on the couch and made a call.

Keeping his calendar clear for the weekend was getting harder and harder. Keeping things running between all the women in his life was getting harder and harder too. It was the only reason that Wednesday night Joy was over his place, in his kitchen, making him dinner.

Jeff had suggested take out, but she insisted on cooking. It wasn't as elaborate as she wanted — she made a mean curry chicken, but the spaghetti, meatballs and garlic bread was fine with him.

Normally, he was good with not watching the clock. Normally, some internal mechanism kept track of time without him having to actually look. But it had been close to six thirty by the time they got in and they hadn't sat down to eat until after seven.

A phone call between himself and Dajah was about due.

"Good?" Joy asked, her eyes bright over the candles she insisted on lighting.

"Yeah, good," Jeff uttered, crunching on a bit of garlic bread.

"You should have let me do that dessert for you."

Jeff forced a smile. "Maybe next time."

Joy wasn't a big eater, but she was a slow one. Jeff was forking up the last of the spaghetti and she still hadn't finished her salad. He felt a pressure on him, the type he hadn't felt in a while. Standing, he took up his plate and hers, startling her silly.

"Where you going with my plate?"

Jeff didn't answer. Simply continued to the kitchen, spying the sauce-stained stove, and the empty, scummy pasta pot. He spotted the open box of pasta, the unclosed package of garlic bread and the greasy baking pan sitting on a burner.

Ignoring the mess, Jeff placed the plates on the counter and headed back to the dining room table. Slipping his arms around Joy's waist, his lips were headed for her neck when the phone began to ring.

There was no need for Joy to ask if he was going to get it. He never did. There was no further need to ask why he had taken away her plate; the reason was obvious. A minute later they were in his bed. Twenty-one minutes after, they were out of it.

Two minutes after that Jeff was waving goodbye to her as she drove her Sebring convertible down the cold, dark street.

Ten minutes after that, Jeff was on the phone with Dajah, the smell of Joy rising up around him with every breath he took.

You dig him?

That was the question Tarika had asked Gina with regards to Collin. Though Gina tried to pretend she didn't care one way or the other, there was no doubt she did. She had never invited any man to her place, not even Rick. Gina had never allowed anyone she was seeing to cross her front door. But Collin was her one exception.

Gina didn't tell Rick just what her plans were, only that she needed him to baby sit Saturday. Saturday afternoon she stood at Rick's front door, a cab idling at the curb, Kanisha having disappeared inside a few seconds before. "So you're going to drop her tomorrow about noon?" she asked Rick.

"Yeah."

"Alright." Gina turned to leave.

Rick stopped her. "Second time in a month," he offered with a smile.

"Second time what?"

"That you're going out ... so where are you headed?"

"I don't even know yet." But there was something in her eyes.

"What, you and your girl can't decide?"

"I ain't hanging with Tarika tonight."

"Oh."

"I'm hanging with that cat I told you about. He's coming over. I ain't trying to have no man up in my place with Kanisha there."

Rick nodded, surprised. He moved past it. "Well, that's smart."

"Yeah. So I don't know. I could go somewhere, I could be home."

"You just be careful, Gina."

"You ain't got to tell me. I ain't letting no man come up on me wrong." She looked back at the cab. Looked back at Rick, sensing how far they'd come. "I'll see you tomorrow." With that, she headed down the steps.

She wasn't giving him jack.

It was a decision Gina made before Collin rang her bell. They could hang, they could chill, they could talk all night, maybe kiss a little, but he wasn't about to get none of her.

She changed the CD in her CD player. Turned off the ceiling light and turned on the side lamps. She looked around her living room and spied a toy in the corner. She took it to Kanisha's room and ducked into the bathroom to check her face on the way back.

This night was about entertaining and she was new to it.

She bought some wine and it was chilling in the refrigerator. Her bedroom door was closed and she was determined to keep it that way. She'd hope they would go out, but it would be okay if they stayed in. Despite her fronting, there was something about Collin she liked.

He made her laugh.

Gina never knew telling jokes could be so attractive. She had never been with anybody who saw humor in almost everything.

Her doorbell rang. Taking one last look around her, she made her way down the steps. Gina barely recognized the close-shaved-headed man before her.

"I told you I was going to cut them."

"Collin?"

"Gina?"

She laughed, opened the door wide. "Come on in." Pointing up the steps. "It ain't much," she found herself saying as his eyes swept her tiny living room.

"Nah, it's cool. Nice." He took off his jacket. Though his shirt was loose, she could see the muscles of his shoulders, the slimness of his waist. Liked how his pants, riding low on his hips, emphasized his behind.

She took his coat and went to the closet. It was packed with things and so she took it to her bedroom, opening the door she swore she wasn't going to open. Put it on her bed.

"So what we doing?"

"Figured we could hang here, if that's all right."

"You want something?" she said, heading to her kitchen. "I got some wine." She went to her refrigerator. Opened the door. While leaning down to get the bottle, arms snaked around her waist. A pelvis pushed against her butt.

She moved away from him. "What you doing?"

He stepped back, arms up in surrender. "It's cool."

"Yeah, well, it damn better be. I ain't rolling like that tonight."

"Can't blame me for trying."

"The hell I can't. Now we can chill here, and I do mean chill, or you can leave now."

"Chill."

"Good." Gina got the wine, grabbed some glasses from the dish rack and headed into the living room.

Another shift finished, Tarika turned down Jamaica Avenue and headed up Merrick Boulevard to the bus terminal, smelling French fries with every step she took. If there was one thing she hated about her job, it was how she smelled after a shift.

Now was no different as she took the lonely, empty block towards her bus. She was off tomorrow and looked forward to sleeping late. For now she just wanted to get home, take a long, hot shower and get out of the clothes that smelled of fast food.

Cars zoomed past her quickly, their headlights, endless beacons that swiped her with their brilliance. Up ahead, buses rumbled out of the terminal and she checked each one to make sure it wasn't her bus. If she missed it, she would have a bit of a wait.

She watched a car come down the street. Watched it slow down. Lights flashed. She ignored it, kept her eyes straight ahead. Then the window rolled down.

He had been thinking about her.

He had been thinking about her ever since she had read him the riot act in the break room and even before then. Since that night at the club she had been on his mind.

Justin thought about how much fun he had had. How she was such a good listener. He thought about how she didn't laugh at his thoughts, his opinions, his personal views of the world. But even with all that thinking, it hadn't been until she basically called his bluff did his heart join the bandwagon.

He didn't know he mattered to her. Justin knew she dug him, but he didn't know the extent until she had gone off on him. She had been so passionate. And bold. Most of the girls he knew would have never stepped up to him. They would have never put their real feelings out there. But Tarika had.

It changed how he saw her, stirred up with all the things he liked about her. Made him come face to face with the fact that yes, she was different, but in a good way. Then Antonio had gotten in his face, claiming Tarika as his own. It only stirred up Justin's pot even more.

So when he spotted her walking up Merrick, he didn't think twice before he began flashing his lights. Without hesitation, he rolled down his window and shouted her name.

Yes, his father would frown upon his choice, but at twenty-three going on twenty-four, the days of direct influence was over. He liked Tarika. It didn't matter if his father wouldn't.

"Tarika."

She heard her name and tried to peer through the windshield, but inside was too dark to see. She slowed, stopped, bent her head and saw College behind the wheel. Frowned.

"Where you headed?" he shouted.

For a hot second she started not to answer. For a hot second she started to right herself and continue on her way. "Home."

"You want a lift?"

"Yeah."

"Get in." She did, her seat belt barely buckled before he was pulling off. "You seeing Tony?"

"Who?"

"Tony. Antonio."

"No, why?"

"Well he's sure acting like it."

Tarika shrugged, her mind in a million places. She glanced at the dashboard. Saw a picture hanging off the rear view mirror. A laminated Polaroid of College swung to and fro. A York College sticker was glued to the dash.

"He told me to step off, that you were his."

"What?"

"You heard me."

"Well he's lying."

"So you're not seeing him?"

"No."

"So you all didn't go to the movies?"

"We went to the movies, but that was it."

The car zoomed across Archer Avenue. "Where do you live?"

"Bricktown."

"Where at?" She told him the street. "So you're not his?"

Her face pinched. The car hit a pothole. Only the seat belt prevented her from hitting her head. "No, I ain't his."

"That's not what he's saying. He said you two got something going."

"I don't care what he say. It ain't true." Up ahead the light turned yellow. College raced his car across the intersection as it went to red. "You trying to kill me?" she wanted to know.

"Just how I drive."

She heard his smile but didn't see it. She couldn't bring herself to look at him. There was too much going on inside of her. Too much she was trying to settle. "Turn here, make a left." He did. "Make another left here."

"So you aren't with him then."

She risked her eyes his way. Lost her breath when his met hers. "No."

"Well, that's not what he's saying. He's telling anybody that listen that you're his."

"Then I got to get him straight cause I'm not nothing to him." She pointed to the window. "Make a right here. Third house on your right."

The car slowed. Stopped. "Thanks." Tarika reached for the handle.

"Wait. What's your rush? What are you doing tonight?"

Tarika had spent the whole ride unsettled. College having a car, asking to take her home, asking about Antonio, gave her no thinking time. But as his hand landed on top of hers, the picture grew a bit clearer.

Maybe she hadn't been wrong about him but she had to make sure. "Tonight? I got plans."

"Can I come along?" It took everything she had in her to tell him no. "Maybe some other time."

"Maybe." She opened the car door. Got out. Said, "Goodnight." And closed it.

Upstairs in her apartment, Tarika headed for the phone. She wasn't sure if Gina was home or not or if she had company. Tarika didn't care. She was bursting and she had to tell somebody.

Tarika had to tell somebody that she hadn't been wrong.

"Where you going?" Collin asked, his mouth slipping away from her breast.

Gina's blouse was up, her bra undone, but her jeans were still on though unzipped and the hand delving into her panties were the only things that would get to go there.

"The phone," Gina said, easing herself up off the couch. It was the break she needed, the chance to pull out and from under the talented mouth and hands of Collin.

She had gone too far with him already and she knew she was only a few minutes at the most, from doing what she promised she would not do, so she gladly went to her bedroom to get the phone. Gladly picked up the receiver. "Hello?"

"Gurrrrrl."

"Tarika?"

"Yes. Gurrrl, I got something to tell you?"

Gina sat on the bed, got comfortable. Began the process of rearranging her clothes. "What?"

"College."

"College?"

"Yeah, you know, the guy on my job. Justin Edison. "

It was the first time Tarika had used his real name in conversation, which told Gina much. "Oh yeah, Justin. You call him 'College' so much, I forgot his name."

"Yeah him ... you busy?"

"Collin's here."

"I'm interrupting?"

"Yeah, but it's all good."

"Y'all wasn't?"

"Halfway there, but your call stopped that. I ain't mad atcha."

"Where's he?"

"In the living room."

"Where are you?"

"My bedroom. Go on girl. Tell me."

"I'm on my way home. Walking down Merrick going to the terminal and this car slows. So I'm like, let me just keep on walking. Then the lights flash and I'm still like, I don't know who that is or what they want, but I'm gonna keep on walking. Then, the window rolls down and I hear, "Tarika." I stop. Look. And it's Justin."

"College."

"Right? So I started to keep on walking and then he asks me if I wanted a ride home. So I say yeah. I get in his car. Check that, his *car*. He has a car and he didn't even offer us no ride? Anyway, I'm in his car and he starts asking me about Antonio."

"Who?"

"This other cat on my job who kinda liked me but ain't about nothing."

"Oh, him."

"Yeah, him. Anyway, Justin's telling me that Antonio is going around telling everybody that me and him hooked up. Telling all these lies and stuff. So I tell Justin that Antonio lying. Justin drives me home right, and we pull up to my place and I'm like, "Thanks" and I'm getting out the car. And he says, get this, "What's your rush?" and "What you doing tonight?" and I'm fucking shocked because a few days ago, he wasn't even talking to me hardly.

"So I play it real cool and say I was going out and he says, check this, "Can I come along?" Gina. Girl, I could have passed out right there. But I'm still playing it cool, right? So I tell him no and get out the car. Just got upstairs and I had to tell you."

"See, didn't I tell you you was somebody important? Don't let nobody run over you, no matter who he is."

"I hear that."

"So where you going?"

"Nowhere. I was just messing with him. He need to know that I ain't no ho. That I don't roll like that. He want to get with me, he got to show he on the real."

"For sure. Well, let me get back to Collin. It's about time for his ass to go."

"Already?"

"Yeah, it's getting a little heated out there and I ain't giving up nothing."

"I hear you. I give you a holla tomorrow."

"A'right."

"Peace." Tarika hung up the phone.

Gina disconnected and went back out into the living room. "That was my girl."

"Tarika?"

"Yeah. You ready?"

"For?"

"Get on up out of here."

"I just got here."

Gina went and turned on the ceiling light. "It was feeling good and all, but I ain't going there with you tonight."

"I didn't say you had to."

She gave him a knowing look. "You ain't had to say jack. You know what you was doing and I know what you was doing too and so you best go now so you don't get your feelings hurt later." Gina grabbed the empty glasses. "You need me to call you a cab?"

Chapter Twenty

The stockroom was long with a low ceiling, crammed full of non-perishables used at the fast food restaurant. There were boxes upon boxes of salt packs, ketchup, sauces and straws. Tarika moved through the towering cartons, a box of paper napkins in her hand.

The size of the box made seeing beyond it awkward but she caught Justin coming her way.

"You got that?" he asked.

"Yeah, I got it."

"You sure?"

"I'm sure." She was trying not to smile, but couldn't help it. Her teeth appeared behind her lips.

"A smile. That's a plus."

She looked away from him, the box bulky. She shifted it up against her stomach.

"Let me take that for you." She let him take it. Headed for the stairs. "Wait up."

"Yeah?"

"You have a good time?"

"When?"

"The other night after I dropped you off. You said you were going out."

"Yeah, I had a good time."

"This weekend, are you doing anything?"

"I don't think so, why?"

"I thought maybe we could go back to the Rubba Dub."

"You asking me?"

"Yeah."

"So ask."

"I just did."

"That's not how you ask somebody."

"Alright, alright. Tarika, will you go with me to the Rubba Dub this Saturday."

"I'll think about," her smile flippant as she headed up the stairs.

Collin called Gina and told her he wanted to come over Saturday, that there was something special he wanted her to see. The more she asked what, the less he told her, so by Saturday afternoon, she was a little anxious.

After two dates and endless phone conversations, she felt comfortable enough for him to meet Kanisha. Kanisha wasn't thrilled with the idea of meeting her mother's friend, but like those other times she had seen her mother with men who weren't her father, it just became the way it was.

At two o'clock, Gina's doorbell rang. Fifteen seconds later she was bowled over by what she saw — Collin Jr.

Gina knew before Collin even spoke it. Knew that the little four-year-old next to him was no one but his son. "Gina, this is my son CJ. CJ, this is Miss Gina."

CJ looked up at the woman, hoping she had goodies in her kitchen. He had enjoyed the train and the bus ride but was looking forward to the special treats he always got when he went visiting with his daddy.

"Son," was all Gina could manage, unable to hide her surprise and the jab to her heart.

"Yeah. Say hello CJ."

"Hello."

"You never even told me you had a child."

"You never asked." Even though Collin was smiling, she could tell her reaction wasn't thrilling him. "Can we come in?"

"Yeah." Gina stepped back and let them pass her. Closed the downstairs door. Locked it. "CJ, why don't you go on upstairs and introduce yourself to my daughter Kanisha. Me and your daddy be there in a minute."

CJ looked back at his father. Collin nodded his head. CJ went.

"Why you wait till now to tell me?"

"What difference does it make?"

"A whole lot. I told you about Kanisha from the get go."

"And I'm telling you about CJ."

"Where's his momma?"

"In the Bronx."

"You still with her?"

"No."

But Gina didn't like the idea that they were in the same borough.

"Who he live with?"

"He lives with her."

"How long y'all been apart?"

"A year, but we're through."

Gina didn't believe it. She knew one thing if she didn't know anything else. A man could say he wasn't going back, but he often made himself a liar.

Tarika and Justin went clubbing that Saturday night. They ended back at her place afterwards. She could tell he didn't expect her apartment, though tiny, to look so nice. She could tell that the outside of the building spoke nothing of the jewel she had created inside.

He ran his fingers over the kitchen wall. "You did this?"

"Yeah."

"How?"

"A couple cans of paint, some rags. It's called 'ragging'."

He peered his head towards the darkened living room. Even though there were no lights on, the sheer drape allowed the soft street light in. He could make out huge throw pillows, dried wheat stalks in tall glass vases. An area rug in the middle of the floor and her stereo system.

Tarika went in and turned on a lamp, the soft charcoal gray walls complimenting the oatmeal colored pictures she had hung up, the throws tossed tastefully in a corner. "I would ask you to have a seat, but as you can see..."

He shook his head. Eased off his jacket. "No, the pillows are fine." His eyes danced around the room. "You hooked this up by yourself?"

"Yeah, I did."

"How did you learn?"

"Learn what?"

"To decorate?"

Tarika shrugged, understanding it was a compliment to the highest. "I read magazines, studied layouts and stuff. Bought a few things here and there."

"Damn, but this is nice." He looked out of the living room. "Your bedroom must be smoking."

"Would you like to see it?"

"I'd love to."

Justin spent the night, clothes on, shoes off. They didn't get in the bed, just on top of it. Tarika gave him the blanket and she took the comforter. They talked until the sun was kissing the horizon. Dozed off with sentences unfinished.

When they awoke, there was no uncomfortable silence between them. When they awoke hours later, the ease they had drifted off to remained.

Sunday morning arrived cold and drizzly. Dajah looked out of the window at the cold rain washing out the March day and smiled.

It didn't matter, not in the real sense of things. Today was a special day. Today her best friend was going to meet her man.

Her man.

It had never been discussed, but every time they got together, Dajah could feel it was so. She had no doubt Jeff felt the same way. They had been seeing each other a little over a month and that was a real indicator as far as she was concerned. She really liked Jeff and she hoped that Frieda would like him just as much.

There was much that could have come from the Sunday dinner at Dajah's place. Much that could have been anticipated. It could have been a real kickback afternoon of too much food, too much wine and a whole lot of fun.

But the Sunday dinner wasn't about any of that. It was about Jeff passing a test.

As far as Dajah was concerned, she had struck gold but she needed that verified. Dajah needed proof positive that the relationship was on solid ground and wanted Frieda and Barry to give it.

They didn't.

While Frieda and Barry greeted Jeff warmly, by the time dinner was over and Dajah was doing the dishes she knew her friends had not been impressed. She had caught both Frieda and Barry giving each other looks over the meal.

Dajah had seen the arch of their brow, slight rise of their eyes, a pensiveness on Frieda's face too deep to ignore. She had planned to get to the bottom of it later, but ended up having a whispery intense conversation about it as she washed up the dishes and Frieda dried.

"He ain't for real," was how Frieda began. "I don't know what his game is Day, but he running game on you."

Dajah nearly dropped the plate she was washing. "What?"

"I'm telling you Dajah. The cat is just a little too intense for someone you've only known a month."

"What are you talking about?"

Frieda moved closer to her friend, her voice dropping to a hissing whisper. "I'm talking about Jeff. He never stopped touching you during dinner. Playing kissy face with you with me and Barry sitting there." Frieda's face bunched up. "It was like he was putting on a performance to impress us."

"He wasn't play-acting Frieda." And he wasn't. That's how it was when they were together, always up in each other's Kool-Aid.

Frieda's hushed tone vanished. "Oh no?"

The two women glared at each other. Frieda turned. Put a clean plate in the cabinet. "You believe what you want to believe, but Jeff isn't doing nothing but playing you."

The evening ended soon after that, Frieda and Barry getting their coats, saying their good nights and leaving out, leaving Dajah to question her emotions, but mostly pondering Jeff's.

With both feet, Dajah jumped in. "You playing me?"

"What?"

"I said, are you playing me?"

Jeff looked up from the couch, a hot and fiery Dajah before him. "Is that what your girl thinks?"

"Answer the question Jeff. Are you playing me?" It hurt a little bit more every time she said it. Hurt that she had asked the question twice and still had not been given an answer. She peered into his eyes, waiting for the slightest flinch, the slightest telltale sign that Frieda had it right.

"Well, if you call enjoying being with you 'playing you,' then I guess I am."

"Being with me? Is that all this is?"

"Is it supposed to be something more?"

She felt dumbstruck. The one question that she always asked but somehow forgot to jumped her soul. "Are you seeing other people?"

"Is that a problem?"

"Yes, it is."

"Why? We have a good time together. I like you, you like me. What's the big deal?"

"The big deal is I don't share a man with anyone."

It was Jeff's turn to be stunned. "You thought it was just me and you?" Yes, that's exactly what Dajah thought. "I never said anything like that."

But he didn't have to say it. He was acting as if she were the alpha and omega. She told him so. "It wasn't what you said Jeff, it was how you acted, treated me." According to Frieda, it was all pretense. According to what Jeff just told her, Frieda had been right. "You better go."

"I never said that Dajah. Ever. Now if you wanted to believe it, then fine, but don't make me the bad guy here."

"I'll get your coat." She came back with it, handed it to him and opened her front door. Down the steps she went, not waiting for him. By the time he reached the first floor, the outside door was wide open.

"This is how you want it?"

"No, it's how it has to be. I don't do share."

Dajah didn't want to be on the phone fifteen minutes after Jeff had left. She wanted to turn off the lights, get in bed, holding her hurt close like a newborn. She wanted to slip into oblivion, forego the thoughts that plagued her, vanish from the world for a while.

She didn't want to have a conversation admitting how blind she'd been. Dajah didn't want to tell Frieda that she had been right. But her emotions were every which way but right and she needed to talk.

Frieda didn't say much, allowing Dajah to spill her heart; saying that she was sorry that it didn't work out when Dajah was done. "I mean that Day. I'm really sorry. You seemed so happy with him."

Even when she got off the phone with Frieda, Dajah could not stop doing replays in her head. She could not stop cycling through the moments she had had with Jeff.

What she'd felt for him had been real. He may have not been on the up and up, but he had given her some good times. For a hot minute, it had been wonderful. That's the part Dajah held on to.

What a difference a beach made.

Terrain-wise, it was the same body of water, the same composition of sand, the same coastline. But the fifteen miles between Jones Beach and Far Rockaway Beach felt continents apart as Jeff walked with Kelly along the boardwalk.

There was no running wild for his dog on this beach. No letting his canine romp free along the weathered boards, the seashell-filled sand. Unlike Jones Beach, the few strollers of Far Rockaway seemed to take offense to an unbounded Kelly. Scampering and screaming as Kelly raced in their direction, some threatened to call the police.

A week since he had spoken to Dajah, a week since he had seen her, Jeff knew that the sunny, almost warm March day would definitely send her to Jones, so he came to Far Rockaway instead.

Jeff felt partially at fault but he wouldn't carry the brunt of it. Dajah had assumed and that was on her. He had never come out and said what they had was exclusive, even though moments came when he thought he wanted just that.

He did feel closer to her than all of the other women he saw, but he wasn't ready to put all his eggs in one basket just yet. Besides, none of his other 'friends' seemed to mind.

But Dajah isn't like all your other friends.

There was a fire to her that the other women in his life lacked. She had him doing the things he used to do and she brought a fresh excitement to his life. Regardless, he wasn't ready for that one on one.

Kelly stopped. Sat. She looked up at Jeff and whimpered. There was no doubt Kelly wasn't pleased with her master's choice of beach.

Being leashed didn't allow her the chance to charge seagulls or search out whatever caught her nose in the sand. This day at the beach was restrictive as a walk through their neighborhood park. Kelly wanted freedom.

Jeff pulled on her leash, urging her to, "Come on," but Kelly refused to move. She looked behind her, whimpered and gave a quick bark.

Jeff dropped down to one knee, nuzzled her neck, that space beneath her ears. "I can't let you loose girl. I want to, but I can't. I have to keep you chained." The dog gave its master another sad look, then got to her feet. "I know you want Jones, but we're not going there today."

Giving the leash another tug, reluctantly Kelly started trotting.

A rough week, Dajah was grateful when Saturday arrived beautiful and sweet. Up with the sun, Dajah cleaned her house, vacuuming the carpet in her living room and bedroom, washed the kitchen and bathroom floors. She dusted, watered her tree and separated her clothes for the Laundromat.

She had been stung badly, so badly, her head churned every time she thought about it, but she wasn't going to get stuck like she had with Rick. She wasn't going to give up chunks of her life to play the mourning game.

She wasn't going to let the latest failure in her life immobilize her. Dajah was going to keep moving.

By the time her place smelled like aisle ten of her supermarket, it was past noon. The evening was planned so she didn't mind the lull. Later she would be heading to Barry's house. He was having a card party and she was looking forward to the fried chicken sandwiches, bottles of cold beer and loud, vivacious games of Bid Whist.

As strategizing as Chess, Bid Whist was one of the few card games she enjoyed that held as much excitement and disappointment as a round at the craps table. Part luck, part strategy, trips to "Boston" were the ultimate high.

Dajah wasn't certain how the exclamation of "Boston!" came to mean that someone was about to win every single book played. But, that mystified expression had birthed others. Her favorite: "*You smell something?*"

Motion. She was in motion. Rick had had her stuck and she

wiggled herself free of him. There was no way she was going to allow Jeff, a man she'd seen just over a month, glorious as it had been, to do the same.

At eleven minutes to midnight, Dajah sat on one side of the dining table, her partner, Joe Pete, on the other. Joe Pete was a big man, chocolate like a Hershey bar and a few years shy of being old enough to have fathered her.

The best Bid Whist player out of the whole crowd, partnering with him meant you rarely lost. Like smooth tracks beneath oiled wheels, he knew how take a basic four bid and turn it into a strong seven.

With near psychic ability, he knew how to read the plays with mathematical precision and how to recover any mistakes you might make. Everyone wanted to partner with Joe Pete and he knew it, but the choice was always his, something he relished.

He'd look around the crowd as if he was still deciding and then nod his head in someone's direction. This night, his head had tilted Dajah's way.

Playing with him allowed her to loosen up, have fun, knowing that he had her back. Partnering with Joe Pete wasn't like playing with Cleta, who hadn't quite figured out the game and often overbid, guaranteeing a loss; or Lester, who got downright hostile if Dajah screwed up.

"You ready?" Joe Pete asked everyone around the table, slapping a card onto his forehead. With five books left to be made and not a single one in front of the opposing side, the mood around the table was electric. "You got them bags packed?" he asked, fixing his gaze on Dajah.

"Sure do."

"Good." Joe Pete grabbed the card off his forehead. Shouted "Pie-Ow!" and he slammed it on the table. It was the big joker. The king of spades fell, the jack, and Dajah gave up her two of diamond.

"That's what I'm talking 'bout," Joe Pete declared, scooping up the book and tossing out the little joker. He played and scooped, played and scooped and played and scooped. Before the last card of the last hand hit the table, Dajah and Joe Pete jumped up.

"BOSTON!" They howled together, slapping each other five.

"All this teaching has made me thirsty," Joe Pete decided. "I'm going to take a beer break."

"I hear that," Dajah chimed, the two of them moving off to the kitchen.

A woman leaving his bed was a tricky maneuver.

Jeff preferred the nighttime.

In the semidarkness, street lamps dusting his bedroom, he could pretend that there was something more, something real, something permanent to what happened in his bed.

In the semi darkness, he didn't have to be 'on,' giving up perfectly executed glances, smiles, the false gleam in his eye that women hardly ever saw as fake. He could close his eyes, draw whatever woman close, entwine with her as if he was determined to pull down the heavens just for her.

He could snuggle, hold her close, long enough to give her a full goodbye, then coax her from his bed, into her clothes and out his front door. In the dimness he didn't have to put himself up to the scrutiny they would sometimes give, searching the whole of him for being on the up and up with his emotions.

But in the morning, with the sun too bright inside his bedroom, he would have to give the greatest performances. Jeff would have to wrap himself in emotions he wasn't feeling long enough to get them gone.

This morning was no different as he watched Jill pad naked to his bathroom, her behind, jiggly, pear shaped and caramel brown. She was back within a minute, her pubic hair on display, revealing a few strands of gray.

Just thirty-seven, the hair below Jill's waist was going places the hair above it had yet to venture. Normally she plucked them out, but she must have forgotten. Jeff had his own and like Jill, every now and then he took tweezers to them. He often wondered what he'd do when there were too many grays to pluck.

"Morning," she said sleepily, beginning the search for her clothes. She found her bra, her blouse, socks and her jeans. But her underwear were missing. "Damn it." Jill stared out into the hallway, anger on her face. "Kelly," she began, charging towards the living room.

Jeff got up too, the both of them knowing what they would find before they found it.

The silky blue underwear was ripped in the crotch and left by the kitchen. "You nasty-ass dog," Jill said, snatching up what remained of her panties. She fixed her eye on Jeff. "This is the fourth pair that damn dog done ruined."

"Bad dog, Kelly," Jeff said moving towards his canine. "Bad dog," he insisted, peering down into the dog's face. He looked at Jill. "Sorry about that."

"Yeah, well, you owe me twenty bucks."

"For a pair of drawers?"

"These were Vicky's and they weren't cheap." Vicky's — Victoria's Secret. "I know for a fact I stuffed them in my bag. That dog of yours went after them."

Jeff resisted the urge to smile. Looked at his dog. Kelly sheepishly returned the favor.

"How come she never eats your stuff?"

Jeff shrugged, the answer inside of him. Kelly only chewed on the clothes of the women she didn't like. The ones she liked, she never touched. "Tell you what, I'll give you forty. Get yourself two pair."

"Yeah, alright. But you need to teach that dog that she can't be going around eating people's drawers. That's just nasty."

"It's not like she does it for spite. She's just cleaning them for you."

"That's nasty and crazy."

"Not to a dog it's not."

"Well then your dog is nasty and crazy." With that Jill left the room. Jeff knew he would never invite her back.

But there was still the issue of getting her out of his front door.

Jill never wanted to leave until he had promised her something, the next date, a phone call, a trip to some restaurant.

She would hold onto him, clinging to his neck like vines until she was certain there would be a next time to them, some verbal referendum that she was more to him then just a night in the sack.

Jeff would give it, careful with what he promised. Often it would be a phone call. Sometimes he would give them an exact time and kept his promise. Even though the phone call wouldn't last any more then three minutes, it was enough that he called.

"Eight o'clock right?" Jill was asking, her body pressed against him, her morning breath none too sweet.

"Yeah, eight."

She released him. Stepped back. "Talk to you later." She left, Jeff standing there until she disappeared down the steps. Closing the door, he took a deep breath and let it go. Glancing at the clock he calculated he had five hours of free time before he had to meet up with Joy.

All he wanted was to go back to bed, but Kelly came into the living room with the leash in her mouth. "Alright girl, let me get some shoes on."

Chapter Twenty-One

It took some getting used to working in the same place with the man Tarika was involved with. It took self-control not to exchange looks, make out in the break room. Hole up in a corner behind boxes stacked six feet high. But the less people that knew about them, the better.

They spent a lot of time talking, Tarika sharing her heart, Justin his. Both sensitive types, they found comfort in opening themselves up to each other. With Justin in college, conversations about Tarika and her own educational status came into play.

He was surprised to learn she never got past the tenth grade but understood the sidetrack when she talked about her life.

"Nobody wanted me," she confessed. "It was like nobody cared what I did. I've been out of my mother's house since I was twelve, ended up staying with an uncle, if you could call it that. I don't think he really wanted me either, but getting paid by the state helped a lot. He never asked me anything. Just told me. 'I want the house cleaned. You got to cook every night,' things like that.

"He had a three-bedroom house and it was just him, but I had to stay in the basement. That funky, nasty, dingy dark basement. Didn't even have a bed, just a mattress on the floor."

"Sounds rough."

"It was. But then I got tired of not doing nothing. I got tired of not having a plan to my day, staying in the basement. Not having no money. That's when I decided I wanted better."

Justin looked around her living room, Jill Scott coming from the stereo. "Looks like you succeeded."

"Yeah, but I want more. Y'know? I mean, working at Em Dee's is good and all, but I don't want to be there forever. I want to own stuff. A house, a car. Have a real life."

"You ever think about going back to school?"

"At my age?"

"You're just twenty-three."

"Four. Twenty-four. My birthday was in January."

"What's the dif? I didn't go back until I was twenty."

"Yeah, but you had a high school diploma. I ain't got one."

"Don't have one," he corrected.

Tarika smiled, self-conscious. "Sorry." That was another thing she liked about Justin. He gently corrected her as often as he could. "Don't have one."

"Well you can get one you know."

"What, a GED?"

"They have programs to help you. Get your GED and then get you into college."

"I ain't, I mean, haven't gone past the tenth grade."

"But you're smart Tarika. You said so yourself that you loved math and science. You can get a degree in math, chemistry or something. Become a pharmacist, a teacher, anything you want."

She looked at him, struck by the excitement in his eyes. "You think so?"

"I know so. You have to at least try. I think York might have some kind of program. I could find out for you."

"You'd do that?"

"Why not?"

The answer made her eyes water. "Because nobody ever really tried to help me. Nobody ever really cared about me like that."

"I do."

"Why?" Justin looked away, embarrassed. "No, tell me. I need to know."

"Because you have a good heart, that's why. Not too many women I meet these days do. I mean I can talk to you about anything and everything and it's cool, you know?"

After years of being looked at sideways every time she spoke about what she was really feeling, she knew exactly what he was talking about.

It was a feeling that revisited her when Justin took her home to meet his folks. Mrs. Edison was kind but there was no missing the disappointment in Mr. Edison's face, or the interrogative questions he asked.

"Do you go to York?" was his first question.

"No, not yet, but I plan to," Tarika had answered carefully.

"So where do you go?"

Tarika knew he was asking about college. "Nowhere. I work full-time."

"She works with me," Justin piped in quickly.

"McDonald's then."

"Yes."

"I see."

And there was no doubt Mr. Edison did. He looked at Tarika seeing all her life, none of it impressive. She slipped her eyes away from Mr. Edison's gaze, grateful when Justin took her hand, told her to come on and took her down the hall to his bedroom.

"Don't pay my dad any mind," he warned behind the closed door.

But it was way too late for that advice and Tarika kept her visits to Justin's house to a minimum.

Gina stood in her small kitchen, washing up dishes from dinner. It was the last bit of chores for the day and she was glad to reach that point.

She'd found routine helped her tremendously, gave her breathing room at the end of the day. The order of things was picking up Kanisha from after school, coming home and starting dinner while Kanisha did her homework.

By the time dinner was ready, Kanisha was finished with her homework and the two would sit down together, share a meal and talk. After that, Kanisha watched television for half an hour, then it was off to bed.

Gina would clean the kitchen and she would call Collin, the two of them talking as early evening settled into late. This evening was no different as she dialed him up. Who answered, was.

"Hallo?"

"Can I speak to Collin?"

"'Ooh calling?"

"Who's this?" Collin lived with his mother, but his mother never answered his phone.

"Ooh dis?"

"Can I speak to Collin please?"

"'E ain't 'ere."

"Do you know when he'll be back?"

"Me don't know."

"Can you tell him that Gina called."

"Maybe I will. Maybe I won't." The phone clicked in her ear.

On fire. That was the only way to describe Gina as she stared at the receiver not believing the conversation. A fire that remained with her later that evening when Collin returned her call.

Like machine gun fire, Gina shot off a round of questions without taking a single breath.

When Collin tried to answer, she shot off another round, of who, why, how come, how she and the like. The biggest one was: "Why she answering your phone?"

The more Collin tried to explain, the less Gina was hearing.

"He could be telling the truth," Tarika was telling her the next evening.

"What? That she had come by to see his mother and just happened into his room and just happened to pick up his phone?"

"Yeah."

"Like hell she did." Gina glared at her friend. "I know the fucking game, Tarika. Know cause I played the shit. Whether that bitch was telling the truth or not isn't the point. The point is how he even let her be answering his phone?"

"Well, she *was* visiting his mother."

"Why his mother let her go into his room in the first place?" Tarika had no answer for that. "You hearing me? I mean what kind of relationship that she got with his mother where she let her answer her son's phone? I don't got time for the bullshit."

"So what you gonna do?"

"I ain't playing those games Tarika cause I know how it ends."

"And how's that?"

"He playing both sides."

"How do you know he is?"

"He her baby daddy, that's how."

"Well, Rick was faithful to that woman, despite what you tried to do."

"Yeah, but I saw him changing in front of my own eyes. I saw him try to get back with me when he was still with her. So I know how it go." Gina took a breath. "Stuff always getting jacked up for me. Why can't nothing go right?"

"It's not jacked up Gina. It's just not easy, that's all."

"No, this is jacked. He all the way in the Bronx with her, with his momma letting her come in and run things." Gina's eyes grew forlorn. "I really like him. Really like him. And you know there ain't many men I do. I'm trying to make a new life for me, y'know? I ain't trying to be in no more drama and that's all this is, a whole lot of baby- momma-drama."

"It doesn't have to be Gina."

"He got a baby, the baby got a momma, there's always baby momma drama." She looked off. Her voice grew scared. "You think this is karma?"

Tarika looked at her friend, knowing she wanted to hear a lie, but she needed the truth. "Yeah Gina, I do."

With Rick and Gina living apart and Kanisha between them, a new routine had come into their lives. Depending on what Gina had planned, Kanisha spent time with Rick at least one day of the weekend.

It was Saturday afternoon and Gina had plans for Saturday night, so she and her daughter made the ten-block trek to Rick's house, the walk guaranteed to put Kanisha to sleep early.

Kanisha headed for her room as her parents finalized their plans.

"I'll drop her about noon tomorrow?" Rick asked.

"Yeah, that'll be good."

"Okay." Rick went to close the door but Gina stopped him.

"You got a minute?"

"Yeah, sure."

Gina came inside. "When you and Dajah was together, how you feel about me?"

The question took Rick by surprise. It was ancient history. "What do you mean?"

"You know, when you was with Dajah, how was you feeling about me?"

Rick hadn't wanted to answer the question back then and he didn't want to answer it now. He shrugged. "I don't know."

"You had to feel something Rick."

"What does it matter?"

"Matter a whole lot."

"Most of the time I was angry at you. You were always in my way. Every time I turned around, you was doing something."

That was a given. Gina needed more. "Besides angry."

"I'm not getting you."

"Was you still thinking about me?"

Rick laughed. "How could I not. You were trying to mess things up."

"No, not like that."

"Like what?"

She didn't want to come out and ask it. Didn't want to appear that she cared that he had started seeing somebody else. But she needed insight into Collin. "Did you ever think you wanted to get back with me?"

The answer was as obvious as the day was long. He *had* gotten back with her, if only for a hot second. "Yeah."

Gina shook her head. "I knew it."

"Knew what?"

She wasn't up to answering. She hadn't told Rick about Collin's child and made Kanisha promise she wouldn't either. The last thing Gina wanted to say was that she was with a man she couldn't trust.

"What Gina?"

She didn't want to, but she was flying in the dark. She needed real answers. "You know that cat I'm seeing?"

"The guy from the Bronx?"

"Yeah."

"Kinda."

"Well, he got a son, with this woman. And she's messing with me."

"Like you did with Dajah."

Another fact, but Rick saying it out loud stung. "Yeah. And Collin be saying she ain't nothing and he's not getting back with her and stuff, but I know what we went through and I need to know if you would have messed with me behind Dajah's back."

"I got to admit there were a few times I was tempted."

"What stopped you?"

"You stopped me."

Which didn't make Gina feel any better. Because if she was certain of one thing, that woman who was Collin's son's mother wouldn't try and stop a thing. If there was one thing she was certain, if Collin gave the slightest hint he was interested, she would be all in his stuff.

"I came real close," Rick was saying, remembering those moments. "Like the next second close. But you always put the brakes on it. It was one of the ways I realized how much you had changed."

"And if I hadn't stopped you and we went ahead and did something, would you have told Dajah?"

"Probably not."

Probably not.

It was the wrong answer. It was so wrong, so unwanted, it made Gina's head hurt on the walk home. If honest, upfront, no-game-playing Rick could have cheated on Dajah and never mentioned it, what did that say about smiling face, everything's-cool-with-life Collin?

For all Gina knew, that heifer could be rolling out of his bed this minute, or he, hers.

Gina wasn't going there. She was not going to let herself get all twisted up over something she had no control over. She would tell Collin when he came over later.

Tell him she couldn't see him anymore.

"Raining cats and dogs," Collin was saying as he stepped into the downstairs foyer, closing his dripping umbrella, stamping his wet shoes. He leaned in to kiss her lips, but Gina moved her head. He kissed the air. "What's up?"

Anger masked her face. "I ain't seeing you no more."

"What?"

"You heard me. I ain't going that route."

"What route?"

"You cheating on me."

"What are you talking about?"

"Talking about you and your child's momma, that's what I'm talking about. I'm not going get played like that. You got to go."

"Go? I just got here."

"I don't care. You got to go."

"You mean to tell me I came all this way in the rain and you're telling me I got to go?"

"That's exactly what I'm saying, Collin."

"I keep on telling you Gina I'm not with her."

"And that don't mean shit." Hurt jumped up into her soul. "So don't try and tell me that it do."

He looked at her, struck by the anguish. "You're really upset, aren't you?" She folded her arms, looked away. Collin leaned his wet umbrella against the wall. Reached for her.

She struggled out of his reach. "You got to go."

"Gina." He reached for her chin. And though she fought the pull of his hand, there wasn't much struggle in her. He peered into her face. "Hey."

A tear came. Then another, turning her lashes to black silk. "You can't walk away from her," she insisted. "You got to go."

"Let's go upstairs," he said softly. "Come on. Let's go upstairs and talk."

Seconds later they were on her couch. Seconds later Gina was baring her soul. "I've been there Collin. I've been her. I know what she can do. I know. And you say ain't nothing going to happen, but I know shit can."

"So what you want me to do, Gina?"

"I want her gone."

"How she's going to be 'gone,' she's my son's mother? I can't make her vanish," a bottom line Gina knew all too well. "She's his mother, how can she go away? I'm not going back, not after what she did."

"What she do?"

Collin's head shook. "Let's just say something that made me walk away."

"What?"

"I'm not going to talk about it."

"That's why you two broke up?"

"Exactly." His head shook. "I can't go back to that."

But Gina had done some things too and Rick had come back. "But that's the thing Collin. What you be saying and what you end up doing be two different things. I know. Rick said the same thing about me, but he came back."

"Did he stay?"

"No, but that's not the point. Point is, even after he swore up and down he was done with me, he wasn't."

"I'm not Rick."

But as far as Gina could see, he was. Both of them had gotten involved with women who had their child and did terrible things. "Yeah, you are."

Collin sat back. "So what you want me to do?"

"What I want can't be."

"Why not?"

"Cause she's your baby's momma. She's there forever."

"So you're going to let her come between us?"

"She was already there before I met you."

"But you're not with Rick."

"That's different."

"How is it different?"

"He stopped wanting me and then I stopped wanting him."

"But the point is you stopped, right? Who says I haven't stopped?"

Gina's head shook. "But it ain't about you. It's about her. And nothing's going to be right until she stops."

"So you're saying it doesn't matter what I want."

She looked at him plaintive. "That's the thing. Sometimes you don't know what you want until it's happening."

Collin shook his head. "He must have been one weak brother."

"Who?"

"Rick."

"Why you say that?"

"Listening to you talk. He obviously couldn't make up his mind."

In a lot of ways, Collin hit the nail on the head. "Yeah, he is kinda weak."

"But that's not me. When my mind is made, it's made. I left her over a year ago. The only time I see her is when I want to see my son. I go pick him up, or she drops him off. That's it."

"But your momma let her roam around your room."

Collin sighed. "Yeah, I know. And I've been trying to deal with that. But it looks like I'm going to have to make that move."

"Move?"

"I've been thinking about it for a while."

"What?"

"Getting a place of my own."

Something in Gina's heart lifted. "You mean that?"

"It's time. Past time. I can't really live my life up in my mom's place. I'd been saving for a car, but maybe I need to take that money and get a place of my own."

"In the Bronx?"

"I was thinking about someplace else."

"Like?"

"I always dug Queens. My job's in the city." He shrugged. "They got buses and trains here just like they do in the Boogie Down."

"You serious?"

"I've been in the Bronx all my life. A change of scenery would be nice." He took her hand up. "So we cool?"

"We a'right," Gina said with a reluctant smile. "But we'll be a whole lot better when you move."

But wanting something and getting it was often miles apart. While Collin had Queens' dreams, he couldn't afford the Queens reality. The places he could pay for were too run down to live in. And where he wanted to live, he couldn't pay the rent.

After a few weeks of searching he told Gina what she didn't want to hear. "Looks like I'll be in the Bronx."

Chapter Twenty-Two

Rick grimaced as the sweat rolled off his brow. He was pressing one hundred and twenty-five pounds with his legs, his personal trainer Dirk, a memory.

Rick had had a love/hate relationship with Dirk for the short time Dirk had been his personal trainer. In the time since, Rick had come to appreciate what Dirk had shown him. Rick took mental note of the paces Dirk put him through and kept up the routine after the free trial period ended. Moments came when he had wished he had Dirk to urge him on, but those times were rare.

"Twenty-five, twenty-six," Rick whispered as he pushed the bar with his legs. Thirty-five was his goal and though he felt making thirty would be a miracle, he struggled for that end line.

In the weeks since he had joined the gym, his body had responded favorably. Where once softness claimed his gut, his arms and the wings of his back, muscle now gleaned. His clothes were fitting better and some pants were too big in the waist.

Mental changes were happening for him as well. With every lift, push and flex, he felt himself grow a little sharper. With every drop of sweat, inhalation of breath, struggle to do 'one more,' the toxicities of his life began to break up and scatter. Rick was evolving.

"One twenty-five. Good."

Rick looked up and saw a firm behind in black spandex pants, the eight inches of brown skin between the sports bra and the waistband.

"Hey Brea," he managed.

"You're coming along well," she told him, headed across the room.

Brea was the head trainer and kept an eye out on those who had used a personal trainer. She had come along before while Rick had worked out, but the most she'd given was a nod. She had never given any words, never any indication of praise, until today.

It fueled Rick. Made the last three of his set easy. Energized, he headed for the dumbbells. Began working on his curls.

Tarika snatched up a medium order of French fries and swerved her body to the right avoiding the straight-from-the-fryer batch heading her way. Scooting around her manager, she went to the bin and plucked up a Fillet O' Fish. Slipping it into the bag, she looked inside as she headed to the counter, making sure the apple pie was inside.

"Ketchup?" she asked the customer.

"No."

Tarika tucked a few napkins in and closed the bag. Eased it across the counter. Eyes to the cash register, she said, "Welcome to McDonald's. Can I help you?"

"What's up girl?"

She knew the voice though she hadn't heard it in months. Her mouth fell open. Closed. "Hey," she said, near shy, fingers on the buttons, a line of people behind him. "What would you like?"

Sha-Keem smiled. The gold cap on one tooth, gleaming. "You."

Tarika shook her head to and fro. "No, serious. What you want. You got to order."

"I told you. You."

She looked at him. He was looking back. "If you're not ordering, you have to step aside," Tarika warned.

"What time you get off?"

"Six."

"A'ight. I'll be back then." Sha-Keem turned. Strolled out of the eatery, a part of Tarika's heart with him.

The West Indian Restaurant on Archer Avenue was filling up with the early evening dinner crowd. Tarika sat in the booth, sipping her soda, eyes everywhere but on Sha-Keem. She felt torn up inside, a part of her still wanting him, the other part knowing better. He himself had said she deserved better than him. That better was now in her life.

"Been hearing such good things about you I had to come see for myself," Sha-Keem said.

"How's Angie?"

His face frowned up. "Who?"

"You know. Angie. That girl you dropped me for?"

"She wasn't nothing."

"She must have been. You left me to be with her."

"I didn't leave you."

"Oh no?"

"No. I ain't walked away. You the one who did the walking."

"Because you told me too. You told me you wasn't good enough for me."

Sha-Keem eyes drifted a little. Came back at her. "And I been missing you every since."

"Oh really?"

"Why else you think I came to your job today? Why I came back?"

She shrugged indifferently, her heart feeling something different. She looked him over. Noticed that while his Roca Wear denim suit was neat and clean, the style was over a year old. She also noticed that the diamond in his ear was gone. The gold chain he wore on his wrist was missing too.

"Where you been?" she wanted to know.

"What you mean?"

"Few times I came through the block I haven't seen you."

"Got picked up."

"How long?"

"Six months. Just got out last week."

Suddenly his reason for showing up, taking her to dinner, talking about missing her became something else. His reappearance in her life had nothing to do with all those years they had had together. It had little to do with how she had gone to see him every day when he was locked in Riker's Island, or carrying his baby and miscarrying.

In a heartbeat the things she thought she'd seen in his eyes, the rekindling of the love they shared became nothing. Getting out of jail and no doubt needing a place to stay was the real reason. Tarika wanted to kick herself.

"Whatever you're going to ask, the answer is no," she said firmly.

"Wait, hold up, who said I was asking you anything?"

"I do."

"I don't want nothing, nothing but to see you. Spend some time with you, that's all."

"After all this time?"

"Yeah."

"No you don't. You just need something, like a place to stay. Well I'm sorry Sha-Keem, I can't help you." She slid out of the booth.

"You leaving?" She didn't answer. "But you already ordered."

"Cancel it. I got to go." Tarika moved past the tables, along the bar and towards the door. She waited until she was a half a block away before she let the tears fall, but she was dry-eyed by the time she got to her bus terminal.

Tarika didn't tell anyone.

She didn't tell Gina and she certainly didn't say anything to Justin, a part of her embarrassed for having had anything to do with a drug-dealing low-life like Sha-Keem in the first place.

Still, she had to admit he had been good for something. It was because of Sha-Keem that she had taken steps in her life to be about something. It had been his words that had encouraged her to make a better life for herself.

Before he had broken up with her, Tarika had no job, no place of her own and no goals. Thanks to him, she had that now and more. They were even, as far as she was concerned. All the years she had been there for him had made her debt to him paid in full.

Besides he would be okay without her help. Sha-Keem was streetwise. He'd land on his feet. Find some place to stay. Some other woman to love him and have his back.

Tucking her shirt into her pants, Tarika stood in the bathroom mirror washing her hands. Three raps came on the door before shouts of "Maintenance," arrived. Before she could even reply, the door was swinging open and there Antonio stood, easing in the bucket on wheels.

"You got all kind of niggas, don't you?"

"What?"

"I saw that other cat that came in here yesterday. Seen him around. Stone-cold thug." Antonio smirked. "Yeah, you playing both ends, ain't you."

"I don't know what you're talking about?"

"Nah? Hmmm. Well then maybe Justin might know. Think if I told him about that cat that you met after work, he'd know?"

"You need to mind your own damn business, Antonio."

"Yeah, and you need to be straight with niggas. I thought we had something going on."

"We did until you played cheapskate at the movies."

"That's what this is about, me forgetting my money?"

"No, that was just the wake up call I needed." She curled up her lip. "You ain't about nothing and nothing is the last thing I need."

"Going to college don't make you somebody."

Tarika looked at him. Shook her head. "You don't get it and I don't have time to make you." She moved toward the door. He was blocking it. "You already on probation. You want your ass fired?"

Antonio moved.

Tarika knew she had to tell Justin about Sha-Keem before Antonio did. She'd been trying to but every time she looked at Justin, she couldn't bring herself to do it.

He made her feel special.

She wanted him to keep on making her feel special. Telling him that she used to be with a drug dealer would change that. Admitting that not too long ago, getting with Sha-Keem had been her only goal, would change how Justin saw her and now he was seeing good things about her and for her.

She was about to take her GED with her eye on college, dreams she had never really had until now.

Smart, Tarika had come to play down her intelligence because everyone said she wasn't, or shouldn't be. Eventually she forgot that she had gotten all the way to Trigonometry before she dropped out of school. Eventually she forgot how doing a book report never was a challenge but a joy.

Nobody cared or wanted to know about her aptitude until Justin came into her life. He was certain that by summer, she would be enrolled in York. How could she tell him that once upon a time her dream had been being a main lady to a neighborhood thug? She couldn't.

But Antonio did.

* * *

"I need a McRib, and two Fillets," Tarika's manager called out from the counter.

Tarika grabbed the McRib and was about to take up two Fillet O' Fish when someone grabbed her arm. "I have to talk to you."

Tarika jumped. Found Justin beside her with fire in his eyes. She pulled back her arm. "I can't now."

"I need to talk to you."

She took the three sandwiches, dropped them into the bag her manager was holding. The manager nodded his head, held up five fingers to indicate 'five minutes.'

"Let me finish this order." She went to the soda dispenser and made the drink, got an order of fries together, feeling Justin's stare, his anger, *his disappointment*.

It was the disappointment that got her the most.

They went down to the basement into the storage room. The fluorescent light was bright and cast thick shadows around the boxes. Justin was staring at her, not saying anything and she wished he would get on with it.

His mouth pinched. "You dating a drug dealer?"

There were so many other things she expected, things like, *"You cheating on me with a drug dealer?"* She didn't expect the simple: "You dating a drug dealer?"

Her answer came easy and gratefully truthful. "No, I'm not dating no drug dealer."

"So how come Antonio is going around saying so?"

"I don't — ," she stopped herself. "I was seeing this cat a while ago, like last year. And he did come into McDonald's the other day and I did meet him after work and he did take me to dinner, but I'm not dating him. I'm not trying to get with him or even see him anymore."

"And he sells drugs?"

"No," more truth because if Sha-Keem had been back on the corner, he would have never searched her out.

"Well you better set Antonio straight because that's what he's saying."

"I tried to set him straight already, Justin and he isn't listening. He just wants me up in his face."

"Well, I'm tired of him up in mine," Justin declared, still angry. "Why you even go to dinner with him?"

"Because I used to love him."

"You still do?" Tarika shook her head no. "You're sure? I mean you went to dinner with him."

"I went with him, but I didn't even stay. I was out of there in like two minutes."

"How come?"

"Because he wasn't what I wanted anymore."

"I can't be rolling like this. I can't be involved with somebody involved in that."

"I don't want him. If I did, I would have stayed at the restaurant, but I didn't."

"But you did before."

"Before I met you, yeah, but you changed everything for me."

Justin believed her. But there was still another issue. "I'm getting real tired of him."

"Who?"

"Your boy."

"How many times I got to tell you, he ain't my boy."

"Well, whoever he is, I'm getting real tired of him."

"Just ignore him. He'll stop."

But Justin didn't have to. The manager knew Antonio was a slack worker and he couldn't have him stirring up trouble between two of his best employees. The manager gave him his walking papers the next day, with the warning that if he came back into the restaurant he would be charged with trespassing.

Dusk.

There was a quiet to the world and even though Gina didn't notice it, she did notice how every day brought a little more daylight. Just past six in the evening, the street lamps were competing with the not quite dark sky as she and Kanisha headed up the street.

"Burgers sound good?" she was asking her daughter as she put her key into the front door of the house.

"Uh huh."

"I think we have some cheese. We can have some cheeseburgers." Gina wasn't up to much more than that. It was Thursday and she was weary from her workweek.

They were making their way upstairs when Gina heard her phone ring. Hurrying to unlock the door, she raced across the tiny living room. Snatched up the receiver. Said a breathy "Hello?"

"Collin dere?"

"Excuse me?"

"Me say is Collin dere?"

It took her a second or two to realize who was calling. Another second to understand that somehow his baby's momma had gotten her phone number. "Sybil, I don't know what games you playing, but don't call my house no damn more."

Gina slammed down the phone and stared at it, on fire, unable to believe who had been on the other end. Before she thought about it, she hit star sixty-nine, listened to the number and hit the 'one' button. She waited while the phone rang and rang. At the fifth ring, she knew they weren't going to pick up.

She hung up, fuming. She dialed another number, waited for them to pick up. "Tell that bitch to stop calling my house."

"What?"

"You heard me? She just called here looking for you and I'm not having it."

"Sybil?"

"Yeah, her."

"When did she call?"

"A few minutes ago. Said she was looking for you, knowing damn well you wasn't here."

"I'm sorry Gina."

"Not as sorry as her ass is going to be if she call here one more time. I ain't playing Collin. You better tell her."

"I don't even know how she got the number."

"It don't matter how. She better not call again, you understand? You handle your business." Gina hung up the phone, seething but more so hurt.

God was putting her through what she'd put Dajah through. Every funky little trick she'd used was being visited upon her. That woman was messing with her head the same way she'd messed with Dajah's and it felt awful.

Beyond the anger and hurt, the feeling of being powerless, under someone else's control, was overwhelming. Gina was sure even if she changed her number Sybil would still get a hold of it. It didn't help that she was two boroughs away.

Gina liked Collin and she felt Collin liked her just as much. But his child's mother was getting in their way.

"Momma, you okay?"

There had been a time in Kanisha's young life that asking such a question would have meant angry words in her face, a backhand to her cheek. But time had changed things for them and asking was as natural as breathing.

"I'm alright Kanisha." But Gina wasn't, not by a long shot.

She made an appointment to see her counselor, pouring her heart out two days later as she sat in Mrs. Jones' office.

"And you think it's karma?" Mrs. Jones asked.

"Yeah. All that stuff I did."

"Did, the key word Gina, as in the past. You've changed a lot since then, am I right?" Gina nodded "Okay. So forgive yourself for all the bad things you did and move on. Don't go around thinking life's going to be bad forever because you've done some bad. Keep on being positive and positive things will happen for you."

But that wasn't how Gina's life worked. She knew it didn't. A part of her knew that Mrs. Jones knew it too.

That night Gina dreamed of Jefferson standing in his kitchen, looking as alive and healthy as ever. He was cooking something good and the smell of food drew her.

He was looking down into the pots, smiling and humming. She opened her mouth to call him, but before she could get the first syllable of his name out, she woke up. *More stuff I don't have no more.*

The thought made her weep.

Chapter Twenty-Three

Her hands felt like claws, digging too deep and too harsh into the skin on his back.

Jeff squirmed away from Lisa's embrace, his orgasm too far away to even want it. He had grown soft inside of her seconds ago, but if Lisa noticed, she was going on as if she hadn't.

Rolling on his back, his condom-enclosed penis flapped wetly against his thigh. Bringing an arm over his forehead, he hid his eyes beneath the weight of it.

"What's wrong?"

He knew her question would come. Some part of him knowing that the question, this moment, would arrive. Jeff sensed, as he always had — some part of him anyway — that the life he led, the life he had purposely chosen, the disconnections he had been operating on since Mya betrayed him, would come to an end.

What he wasn't prepared for was confessing it. What twisted his stomach was opening up his mouth and saying: *"Us together is about sex and I want more than that, just not with you."*

He could have said those words to Syreeta and she would have been okay with it, cried perhaps, but would have allowed him to get up, get dressed and go. But Lisa wasn't Syreeta. Lisa had been with him the longest and would no doubt argue against his conclusion.

She had been there from the beginning of his waywardness. She had clocked in many hours of giving him all the space he needed. She was deeply vested into this person he had become, staying by him through thick and thin. No, she would demand more than that simple summary.

"Jeff?"

There was a little panic in her voice now; a slight rise of fear and uncertainty. He knew she would reach out and shake him a little if he didn't respond. But the words were locked in his throat.

He rolled to his side, sat up, feet on the floor, head hung down a bit. He felt her cool hand on his cooling back and resisted the urge to flinch. He swallowed, moved different words to the front of his mouth; different words — the kind that wouldn't hurt as much.

"Nothing, everything." He forced his head in her direction. "I got to go." He stood and began searching the gloom for his underwear.

"Go?"

He stopped his search to look at her again, sorry in the worst way. He had signed her up for this journey and she had come along willingly, but it had been truly a road to nowhere and nothing was what she was going to get. "Yeah, I got to go."

For four years she had been faithful to him in a way he refused to be faithful back. For four years she had played the happy camper thrilled to be at Camp Jeff. Now that her stay was over, there would be no little ribbon given, no final fun-filled night around the camp-fire, just a maw of time she'd wasted with a man who did not love her back.

Jeff wondered how she would survive that, if she would survive it. He found himself wondering what her life was going to be like tomorrow when she awoke with the knowledge that he was gone from her life.

Would she cry? Call her girlfriends or suck it up? Would she badger him, harass him, try to change his mind? Would she get desperate, obsessive, hate him forever?

Jeff reached down and got his underwear, his slacks. Headed out the room. There in the soft hush of Lisa's sea-blue bathroom, he allowed the answer to her question — *"What's wrong?"* to come.

What was wrong was Dajah wasn't going away.

She was not going to disappear from his memory, his mind, but more importantly, his heart. He could not just dust off his hands and get busy with whomever he chose for which evening.

Dajah wasn't going to become just another failed conquest; a little-young-thing that didn't fall for his okey-doke. She was better than that. More than that. Special.

It took weeks of marathon dating, weeks of bedding women just for the hell of it to accept that she evoked something in him that nobody had in a long time.

It took weeks of hope and days of fear every time he went to

Jones Beach to get a grip on how he felt about her. It took pulling out his sketch book and sketching like he hadn't in a long time to accept she had opened something in him that been repressed for so long.

Once the knowledge came, it became a question of what he was going to do with it. Once the knowledge came, it became a question of whether he was ready to sever all those loose ties and attempt that true commitment.

Once the knowledge came, the question: *Are you ready?* moved through him with the answer riding its coattail.

Yes, he was.

Beyond the door waited the first person he would tell it to. The first person who would hear that he was going back to the Jeff he used to be. Back to real commitment, a real relationship.

Sliding the condom into some toilet paper, Jeff put on his underwear, his pants, looked himself in the mirror, then headed back towards the bedroom.

She was dressed in a silk bathrobe, the white shine of the material complimenting the rich chocolate hue of her skin. Her hair was tussled and her eyes were wide. Fear was doing a slow tango inside of them, hints of anger clinging to the sides.

It made the words inside of Jeff congeal. He swallowed, swallowed again. He owed her so much more than this moment, but there was nothing else he had for her. He hoped she would suck it up. Accept it. "Remember the day we met?" he found himself asking, a sincere smile coming into him.

She blinked, confusion swirling up in her fear. "What do you mean?"

He sat on the bed. The conversation would not be brief. "You remember that day? I was out at the track, doing my nice, smooth four miles an hour around the track and you whizzed past me, a vision in white."

Lisa looked off, trying to mentally snare the incident. A soft smile came into her. Ease shifted down the tension in her shoulders. "Yeah, I remember."

"All white," Jeff offered, shaking his head in old amazement. "White top, white shorts, white sneakers, white headband. I couldn't have missed you if I wanted to."

"I was into white back then."

"Yeah, I remember. And you had on some type of perfume."

"Body spray."

"Yeah, body spray and it caught the wind right and slipped up my nose and soon I found myself running to catch up with you."

"Which made you struggle because I was moving."

"Yes, you were. So I set pace with you, trying to catch your eye and you were just ignoring me."

"Because I didn't know you."

"Yeah, but you wanted to ... " his voice trailed off. He shifted on the bed. Reached for her hand. "That guy you met that day, the Jeff you saw that day, it wasn't the real me."

Lisa took her hand back. "What do you mean it wasn't the real you."

"It was the hurt me, the dejected me, the sad me, the angry me, but it wasn't the real me."

"What are you trying to say?"

He found her eyes. Forced himself to look at her. "What I'm trying to say is, back then I had just had my heart torn out and tossed into a meat grinder and I was looking for revenge." Jeff looked off. "Got it too. Sometimes I'm amazed at how easy I got it."

"What are you trying to say?"

He sighed, the hard heavy part, struggling up his throat. "I'm trying to say that for the last four years I've wasted your time and mine. For the last four years, I've been holding onto a hurt that I've let hurt me too long. For the last four years I've been running away from real relationships and I'm tired of running."

"So what we had wasn't real?"

He looked at her, waiting for the absurdity of her statement to find her. "You know it wasn't."

Lisa looked off. Looked back at him. "No, it wasn't twenty-four-seven with us, but we were together."

"And what do you think was happening when we weren't?"

That was the one question Lisa never really asked herself, not ever. The one question she'd been avoiding and ducking since she'd met Jeff. She wasn't up to answering it now. Her head shook. "It doesn't matter what was happening when you weren't with me. All that matters was what happened when you were."

His eyebrow went up. "I ran a good game Lisa, that's all. I knew all the moves, what to say, when to say it. But it never came from here." He touched his heart. "Not in the way it was supposed to. You know that."

She did but when she was with Jeff, he made her feel like she was his all. When she was with him, those other women he saw didn't exist, not until he walked out her front door or she, his.

He saw her at least once a week; called her twice as many and they had shared quite a few New Year's and Christmases together. He bought her nice things, was attentive and never forgot a birthday.

"So it was all a lie," she found herself asking.

"No, not a lie, but not how a real relationship is supposed to go."

"Because you never wanted one."

"Exactly. My point exactly. And now I do want one."

His words made her smile but the tone in which he delivered them — pain-filled, halted the effort. She pressed on. "So, we'll have one." But even as she said that, Lisa knew it wasn't an option or even his consideration.

"We can't."

"Why?"

"We didn't have one for all those years. How could we start now?"

There was a truckload of insinuation in his question. A truckload of funky, unkind, implication in all that lay beneath that bottom line. Anger flared up in her voice. "You are really something, you know that? All those years of being with you and now you're saying I'm not good enough?"

"It's not about good or bad Lisa. That's not what this is about."

"So what is it then?"

She wasn't really listening. She was stewing. Jeff answered anyway. "It's about the Jeff I used to be, before you, before that other mess. It's about someone coming into my life and taking me back to that, that's what it's about."

"Who?"

"You don't know her."

"Syreeta?"

"No, not Syreeta. It's not Jill, not Joy, none of them. It's someone I recently met."

"And she's done what I couldn't." It wasn't a question.

"Yes, she has."

Lisa stood up. "Fine Jeff. Just fucking fine. You finished?"

He looked at her, but could not hold her gaze. "I guess I am."

"Then will you kindly get your shit and go." With that she walked out of the bedroom. But there were more words for him as he went to leave the final time. "You can't do what you've done to people and not get some payback. You remember that, hear? And when she do to you what you've done to me, don't expect me to be here waiting to pick up the pieces."

The words bounced off of Jeff like Teflon. As far as he was concerned, they were without merit or weight. He had already experienced the pain and suffering she was forewarning. For the last four years he had been in that desert.

His oasis was finally up ahead.

When Jeff got in, he wasn't surprised that Kelly had crapped on the living room area rug. He was just disappointed.

It had been a while since he had taken Kelly on her weekend romps along the sands of Jones Beach, and Far Rockaway just wasn't cutting it for his dog, he knew that. But until recently, he didn't want to run into Dajah.

Still, discipline was discipline. Grabbing his dog by her collar, he dragged her across the floor. Kelly knew what was coming and didn't want it. She tried to find traction against the hard wood. But Jeff was stronger and soon Kelly's snout was being rubbed against the pile.

"Not in the house, Kelly," he insisted. "Not. In. The House."

When Jeff released her, Kelly went scampering to the kitchen. Jeff followed her, getting a paper towel and wetting it. Then with the care of a mother tending a newborn, Jeff wiped his dog's nose, feeling the brunt of his dog's punishment. In truth, it was his fault.

His marathon dating life and fear of a woman named Dajah had totally interrupted his dog's routine. If things went the way he hoped, both his and his pet's life would have normalcy again.

Leashing up Kelly, he took her for a late night walk in the park. When he got back home, he sat himself down and picked up the phone. He had some news he needed to share. He had waited all too long to share it.

"Congratulations," was how he began.

"Jeff?"

"Yeah."

"This is a surprise."

"Why?"

Dajah laughed. "Because I don't do share and the last time I checked, you did." Still, it was nice to hear his voice again.

"Well things have changed."

"Really."

"Yes, really. Good change, the right change. Long overdue change."

Change. Something different. Something other. "So what happened?" She truly wanted to know.

"You happened."

"Me?"

"No one else but."

"What did I do?" But Dajah suspected what she'd done. She'd given him a taste of her power and her glory and had refused to lower her standard on what she expected in a relationship.

"You made me think, feel, question. You made me want something I haven't wanted in a while. But mostly you reminded me of how life used to be and I miss it."

"Being with just one person?"

"Yes."

"So why did you stop?"

His throat grew tight. "A woman I met. Her name was Mya."

"Mya?"

"Yeah."

"Sounds a bit like my name."

"I know."

"What happened?"

"We met and got together. I fell in love. Thought she had too. But her history had messed up her mind. She was going through that bad-love-is-good-love thing, except she didn't know it and neither did I until we were supposed to get married."

That surprised Dajah. "You were getting married?"

"Key word: Supposed. Anyway. Date set, invites, the whole nine and she runs into an ex and cheats on me with him. Tells me. I was torn right in two. She tried to get back with me, but I was too angry to let her. Anyway, she does some soul searching, writes me a letter, explaining how her parent's screwed-up marriage made her see love all wrong. She got herself together and went on and met somebody else. Told me I had to get on with my life too."

"Did you?"

"Not really. I stopped believing in the happily-ever-after thing."

"That's when it started?"

"Yep."

"How long ago?"

"What? Four years and some change?"

Dajah was silent for a second. "That's a long time."

"Yeah, but it didn't feel like a long time until I met you. You came along and I started remembering the old me. The things I used to do, like drawing."

"You stopped drawing?"

"Yeah, I did. Mya happened and I just wasn't interested in it anymore. Then I meet you on the beach one day and within a few days, I'm sketching like I never stopped."

"I guess my stuff is mojo," she said with a laugh, glad for the phone call, her abilities, his coming around. Dajah was glad the good times weren't lost forever. But more importantly, she was glad she held her ground, didn't give in, give away what was precious, important.

"No. I haven't met anyone like you in a long time," he went on to say. "You got real balls and I like that."

She was quiet for a moment, much behind them. Even more in front. "So how have you been?"

The truth was on him, in him, about him and through him. "Tired. Very, very tired. I didn't know running from something could be so hard."

"So you admit it."

"Admit what?"

"That you were running."

"I didn't know it at the time, but I do now and it's nice being off that treadmill." He paused and Dajah knew what was coming. "You want to get together tomorrow?"

But instead of an answer, she gave a question of her own — the one she'd made the mistake in not asking before. "You tell all the women in your life it's over?"

"Some. Not all."

"Well, when you have, then give me a call and we'll see about getting together."

"You're a tough one aren't you?" There was a delight in his voice that warmed her.

"No, I just know what I want and need. I forgot for a hot minute, but that's over."

"Makes sense," he decided.

"What makes sense?"

"Why you were at the beach in the dead of winter. Heartache sent you there."

"I wouldn't call it heartache."

"No?"

"Well, I mean, yeah, but not like a sobbing wreck heartache."

"What then?"

Dajah sighed. Tried to gather the sum of it all into a single train of thought. "It was more like emotionally, I was scattered. I needed to get myself grounded again."

"So, what was his name?"

"Why?"

"Just curious."

"Rick." But the name felt weird on her tongue.

"Rick?"

"Yeah, Rick."

"What happened?"

"Let's just say that he had a hard time dividing his attention between me, his daughter and his daughter's momma."

"Oh."

"Exactly. I broke my biggest rule over that one. I swore up and down I wouldn't do it again."

"Makes sense," Jeff said after a while.

"And that's all I'm allowing in my life now — things that make sense. Anyway, you have some phone calls to make, so I'm going to let you get to them."

"Who says I was going to make them tonight, or that I even will? I mean, technically, I can tell you that I did, but didn't. How will you know?"

Dajah chuckled. "Oh, I'll know. Fool me once, shame on me. Fool me twice, it ain't gonna happen." Not anymore.

"Okay, I get your drift."

"Good. Talk to you later." Dajah hung up. After years of wanting someone who treated her the way she wanted, the opportunity had finally arrived.

It took three days for Jeff to make those phone calls; three days of preparing himself for the cursing out and the tears. While none of the women were happy he was saying goodbye to them, they were extremely unhappy when they found out why.

They all wanted to know who she was, what made her so special. Jeff didn't relinquish a name or exactly what she had done to turn his head, but he did tell them that it was what he wanted and there was no changing his mind.

Some cried. Some hung up only to call him back. Some tried to get a face-to-face to plead their case. It was the longest three days of his life.

But when the fourth day arrived and the dust settled, he picked up his phone a fourth time in as many days, making the only phone call he had been looking forward to.

"They're gone, so now can I see you?"

Dajah told him yes.

She was back at Jeff's apartment, but this time was different. This time when Dajah entered Jeff's apartment, it was a whole new perspective, a verified outcome.

This time when Dajah entered Jeff's place, she knew whatever did or didn't happen between them would be real and valid on both sides.

She was easing off her coat when Kelly appeared, paws landing on her breast, sharp nails catching on the mohair of her sweater.

Dajah scratched the red head, allowed the long wet tongue to lick her cheek, pleased that Kelly not only remembered her, but missed her.

"Hey girl. Hey. How've you been hmm? How've you been?" She gave the dog one more good head scratch and eased her away. Kelly sat looking up at her, the thick, furry, red tail sweeping the floor.

"Okay Kel, that's enough." Jeff's words got the dog moving, Kelly walking off to the corner and plopping down on a small area rug. "Let me get your coat." Dajah handed it over, looking around. "Have a seat." She took one on the couch.

Jeff disappeared down the short hall and when he came back, he had a long cedar chest. "I'm going to draw you again."

"How come?"

"Because this is our real start and I want to capture you." Looking around, he pointed towards the window. "Over there will be good." Dajah leaned against the wall. "No, on the floor. Casual."

She got down on the floor, folded her legs Indian style.

"No, relax."

"I am relaxed," but her smile was making her lips twitch.

"Relax," he insisted.

"Should I keep on smiling?"

"Do you want to keep on smiling?'

Yes, she did. Dajah wanted the feeling she had never to leave her. The joy to always be her's. She wanted forever the man who knew so much, had so much, could do so much. She wanted Jeff for a lifetime. "Yeah, I'll keep smiling."

Her eyes shifted to the paper he was drawing on. "Un uh, don't look down, just look straight like you're looking at me."

It was hard but she did and in less than four minutes, he was finished. "Wow. You are good."

"It's not hard."

"Easy for you to say. Do you do murals?"

Jeff laughed. "Never attempted one, but I'm sure I could if I had to." He thought for a minute. "They're having the big art show down at the Jacob Javits Center in a few weeks. Want to go?"

"Sure. Why not."

"Great. And after we can go to this restaurant in Soho."

"You ever walk around the city at night this time of year?"

"Not in a while, but yeah."

"Instead of going all the way downtown, let's do that."

Jeff thought about it. Nodded his head. "Cool."

Her better half.

She had one now. Verified and certified, Dajah was the exclusive in Jeff's life. So it was with great joy that she got on the phone with Frieda to share the latest in life. It was with real splendor as she revealed how her stance had paid off, no ifs, ands or buts about it.

"All because I didn't ask that first time," she was saying to her friend over the phone. "The most important question I'm supposed to ask and I just didn't."

"Maybe if you had asked back then, he wouldn't have gone through the process that he went through. I mean, if you had gotten your answer before the end of that first date, that would have been that and he would have never gotten the chance to know you like he did and come to appreciate what you bring to his table."

"Maybe."

"So, everything happened just the way it was supposed to."

"Yeah, but what was the 'Rick mess' about?" A far away history, it still bothered her from time to time. It bothered Dajah that she had given so much and gotten so little in return.

"I think you were suppose to get Rick to get his 'house' in order. I think you were suppose to make Rick realize that that little girl wasn't the one for him, that he deserved better."

"Just not with me."

"Right. But then, if you hadn't gone through all that mess, you would have never been out at the beach in the middle of winter and ..."

"I would have never met Jeff."

"Bingo."

But it didn't seem like a grand prize. Yes, she had wanted a man like Jeff all her life, but what she went through to get with him still turned her gut.

"Sometimes you got to give a lot to get more," Frieda was saying.

"Yeah, but I just wished it could have happened sooner and easier."

"What does that matter now Day? The Rick drama is behind you and Jeff is with you. Everything else isn't important."

Dajah thought about it. She knew she still had a ways to go before she could forget all that had been, but she made a deal with herself to embrace all that would be.

Chapter Twenty-Four

Touch and go and on the lookout, that's how things were proceeding for Gina as she struggled to believe in what she had with Collin. To his credit, there had been no more calls from Sybil and to his credit Collin hadn't disappointed her about anything of late.

This was the main reason Gina was waiting outside the subway station in Manhattan, rain coming down and Kanisha by her side. It was Easter Sunday and Gina and Collin had planned to take their children to the Easter egg hunt in Central Park together.

Rain or shine, the Easter egg hunt always went on as scheduled.

The temperature was in the low forties and the sky had dripped and poured throughout the day. Regardless, parents dressed their children up in their Easter finest and came out to participate.

Brand new patent leather shoes became coated with muck. Pretty pink tights held splotches of dried mud from tromps through the soggy, dead grass. Shirley Temple curls unfurled and sagged and mud-splattered Roco-wear, Fubu and Sean John denim outfits were everywhere you looked.

Gina stood by the entrance of the subway station, a large umbrella over her head, a small one over Kanisha's. The puffy, lemon cream-colored crinoline of Kanisha's Easter dress poked out from beneath her little down jacket like a tutu. Her patent leathers shoes with the one-inch heel was still trying to hold their shine

When Gina had selected her own outfit, it was with the notion that Central Park would be sunny and dry. She never thought she'd have to stand around in the rain waiting. But that's exactly what she was doing and her narrow-toed shoes was sodden and pinching. The bottom of her soles had started to burn.

It had been a long, cold, wet journey from their apartment in Jamaica, Queens to the subway station at the edge of Central Park.

The twenty minutes they had been waiting only made the journey colder and wetter.

Gina looked at her watch. Looked up the street. She scrunched her toes up inside the tight, wet shoes, trying to warm them, get the blood going. She pulled out her cell phone and dialed a number. Listening to it ring, it went unanswered.

She looked up the street again, down behind her into the bowels of the subway. Whispered softly to herself, "Come on." No sooner had her plea left her did she spot Collin coming down the street and his son, CJ, by his side.

There before her was the reason she had taken a bus and two trains into the heart of Manhattan on such a cold, miserable day. The reason why she wore her ninety-dollar shoes in weather that would ruin them. Why she had done her hair, put on some make-up and had stood out in the cold drizzle with her daughter.

She broke out into a smile. Tapped Kanisha's hand. "There they are. Come on." Mother and daughter headed up the street, the wait over — a new drama about to begin.

"Hey," she said, reaching for Collin. She felt him stiffen. Felt his pull back. Watched his body shift to the right.

It was then that Gina noticed the woman behind him, a smile on her face as chilly as the day.

"Gina, this is Sybil. Sybil, Gina."

Sybil, CJ's mother and Collin's ex. Sybil, a perfect name for her because only a witch would invade their plans like she was doing.

The hurting feet, the chill that seeped into her body grew worse as the question Gina longed to ask bunched up on her tongue. As the group of what should have been four, but was five, made their way to the Easter egg hunt site, Gina wanted to know one thing: *Why was she here?*

She wanted to ask but Sybil was only three feet behind them. Gina sensed just letting Sybil hear her question would mean Sybil would win. There was no way Gina was going to let her. Gina was in the middle of a battle. It was a war in which she herself had waged.

She understood fully what Sybil wanted. Gina wasn't going to give it to her.

She wasn't going to get loud. She wasn't going to get funky.

Gina was going to keep a smile on her face and ignore the bitterness of her heart, the pain in her feet. She was glad she had worn her outfit despite the elements. Glad that her short leather jacket emphasized the curve of her hips, the roundness of her behind.

Gina was glad she had kept the zipper on her jacket zipped only midway; that the wrap shirt showed pretty brown cleavage, a place that Collin had looked at often. She was glad that she looked good and sexy, unlike Sybil who had on a long trench coat like she was going off to some job. The dark-brown Timberland boots were unflattering as well.

After the hunt, Collin would be coming back to her place for dinner. After the hunt, Sybil would be going home all by her lonesome.

"You okay?" came a voice from behind Gina.

Gina looked back. "Excuse me?"

"Me say, are you okay? Dem shoes cute and ting but ya walking funny like dem hurt."

Gina found the woman's eyes. Smiled a caustic smile. "Hundred dollar shoes don't hurt."

"Just dat da way you walking."

"My walking is just fine." Gina turned her head back around. Felt Collin's hand brush against hers. It was enough to make the smile she held genuine.

Since Sybil had on the boots, she followed the children around as they hunted for eggs. Gina kept a close eye on Kanisha, not trusting Sybil to do it.

Collin took the opportunity to explain. "She's taking CJ to her mother's house in Brooklyn for dinner after this. It's the only reason why she's here."

"You still coming back with us, right?"

"I got to take the ride with her."

"Why?"

"There's this cat I got to go see."

"Today?"

"Only day I can. He's leaving for Jamaica tomorrow and I need him to take something for me."

Gina's eyes narrowed. "Something like what?"

"No drugs or nothing like that, but I need him to handle some business for me back in Jamaica."

"What kind of business, Collin?"

"Family business, that's all Gina."

"Why couldn't you have done it yesterday? Why you have to do it today? You know we was supposed to be together."

"I know and I will. Just that I have to take a run out to Brooklyn first, then I can come by."

But Gina didn't like it. Suddenly the idea that she wasn't going to let Sybil win this round became moot. It wasn't Sybil she had to worry about. It was Collin.

No doubt he had somebody he had to catch up with in Brooklyn, but Gina knew for a fact that first he would go to Sybil's mothers house, if to do nothing else but dry off. No doubt he would insist he couldn't stay, had other places to be, but they would ask him to stay for dinner. Even if Collin said no, his son would beg him.

The outcome would be what should have been a quick trip to Brooklyn before heading to her place would become hours.

Her cool vanished. "You lying Collin and you know it. You ain't just running out to Brooklyn. You going to be there for a while."

"No Gina. No. I just got to run over Oliver's place, give him some papers and then I'm back on the train."

"So you're not going to her momma's house."

"Well yeah, I got to at least pop my head in. Say hi. I can't go all the way to Brooklyn without dropping by."

"'Specially today, right?"

"What do you mean?" Gina looked at him a long time. Rolled her eyes and walked away. He called after her. When she didn't respond he caught up with her. "How come everything I say is suspect?"

Gina didn't answer. Allowed her eyes to do the talking. They drifted and settled on the woman in the trench coat and the Timberland boots. "You think if I wanted her, I'd even be here today? Here on this funky, nasty, cold-ass day? The only reason why I'm here is because of you."

"How do I know that Collin?"

"Because I'm telling you."

"You say you here because of me? Fine. You go to Brooklyn, you pop into her momma's, give your hello, go by that cat's house and then get your ass on the train to me, you hear?"

Gina headed onto the field, ignoring the heels of her shoes sinking into the mud. She called out to Kanisha, waved her back. Told Kanisha they were leaving.

The heat, turned off a few days ago was missing in action when Gina got back home. She expected some toasty warmth when she stepped through the front door. She expected the cast iron radiator pitched under the double window to fill the tiny foyer with the smell of dry, dusty heat. But the air smelled of nothing.

She placed her cold hand on the cast iron. Not a drop of warmth there. She was wet and Kanisha was wet and beyond getting out of their soggy shoes and drenched coats, they needed to warm up.

Upstairs, Gina turned on the oven and cracked the door open. Standing before it, both she and Kanisha stripped down to their undies. Made a pile of their wet things.

It didn't feel like Easter Sunday and not even the colorful plastic bag full of candy-filled plastic eggs made it so. Even with the glazed ham Gina had made and the roast chicken and collards made with smoked turkey because Collin didn't eat pork; even with the candied yams, the macaroni and cheese already prepared, it felt like just another rainy Sunday.

When they warmed up a bit, Gina told Kanisha to go change into her pajamas and Gina found her flannels. Collin said he was coming by later, but she knew he would call later to say he was delayed.

The doorbell rang.

Her heart leaped. Gina dashed down the stairs, misery leaving her, a fast smile coming on her face. But when she looked out of the rain-slicked pane, her smile vanished. No, it wasn't Collin, just her mother with a huge Tupperware container in her hand.

"I made a coconut cake. Didn't feel right eating it all by myself."

Gina hadn't made any plans with her mother because they

never made plans together on Easter or any of the other holidays. But hearing her mother say she didn't want to eat the cake by herself changed the picture a bit. It made her remember Jefferson was dead and he had been all her mother had.

"We ain't eat yet. We just got in."

"Well then, you can have this for dessert." Her mother handed over the cake, "Don't eat too much. It's rich." Doreen Alexander hesitated for a second, then spoke, "Well, happy Easter." She turned. Opened her umbrella and headed down the stairs.

"Wait Momma." Doreen turned slowly, relief moving through her. "We got a bunch of food. You welcome if you ain't eat yet."

"I don't want to be no bother," Doreen said quickly.

"Ain't no bother. Just me and Kanisha."

Gina's mother smiled, made her way into the hallway and then up the stairs. Despite the chill in the air and the fumes from the gas stove, it was one of the best dinners Doreen Alexander had had in a while.

You couldn't dance with the devil and expect not to get burned. Gina wasn't sure where she had heard the expression, or if she had read it in a book, only that it made a lot of sense to her. Easter was the reckoning.

Her mother had stayed only a little while, long enough to eat and spend a few minutes with Kanisha. By five o'clock that rainy Easter day, the sun was gone and what remained of the daylight was dark, dreary and wet.

It didn't help that Gina didn't have any heat and her request to her landlord was not granted. "After the first. No more heat till October," she was told. It didn't help that the stove only made the kitchen comfortable and her bedroom in front felt down right icy.

It didn't help that Collin didn't call till ten o'clock that night, full of an apology she couldn't use. Or that the baked chicken she had made just for him, the collard greens she had used smoked turkey instead of ham hock and the potato salad she'd prepared without onion because that's how he liked it, was for someone who hadn't shown up.

The writing had been on the wall from the moment she'd found out Collin had a son. And as much as she liked him, as much as he made her laugh, made her feel special, Gina wasn't up to any baby-momma-drama.

She didn't want to say goodbye to Collin. Knew she'd missed him terribly. But she knew about sharing a man. The women always lost.

At six thirty-seven on a Monday afternoon, Gina called Collin and told him she couldn't see him anymore. At eight forty-five that night, her doorbell was ringing, Collin coming to plead his case. By eight fifty-eight, thirteen minutes after he arrived he was leaving.

Collin didn't want to end things, but there was no doubt Gina already had.

A year ago if someone had told Gina that she would be going to visit her mother, just for the sake of visiting, she would have cursed them out, then called them a lying ass.

But life had changed and how she felt before wasn't how she felt now. There was no love fest when she showed up at her mother's front door, but there was a much needed feeling of connecting, a connection that had began at their impromptu Easter dinner.

Much of their conversation centered around Jefferson, the digging up of memories did both women good. Gina never stayed longer than an hour, enough time to share a meal and a few memories, but the more she visited, the easier her relationship with her mother grew.

It was after one those visits while she and Kanisha were making their way home, Gina ran into Mustapha.

She hadn't seen him in nearly half a year and had considered her days with a high-ranking drug dealer over, but when he rolled up to the curb in his Hummer H2, the music so deep and loud it entered her bones like ecstasy. When he slowed, rolled down the window and shouted, "Where you headed?" she didn't stop to think.

"Home."

"You want a ride?"

She did. The day was warm and the trek to the bus stop was a few blocks away. Standing and waiting for a bus, or getting a ride in a Hummer H2 that looked showroom fresh was a no-brainer.

Gina put Kanisha into the back and she hopped into the front. Bopped her head to the beat as Mustapha pumped the music.

"Month of Sundays," he shouted over the thump of the music, then turned it down.

"Ain't been that long." But Gina knew it had been. Her relationship with Mustapha had been so brief, she couldn't even call it real. The attraction had lasted less than a month.

Though she had been with him a few times afterwards last year, it had been out of loneliness and boredom. Not because she liked him. She didn't.

But she did like the way people on the street were staring at his bright yellow ride. She also liked the fact that she was riding in the passenger seat.

"You just disappeared."

"I had things to do."

"Oh yeah?"

She looked at him, saw the smile that had snagged her so long ago. "Yeah."

"Like what?"

"Like getting my life together."

"Hmm. Imagine that."

"What that mean?"

"What you think it mean?" He reached up in the sun visor. Produced a Tiparillo, except Gina knew it held more than cigar leaf.

"You got to do that now?'

"Why not?"

"My kid's in the truck."

Mustapha sucked his teeth, rolled his eyes and reached for the lighter.

"For real Mustapha. Don't do that with her in here."

"My ride, bitch?"

It was a Twilight Zone moment and for the second time in her life Gina wondered how she even thought she liked a man like that. Not only did he not care about her, he obviously had no concern for children.

"Stop the car," Gina said hotly.

"What?"

"I said stop the car."

The oversized square of metal screeched to the curb. He looked at her with hot eyes. "Go on, get the fuck out."

Without missing a beat, Gina turned towards the back seat. "Take your seat belt off and open the door." Kanisha did. When her daughter was standing safely on the sidewalk, Gina got out too.

She didn't slam the door — not because she didn't want to. She did. But Mustapha was a crazy fuck and it was best she did nothing to make him show how much. Taking her daughter's hand, Gina headed in the opposite direction.

She couldn't do it anymore. Couldn't do it alone. She tried, but every time she turned around there was some stumbling block, from Jefferson dying, to meeting Collin and being unable to deal with his issues. The incident with Mustapha — just icing on a rotting cake.

Gina just wanted to feel better. Climb out of her skin. Get high.

She still had that envelope. Still had what was in the envelope. She had held onto the bag of weed initially as a reminder of how far she'd come, at least that's what she told herself. But the truth was, she feared this moment in her life and knew the time would come when she wanted to get high.

It was right across the room under her dresser in a shoebox. All she needed was one little joint. She didn't need a spliff, just a slender rolled joint of goodness.

Gina looked across the room at her dresser and then peered out of her bedroom. Kanisha, tired from a day out, was fast asleep in her bed. Her eyes drifted down to the cornice on the bottom. She tried to see what lay beneath it, but the fake carved wood blocked her vision.

If she tilted her head, she could see the shoebox. If she craned her neck, took a few steps, bent down, reached in and pulled it out, the pain would go away.

There across her room, underneath her dresser awaited heaven. Gina wanted some.

Gina sat before her counselor, her story of how she'd gone through the nickel bag of weed without blinking, finished. The disappointment and disgust she felt the next morning was shared too.

Mrs. Jones leaned back into her chair, swiveled it a bit and let out a short laugh. "Who said it was? Whoever said life was going to be easy Gina, especially when you've done things to make it rough?"

"But you don't understand Miss Jones."

"What don't I don't understand? I understand a whole lot more than you're giving me credit." Mrs. Jones leaned forward, rested the nubs of her elbows on the desk. "You got a father after not having one for most of your life only to lose him. Your relationship with Rick is over. You're living on your own for the first time ever, taking on responsibilities you never had before. You met a guy who you thought was working for you but his situation is stressing you *and* you put yourself into a situation a few days ago that not only threatened your welfare, but your daughter's ... I understand, Gina."

"So why I do it? Why did I get in Mustapha's Hummer?"

"Because life was hard and getting a ride home in a nice flashy vehicle seemed like a nice little break, that's why."

"I should have known better."

"And now you do. I think the fact that you nearly broke down my door to see me after the weekend says it all."

"Oh yeah, what it say?"

"It says that Gina Alexander is growing up and finding out that it's not going to be easy and she's going to make mistakes. But it's okay. None of us are perfect and all we can do is keep trying. Don't let one failure stop you."

"Yeah, that sounds all good, but it ain't helping me."

"You got to give it time, Gina. You spent twenty-three years digging this hole. It's gonna take a little time to make your way out." Mrs. Jones pulled out her appointment book. Flipped through some pages. "I want to see you next week. Wednesday at six."

"And what am I supposed to do till then? What if I want to get high again?"

"That's your choice and nobody but you can make it. If you want to get high, I'm not going to send out the 'don't-get-high' police to stop you. You have to stop yourself, understand?"

Gina hated it when she used that word "understand." It meant discussion over. She didn't respond.

"Understand, Gina?"

"Yeah, I understand."

"Good." Mrs. Jones stood up. "Now come and give me a hug." Gina did but she wasn't feeling it.

By the next Wednesday, Gina felt as if she had been swimming through sludge. It didn't help that she had been smoking marijuana every single night before she went to bed, all the while promising it was her last time.

Gina had let herself down and there was a whole line of people behind her that she had let down as well. But right now she was only facing one of them: Mrs. Jones.

"How much?" Mrs. Jones began.

"How much what?" Gina asked defensive.

"How much have you smoked?"

"Just one."

"One what?"

"Nickle bag."

Mrs. Jones gave her a look full of disappointment. "We're cool and I make it my business to keep whatever is said between us between us. But you have violated the terms of your probation and by law I'm supposed to report you. You want to go back to jail? Is that what you want?"

"No."

Mrs. Jones put her hand to her ear. "Excuse me, you say something?"

"I said no."

"Well you have to do more than say it Gina. You have to mean it. You may want an easy life but I'm sorry sister, you're not getting one. The sooner you accept that, the easier it will be to deal with it without drugs, you hearing me?"

"Yeah."

"Good. Now, when was the last time you and Kanisha did something with Rick?" Gina snorted, shook her head. "Can't remember?"

"Nope."

"If it's been that long then it's been too long. It's time to start up again."

"Rick don't want to be bothered with me."

"I'm not saying he has to. But what I am saying is the both of you have to maintain a balance for your daughter whether you all want to or not. Kanisha didn't ask to come here, but you two chose to bring her here so both you and Rick got to handle your business. Get in contact with him and make some plans for the three of you, whether it's taking in a movie or just an hour in the park, you plan something. Your daughter not only needs that but deserves it." Mrs. Jones made a note in the file. "And I think it'll do you some good too."

It had started simple enough, an unplanned meeting at the health bar at the gym that led to easy conversations over Smoothies. Rick asked for pointers on his workout and Brea, the head trainer, told him.

Three minutes into her advice, she pulled back. Smiled. "I'm up here giving you advice that other people pay for." She shook her head. "You want to know another thing, you're going to have to pay."

"All I did was ask. You didn't have to answer."

"You're right, but don't do it again." She took a sip of her Smoothie, glanced at her watch. "I got to get back. Take care." She slid off the stool.

Rick called her back. "Wait. How much do you charge?"

"How much do you make?"

Rick's brow went up. "That much?"

"I'm the top trainer here. You want the best, you have to pay."

"What about dinner?'

"What about it?"

"It's free right? I mean I don't have to pay you for your time if I take you to dinner."

She shook her head, laughed and continued on her way.

He caught up with her as she was heading up the stairs. "No, I'm serious."

"I can't go to dinner with you Rick."

"How come?"

She tried to find an answer. Couldn't.

The gym energized Rick. An upcoming date with Brea energized him even more. He was buzzing as he let himself in, a long, hot shower on his mind. He had just adjusted the temperature and had stripped down to his underwear when the phone rang.

Picking up, he heard Gina's voice. "Hey Rick."

"Hey."

"You busy next Saturday?"

"Saturday evening, yeah. Why?"

"We haven't done anything together with Kanisha lately. I thought maybe we could do something this upcoming weekend."

"Something like what?"

"I don't know. A movie, the park, something."

"She wants us to?"

Gina didn't know. She hadn't asked Kanisha. She wanted to make sure Rick was for it first. "Probably."

"She didn't ask?"

"No. I just figured that it would be nice. The three of us, for a few hours."

It had been a while since they had done anything together. "Sure. Why not."

"Okay then. I'll ask her what movie she wants to see then call you later." Gina hung up, a bit of movement in her heart. Still too fragile to bloom, it resided in the place between uncertainty and joy.

Chapter Twenty-Five

"'Z'. 'N' is the symbol for zinc."

Tarika nodded her head. Tried to find something in her brain that would make the fact stick. "Okay, give me the next one."

"K."

She looked off trying to see the symbol in her head. The actual element next to it. A yawn left her. She tried not to let a second one come.

"K," Justin repeated again, leaned against a floor pillow in her living room, willing her to get the answer.

Her hand went up. "Give me a minute." But it was no use. She had worked a full day at McDonald's and had an early rise tomorrow. She needed sleep and her brain was halfway there. She shook her head. Looked at Justin solemnly. "I'm just too tired to think."

"The answer is potassium ... your test is in four days."

"I know that. Don't you think I know that?" It was the first time she had gotten angry at him and it caught them both by surprise. With the test so close she was full of fear. Justin had suggested the GED prep program but she had decided against it.

Beyond saving two hundred and ninety dollars for the course, which she didn't really have, Tarika felt smart enough to take the test without the preparatory class. She knew people who dropped out of the tenth and went on to get their GED. She had been certain she could do the same.

With three evenings left to cram, now she wasn't so sure. She got up from the floor. "I can't do it anymore."

"What do you mean you can't?"

"I'm tired Justin. Worked all day, got to get up early tomorrow. It's already close to eleven. I'm tired."

"Tired? There's no such thing when you're getting a degree. It doesn't matter what you did all day, when it's time to study, you have to study."

"But I'm not in college. It's just a stupid-ass GED." The hurt in her voice was full.

"Its more than just a stupid ass GED. That GED is going to get you into college."

Tarika shook her head. "Adult Continuation Education programs ain't college."

"Don't say ain't," he reminded softly. He saw so much in her, so much to her. Justin had seen a few 'Tarika's' in his lifetime, young women whom life never really gave a chance. It was his belief that all they really needed to pull themselves up was some support; someone to be behind them, believe in them, push them when the going was rough.

He stood up. Opened his arms. "Come here."

But Tarika wasn't going. She needed him to understand something more than she needed his arms. She needed Justin to understand that she might not pass the test. That she wasn't as smart as he thought. She stood her ground.

"Come on over here."

She folded her arms, rooted. "I can't do it."

"Of course you can do it. You're just a little uptight about it, that's all."

"I can't. I'm not ready."

"You're just a little tired now, like you said. We'll stop, pick up tomorrow." He moved closer to her. Slipped his arms around her tense body. "It's okay to be scared Tarika. There's nothing wrong with that, but I know you can do this."

She wished she had his faith.

Kanisha bounded down the stoop, skipped along the walkway and bounced up to Rick's vehicle. She pulled open the back door, climbed inside, her face a bowl of sunshine as she sang "Hi Daddy."

It was a simple moment, ordinary and everyday at one time, but it had been a while since he had experienced it and it caught him off guard. Made a lump grow in his throat. Rick swallowed it back. "Hi baby."

The sound of a front door closing reached him. Rick watched Gina lock the door and head his way, the sneakers on her feet, a different look for her. Rick couldn't remember the last time he had seen her wear a pair.

"Hey," she said, sliding into the front seat, lips a glossy brown, pale blue sunglasses on her face.

"Hey."

"We're going to Valley Streams."

"Okay." The Navigator eased from the curb. Rick glanced at her. "I can't remember you ever wearing sneakers."

"Just giving my feet a break. I was watching a program on TV about heels and they say you should switch up what you wear. Wearing heels all the time shortens something in your legs."

"Yeah, I think I saw that too."

"Did you see that lady who could hardly walk in flats?"

"The old lady with the gray hair?"

"Yeah her. I was like, man. I don't want to be like that."

"So, how does it feel?"

"Weird. My legs hurt a little bit. But I'll get used to it." It was Gina's time to do the looking. "You looking all fit. Must be working out hard."

"Yeah. Every day after work."

"Every day?"

"Don't miss one unless I'm sick."

"Well it's looking good."

"Thanks."

"Collin called me."

"That guy?"

"Yeah. He still trying to convince me it can work." Gina shook her head. "But I know better."

"It could Gina."

"No, because his baby's momma ain't ready to let go. And I don't have time to wait for her to. Collin was cool and all, but I can't get with that."

Rick nodded. "I hear you."

In the darkness of the movie theatre, with Kanisha between them, both Rick and Gina fell asleep. If Kanisha noticed, she didn't seem to mind. "It was the best movie ever," she declared as they headed out into the warmth of the day. "I want it on DVD."

"It's not even out yet Kanisha," Gina said with a chuckle.

"But when it is, I want it."

"Well, what are you going to do to get it?" The question puzzled Kanisha. "I mean, it's okay to want something, but you got to do the right things to get it. Right Rick?"

"Yep, you sure do."

Kanisha frowned up her face. "Things like what?"

"Well, things like keeping your room clean or doing well in school. Not getting into any trouble. Stuff like that."

"You used to get stuff Momma and you wasn't so good."

"Yeah, I know, but I'm paying for it now."

"It's costing you money?"

"No, not money. But other things. Things more important than money, so you got to remember if you want good things to happen to you, you have to be good."

"Okay."

Gina wasn't aware that Rick was looking at her closely. She did not see the small smile that dusted his lips, the way his head nodded in gentle agreement. If she could have climbed into his head, she would have seen his thoughts: *Bravo Gina, bravo.*

Red Lobster had a light crowd so getting a table didn't require a wait. Rick, Gina and Kanisha settled into the booth and studied the menus. They had their orders ready by the time the waitress came by.

"Remember when we used to come here all the time?" Gina asked.

"Yeah, I remember. Felt like we were here for breakfast, lunch and dinner."

Gina turned up her nose. "Now I don't even see what the big deal was."

"Me neither," Rick said with a smile.

"I can't believe we used to bring Kanisha here for her birthdays."

"All the time."

"I think that was more for us."

"For you, maybe. Me, I always wanted to give her a real party. You were the one always insisting on Red Lobster."

"Back then it was like the 's' y'know? Now?"

"Kinda ghetto, right?"

"Yeah." Gina shook her head. "Damn, but I was weak."

"No, you just hadn't grown up yet."

"I wasn't trying to either."

"Well, you're trying now, that's the most important thing."

"You was a little immature too."

Rick's face turned up. "When?"

"All the time. That's why it was so easy to play you."

"Yeah, you did, didn't you. Like a piano."

"Because you was weak. Not now, but back then? I say 'roll over and you be like 'how many times Gina?'"

Rick laughed, embracing the truth, knowing it no longer could hurt him. "Yeah, you right. I be like 'Gina where you going now?' and you be like 'Out Negro. See you when I see you.' Of course you didn't say Negro."

"Yeah and I remember when I said it one day and you was about to give me a beat down."

Rick chuckled. "I remember. I was like seconds off of you." They looked at each, the chuckles still dancing in their eyes.

"It was rough Rick and I don't know how you stayed with me," she looked at Kanisha. "But we did get something good from it."

"We sure did Gina. We sure did."

Gina reached for her glass of water. "So, anybody snatch you up yet?"

"Nah."

"No one?" Rick shook his head no. "Well don't worry none. You keep working out and they're gonna be lined up at your front door."

"I don't know about all that Gina."

"Yeah, well I do. It's rough out there. The pickin's slim. You got a lot to offer somebody. Don't you ever forget that."

Gina's words shouldn't have mattered, but it did to Rick. A whole lot.

Dajah grabbed the Frisbee and pitched it through the air. She watched as Kelly bounded after it and prepared herself for its slobbery return. Above her the sky was Italian-icy blue and the sun warmed the sand beneath her feet.

Kelly came back, Frisbee in her mouth and Dajah took it. "One more throw and then I'm taking a break." She tossed it, took a seat in the sand next to Jeff and tapped his thigh. "Your turn."

"You're quitting already?"

"Yep."

"You weren't at it a good five minutes."

"Yeah and my arm's tired."

"I didn't know you were so weak," Jeff said with a smile.

"Yeah? Well you know it now. Get up. Here comes Kelly."
Jeff got up.

Standing by his car, they dusted as much sand off their feet and bottoms as possible. Got inside. "So, what's for dinner?"

Dajah had been thinking about Italian all day. She remembered a restaurant she had gone to a few times in Astoria. They had the best Italian food she ever tasted. Their shrimp Parmesan was to die for. "I know this great Italian restaurant."

"Where?"

"Astoria."

"Sounds good."

Rick bent down to get his daughter's hug, her soft-lipped kiss. "We're going again, aren't we daddy? We gonna do it again?"

"We sure are Kanisha." He kissed her cheek. "I love you. You be good." Rick stood up. Looked at Gina.

"Thanks," she offered softly.

"For?"

"For taking time out for us."

"It's what I'm suppose to do."

"Yeah but what you supposed to do and what you do ain't always the same."

"Well thanks for asking. I didn't realize how much I missed doing stuff like that. Kanisha hasn't looked so happy in a while."

"Yeah. She gonna be talking about it all week." Gina reached out, her hands going on his shoulders. Before Rick could react, she kissed his cheek. "That's for caring."

"About?"

"Me and Kanisha." She turned and headed towards the house. Stopped. "I put you through a lot of stuff and I ain't never said sorry. But I want you to know I am. And I hope you meet somebody nice."

Rick started to say something, but just nodded and smiled. If fate was going his way, he already had.

Dante's on Astoria Boulevard in Astoria was a few blocks down from the Astorian Manor. Saturday night found a waiting time of half an hour. Dajah and Jeff put their name on the list and headed to the bar.

"Smells good," Jeff said, sipping his White Russian.

"Is good," Dajah answered, breathing deeply on the heavily aromatic air.

Jeff rapped the bar. "Real Mahogany. You don't see that much anymore." He pointed to the wine rack made of iron. "And I bet you a week's salary that came from Italy."

Dajah smiled, marveling at him. "How do you know so much?"

"Architecture. I studied all kinds of things when I was in school. Just about every place I go, I notice things like structure, design, even what period."

"Yeah? Well how old do you think this restaurant is?"

Jeff glanced around. "The restaurant itself," he shrugged. "But the structure? The frame work, over a century."

"Really?"

Jeff nodded. "See the cornice up there, up near the wall? Hand tooled."

"How can you tell?"

"I can tell by the smoothness of the wood, the tone of the varnish."

"Tone?"

"Not like in making music tone, but the coloring, the shading, the aging."

Dajah shook her head. "You are probably the smartest man I ever met."

"Is that a bad thing?"

Dajah was about to answer when she sensed eyes on her. She looked toward the entranceway. Saw someone watching her. Rick.

He was standing there with a woman. A fox of a woman. A woman who wore the tiny little skirt and half-boot heels with as much finesse as a super model. A woman that looked healthy and vibrant enough to have a fresh clean look without anything more than lip gloss. A woman who seemed, in the quick second Dajah looked, to have enough confidence to set the world on fire.

* * *

He didn't expect her here.

Rick didn't expect to see Dajah anywhere ever again. Yes, he had brought her to this very restaurant on many occasions, but had been coming here for nearly two months and he had never seen her.

But there she was with a man.

Older but well put together. Older, but he had the air of substance and style. Smooth. A somebody.

"You okay?"

Brea's voice snapped him from his thoughts, pulled his eyes from Dajah across the room sitting at the bar. "Yeah. Fine."

"You were just standing there like you saw a ghost."

Rick blinked. Got his heart to settle to a less fast rhythm. "No, not a ghost. Just an old friend. Come on." He took Brea's hand and headed into the bar.

Dajah saw him heading in her direction. She looked away. Inhaled and let it out quick. "He's here," she whispered.

"Who's here?"

"Rick."

"Your ex, Rick?"

Dajah nodded slightly but furiously. "Yeah. He's heading this way."

"You're going to say hello?"

"What?"

But Jeff never got a chance to repeat his question. Rick came up behind them. Called out Dajah's name. She heard it and contemplated answering. She caught herself. What was she hiding from? Why should she?

She turned, a smiled plastered on her face. "Rick. Hey."

He leaned in to her, kissed her cheek. "Hi. Good to see you."

Dajah nodded, forcing her eyes not to look at the woman beside him. "Good to see you too." She indicated Jeff sitting besides her. "This is my friend Jeff. Jeff, this is Rick."

Rick eased back, took Jeff's hand. Gave it a firm shake. "Nice to meet you."

"Same here." Jeff answered.

Rick eased Brea forward. "And this is my friend Brea. Brea, this is Dajah."

"Nice to meet you."

"And Jeff?"

Jeff smiled, nodded, took the woman's hand. "Yes. Nice to meet you."

Then they were out of words, intros and smiles. Rick looked around. Spotted a booth about to be emptied. "I see some seats," he said to Brea. He took one last look at Dajah. "It was good seeing you."

"Same here."

"You guys have a great evening," were Rick's parting words.

Dajah found her breath. She looked towards the mirror at the bar. Shook her head. "Wow."

"Wow?"

She looked at Jeff. "Yeah," blinked twice, "Wow."

"What?"

"This whole thing."

"Why?"

She didn't know, only that the sight of Rick had stopped her heart. But by the time he had come up to her, it had started again with more gusto than it had in almost a year.

Brea was watching him closely, a Madonna smile on her lips.

Rick raised up his hand. "Don't ask."

"I wasn't. But if you want to tell me, I'm all ears."

He took up his drink. Indicated that she should raise hers. "Here's to new beginnings."

She clicked his glass. "New beginnings," her eyes shifting, taking in Dajah at the bar.

"So you decided what you want?"

Rick's voice snatched her attention. "I'm watching my carbs, so it will probably be a salad."

"Just salad?"

"Well, maybe some fish or something."

"Do you always watch what you eat?"

Brea smiled. Waggled her finger. "My body is my career. If I don't keep it looking good ... "

Rick nodded. "I hear you." His eyes roved over the tight top with the exposed cleavage. "And for the record, your body looks good."

"So does yours."

Rick's eyes raised. "Coming from you, that's a real compliment."

"I tell it like I see it."

"I like that in a woman."

Brea picked up her drink, took a sip, her eyes never leaving his. "Yeah?"

"Yeah."

In the fifteen minutes they waited for their table to be ready, Dajah found herself sharing her heart, the moment. "I hope it works out."

"What?"

"Rick and his friend. I hope it works out for him. He's really a good egg, just misguided . . . he told me him and Gina were over but I didn't really believe it until tonight."

"What about us?"

"What about us?"

"Are you hoping we work out?"

"What's to work, it's done." She said, surprised.

"Is it?"

"You know it is."

Jeff smiled. "Just testing."

"And I passed," Dajah said quickly.

"You sure did. You've taken me where nobody has in a long while and it's a good place."

Dajah looked at Jeff, a soft gratitude in her eyes. "Ditto."

Chapter Twenty-Six

Tarika didn't have to see the results of her test to know she didn't pass. Whatever knowledge she had had, whatever knowledge she tried to cram into her brain had vanished by the time she walked into the education center on Archer Avenue.

The test, taken over two days in May, was a washout.

She would have to take the prep course. She would have to set aside time and save up some money for the six-week course. The next series would be given in the summer and it seemed a lifetime away. She no longer wanted to try.

"How are you going to back down now?" Justin asked her. "As far as you've come?"

"But that's just it, I can't go no further. All that stuff about college was just some dream."

"Isn't everything you want a dream in the beginning? Isn't every single goal you get starts with wanting it to happen?"

They were in his room, a room he had outgrown years ago. Books were stacked on the floor and his closet was filled to capacity. Track trophies were lined along shelves and a few were lined against the wall.

A York College banner shared space with one from John Bowne High School. His bed, a queen size, took up most of the space and his stereo equipment was wedged up against the footboard.

Tarika didn't like coming here because it always felt congested to her. Now as she looked around, all she wanted was some air. Justin's sneakers were funking up the room and even though the window was opened, a rankness rode the breeze.

"Can we go for a walk?" she asked.

"A walk?"

Tarika looked at him. "Yeah. Up to the park or something."

His brow raised. "A *long* walk?"

"Yeah."

"Like your favorite Jill Scott song?"

It was things like that that made Tarika appreciate Justin. She had never come out and said how much she dug Jill Scott, but Justin had picked up on it. In truth, she did want to take a walk through the park. She had always wanted to take a long walk with a guy she was digging.

Sha-Keem had laughed at her suggestion. After that she never mentioned it. But somehow Justin had sensed it and it took some of the gloom from her soul. Made her smile. "Yeah, like the Jill Scott song."

"You're going to sing it for me?"

"Sing what?"

"That Jill Scott tune you love so much — "A Long Walk.""

"Who says I can sing?"

"I do. I hear you when you're in the shower and girl, you got pipes."

It was another thing about her that had gotten crushed by other people's opinions. Yes, Tarika could *sang*. She could wail. But she no longer did it in front of anyone. Still Justin had heard her and recognized her ability.

"You want me to sing to you," she said, nonplussed.

"Yeah. It'll be just like the video. I'll be the cat, you'll be Jill Scott and you can sing as we stroll down through the ghetto."

"What you mean the ghetto? This ain't the ghetto." Tarika knew because she lived in the ghetto. The section of Queens Justin lived in was far from it.

"Yeah it is, you just don't know it."

She shook her head, laughed. "You crazy."

"'Bout you." He got off the bed. Slipped on his sneakers. Grabbed his cell, his keys. Opened his bedroom door, the sound of the television playing in the living room moving down the hall. They left his bedroom, moved to the living room.

"Pops?" Justin said. Mr. Edison looked up. "Me and Tarika are going to take a walk. We'll be back."

Mr. Edison looked at his son, the young woman in his life and nodded. He didn't smile and never did, disliking the latest girl his son had brought home. He had hoped it was just a phase for his son, but time had shown him different. Worse, his wife liked her.

"Goodbye, Mr. Edison," Tarika said in her best voice.

"Goodbye, Tarika," he offered back, as if just the sound of her voice was annoying. She was not his choice by a long shot, but as his wife was quick to remind, Justin was way past twenty-one.

The stronghold Mr. Edison once held had slipped greatly. With his wife taking his son's side, he knew he was outnumbered. He didn't fight it, but nothing could make him like it.

Stepping out in the sunny, warm afternoon, Tarika let a smile go. Mr. Edison's attitude was bothering her less and less these days.

Justin took up Tarika's hand. "Ready?"

"Yeah."

"Okay. Start singing."

She smiled so hard her mouth hurt. "You serious?"

"As cancer. Come on, how does it go? *You're here, I'm pleased.*" Off key and screechy, his redemption hurt her ears.

"Hush," Tarika said. "You're going to make the dogs start howling."

"Well if you don't sing it, I will."

She looked at him, trying to judge if he was serious or not. Looked off, gathering the will to sing out loud to him as they walked down his block. Tarika started, *"You're here,"* got choked. Laughed nervously. Cleared her throat. "Ah-hum ... "

Her eyes closed as she went into herself where it was just her and Jill Scott, their voices, the music and nothing else. By the second verse, her eyes were opening, the strength and joy of her voice coming through with vibrato and joy.

"... I was blind but now I see." Tarika could see now, clear and fully, her voice, deep, mellow, easy and affirmed. Jill Scott's word, speaking all she ever wanted to say to Justin. Speaking everything Justin wanted to hear.

Passersby stared at her, smiled, pulled in by the wonder of her voice, the boldness of her act. Something good stirred up between herself and Justin. It was a halo of light around them.

Her head was back, her mouth opened. Eyes pinched, Tarika was deep into the song. Justin, into her groove as well, provided the bass beats. Together they headed towards the park, syncopated motion of song and bass line. Two people who had found a rhythm within each other and weren't afraid to show the world their harmony.

"That was incredible," Justin was saying as the last word faded from her voice.

Tarika's eyes dazzled. She was breathless, excited. Hyped and awed. "I can't believe I did that."

"I can. You definitely need to join chorus when you get to York."

"You keep on saying it like I'm there already."

"You are. You just have to do your part, like take the course and pass the test."

"You really think I can do it?"

"I know you can."

Tarika smirked. "How come you know?"

"Because when I look at you, I see so much for you. I see all that you want for yourself. I know where you've been and how far you've come, that's why."

"And?"

"It's like that old ass record — Aint No Stopping Us Now. As long as I'm here, nothing's going to stop you. I'm not going to let it."

"*He's so sweet and good ... good.*"

"Uh oh, she's gonna give me another song y'all."

The words just came out of her mouth without prompting. Jill Scott's "He Loves Me," coming out of her like breathing. Her favorite CD made reality by Justin. The songs that touched her like no other music could, turned into real life.

By the time she finished, she was misty-eyed. Justin was just as affected. "Nobody's ever sung to me before," he offered, staring into her face, marveled, as if for the first time. "Nobody."

"Nobody has ever really made me want to sing till you."

There in the park, at the end of their long walk. He kissed her and Tarika knew that her world was forever changed, for the better.

Gina was dreaming. She knew because it was the same dream she had had a while back. She was dreaming of Jefferson, standing in his kitchen, looking alive and well, cooking her up a meal, a smile on his face.

She knew she had to act fast. She knew she had to say his name before she woke up. She knew that if she didn't, she would get cheated of something; something important and real. But once again, her mouth wouldn't open.

She decided another course of action. In her dream, her feet took flight. But even as she neared Jefferson, even as steam rose up around his smiling face from the big pot of which he was stirring, she felt herself moving towards consciousness.

Gina felt the dream, Jefferson, the smells, the steam, fading to black.

In the next second, all of it was gone.

Opening her eyes, Gina knew. She had to find out where Jefferson was buried.

She was taking the bus to work when an idea came to her.

The funeral home on Sutphin. They would know where the body went, that much she was certain. What she wasn't sure of was whether they would tell her or not. She wasn't a blood relative. She didn't have any legal right to the information. But Gina knew she had to try.

She also knew she had to sound more educated then what she was. She had to sound like she was somebody important.

There once was a time in Gina's life where she thought any black person who talked like a white person was a stone-cold Oreo. But working at the library showed her the importance of it. She watched how people reacted to co-workers based on how they sounded. Those that sounded 'white' got the most respect.

She found herself practicing a 'white' voice. It sounded clumsy and stupid to her own ears, but she kept on practicing, repeating the same words over and over until she got it right. But when she called the funeral home and a man answered, she lost all pretense.

Instead, she told the truth. By the time she hung up, she had the town, the state and the name of the funeral home that had handled the final service.

The travel agency was right next to the real estate office Gina had visited not so long ago. Gina hoped to get tickets over the Internet using the computers at work, but she didn't have a credit card, so she had to do a face-to-face cash transaction.

She knew the cost of the flight from JFK Airport to Durham, North Carolina, wouldn't be cheap, but she never expected it to cost nearly fifteen hundred dollars. For that much money Gina figured they could take a cruise.

"It's your time frame," the woman told her point blank. "You want to fly out in three days and that doubles, almost triples what you would pay if you waited."

But Gina couldn't wait. She had waited long enough. "Go ahead, book it."

"Do you have a place to stay when you get there?" Gina hadn't thought of that. Told the agent no. "Well I can find some hotels near the airport if you like. Ones with a shuttle to the terminal and back, save you some money."

Gina told her okay.

When Doreen Alexander heard that Gina had not only found where Jefferson was buried, but had purchased tickets for them to go the upcoming weekend, Doreen was overcome. She had never known her daughter to care too much for anything. Yet she had found Jefferson and paid for her plane fare.

"I needed to know where he was Momma," she confessed. "He's been on my mind a lot and it didn't feel right not knowing."

"I don't know what to say," Doreen told her.

"Say you'll go," all Gina wanted to hear.

"That's not what I mean."

"I know it ain't. But the most important thing is we're gonna go see Jefferson this weekend."

Doreen knew her daughter was absolutely right.

Saturday afternoon Gina, her mother and her daughter boarded the plane at JFK. A few hours later they were leaving the terminal in Durham. A few hours after that they were standing at Jefferson's grave site.

There was no marker, no flowers, nothing but turned earth. According to the person in the office, Gina, Doreen and Kanisha, had been the only visitors to his grave since he had been buried. When Gina asked about a headstone, she was told that none had been ordered. When she offered to get one, she was told it could only be done through the family.

Gina knew what she had to do.

She never thought she would be back to the house again. Gina never thought she would stand on the stoop or ring the bell. But when she got back from North Carolina, that's where she found herself.

She could see the heavy drapes that used to cover the windows had been taken down and mini blinds were in their place. The windows were open but no loud music poured out. Gina tried not to look in while she waited for someone to answer.

She felt somebody behind the door and her suspicions were confirmed when someone spoke. "What you want?"

"I'm here about Jefferson and the money."

Magic words — the door swung open. Before Gina wasn't one of Jefferson's grandchildren but one of his daughters. Gina didn't know which one.

"You ready to return it?"

"I never had it, but that ain't why I'm here. I'm here to make a deal."

The brown eyes looked at her quizzically. "What kind a deal?"

"Your daddy ain't got no headstone. The man at the cemetery—,"

"How do you know where he buried?"

"Don't worry about how I know. That's not the issue. The issue is, the man at the cemetery office said nobody has ordered one. I want to order one but I can't because I'm not blood."

"Oh, so you think I should?"

"That's not what I'm saying. I'm saying if you go with me to get one, I'll pay for it and then give you some money for your trouble."

"How much money?"

"Five hundred dollars."

It wasn't a fortune but it was more than the daughter had on her. Besides, if Gina wanted to buy a headstone, that would save her both time and trouble. "A thousand."

"Five hundred."

"I'm sorry, but five hundred ain't enough."

Gina kept her face even. Shrugged. "A'right." Turned and started down the steps. She knew she wouldn't get far. That greed would have the daughter calling her back.

"Wait. I'll do it."

Gina turned back around, keeping the smile undercover. "You got a car?"

The woman told her yes.

"Alright, here's what we'll do. There's this monument place out on Merrick Road. We'll go there, and I'll pick out something. You place the order. We leave there and come back here then I'll give you your money."

"Well I got a better idea. We'll go out to that monument place, you pick out what you want and give me the money. Then I'll place the order."

"Ain't happening," Gina said firmly.

"Then I'm not going."

"Suit yourself." For a second time, Gina turned about, headed down the steps.

"All right, all right, we'll do it your way."

It was one of the longest, tensest, most grilling car rides Gina ever took in her life, but she managed her way through it. As good as Jefferson had been to her, there was no way she could allow him to remain in an unmarked grave.

Gina and Tarika sat on the park bench, eyes on Kanisha who was on the swing. There was a time in their life where a trip to the park was an everyday occurrence. Now it was a rarity.

Slowly and carefully, Kanisha placed one foot first then the other onto the metal swing bottom. With utter concentration, she straightened herself up. Tiny hands fixed around the chain-link metal and bottom lip in her mouth, she bent her legs and pushed her pelvis forward.

"Look at her," Gina said, pointing to her daughter. "The child is trying to pump."

Tarika laughed. "I remember it took me forever to learn how to do it. But once I got the hang of it, I didn't want to stop."

"Yeah, I remember. All you wanted to do was 'pump.' By yourself, with other kids, you didn't care, just as long as you could. It was fun coming to the park with you. All I had to do was sit and swing, you did all the work."

"I did like that, didn't I? I guess because it was the feeling of doing something, of getting somewhere."

"Somewhere where? Back and forwards?"

"It didn't feel like back and forwards," Tarika confessed. "It was like flying high above everybody and everything. All the wrong stuff at home was forgotten when I pumped. I guess that's why I liked it so much."

"I guess."

"So you're going to go back down there?" Tarika wanted to know.

"Yeah. They said the headstone would take about three

months. I figure maybe the end of September. I don't want to go down when it's too cold."

"I hear you. And that was such a sweet thing you did too."

"I had to. Them heifers wasn't even thinking about giving him a headstone." Gina shook her head. "I never understood why they never treated their daddy like he was something important?"

"A lot of people treat people in their life like they're not important."

"Yeah, but still. That was their father. You know how many people out here wish they had one?"

Tarika did. "You know I know."

"I don't ever want Kanisha to be like that, treating Rick any o' kind of way. I want her to always respect him and care for him."

"I think she will."

"No, she was trying it, believe it or not. Of course I didn't help none. I was like, she don't want to be with him, then I ain't making her. But I think that had more to do with me, than Kanisha."

"Why you say that?"

"Because at the time I was just mad with everything and everybody." Gina looked off. "But now? It's okay. I think finding Jefferson and getting him that headstone helped me a lot."

"Me and Justin's going to Rubba Dub. You want to come?"

"Nah."

"Oh come on Gina. You ain't, I mean, haven't been nowhere since the last time we went out for your birthday."

"And?"

"You need to get out. Have some fun."

"I don't know girl."

"You'll think about it at least?"

Gina said she would.

The summer night was hot, humid and muggy. Air condition units jammed tight into windows burred and dripped and portable fans pushed hot, muggy air around living rooms. Music flowed from open car windows and people were out on the streets looking for relief from the night-time heat.

The crowd inside the Rubba Dub was thick and as much skin as the law allowed was visible everywhere you looked.

Tarika, Justin and Gina sat at a table, sipping drinks and checking out the crowd. Even though Gina felt like a third wheel, she was glad that Tarika had invited her to go with them.

"You ready?" Justin asked Tarika.

"Yeah." She looked at Gina, mouthed "Be back," and the two of them headed for the dance floor, becoming swallowed up in the crowd.

Gina sat back, sipped her drink. Looked around. She was happy for her friend. Happy that Tarika had found someone good in her life and wished the same for herself. She missed Collin more than she would ever admit but was glad he had stopped calling.

In a few weeks she would be taking the GED prep course with Tarika and while the idea was exciting, it was scary. Unlike Tarika, Gina didn't have the smarts, but she knew that in order to get somewhere, she needed more education.

"Can I have this dance?"

She never saw him approach, but knew the voice. She didn't look up. "No."

He took a seat. Reached for her hands. She snatched them away. "Gina."

"Ain't nobody asked you to take a seat." She would not look at him.

"I been missing you something awful."

"Tell it to somebody who care."

He reached for her face. "Gina," his fingers brushing her cheek.

"No, Collin. No."

"No what? I haven't said anything."

She fixed her eyes on him. "You ain't got to say anything. I ain't going there with you."

"Going where? Where you think I'm trying to take you?"

"Through baby-momma-drama."

"Now why would I want to do that?"

"Not you. *Her.*"

"Sybil?" He shook his head. "I don't know why you think she got something on me."

"Easy. She's your baby's momma."

"And that's all she is." He looked towards the dance floor. Looked back at her, but her eyes were elsewhere. "You here alone?"

"No."

"With some cat?"

"Yeah." Which was the truth. She was here with Justin even if Justin was with her girl.

"Where he at?"

"Don't worry about where he at."

He reached for her hand again. "Come on and dance with me."

She snatched it away. "What part of no don't you understand?"

He jumped up. Slid his chair closer to her. So quickly it seemed warped speed. Suddenly his arms were around her tight. She struggled. "Get off of me."

But he held on. "I'm not going nowhere."

"I ain't playing Collin."

"Neither am I."

Gina went still. Barely breathing. Barely blinking. She didn't move. Put a bored expression on her face as he continued to hold her, his breath near her neck. They went on that way for thirty seconds before she was forced to give up the ghost. "You finished," she said evenly.

"Are you?"

"Yeah."

He eased up his hold. Slid back. Stood. Extended his hand. "Dance with me."

She looked at him, eyes rolling. Looked away.

"I'll stand here all night if I have to."

"Go right ahead."

But after forty-five seconds of that hand being extended her way, Gina took it.

"Do you like it, Kanisha?"

Mouth full of popcorn, another gathering in her small hand, Kanisha nodded. Mumbled 'Um hum."

Brea looked at Rick. Smiled. Mouthed the words 'told you so.'

They were at Rick's place, the three of them taking in a PG movie on HBO Family. Gina had gone out and Rick was babysitting Kanisha. With Saturday night being Rick's time with Brea, he had invited her over too.

Unlike the first time Rick had introduced his daughter to the new woman in his life, Kanisha had no problems with it. Her five-year-old mind understood that her mother was seeing other men.

And once again her daddy was seeing other women. They didn't seem to mind and so she didn't either.

Rick took a handful of popcorn, munched on it. It did taste like regular popcorn even though it was lite popcorn with half the calories of the regular. Rick had been certain Kanisha wouldn't like it. But he had assumed wrong.

Being with Brea took some adjustment. Keeping fit was her livelihood and beyond working out every morning, no matter where that morning found her, she ate differently. She was getting Rick to eat differently too.

He found himself with more energy than he ever had before and the stresses of the job were no longer that stressful. But on certain things he drew the line on. Like her favorite drink of all time — Crystal Light. That he couldn't get with.

The credits began to roll and Kanisha gave a yawn. She handed her bowl of popcorn to Brea and scooted off the couch. "I'm sleepy Daddy."

"Okay, let's get you tucked in."

"You say prayers Kanisha?" Brea wanted to know.

"What's dat?"

"You know. Before you go to bed. You get down on your knees and put your hands together and thank God for all his blessings."

"What's blessings?"

"Oh, stuff like, having your mommy and your daddy. Having fun at school. Good food to eat. A nice place to stay." Kanisha shook her head. "Well, how about if I teach you the prayer that I used to say when I was a little kid. Would you like that?"

Kanisha looked to her father. "Can she daddy? Can Miss Brea teach me?"

Rick smiled, choked. Embarrassed. "Sure."

They went to Kanisha's bedroom. Brea got down on her knees. Kanisha got down too. Brea folded her hands together. Kanisha did the same. "Okay, now bend your head and close your eyes." Kanisha did. "Now just say what I say. "Now I lay."

"Now I lay."

"Me down to sleep."

"Me down to sleep."

"I pray the Lord."

"I pray dalord."

"My soul,"

"My soul."

"To keep."

"To keep."

"If I should die?"

Kanisha took a breath. Opened her eyes. "I don't want to die."

Brea smiled. Eased a hand along Kanisha's shoulder. "No sweetie. You're not going to die. It's just how you say this prayer."

Kanisha looked up to her father. "Daddy. Am I gonna die?"

"No Kanisha. You're not. It's okay. Say it."

"If I should die."

"Before I wake."

"Before I wake."

"I pray the Lord."

"I pray dalord."

"My soul to take."

Kanisha hesitated. Looked back at her father. Rick nodded. She closed her eyes. Repeated the line.

"God bless Mommy."

"God bless Mommy."

"And Daddy."

"And Daddy."

"And Grandma."

"And Grandma."

"And Grandpa."

"You mean Grandpa Al?"

"Sure."

"What about Grandpa Jefferson? He dead but can I ask God to bless him?"

Brea smiled. "You can ask God to bless anybody, whether they're living or dead."

"God bless Grandpa Jefferson even though he in heaven and I don't see him no more."

"Anybody else you want to bless?"

"God bless my friends. God bless everybody."

"Is that it?"

"Yeah."

"Okay, so when you're finished, you say Amen."

"Amen."

"Good girl." Brea rose from her knees. Eyed Rick. "Okay, you can get in bed now." Kanisha did. Rick tucked the covers tight. Kissed her forehead. "Goodnight sweetheart."

"Good night Daddy. Good night Miss Brea."

"Good night Kanisha."

They left the bedroom. Closed the door. "You never taught her to say her prayers?" All Brea wanted to know.

Rick looked guilty and sheepish. "Just never thought to."

"And I guess you don't say any either."

"Not in a long time."

"Well, there's no time like the present." She decided. "You can't go around in this world living in a vacuum Rick. You got to recognize your blessings and thank God for them."

"What? You religious or something?"

"Religious? No. Spiritual, yes. You don't have to go to church to believe in God and thank Him for all that's He's given you."

"I guess you're right."

Brea raised a brow. "I know I'm right." She looked back towards Kanisha's bedroom. "You have a precious little soul in there. You have to do everything to keep it that way."

That's all Rick had ever tried do from the moment Kanisha had been born. But saying that would reveal too much of his history. He just nodded, uttering, "I hear you." Picking up the bowls of popcorn, he headed to the kitchen. "You want something to drink?"

"Got any more Crystal Light?"

"You have to make it yourself."

Brea got the canister, the bottled water, a glass and a spoon. Felt Rick's unease. "I'm not going to try and tell you how to raise you daughter. That's not why I'm here and I'm not really interested. She already has a mother and father. But something as simple as a prayer, I can do."

"I used to say it all the time when I was a kid."

"So what happened with Kanisha?"

"Gina."

"Her mother."

"Yeah."

"She must have been something."

Rick looked off. "She certainly was."

"But you guys are cool now, right?"

"Most def. She's living her life and I'm living mine."

Brea smiled. "Well that's good to hear. Like eating healthy and keeping fit. I don't do drama."

"Me neither." He took some wine out of the refrigerator. Got a glass.

"You didn't tell me you had wine."

"You didn't ask. Besides, all you drink is that Crystal Light."

"No, I do wine too. Pour me a glass."

"You sure? I wouldn't want to mess up your carbs or nothing."

"Do I detect some bitterness."

"No. No bitterness."

"Don't hate," she said with a smile.

Rick shook his head. "No, I'm not hating." He reached for, brought her near. "Not hating by a long shot."

The briny breeze coming off of the East River danced and curled around Dajah's arms as she sat at the Pier Seventeen Restaurant along the east side of the Manhattan shore. Not too hot, not too cold, the breeze was delicious, as was the food she was eating.

Across from her, Jeff was easing a plump piece of lobster from a claw. She watched even as she bought her own to her mouth. The plastic bib she wore was slick with lobster juice and her plate was scattered with bits of broken shell.

"How did you do that?" all she wanted to know.

"Do what?"

"Get that nice big chunk of lobster out that claw? I had to dig mines out."

Jeff looked at the morsel at the end of his fork, looked back at Dajah. "You want it?"

Yes, she did. She wanted him to pass it over so she could dip it into the drawn butter, squirt it with the wedge of cut lemon and pop it into her mouth. But she told him no.

"You sure. You can have it if you want."

It was a perfect specimen. Every bit of the meat whole and plump. Mouthwatering. "No. I'm fine." She looked down at her plate, the best part of her lobster gone, one claw left behind.

"Here, let me." Jeff picked up the claw, eased her seafood fork in, twist and turned it a few times and then slowly withdrew the solid piece of meat. He handed it back to her and Dajah took it gratefully.

Dajah always loved the summertime, and summer nights were the best. Especially when it meant an evening of Alvin Ailey and dinner on the pier with someone she was really digging and he was digging her back.

She ate the lobster. Wiped her hands with a wet wipe. Picked up her drink and took a long sip, satiated. "Can we stay here forever?"

"Stay here." It wasn't a question.

"Yeah. Just pitch a tent over there and live."

Jeff laughed. "Sure we can until they arrest us for vagrancy."

"I don't know why I love water so much. I mean, I'm not even a water sign. I'm a fire sign, but I can never get enough of a body of water."

"Well I'm glad you do. How else would I have met you?"

A waiter came to their table. "Is everything okay?"

"Great," they said in unison.

"Would you like dessert?"

Jeff looked at Dajah. "You want?"

"Yeah, but there's no more room."

Jeff told the waiter no. Waited until the waiter left. "What are your plans?"

"For?"

"The future?"

Dajah shrugged. She had a job she liked and was moving up along the ranks of accounting nicely. She had an apartment she liked and a man she liked even more. "I don't think I have any real ones. Why?"

"Thirty-nine."

"Thirty-nine?"

"Yeah. Me. I turn thirty-nine this year."

"Oh."

"Yeah." Jeff looked off, getting his thoughts together. His nerve. "I'm not trying to rush you into anything, but so close to forty, I have to start considering my future."

"You talking about marriage?"

"I guess I am."

Dajah sat back. Marriage was a big word and just as big a step.

She had never really thought hard on it, though she had thought about it. She told Jeff so.

"So, it is out of the question?" he wanted to know.

"Out of the question? No. Make a decision right now this minute? I can't do that."

He nodded to himself, affirming some private notion. "I understand."

"I'm not saying I won't. And I'm not saying that I don't think you would be perfect for me. Because you probably would be. It's just kind of sudden and we haven't known each other that long."

"I hear you, Dajah."

"No you don't. You're sitting over there licking wounds because you think I'm saying no." She reached over and took his hands into hers. "I'm not saying no Jeff, not by a long shot. I never met anybody more perfect for me. But what I am saying is not right now, this minute."

"I just never thought I'd turn out like my parents."

"What do you mean?"

"Being close to fifty before I had a kid."

"Your parents are that old?" Jeff nodded. Parents hadn't entered their equation yet. As far as they were concerned, that was a ways off. "Well, you turned out great."

He smiled. "I did, didn't I?"

"Oh, listen to you talk." She took a breath. Let it go. "Right now, what we have is good. But we're still new to it. Let's just see how things are going a year from now."

"O'four."

"Yeah. July, two thousand and four, let's see how we feel."

"I already know how I'll feel."

Dajah smiled. "Yeah?"

"Yeah."

"That's because you've only seen my best behavior. You haven't caught wind of my worst."

"Haven't I?"

"No, you haven't. I can get funky with the best of them."

Jeff shook his head. "I doubt that."

Dajah raised her brow. "That's what you think. I can be quite demanding you know."

"I already know that. It's a part of you that I like."

"Alright, make sure you remember that."

He leaned back, shook his head. "Dajah Gingham. Not easy on the tongue at all."

"No, that would be Dajah Moore-Gingham. I've been a Moore all my life. I'm not about to let that go."

"I don't expect you too. Besides, 'Moore' is a good thing ... you know I thought I had found that special person before, but now, being with you, I do believe that this time I got it right."

Dajah raised her glass. "Yeah, this time I think it could be the real thing."

Jeff raised his glass, clinked hers.

━━◆━━

THE END

Acknowledgements

I think of my life, this point in my life, and all I see the joys and the sorrows; the defeats and the triumphs. But more importantly, I see clearly that God has been with me every step of the way. He will not give you anything you cannot bear. If He brings you to it, for sure He will make sure you get through it ...

Having said all that, it's thank you time.

As I worked on this book, my first real live baby — something I gave birth too from start to finish — I found myself looking back on my life, gathering up all the people who have helped me not only become the writer I am today, but more importantly, the person I am today.

I'm starting at the beginning here — like third grade beginning.

I have to so say 'thank you' to Miss Bellinger, my 3rd and 5th grade IGC (Intelligently Gifted Children) teacher (yes, I had her twice!) from P.S. 45 on 150th Street in Jamaica, Queens New York. She made us work hard, use our minds on a daily basis and wouldn't allow us to do anything less then our best.

So, to you Miss Bellinger, wherever you are, the former Margaret L. Johnson, of the your former 3rd and 5th grade IGC classes at P.S. 45 in Jamaica, Queens, New York, between 1964 and 1966, says *Thank You* ...

To my mom — Alma H. Johnson. I love you deeply and completely, even when we have our moments. Again, I thank you for raising me up right and being behind me. You were the first person to step up to the plate to help me accomplish this goal. Words will never say how much I appreciate both it and you.

To my husband Terence A. Hodge, the love of my life. What can I say now that I haven't said in the past? You brought so much joy to my life. I'm truly blessed that you chose me. We received what most people won't get in a lifetime — *Amazing Love*. To quote our wedding song: *I will love you so, for always ...*

To my children Jon and Chris. Though you two are still not old enough to read my novels (smile), I just wanted the world to know how much I love you, appreciate you and thank God for the both of you. I look into your faces and see all of life's wonders ...

To my Amen Corner: My mom Alma H. Johnson, Audrey Lawrence, Vanessa Benton, Salimah Muhammad, Tara Bidwell and Victoria Christopher Murray. Thank you for being there for me. You all have made all the difference in the world. I love you all tremendously.

To my girls: Bettina Stafford, Cydney Rax, Cynthia Simmons, Diane Prince (yes, Diane, you too — lol) Elizabeth Goodrow, Evelyn Richardson, Millie Banrey, Sophia Johnson, Stacy Moore, Terrie Russell, Terryl Manning, Tracy LaVonne Johnson, Valarie Escoffery and Vivian Smith. Where would I be without you?

To the guys: Phill Duck and Timmothy B. McCann. To Deacon Roscoe Campbell, Deacon James Brock and Shawn Moore from the Sardis Missionary Baptist Church. To Herron Johnson, Thomas Gaskin of MARTA, Ricardo Burke, Eugene Frederricks, Tee Newkirk, James Miller and Mervin Seraphin — thank you all so much. You have been a wonderful support to me. And to George Walter Xaverian Bellinger, Jr. — I love you more. Thank you for loving me first ....

To the church family of Sardis Missionary Baptist Church. To my neighbors Lee and Barbara Evins. To Eartha Alston, Doris Maye, Brenda Knight and Claudia McGuire. To TaMeka Gates of MARTA. Thank you for being there when I needed you most.

To my family Alma H. Johnson, Jessie C. Rhoden, Traci LaVonne Johnson, Nicole Rhoden, Derrick Stokely, J'nea Woods, Missy and Ana Batchelor (my Philly niece — yeah, you.) To my family Mercedes Hodge Joseph, Felicia Bijlhout, Melva Scarsborough, Bernadine Thomas Cijntje, Joan Foy, Tomas Foy, Clinton Foy, Ralph Foy, Sister Betty, Tomasita Foy, Justin Foy, Michael Annan, Atchinson Annan, James Ato Annan, Gene Wilson, Elsa Wilson, Cornelius Wilson, Andrea Wilson and Alfred Joseph. Your love and concern means so much.

And a really, really, really big thank you to my Sutton Place Crew: Brenda Conner Bey Miller, you have been many things to me over the years — mentor, rabbi, my priestess and loving friend. Now I have both the honor and the pleasure of adding one more 'thingee' to who you are to me — my editor. Thank you from the bottom of my heart for editing my book. You are an incredible woman and I love you very, very much.

Cydney Rax — you are my cuz fo' sure. Thank you for being additional eyes for my manuscript. You've always brought me good news and kept me abreast on what was going on in the literary world with regards to my career. Thanks for always having back and laughing at my corny butt jokes. May your own literary star continue to rise.

Stacey Moore — I knew from the moment I met you what a sweetheart you were and since that time, I know it more and more. Thank you for being the copy editor for This Time. Your help and friendship is immeasurable. (P.S., if you spot typo's in this Acknowledgement, I apologize, but I didn't want anyone — not even you, the copy editor, to see my acknow's till the book was out. I hope I got the comma's in the right place - lol

Salimah Muhammad — you are so on it. Thank you for doing all that footwork for me and not taking 'no' for an answer.

Cathleen Toelke — you are a true artist, in both heart and abilities. You are truly a special talent. I cannot thank you enough for working with me. I am so proud to have your artwork on my cover. Thank you for that honor and privilege. You are a true gem.

To my author buddies: Timmothy B. McCann (my 'through the trenches' buddy), Phill Duck (my Literary Son — watch out world), Thomas Green (my fellow author by way of the Boogie Down Bronx), Cydney Rax (my 'Cuz' fo' sure), Victoria Christopher Murrary (I am so glad you are in my life) and Brian Egerston (nobody reads a body of work better then you do ...) Thanks for your encouragement and your belief in me. It means a lot. To Brandon Massey and Travis Hunter, there are only a handful of folks I will travel across town to celebrate book releases for. You guys are like two of the three. Janice Sims, one day we will meet face to face, I promise! Linda Dominique Grosvenor, keep on doing your thing.

To Carol Mackey and Black Expressions, Sista Tee and RAWSISTAZS, Shunda Leigh of Circle of Friends II/Booking Matters, Nia of Medu Books, Alvin Romer of Romer Review, aNN Brown, Phyllis McLaughlin (where you at?). Angela Reid and Imani Book

Club — thanks for coming to the other side of town to see me. G.R.I.T.S. Online Reading Club, Harriet Klausner, R.E.A.L. Reviewers, Book-Remarks.com, Yasmin and the APOOO crew, Jeanette Frommi (Wallington) and the Motown Review Book Club, Jeri Tolliver of 1230AM WDBZ The Buzz, Jay Butler of WQBH in Detroit, Maxine Thompson of VoiceAmerican.com, Bill Thompson of MetroSource Network. Hollywood Hernandez (thanks for keeping me smiling) Wali Muhammed and Jay Butler. Your support for me has been incredible. Thank you all.

And finally, to all the bookstores that carried my books, all the book clubs that read me; to all the readers who love themselves some *"margaretjohnsonhodge"* and even to all those who read my books and didn't, I often say that without you, I'm just somebody telling stories for my own benefit.

THANKS FOR LETTIN' ME INTO YOUR LIVES ONCE MORE ...

Peace, love and, blessings,

Margaret